M000280030

PRAISE
PATIENCE GRIFFIN'S BOOKS

"Griffin has quilted together a wonderful, heartwarming story that will convince you of the power of love."
-New York Times bestselling author Janet Chapman

"Griffin's lyrical and moving debut marks her as a most talented new-comer to the romance genre."
-*Publishers Weekly* starred review

"A fun hop to scenic Scotland for the price of a paperback."
-*Kirkus Reviews*

"Start this heartwarming, romance series!"
-Woman's World magazine

"With the backdrop of a beautiful town in Scotland, Griffin's story is charming and heartwarming. The characters are quirky and wonderful and easy to feel an instant attachment and affection for. Be fore-warned: You're likely to shed happy tears."
-RT Reviews

"Ahhh, this series is my own little vacation to a land I love, even if the land in this series is a fictional Scottish fishing village where the men are braw, kilt-wearing, and have full respect for women."
-Gourmonde Girl

"The best thing about this series is the way that it touches you as a reader. The characters are deeply written, with flawed characteristics that make them seem familiar – like real people that you know and see every day."
-Ever After Book Reviews

"I dearly loved this romance, and I dearly love this series."
-Book Chill

"Patience Griffin gets love, loss, and laughter like no other writer of contemporary romance."
-Grace Burrowes, New York Times bestselling author of the Lonely Lords series and the Windham series

"Patience Griffin, through her writing, draws the reader into life in small town Scotland. Her use of language and descriptive setting had me feel like I was part of the cast."
-Open Book Society

"Griffin has a knack for creating characters that I find engaging from the opening page. I love the Kilts and Quilts series."
-The Romance Dish

"I love Patience Griffin!! These Kilts and Quilts books are among my favorites EVER!!!"
-Margie's Must Reads

"Ms. Griffin paints a vivid picture of Gandiegow with the ever meddling members of the Kilts and Quilts. Fans of LuAnn McLane and Fiona Lowe will enjoy The Accidental Scot."
-Harlequin Junkie

(About *The Laird and I*) "I have read it. I'm reading it again. *laughing* It is like putting on your softest nightgown and slippers."
-Becky, a reader

"This author has a way of choking me up in parts and that does not happen a lot to me. If you are looking for a great series to fall in love with then I suggest you give this one a try."
-www.AHollandReads.com

""Patience Griffin seamlessly pieces compelling characters, a spectacular setting, and a poignant romance into a story as warm and beautiful as an heirloom quilt."
-Diane Kelly, author of the Tara Holloway series

⸿◯◖

BOOKS by
PATIENCE GRIFFIN

———————— ⅏ ————————

KILTS AND QUILTS® SERIES:
ROMANTIC WOMEN'S FICTION

#1   *TO SCOTLAND WITH LOVE*

#2   *MEET ME IN SCOTLAND*

#3   *SOME LIKE IT SCOTTISH*

#4   *THE ACCIDENTAL SCOT*

#5   *THE TROUBLE WITH SCOTLAND*

#6   *IT HAPPENED IN SCOTLAND*

#6.5 *THE LAIRD AND I*

#7   *BLAME IT ON SCOTLAND*

#8   *KILT IN SCOTLAND*

———————— ⅏ ————————

From the author of Blame it on Scotland

Kilt in Scotland

A
Kilts and Quilts®
Novel

Patience Griffin

Kilts & Quilts®
PUBLISHING

COPYRIGHT

Copyright © 2019 by Patience Griffin
First Printing October 2019

All Rights Reserved

———

This book and parts thereof may not be reproduced in any form, stored in a retrieval system, or transmitted in any form by any means—electronic, mechanical, photocopying, or otherwise without prior written permission of the author and copyright holder, except as provided by the United States of America copyright law. The only exception is for a reviewer who may quote short excerpts in a review.

Cover art by Amy Lockard Ness

Cover design by Kathleen Baldwin

ISBN 978-1-7320684-4-5

This is a work of fiction. Names, character, places, an incidents are either the product of the author's imagination or are used fictitiously, and any resemblance to actual person, living or dead, business establishments, events, or locale is entirely coincidental.

Published by Kilts & Quilts® Publishing

DEDICATION

This last year has been incredible and I have a lot of people to thank for helping me with this book...especially PhD, who bought me salads for those nights when I was too busy to cook and for accepting that I'm at my computer night and day.

Special thanks goes to Amy Lockard Ness for creating the beautiful artwork for the cover. You are such a talent. Oh, how this cover makes me smile.

A big thank you goes to Sue Carter and Carin Shaughnessy for being my pattern writer, quilt piecers, and most importantly my friends. You two make me smile and laugh. A lot!

I'm blessed to have Cagney, who drops everything to give me a readthrough.

Thank you to Duckie for stepping in to be my assistant.

I'm so lucky to have made a friend in Karen Gibbs, a fabric genius, also the Creative Director at Banyan Batiks. You've made my fabric journey so much fun!

For Kathleen Baldwin for creating my book cover and for being on the other end of the phone to talk about writing, family, and well, about everything!

PRONUNCIATION GUIDE OF NAMES

Aileen (AY-leen)
Ailsa (AIL-sa)
Bethia (BEE-thee-a)
Buchanan (byoo-KAN-uhn)
Cait (KATE)
Deydie (DI-dee)
Moira (MOY-ra)
Ryn (ren)

DEFINITIONS

Blue Badge Guide—An accredited tourist guide who must complete a 1,300-hour training course, plus exams to lead tours in Scotland
céilidh (KAY-lee)—a party/dance
Coach—bus
Dreich—a word to describe cold, dreary weather
P&L—profit and loss statement
Tatties—potatoes
Torch—flashlight
Tavon—pronounced ˈtæv-ɪn
Trackies—sweatpants
Wynds—pronounced wʌɪnd—narrow street or alley

1

GLASGOW, SCOTLAND
GUY FAWKES NIGHT

Remember, remember the fifth of November
Gunpowder, treason and plot!

TILLY DIXON COULDN'T GET out of her head the chant
that she'd heard on the street earlier. Between the stress
of finishing the next book in the Quilt to Death series and the
noise of Glasgow gearing up for Guy Fawkes Night, Tilly was
wound tighter than usual. Her muscles ached. Her eyes hurt.
And her brain was fried. She closed the lid of her laptop and
stood, stretching, trying to ease the tension from her body.

She felt older than forty-two. Her sister, Marta, younger by
two years, had plenty of spring in her step. *Spring,* though,
wasn't quite the right word. Marta strutted through life, pa-
rading around like a queen bee. Tilly trudged. Hours of
slumping over a computer and waiting on Marta hand and

foot caused Tilly's misery.

Tilly bent over and tried to adjust the computer chair again. But it was no use. She missed the little things when they were abroad. Her worn, comfortable chair in Marta's New York apartment for one. They always roughed it when they were here in Scotland, but it seemed as if Tilly was the only one who suffered.

Marta didn't seem to have a worry in the world. And she didn't care one whit that the accelerated deadlines of the last three books with Three Seals Publishing had nearly killed Tilly.

Stiff as a corpse, Tilly went to the window of her sister's fifth-story apartment and gazed out. Marta loved the city. Tilly didn't. *Too loud. Too crowded.* She preferred the peace of the Scottish countryside, or the lapping waves along the beach of one of the fishing villages. A place like Gandiegow, which she and Marta had visited once. The memory made Tilly sigh.

November evenings came early in Scotland, the sky ink-black at only four in the afternoon. Anticipation of the celebratory bonfire lay upon the crowded streets below. Tilly wasn't looking forward to the crack and boom of the fireworks later, hating how they frazzled her poor nerves more than they already were.

The apartment door opened and Tilly turned to see her sister flounce into the room as if she was a twenty-something and not middle-aged. Her new editor, Rance Bettus, trailed behind her and Tilly cringed. It wasn't just his slicked-back hair, or his fading good-looks that made her skin crawl. His skeevey, unethical behavior was repulsive to Tilly, but apparently, flypaper to Marta. Over the years, there'd been scads of men just like him. Charmers, looking for something in return—money, fame, power—all subpar men. *Not the kind of men I write about.* The way Marta and Rance were acting, the affair was in full swing, despite Rance being newly married to another.

The affair aside, Tilly couldn't stand Rance for a lot of reasons—he smoked, he was loud, and he treated Tilly as if she wasn't even there. But at the top of Tilly's list was his awful taste in books—*all things dystopian*. He'd told Tilly once that he couldn't get enough of the rising body count in *Hunger Games* and *Game of Thrones*.

He stood in the doorway carrying a cardboard box the size their author copies usually shipped in.

"Set them on the desk," Marta commanded.

As he made his way across the room, Rance leered at Marta, skimming her with his eyes, as if he were using his irises to peel off her body-hugging designer suit.

Tilly gagged, a common occurrence when the two of them were around.

Rance wasn't paying any attention and she had to rush to move her laptop before he crushed it beneath the carton.

She adjusted a flap on the open box so she could look inside. "What's this?"

Marta pulled out a novel and tossed it to her. Tilly wasn't expecting the pass and fumbled it. The book was upside down, so she shifted it, bringing the sinister-looking cover into view.

When the title and author registered, it knocked Tilly sideways.

"You wrote a book?" It couldn't be. *Tilly* was the writer in their family of two.

But it was indisputable. **MARTA DIXON** was splashed across the top, just like the other nine novels in the Quilt to Death series —a collection of cozy murder mysteries set in the Highlands and centered around the Buttermilk Guild. Tilly turned the book over to see the spine, and sure enough, *#10* was printed there, plain as day.

"Hot off the press," Rance said cheerily. "We better hurry if we're going to make the launch party in time."

"Launch party?" This was crazy. Tilly would've known. "A launch party. . . for this book? I don't understand. I'm just finishing book ten! I thought we were in Scotland for a break."

Marta snatched the paperback from her. "I told you, but you must've forgotten. *Again.* I've been working on this book for several years now."

Which explained why Marta had sequestered herself in her office last year for months, and then Marta had a series of meetings with Three Seals Publishing. When Tilly had asked what the meetings were about, Marta had claimed they were *the same-old-same-old.*

Marta waved a hand in the air. "It makes no sense that you've been slaving away on book ten. You see, the book is done. I'm afraid you're losing it, Tilly."

That was a lie. More often these days, her sister would insinuate that Tilly had gone mental, forgetting things Marta had never told her. Always, it turned out, things Marta didn't really want her to know. But Tilly certainly wasn't imagining the stabbing pain she felt now. Maybe it was the knife her sister had just plunged into her back.

Marta straightened her scarf, not meeting Tilly's eyes. "You've probably also forgotten that this is the last book. The series is done."

"Done?" Tilly couldn't breathe. She wanted to push up the window to get some air. She just couldn't believe it was true.

Five years ago at a quilt retreat, Marta had come up with the idea of writing a mystery series featuring a group of quilters and suggested that the two of them split the responsibilities. Tilly would write the novels while Marta did everything else, including being the face of the brand. Whenever Tilly felt like she was being taken advantage of, Marta would remind her: *You have the easy job—writing. I'm the one who has to do all the heavy lifting. It's not a walk in the park being Marta Dixon and running this empire. Besides, you hate the limelight. You always have.* It was true. Tilly would rather sit in a room alone with the Buttermilk Guild pouring from her fingertips than sign books with a mob of strangers surrounding her.

Marta's charisma had made the Quilt to Death series a huge success. Tilly stayed in the shadows where she felt comfortable, the ghost writer behind the scenes and, to the outside world, Marta's assistant.

Tilly crumpled into a chair. "Why would Three Seals sign off on this?"

"I made them an offer they couldn't refuse." Marta didn't elaborate but instead tapped the book against the desk. "We're done discussing this. The book was released today. The fans are waiting. Now, go get dressed. The book signing starts in an hour."

"Book signing?" Tilly felt another whammy.

Marta rolled her eyes. "Yes, the book signing is at the bookshop across the street." She shook her head as if she felt sorry for Tilly. "You must've forgotten that, too."

Tilly stood up and looked through the window and down at the street. A line had formed outside the bookstore.

Marta laid the book on top of the box. "Three Seals has assigned me a new publicist for this book. Her name's Diana. She seems okay. She and her team are there waiting on us. It's a big night." Her sister looked around as if she'd lost something. "Where's the quilt for the new book? Diana wants to hang it up behind the table where I'll be signing books."

Tilly exhaled, feeling as if Marta had dropped an elephant squarely on her chest, breaking her heart in the process. "Is that why you wanted me to get the quilt done so early?" Usually the quilt and corresponding pattern didn't need to be ready until the novel was released.

"Seriously, Tilly. I think you're slipping. I told you all about this."

But Marta had said nothing. And both she and Marta knew it.

ಬಾರ

GANDIEGOW, SCOTLAND

Deydie hobbled to Quilting Central as fast as she could, paying no mind to the North Sea as the spray hit the walkway, splattering her sturdy Wellies. She wasn't a spring chick anymore, and this wet morning had her feeling all of her seventy-nine years. But she was on a mission. She'd heard from Bethia, her dearest friend, that *it* had arrived.

Deydie reached the entrance to Quilting Central and slung open the door. As it was still early, the tables and sewing machines sat unattended. In the reading corner, though, she found the lass she'd been looking for and rushed to her. "Sadie, where is it?"

"Where's what?" Sadie looked guilty as hell, as if she'd messed around with Deydie's scissors and ruined a piece of Deydie's favorite fabric. A capitol offense.

"Ye know what!" Deydie yelled. "The new book in the Quilt to Death series."

Sadie glanced down at the paperback in her hand and winced as if the book had burned her. But instead of dropping it, she clutched it to her chest.

"That's it, isn't it?" Deydie barreled toward her. "Marta Dixon's new book?" She thrust out her hand. "Give it here!"

"I can't."

"Why not? Ye know the reason I have to read every one of those books." Deydie had a love-hate relationship with the

6

Quilt to Death series. She loved the books...but not the author.

"I know, but you shouldn't read *this one*. You're not going to like it."

"Hand it over." Deydie reached for the book, but Sadie jerked away.

The lass had the audacity to take two steps back, acting as if she didn't know Deydie owned a broom and knew how to use it on the backside of anyone who crossed her.

"I won't give it to you," Sadie said bravely.

"Ye American lassies can be so full of yereselves." Deydie reached for the book again.

"Trust me." Sadie's sympathetic gaze said Deydie was a simpleton. "I sped read the book this morning, when it came in the post."

"Why are ye acting strange?" Deydie looked around to see where her broom might be. "Did ye break the spine?"

"No," Sadie said defensively.

"Did ye dog-ear the pages then?" Deydie saw her broom near one of the longarm quilting machines...all the way on the other side of the room. "If ye don't hand it over right now..."

Sadie shook her head.

"What is it? What's wrong with ye?"

"Nothing's wrong with me." Sadie looked side to side as if someone else in the empty room might explain what was going on. "It's the book."

"What makes ye think I'm not going to like it? Spit it out!"

Sadie glanced down once more, staring at the book as if an awful secret lay inside. "Are you going to get mad at me if I tell you what happens in the end?"

Deydie glowered at the lass, wanting to shake her. "Any madder than I am right now?"

"Okay. But don't take it out on me." Sadie reluctantly handed it over.

"Ye've aged me another year," Deydie grumbled. "Ye're acting as if someone died or something." She thumbed through the pages and grinned. "No quilting for me today. I'll just spend my time with a good story."

Sadie gently touched Deydie's arm, getting her attention. "Someone did die."

"Who?"

With trepidation in her creased brows, Sadie gave her a sad smile. "The Buttermilk Guild died. All of them. Ms. Dixon killed them off in the epilogue. On a ship, during a quilting cruise. They all drowned during a storm."

Deydie glared at Sadie. "She couldn't've."

Sadie acted as if she had to hurry through the next bit. "The Detective Chief Inspector, though, went back to his fiancé in Edinburgh and got married. At least that part had a happy ending."

"I don't care about that *mush!*" Deydie's old chest felt heavy. "Why would Marta Dixon kill off *my quilters?*" *Dammit.* "I mean, *the quilters.* Why would she do that? This is only the tenth book in the Quilt to Death series. I thought it would go on forever." Deydie's despair made her blood run hot. "I'll take Marta Dixon to task for what she's done. Aye, I will!"

"We aren't the only ones who are upset," Sadie said timidly. "I checked online. Everyone who's read the book is complaining, too."

Deydie smacked the paperback on the table. "I'll tell ye what. I'll do more than complain. When Marta Dixon shows her face in Gandiegow again..." She blew out a breath and was genuinely surprised when it wasn't pure flames. "I'll kill her. That's what I'll do. I'll kill her!"

☙☙☙

GLASGOW, SCOTLAND

Diana McKellen gazed around the bookshop, making sure everything was in its place—the podium, the rows of chairs, the table for signing, and the stacks of the latest Quilt to Death novels.

The only thing missing was the author and the quilt she was supposed to bring with her.

Diana couldn't shake the feeling something dreadful was going to transpire tonight. *You're being silly.* The awful thing had already happened—*the killing of the Buttermilk Guild, and along with it, the series.* It was a terrible way to spend her birthday week—thirty-five yesterday.

Diana knew Three Seals Publishing had hated to end the successful series and had tried to dissuade Marta from killing off the Buttermilk Guild. But Marta had stood firm and went so far as to decline an advance on the next series, taking a slightly higher royalty on the ebook. Ending the series was still a huge gamble. For months, Three Seals had been discussing, strategizing, and preparing for the backlash, knowing readers wouldn't take the brutal end to the series lying down. And readers were already weighing in. The news of the quilters' death had traveled fast. Initially, they'd managed to set up double the usual number of appearances for Marta's new book, but since this afternoon, shops and quilt guilds were canceling their events at record speed. Bookstores were pulling orders. And shockingly, death threats were pouring in. Who knew quilters could be so violent?

But Diana had come prepared with a multilayered plan, and because of the cancellations this meant they were moving to plan B.

Diana looked out the bookstore window to the line, which was growing. The fans didn't look upset, though. They smiled and chatted with one another, seeming excited. *Weird.*

Parker, Three Seals' media guru from the New York office, sidled up to her, slinging her long blond hair away from her face, revealing the two cameras hanging on her shoulder—one for still photos, one for video. Parker's name matched her fun, bubbly, and sometimes quirky personality. She was full of energy and a lot of fun to have as a business trip partner. Parker smiled brightly. "I'm shocked at the line outside, aren't you?"

Diana shrugged, feeling befuddled herself. "Either they're loyal, die-hard fans or they haven't heard the news yet." She tilted her head in the direction of the store owner. "I had to do some fancy footwork with that one to keep her from calling off the book signing."

Parker checked the lens on one of her cameras. "I think she would be ecstatic to have the extra foot traffic."

"She didn't want to deal with unhappy customers...and possible returns. I don't blame her."

"It's amazing the publishing house was able to keep this under wraps."

"I know. News like this usually leaks out."

Parker nudged her. "You know what people are calling you, right?"

"*The Fixer*." Diana had heard it before. Over the years, she'd earned the *Fixer* name by fixing authors' faux pas and embarrassing behavior. But this time they were expecting a PR miracle. Sometimes there was no recovering from a book-idea-gone-wrong, like when Helen Fielding had killed off Mr. Darcy in her *Bridget Jones* series. Sometimes, readership was lost. But Diana was going to do her best to make sure the last Quilt to Death novel didn't crash and burn. She herself was a fan of the Buttermilk Guild and didn't want the memory of them to turn into ash.

Parker looked at her expectantly. "So...what's the plan this time?"

Actually the plan was complicated with contingencies A, B, and C. But Diana wouldn't bore Parker with the details. "One of the things Marta needs to do is the usual on-camera interviews to explain why the series ended the way it did."

Parker grimaced. "Why didn't she just have the Buttermilk Guild ride off into the sunset? I love those old gals."

"I love them, too," Diana commiserated.

The back door opened and Marta—tall and straight—strutted in, wearing her signature white winter suit, offset by her blood-red scarf. The woman certainly had *presence.*

"I'm here," Marta sang.

Tilly, a smidge taller than Marta, and the mousy one of the two, came in after her, holding the latest quilt in her arms. Rance followed behind them.

Diana glanced at her watch. Marta had cut it close. There were things that still needed to be done—like hanging the quilt behind the signing table. More importantly, Diana needed to speak with Marta before the event started.

Diana walked over to her and handed her the itinerary. "Nearly everything is ready. We'll have you wait in the back, while we open the doors and get as many in as will fit."

Marta motioned to her sister. "Tilly, make sure my table is set up properly."

As if shell-shocked, Tilly stared at the two ceiling-high vertical banners of the dark and ominous book cover looming on either side of the signing table. This cover design screamed that inside was a serious departure from the other books. The previous Quilt to Death novels had playful watercolor drawings on the covers, making murder-solved-by-amateur-sleuths look like a fun read.

But not this one.

"The cover looks even worse blown up like that," Tilly whispered.

"Tilly!" Marta yelled. "What's wrong with you?"

Tilly didn't budge.

Marta marched over and yanked the quilt out of Tilly's arms and thrust it at Parker. "Here."

Parker looked a bit stunned, as if she'd been put in charge of a baby bear.

"I'll take it," Diana said. The bookstore owner rushed over and retrieved it from her.

Marta glared at her sister. "You're useless tonight."

So the rumors about Marta Dixon were true; she treated her sister like crap. Diana had only met her at one meeting and she'd seemed charismatic then. But now, the whole room was filled with awkward tension. The bookstore owner bit her lip and busied herself with hanging the quilt behind the book signing table. As the whimsical quilt unfolded, Diana saw a rook appear in the center, surrounded by bright stars and a few small rooks thrown in around the edges.

Rance stepped forward and draped an arm around Marta. "I'll make sure your table is set up. *I know how you like it.*" The sexual overtone made the situation even more uncomfortable.

The few interactions Diana had had with Rance confirmed her initial reaction to the man. She didn't care for him at all. But by the way Marta was beaming at him, apparently, she did.

Diana touched Marta's arm. "We should talk first, before everything begins."

Marta pulled away. "About what? I've done thousands of these events. You can't tell me anything that I don't already know."

"I'm afraid this one will be different. You should be prepared. Because you killed off the Buttermilk Guild—."

Tilly gasped, and all color from her face drained away.

"What? The Buttermilk Guild is dead?"

"You didn't know?" That's strange, Diana thought.

Tilly hung her head and shook it slightly.

How could she not know this important detail! Tilly was Marta's assistant, and one would assume she had read the book before it went to print.

Tilly appeared stricken, absolutely devastated. Diana was torn, because the clock was ticking. "Do you need to sit down? You don't look well." Diana's PR brain went to the worst-case scenario and it wasn't pretty. There would be a huge mess if an ambulance had to be called to carry Tilly away.

"She's fine," Marta insisted.

Diana didn't think so. "Parker, can you find Tilly some water?"

"Sure, boss."

Diana welcomed *boss* now over the *Fixer*, as she wasn't sure she could fix anything right now. "Marta, there's going to be some backlash—" Diana would have to be careful here with her words, for Tilly's sake "—because of the conclusion to your new book."

But Marta was half-distracted. "Poppycock." She glanced down at her scarf and adjusted it. "You're making too much of this Buttermilk Guild thing. The readers are going to be fine with it."

Rance echoed her sentiment. "No one is going to care about the demise of those old biddies."

Tilly gasped and gawped at Rance as if he'd said that he'd killed the Buttermilk Guild himself.

Diana turned to Rance. The man was oblivious to what this could do to Marta Dixon's sales. Had he not been in touch with Three Seals today? But Diana couldn't worry about Rance's grasp of reality right now. She had to get through to Marta. "Please listen to me." She gave her a pointed look and held her gaze. "You've been getting death threats since the book came out today."

That got the self-absorbed author's attention. She glanced around nervously. "Death threats? Well, I need protection! Three Seals had better get me a bodyguard."

"I'll protect you," Rance said.

Marta glared at him. "This was *your* idea. *You* said I should kill off the quilters. That it would make things more interesting. *Edgier*."

Rance put his arms out. "Listen, baby, don't worry about a thing. You wanted to get away from that soft writing anyway, and into true crime. Didn't I get you a four-book contract—"

There was a thud. Diana turned, worried it might be Tilly hitting the floor, but it was only Tilly's bag. Surely she wasn't just finding out about Marta's new book deal!

Rance went on. "It's all going to work out fine. It's gonna be great. You'll see."

Marta shook her head and spun on Diana. "Get me a bodyguard. Tonight!"

"I'll work on it."

Marta glared at Tilly. "What are you doing just standing there? Make sure my table is right. You're my assistant, aren't you?"

Though Tilly looked like death, she obediently went to the table and began shifting the books—giving Marta extra room, laying out a packet of tissues, a bottle of water and a few lozenges.

Rance took Marta by the arm, and with the bookseller on the other side of her, ushered Marta to the back room to wait. As Parker tested the lighting one more time with her meter, Diana checked her watch again and headed toward the front door.

Once there, she stepped outside. "Is everyone ready?" she

yelled to the crowd.

A resounding "aye" rose up.

She held the door wide as the fans crowded in. Some had canvas tote bags filled with Quilt to Death novels and quilts. "Remember, Ms. Dixon can only sign two outside items, plus an unlimited number of in-store purchases." One of the store clerks stood just inside the door and marked outside items with a sticker. The tension of the day eased away as fans flocked to the mystery shelves to buy more books about the Buttermilk Guild.

"Take your seats as soon as you can so we can get started." Both cash registers were dinging and Diana smiled. Her worry had been for nothing.

The chairs filled quickly and people filed along the back of the store, three deep. Diana nodded to the store owner. "It's time."

A moment later, Marta strutted out to applause, going straight to the podium. A line had already formed at the microphone for the question and answer portion.

"Welcome, everyone," Marta started, all confidence. "I love seeing my adoring readers and I have great news to share with you, my darlings. I'm starting a new series."

The crowd *oo'ed* and *ah'ed*.

"It'll be something a little different. Starting tomorrow, I'll post hints and sneak peeks on my website but tonight, how about I read the first chapter of my new book?"

Everyone seemed to lean in as Marta read. She had a great Scottish accent for each member of the Buttermilk Guild. She really did know how to hold an audience and keep them on the edge of their seats.

When Marta was done, she closed the book and flourished a hand in the air. "Let's open it up for questions now."

Diana reached over and turned on the microphone for the

people in line.

The first woman stepped up, holding a miniature milk can with Buttermilk Guild plastered on the side in blue letters—a promotional giveaway for the previous book. She leaned into the microphone. "Your new book came in the morning post and I read it first thing."

Marta took the microphone from the podium and stepped closer to the woman, beaming, as if the woman had just complimented her newborn. "And how did you like it?"

The woman's expression turned hard and ugly. "What made you think you could get away with murdering the Buttermilk Guild?"

Before her words could register with Diana, the angry woman ripped the lid off the milk can and threw the contents at Marta. *Blood!* It went everywhere, but mainly it hit Marta in the face. Her white suit soaked up a good portion of it, too, as if it'd been thirsty.

The crowd went crazy.

"What in the hell is wrong with you?" Marta yelled.

But the woman had fled and was almost to the door. Everyone must've been in shock, because no one stopped her as she tore out into the night.

Diana was mobbed by people who'd gotten splattered. Out of the corner of her eye, she noticed Parker, her video camera held up, the recording light on. *Good girl.* Hopefully, she'd gotten some footage that would help the authorities capture the milk-can-carrying woman.

"I'm going to kill that bitch!" Marta shouted into the microphone.

The crowd went silent, stunned at seeing the real Marta Dixon for the first time.

Diana rushed to her, taking the microphone away.

"I told you I need a bodyguard!" Marta screeched.

Diana tried to push her toward the back room.

"Three Seals is going to pay. Do you hear me?" Marta howled. "Where's Tilly? I need someone to clean me up."

The young store clerk ran toward her with paper towels, unrolling sheets as she came.

Instead of being grateful and thanking her, Marta barked, "Give me those!" She snatched the paper towels and scrubbed her face without a kind word to the young woman.

Up close, Diana realized it wasn't blood at all. It was too thin. Was it dye? She looked over to see the store owner on the phone and assumed she was talking with the police.

"Excuse me." An old lady touched Diana's arm. "Are you in charge here?"

Diana was torn, as the chaos in the room wrestled her attention in what seemed like a thousand directions. She wondered if she should stop people from leaving or if she should go to the store owner and make sure she was all right; of course, Marta was her responsibility—but Diana decided to see what the woman in front of her needed first. "What can I do for you?"

"My quilt is gone. Someone must've taken it by accident."

Diana pointed toward the store owner. "That's who you need to tell—"

There was a scream from the back of the store. Diana ran toward the sound. It was the young store clerk, but she wasn't handing out stickers now or giving Marta paper towels. She stood at the opened back door and screamed again, her face contorted in horror at what was outside.

"What is it?" Diana pushed through the shocked crowd to get there first.

The alley was dark, but a streetlight shone on the face of Rance Bettus, sitting against the building with his legs outstretched. It wasn't unusual for Rance to be outside smoking.

But he should be standing, not sitting. And his face…

His face held a blank stare. The look of someone who was dead!

Wrapped around his shoulders was a quilt. Diana recognized it—the quilt on the front cover of the very first Quilt to Death book. Blood was soaking through the quilt on his left side, closest to the door.

A note was attached to the quilt with a straight pin:

FROM THE BUTTERMILK GUILD

The store owner rushed out, took in the scene, and was clearly shocked. She led the inconsolable clerk back inside.

Marta stuck her head out. "What's going on?" She emerged and gave Rance a poke with the toe of her shoe. "What in God's name are you doing down there?"

Rance's body moved…and slowly fell over to the side.

Marta looked at Diana with her eyebrows pinched together, incomprehension on her face, as if she was a small child. "Is he okay? Why isn't he getting up?"

Diana knew shock could take many forms. She'd witnessed it in her mother. She'd experienced it herself.

Empathy washed over her. Gently, she put her arm around Marta's shoulders. "He can't get up, sweetie. I believe he's dead."

2

—————————————

RORY CRANNACH PUSHED up the yellow police tape and walked into the bookstore. He hated Guy Fawkes Night and the memories that came with it. But it was more than that. There were never enough police officers to cover the mayhem that inevitably broke out. He wondered if the bookstore had been a victim of the rebellious holiday.

He scanned the interior, noting that the place was crowded, and he cringed. Securing a crime scene could be difficult, but with this many people, *impossible*! He had no way of knowing what evidence might've walked out the door already, what evidence had been contaminated, or what evidence had been strewn around. The place should've been locked down after the crime. At least a small band of officers had arrived quickly—*considering the night*—and had made an effort to stop the in-and-out flow of traffic. What were so many people doing here at the book shop on this night of all nights? Luckily, Rory had only been a few blocks away when he'd gotten the call. *A hell of a night for a murder.*

He pulled out his badge and displayed it. "I'm Detective Chief Inspector Crannach. Who's in charge here? Where's the owner?"

A woman near the entrance raised her hand. "I'm the owner."

"Tell me what happened," he said.

The owner gestured to the beautiful thirtysomething beside her. "You should speak to her. She's the one in charge of the event."

"First," he replied, "are there security cameras inside?"

"Aye. But I checked. The cameras had been disabled...from my computer."

"Maybe we can get some prints from the keyboard."

She hung her head. "Probably not. Ye'll only find mine. I wasn't thinking about fingerprints. Just trying to be helpful."

"It's all right." He couldn't fault the owner; she was clearly upset.

The lovely woman stepped forward and held out her hand. "Diana McKellan." Her accent revealed she was an American, while her sleek purple dress had big city sophistication written all over it. "I'm with Three Seals Publishing, heading up the PR campaign for Marta Dixon's new book." She gestured toward the table with the banners behind it. "If it helps, my assistant had her camera running. However, I'm pretty sure she didn't catch the killer in the act."

"Why's that?"

"She was in here with us."

"I'll need that footage," he said.

Ten feet behind Diana, two tall women stood, one with blood covering her face, hands, and suit; the other one with paper towels, dabbing at the face of the first one.

The bloody one stomped her foot. "Tilly, stop it! Just take me back to the apartment. Now!"

Tilly, the non-bloody one, was hunched, submissive, and halted her ministrations as soon as the first one barked. She looked to be cowering more than before.

Rory raised an eyebrow, as if to ask the American lass who the drama queen was, and the American picked up the cue.

Diana sighed. "Marta Dixon, the author of the Quilt to Death series and the reason we're here. The other one is her sister, Tilly, who's also Marta's assistant."

Rory projected his voice to the group. "No one is going anywhere until I can get your statements." He looked at Marta more closely and realized her face might be stained red with dye instead of blood.

The bell over the door rang and two of his team members arrived—Reid McCartney and Corey MacTaggart. Thank goodness.

"Where do you want us to start?"

"Let's take a look at the crime scene and then we'll get going on the statements." He turned back to Diana. "Where's the body?"

"Right out back. I'll show you." She seemed calm, which made him suspect her right away. The rest of the store's occupants were visibly shaken.

He followed her to the back, taking mental notes to jot down later.

Probably five-six without the stilettos.

Easy measured steps—another clue she might be the killer.

Nice backside.

The last thought, though, wouldn't go in his report.

Diana opened the back door and went through. "Here he is."

Rory stepped out and took in the man on the cobblestones,

lying in a perfect L-shape. A quilt was wrapped around his shoulders, a pool of blood at his side. Rory read the note. He'd seen a lot of murder victims, but this one was bizarre. *From the Buttermilk Guild?* Who the hell was the Buttermilk Guild? What did the note mean? "Did anyone tamper with the crime scene?"

"Well..." Diana started.

Tilly appeared out of nowhere. "Marta kicked him." For someone who seemed so awkward, she had certainly walked up on them quietly enough.

Diana tilted her head to the side. "I wouldn't say Marta kicked him exactly. More like she nudged him with her foot." She looked Rory straight in the eye and spoke matter-of-factly, "Rance was sitting up when we found him."

"Rance?" Rory inquired.

Diana nodded. "Yes. Rance Bettus. Marta's editor. From New York. I can get you all his information."

"Aye. I'll need it. Who discovered the body?"

"The clerk found him," Diana added. "She's inside, sitting on the loveseat right now. She's really upset."

McCartney and MacTaggart peered through the doorway. "Are you ready for us?"

"Yes," Rory said. "McCartney, take yere photos. MacTaggart, talk to the store clerk." Rory wanted to question the Yank himself. "Diana, where were you when this happened?"

She looked puzzled. "I don't know. I guess I was standing at the side of the room, while Marta spoke to the crowd." She paused for two seconds and then, "Am I a suspect?"

"At this point, everyone is."

He squatted down and used his pen to lift the quilt above the pool of blood. *Hmm. Perhaps the killer knew what he was doing.* On the victim's arm, there was an incision, indicating the brachial artery had probably been cut. He lifted the quilt a little higher and saw a strange tool with a circular blade lying underneath. He'd need an evidence bag. He pulled his pen away and the quilt dropped, covering the wound again.

"Excuse me," a woman said from the doorway, clearly speaking to Diana. "I was telling ye about my quilt. It's missing."

Diana walked to the doorway and blocked the view, as if protecting the woman from seeing the dead body. "Yes. Let's go back inside."

Rory stood and listened.

"I brought it here for Marta Dixon to sign. I was wondering if you'd seen it." She looked behind her at Marta, as if to get her to sign it now.

Diana walked through the doorway, arms out a little to the side, as if moving the Caledonian cattle along. "Would you like me to help you look?"

Rory followed her, too.

"We've checked everywhere for the quilt," the woman said. "It's special to me. My first Buttermilk Guild quilt. Ye know, from the first book in the Quilt to Death series?"

Diana nodded.

The woman continued. "I figured I could only bring one quilt to this event for Marta Dixon to sign. My plan is to bring the rest of my Quilt to Death quilts to my local guild meeting tomorrow night for her to sign them."

Rory put himself in the conversation. "The missing quilt...what does it look like?" But as soon as he said it, the unsettled expression on Diana's face registered, and he knew the answer. "Miss...?"

"Judy Keith."

"Miss Keith, let's go sit down for a moment." He'd have to break it to her gently. His mum and grandmother had cherished their quilts and he bet Judy Keith wouldn't be happy her quilt was now evidence in a murder case. *Nay,* nor would she be getting it back. But who would want it, anyway, with a good portion of it soaked in blood?

He settled them on chairs that were set out for the event and explained where her quilt was. He questioned her thoroughly, finding out she'd set the quilt beside her chair before the event began. Anyone could've made off with it, as the bookshelves were close to her seat—perfect cover for a snatch-and-go scenario.

When he was finished with Judy Keith, he dismissed her and went to find Diana again, who seemed to be consoling the bookstore owner.

Rory cleared his throat. "Ms. McKellan, let's get back to your statement now."

"How was Rance murdered?" Diana asked. "With a rotary cutter?"

So that was the tool with the circular blade. "Why would you ask that?" It was an awfully specific guess, Rory thought. Was she just trying to throw him off her scent?

She gazed at the bookshelves behind him, as if her memory lay there and she was scanning it. "In the first Quilt to Death novel, the killer wrapped the victim in a quilt, made by the Buttermilk Guild."

"And?" he prompted.

"He used a rotary blade to slice an artery or something. Marta did a good job of not putting gore into the book, but it seemed pretty gruesome to me to bleed to death that way." Diana shuddered, as if murder was unappealing. But he wasn't marking her off his list of suspects just yet, even though she'd given him some information that might be useful.

"Hmm," he said.

"Is that what happened to Rance?" Diana probed. "Was he sliced with a rotary cutter?" If she was guilty, she was pretty good at playing as if she wasn't.

"We'll have to wait for an official cause of death." But Rory was worried.

"Do you think this is the beginning of something worse to come because the murder was inspired by the first book in the series?"

"Let's not jump to any conclusions." But the thought latched on and gnawed at him anyway.

"What if someone is going to reenact the murders in all the Marta Dixon books?" Diana speculated.

"How many books are there?" Rory asked, hoping it was only a few.

"Ten." Diana chewed her lip, as if something else was worrying her. "I guess I better tell you now, there's been death threats. Against *Marta*, not Rance," she clarified. "They've been pouring in all day."

"Death threats? More than one?" This was becoming more complicated.

Diana explained about the Buttermilk Guild being killed off and how the fans of the Quilt to Death series were in an uproar. "I can't imagine why someone would kill Rance, though." She frowned then, as if an idea had come to her.

"What?" he asked.

She looked around, seeming to take stock of who might overhear her. She leaned closer to him. "Can we speak in private?"

"Sure." Rory was torn. He wanted to question the rest of the people in the store, probably mostly gawkers, but he didn't want to give *this Diana McKellen* time to work on her alibi, if that's what she was up to. Something was up, though, because she smelled too good to be innocent. "Does the store owner have an office?"

"I'll show you."

He followed Diana to a small office and shut the door behind him, and then waited for her to speak.

She was back to chewing her lip. Aye, it was cute, but she was a suspect, and he took his job seriously.

She hugged herself. "I hesitate to say this, because I don't know anything for sure."

"Tell me what's on yere mind and I'll decide if it's relevant or not."

"The rumor is that Rance and Marta were having an affair."

"Are either of them married?"

She nodded. "Rance is married to the publisher's daughter. And Marta just got out of a relationship. I heard her boyfriend Leo had to go to some kind of institution to recover. Leo Shamley," she provided, as he wrote the name on his notepad.

Diana looked down at the floor. "This feels like gossiping. I've only heard of Leo. I've never met him."

If he wasn't a DCI, he would've given her points for not wanting to *natter on* about others. But as it was, this was information he could use. "Anything else?"

"It's rumored Marta is paying for Leo's stay at the resort or whatever it is. It's expensive. Like, five figures a month."

"Do you have Shamley's number?"

"Maybe." Diana pulled out her phone from her sparkly black purse. "I saw on Marta's paperwork that she has Leo listed as a contact. It'll just take me a second to find it."

"While ye're doing that, tell me why Marta Dixon has red dye on her face and her clothes. That's not from kicking the body."

Diana glanced up, but then held his gaze. "Murder isn't the only excitement we've had here tonight. A woman in the audience threw a container of dye at Marta. The woman ran out before anyone could stop her."

"Did ye get a good look at her?"

"Not really. It happened so fast. But I bet Parker got it all on tape. You know, the one I pointed out earlier?"

"And the death threats toward Ms. Dixon?"

"Three Seals, our publishing house, has been forwarding them. Thirteen of them. I can print them out for you, if you'd like."

"Aye."

"Oh, here's Leo's phone number."

Rory wrote it down. "Do ye know the name of the place he's staying?"

Diana bit her top lip, as if that would help her concentrate. "I believe Marta said he was at Malibu Hills Spa & Treatment Resort, or something like that. It's a place where the rich go to decompress. Give me a second to double check." She typed it into her phone, then slid it over for him to see.

"Thanks." He wrote down that number as well.

This Diana was a lot of help. She seemed too forthcoming and straightforward to have committed the murder, but it was too early to take her off the suspect list. If he had more time, though, he'd like to dig deeper to find out where her calm-in-the-face-of-the-storm came from. But there were others to interrogate.

He looked down at his pad, double checking that he had her phone number, in case he needed to reach her. He did. "That's all I need from ye at the moment. You may leave."

"Okay." She gave him a perfunctory smile as she stood. "I'll see if I can use the shop's printer to print the death threats now."

Rory watched Diana go, but then pulled out his phone to call Leo Shamley, Marta's ex-boyfriend. He didn't pick up. Next, Rory called the spa. After he explained who he was and what had happened, the Malibu Hills receptionist was forthcoming.

27

"Mr. Shamley has left," she admitted. "We haven't seen him for several days."

Leo could be another victim of murder, like Rance lying in the alleyway, but more than likely, he had just become Rory's number one suspect.

He flipped to a fresh sheet in his notepad and went to the door, addressing the group, "I'd like to speak with Marta Dixon next."

Marta stepped out from behind the other Ms. Dixon. She seemed genuinely upset as she walked toward him. But she also carried herself with poise, along with a modicum of underlying hostility.

Once inside the room and the door closed, she put her hands on her hips. "How long is this going to take? I have to get out of this suit."

"Have a seat, Ms. Dixon. I'll make this as quick as I can." *But I'll take as long as I damn well please.*

Now that Marta was in the room, the small office buzzed with negative energy. He quickly asked the standard questions and learned Marta owned three residences—one in Malibu, one in New York, and one here in Glasgow. The most interesting thing she revealed was that Rance Bettus was a smoker, maybe the reason he'd stepped out from the bookshop in the first place, only to be murdered. Then Rory asked the most important question of all. "What was the nature of yere relationship with the victim?"

"Rance?" Marta looked a little stricken, but she recovered and straightened herself. "He is...*was* my editor."

"And?" Rory pressed.

She rolled her eyes, as if to give up. "We were involved. Nothing serious, though. What does it matter now?"

"And his wife? Did she know about the affair?" Rory asked directly.

Marta acted as if she'd been caught with her hand in the cookie jar. "I don't know." Her voice was hard and she'd said it as if she didn't care whether Rance's wife knew or not.

"Moving on. When was the last time ye spoke to—" Rory flipped the page back to find the name "—Leo Shamley? Yere ex?"

She sucked in her breath. "How do you know about Leo?" She looked at the door and frowned. "*Diana.*"

"Did ye speak with Mr. Shamley yesterday? Today?"

"No," Marta said coolly, as she eyed Rory with a degree of shrewdness. "I called Leo before I left New York. On Halloween night."

"Five days ago," he said. "What did ye talk about?"

She looked as if she was going to tell him to *walk off*. She shifted in her chair and then folded her hands in her lap. "I knew Leo would be feeling lonely. For the last two years, we dressed up as famous couples and went to the Hartford Hill's Halloween bash. All the big names attend, you know." She brushed some imaginary dust from her shoulder.

"What did Mr. Shamley say?" He decided to make it clear. "How did he respond? Was he happy to hear from you?"

"Of course, he was happy to hear from me." She screwed up her face and Rory knew there was more.

"Was he angry?"

"Not exactly. He just didn't seem like himself."

"In what way?"

"I don't know," she said. "There was something in his voice. He sounded strong, determined, which was out of character for him. Leo's a good-looking man, perfect for the photographers at A-List events; that's important in the business I'm in. But underneath his charm, Leo is really a marshmallow, you know, not much of a backbone. But Halloween night, he sounded as if he'd grown one."

Rory could understand why someone with Marta's personality would want to surround herself with spineless people. Minions were much easier to control than *Alphas*.

Rory went straight to the point. "Did Leo know Rance?"

"A little bit. They met at a Three Seals cocktail party at the MWLM conference."

"MWLM?"

"Mystery Writers Love Murder. It's a great organization. They put a conference on in New York City every spring."

"Tell me, how did Leo react when you broke up with him?"

Marta looked away, staring at a stack of publishers' catalogues on the office shelf. "He took it badly."

Rory would have to choose his words carefully here. "Was he upset? Violent?"

"Heavens, no. He cried. It's the reason I paid for the spa. He's getting therapy there."

"Speaking of the spa, did ye know Leo has left?"

Marta halted. "What? How do you know that?"

"It's my job to know," Rory said.

"There's no reason for him not to be at the spa," Marta said. "I paid up through the New Year."

"Do you think Leo would want to exact revenge for you breaking up with him?"

Marta guffawed. "Leo is harmless. He wouldn't kill a mosquito if it bit him. Actually, he wouldn't know how to."

Rory was surprised that Marta seemed oblivious to the logic that her ex could be the killer.

He leaned toward her to drive home the point. "I assure you, he's gone. The Malibu Hills receptionist said he'd been missing for at least a couple of days. Do ye know where he might be?"

She shook her head. "I don't know. I'm really the only family he has."

"Do you think he would come to Scotland to find you?"

"No. Maybe." She paused, then screwed up her face. "I don't know. I told you, he seemed different on the phone. How do you expect me to know what he's thinking?" She looked down at her ruined clothes as if her disheveled appearance explained her lack of knowledge.

"Sometimes," Rory started, "when people get hurt, they become capable of doing awful things." He'd seen it more times than he cared to think about. Crimes of passion kept him very busy.

"Leo couldn't have done this to Rance," Marta said stubbornly. "Talk to Tilly. She'll tell you about him."

"I'll do that." Rory pointed to her phone, which she'd laid on the table between them, when she sat down. "But first, ye'll find me a picture of Leo and text it to me." He slid his card with his mobile number over to her.

She glared at him. "He didn't do it." But she swiped her thumb over the screen anyway, exhibiting combativeness, rather than cooperation. A second later, she snatched up his card to complete the text, muttering, "Here's your picture." Afterward, she stood, holding her phone at her side. "Anything else?" But her tone was contrary to her words.

"Send yere sister in to see me."

A minute later, Tilly crept into the room, her eyes darting this way and that, as if she was a small mouse watching for a hawk as she stepped into a clearing. Tilly's awkwardness seemed to be her defining trait, while Marta's might be the negative energy she exuded. Rory couldn't help but wonder what might have happened in their screwed-up childhood.

He stood and pulled out the chair for her. "Have a seat." He'd hoped to put her at ease, but her eyes went wide, and he knew his attempt had only made both her, *and him*, more uncomfortable.

When she slipped into the chair, he couldn't help but feel sorry for her. He'd seen the way Marta treated her—like an unwanted dog. Tilly seemed like the type who was willing to be kicked over and over, but always faithful, hoping for a little love and attention in the end.

Expediently, he asked his questions and learned Tilly had been positioned off to the side, behind Marta, while Marta gave her speech.

"Did ye see the woman who threw the dye at yere sister?" Rory had noticed earlier how Tilly didn't have a speck of red dye on her face. And her clothes, *well*, it would be hard to tell, as she was covered in dark gray from her dark baggy slacks to her nondescript tunic.

For a moment, something flickered in Tilly's eyes, maybe embarrassment. "It was awful. Marta was really upset. I hid behind the bookcase when the woman with the buttermilk can started yelling." Which explained why the dye was nowhere on Tilly, and everywhere on Marta.

"Can you tell me if Rance had any enemies?"

Tilly looked embarrassed and whispered, "Rance is married. *Was* married, I mean. Maybe his wife found out he and Marta were...dating."

Rory made a note to find out about his wife's whereabouts this evening. He put his pen down. "Do you know if Leo knew about Rance and Marta?"

She nodded. "He did. I was there when Marta told him."

"How did he take it? Was he angry?"

Tilly looked more uncomfortable, if that was even possible. "He cried. Marta had to call his sister to come and take him away."

"Where was this?" Rory asked.

"In Malibu," Tilly said.

"What's his sister's name and where does she live?"

"Her name is Tiki."

"Last name?"

"Shamley. She never married. Like Leo. She lives in Los Angeles. I can give you her number if you need it."

"Yes. I'll need your mobile number, too." He offered her a clean sheet in his notebook.

When she was done, she passed it back.

"All right then," he said. "Thank ye for yere time, Ms. Dixon. Ye and yere sister are free to leave."

One by one, he spoke with everyone in the store. When he finished, only the store owner and Diana remained.

Diana handed him a stack of paper, maybe sixty sheets in all. "Here are the death threats."

"You said there were thirteen."

"What can I say? The number grew as news about the Buttermilk Guild got out."

Rory offered her his card. "If any more threats arrive, send them along. We'll check out every one. And if you think of anything else, ring me up."

She was chewing her lip again. "Can you do me a favor?"

"Depends."

"Marta needs a bodyguard. Can you point me in the right direction?"

"I know a couple of people. I have your number. I'll get you some names and their contact information, when I get home tonight."

The store owner hung the Closed sign in the window and picked up a quilt with a rook sewn into it. She walked over to Diana and held it out. "Will you get this back to Marta?"

"Sure," Diana said, examining the quilt to see if any dye had gotten on it.

He nodded to Diana, but spoke to the both of them. "How are you getting home tonight?"

The store owner pointed up. "My flat is above stairs."

"And you?" Rory asked Diana.

"My hotel is a couple of blocks away." She gazed out at the crowded streets. "I should be fine. A lot of people are out tonight."

But he wasn't taking any chances; someone had murdered an employee of Three Seals Publishing tonight. And Diana was a Three Seals employee, too.

"I'll walk you," Rory said, before thinking it through.

3

DIANA WALKED BESIDE Rory, her insides churning. She must be in shock. She was half numb and half jumbled, like a stone in a rock tumbler. She felt pretty certain though, by the time this was over, she wouldn't be as polished and beautiful as a gem.

She glanced over at the policeman—*Detective Chief Inspector Crannach*. He was six-feet-something with perfect light brown hair—the kind of rugged-looking hair she wanted to run her hands through. He had a sexy five o'clock shadow, and earlier at the bookstore, she'd noticed he had the most piercing aqua blue eyes she'd ever seen.

If not for the dead body tonight, she could almost imagine they were on a date. What was she thinking? She didn't waste time on whimsical, romantic longings. She was a down-to-earth New Yorker. Even more importantly, she never dated cops.

They looked like they were out on a date, though, didn't they? Rory was wearing jeans and a black leather jacket with a white Oxford underneath, the top button undone, showing some manly chest hair. Yeah, she had a thing for *men looking like men*, and not like they'd been using the same place she had her bikini wax done. She was decked out in her purple zip-front silk-blend dress and wrapped up twice in her double leather belt. Her heels made her feel like she was closer to his height, as her legs were nearly long enough to keep up with his stride.

But this wasn't a date. Besides, the current generation of men seemed to be lost.

Like all the rest of her *Sex and the City* peers, Diana had bought into the fairytale for a little while, but in the end, she'd been burned. Mr. Big and the happily-ever-after at the finish was a fantasy and nothing more.

She peeked over at the Detective Chief Inspector. She had to hand it to him; he wasn't the *coming-on-to-her* type. If she looked up Rory Crannach in the Merriam-Webster dictionary, there'd be only one definition beside his name: *Serious*. Serious about his job, nothing else.

Okay, maybe a second definition: *A straight arrow.*

And she had to add just one more: *Brooding.*

Oh, what was wrong with her? She could admit she was attracted to him—who wouldn't be? But *now* wasn't the time. And he was a cop! She should be a blubbering mess, like the clerk who'd found Rance dead. Or at the very least, she should be more unnerved than she was.

But being in the presence of Rory Crannach made her feel safe.

"Thanks for walking me to the hotel."

"It's the least I could do. There's a killer on the loose." His voice was hard. Again, she couldn't help but see him as the epitome of seriousness. "You need to take precautions, Ms. McKellen. Be on the lookout." He stopped and stared at her.

"Where are you from?"

She laughed as if he could lecture *her* on taking precautions. "New York City."

"Ah. Then you understand a little."

"I can take care of myself all right," she said, defensively. She and her sister had been taught growing up that safety depended on being constantly aware of your surroundings. As all New Yorkers were.

"What I mean is, one person from your place of employment is dead. I just don't want it to become two."

That was sweet of him to say. *Sort of.* Except he wasn't trying to be charming.

"When are you headed back to New York? Tomorrow?"

"We have other events scheduled here in Scotland." Diana expected many more venues would cancel once the news got out about the Buttermilk Guild's demise—and Rance's. "Marta is scheduled to speak at the local quilt guild tomorrow."

Rory took her arm and guided her to a lamppost, pulling out his notebook. "Give me the details. I'll make sure someone is there."

Diana thought he might be overreacting, but she didn't mind. "I'll arrive at Marshdons Community Centre at six. Marta will get there about six-thirty. The meeting starts at seven." She paused, wondering what he was thinking. "You don't really believe there will be another murder, do you?"

"Just being cautious, Ms. McKellen."

She resumed walking. "I told you earlier to call me Diana."

"Diana," he said, as if practicing.

"So," she said, trying to be conversational. "Where do you live? Here in Glasgow?"

"I have a flat here, but I go where I'm needed."

"Is there a chance you'll find Rance's killer soon?"

"Aye. There's a chance." Apparently, that was as much information as she was going to get from him.

They reached her hotel. "This is me."

He nodded and waited, as if he was going to make sure she got in all right.

Now that it was time for them to part, she didn't want to. What if someone was waiting for her in her room? And not a *nice someone* either.

Rory's eyebrows came together, as if he'd just had the same thought, too. "If you don't mind, I'll check your room for you, to make sure it's clear."

Diana wondered about Marta and if she was scared tonight, too. But then, Marta lived in a secure building with a scan-in badge and a security guard. Still. . . "You won't forget to send me the names of bodyguards for Marta, will you?"

Rory held the door open for her. "Text me about it."

As they walked in, she pulled out her phone to type in his number from his card. As they passed the front desk, Diana tried not to imagine what the concierge thought of her returning to the hotel with a man in tow. The hotel staff didn't know her from Adam, but she still couldn't stop wishing Rory would flash his badge and say, *"Official police business,"* just the same.

When they got to her floor, he followed her down the hall and took her hotel keycard from her to open the door.

"Wait in the doorway," he said as he pushed the door open.

Diana watched him walk in, scanning every inch of the room, and she cringed. He could see her clothes scattered about on the bed, her pushup bra hanging on the door handle of the bathroom, and an unopened box of tampons on the counter next to the electric teapot. *Oh, no!*

He turned to her, as serious as ever, betraying no indication he'd seen her messy life strewn about. *But I was in a hurry to get to the bookstore!* she wanted to explain.

"All clear," he said.

"Um, thank you." He walked to her door, but turned back and stared at her red face. "You have my number. Call if you need anything." The door closed behind him.

"Oh, my!"

⋘⋙

Rory stepped into the elevator and ran a hand through his hair. *At least that's over with.* Thank goodness he wouldn't be hearing from Diana McKellen again, because something about her took him off his game. Besides, he was too busy for a bird like her. *Fine dinners. Galas. The theater.* She was too New York for him. He'd rather meet a Scottish woman at the pub and have a few laughs than get tangled up with a complicated woman like Diana McKellen. Once again, he wondered...why had she been so calm in the face of death? *Aye,* it was best he wasn't going to hear from her again.

His phone dinged. He looked down and read the text.

THIS IS DIANA. YOU SAID FOR ME TO REMIND YOU TO SEND THE NAMES OF BODYGUARDS.

Oh, hell. He wasn't quite rid of her yet. Against his better judgement, he saved her number. *Och,* he could've just responded to her and deleted her digits. Instead, he walked in the direction of his flat, pretty sure he was going to use her number to see her again. And it would have nothing to do with a crime scene.

4

T HE NEXT NIGHT, a few minutes before six, Diana pulled into the dark parking lot across the street from Marshdons Community Centre. She was glad the lights were on inside the building. Unfortunately, the two streetlamps outside were dead and the empty parking lot was spooky as hell with a stone wall on one side and a cemetery on the other.

The burning anticipation she'd felt all day at the prospect of maybe seeing Rory again was instantly replaced with alarm at the predicament she was in. *Alone. Vulnerable. Unarmed.* Was the killer waiting for her?

Diana remained in the car with the doors locked and took out her phone. The only person she could think to call was *him*, the Detective Chief Inspector. But what could she say? *Can you get here now? I'm scared!* But when he'd texted her with the bodyguards' information, there had been no salutation, no *see you tomorrow night*, just names and numbers. He'd never said *he* would be here at all. He'd only said he'd send someone.

"I wish Parker hadn't been running behind." Parker planned to grab a cab and make her way to the meeting by herself.

The front door to the community center opened and a large figure stepped outside. Instantly, Diana was no longer scared, only relieved. And shocked. It was Rory! If she was fifteen again, she would've thought her heart soared.

She put her phone away, feeling ridiculous, and got out of the car. She went to open the back door to retrieve the signage for tonight's event. Rory must've seen her, because he began walking in her direction. She ogled him for a moment, but stopped herself the instant she realized how nonsensical she was being. She wasn't a stupid woman who fell for good looks and that sexy Heathcliff quality. She gave herself a mental shake and got back to business. She ducked her head into the car, took a calming breath, and pulled out the first box.

When she stood straight again with the box in her arms, Rory was there.

"What are you doing here?" she asked. "You said you were going to send an officer."

"Pressure from above," he grumbled. "They wanted a senior officer to be here tonight, in case there is another international incident. Normally, I'm not reduced to babysitting detail."

"I'm glad you're here," she admitted. He made her feel so safe.

He reached for the box. "Let me get that."

"Thanks. That would be great. It'll save me a trip or two." *And it would save me from being out here alone in the dark.*

Using his head, he gestured to the car. "Add another box on top. I can take both."

She did as he asked...*or rather, as he commanded.* "If you didn't want to be here, then why are you here so early?" Finally, she grabbed the tube with the Quilt to Death banner and the Rook quilt before walking with him to the community center.

"I came early to do a search and get the layout of the building. When the place starts to fill up, I'll be able to keep an eye on everyone and everything."

"Smart," she said. "Have you gotten started yet?"

"I just finished."

"But how did you get in? Is someone else here?"

"The guild president, Cheryl. She's in the kitchen." Even though his hands were full, he balanced the boxes and held the door open for her.

As she crossed over the threshold, she closed her eyes and breathed him in. Just a hint of woodsy aftershave was enough to make her want to breathe him in again. So much for being over men.

A round woman in her sixties rushed to them.

"Cheryl," Rory said, "This is Diana McKellan."

"It's lovely to meet ye in person." Cheryl had laugh lines around her eyes and a pleasant expression on her face.

Diana gave her a grateful smile. "Thank you for agreeing to have the meeting anyway."

"My board and I made calls to all the members today. We told them if they couldn't be nice to Marta Dixon this evening, then they should stay home."

Three more women arrived and helped Diana set up the signing table, hang the banner and quilt, and place a bookmark on each chair. She learned they were on the guild board, too. Thirty minutes later, Marta's entourage showed up—Tilly first, carrying a box of books in her arms while lugging Marta's Louis Vuitton bag over her shoulder. Next, a very large man—a man much beefier than Rory—stalked in behind her, his eyes darting this way and that. When he saw Rory, he broke into a grin. The two men clasped hands like old friends.

"Good to see you," the beefy one said in a French accent.

Rory looked happy to see him and told Diana, "This is Jacques Boucher."

Diana had spoken with him on the phone and was exceedingly glad he could take the job of protecting Marta. But when she saw the embattled author, Diana was taken aback. The makeup caked on her face did little to hide the stain that covered half of her features from her scalp to her chin. However, it was Marta's red and watery eyes and her too-friendly-for-her smile that disturbed Diana.

She pulled Tilly to the side. "Is Marta all right?"

"I gave her a couple of Valiums. She was pretty upset when Rance's murder sank in." Tilly looked a little sheepish. "Maybe you could take this opportunity to talk to Marta. Convince her that the series can't end, that it has to go on."

Diana had to work hard not to roll her eyes. "How exactly could we undo the Buttermilk Guild deaths?" An even bigger obstacle would be to get Marta to write something other than true crime. In the meeting Diana had sat in on with Marta, she'd been adamant about ending the Quilt to Death series.

"I don't know." But Tilly looked hopeful. "I thought with Rance gone, Marta would see reason."

Diana shook her head. "Sorry, Tilly. I don't believe the Buttermilk Guild is going to come back." She glanced over at Marta. "Good grief! Is she *drooling*? Do you think she'll be able to give her presentation?" What a disaster! After all the wrangling Diana had to do to convince the guild not to cancel the engagement. "On another subject, I need to talk to you about what's on the docket for tomorrow. We have a change of venue."

"Tiillllly?" Marta called goofily. "Come talk to me."

Diana tried to take a calming breath. "Can you get her a cup of coffee first?"

"Sure." Tilly went to the kitchen area.

Jacques took up his position beside Marta, allowing Diana to finish the prep for the guild presentation.

When Parker arrived, Diana swooped down on her.

"Make sure not to get any close-ups of Marta's face. Besides her red-stained skin, she's more than a little strung out on Valium."

"Sure, boss. I'll take some pictures of the setup before the place gets crowded."

Rory didn't mingle with the quilters or Jacques, but stood where he could see both doors as the quilters arrived. When two guild members made their way to the kitchen to drop off plates of cookies, he shifted positions to keep an eye on them, too.

But as it turned out, the expected fifty members shrank to seven, most of them on the board, who had either been required to come because of their position, or threatened by Cheryl, the president.

"*Och*, I'm so sorry," Cheryl exclaimed at 7:01. "I think we're it. We better get started."

Diana patted her arm. "It's not your fault." *It's Marta's.* And the publisher for not finding a way to keep Marta from *offing* the Buttermilk guild. "Why don't we make it a cozy gathering? Informal."

Chairs scraped the concrete floor, as they moved into a semicircle around Marta's table. Everyone helped, except Marta, who sat behind her station, glassy-eyed. Diana was certain, if Marta had been her normal *diva-self*, she wouldn't have gone along with changing the event into something so casual and intimate. She probably would've thrown a fit and stormed out, blaming Diana that so few people had shown up.

Cheryl positioned herself to the side, clapped her hands twice, and the room went quiet. "I'm glad everyone could make it this evening." Her frown conveyed her disappointment at the small turnout. "Our guest needs no introduction, as we are all fans of the Quilt to Death series. Ms. Dixon, thank you for honoring our quilt guild by speaking with us. I'll turn it over to ye." Cheryl took her seat to the far right and waited.

Marta gave them all a goofy grin, but didn't say a word.

Diana quickly moved to the front. "Since we have a room full of fans, who would like to be first to ask a question?"

A woman with a bouffant hairdo raised her hand. "I will."

Diana checked first to make sure Bouffant wasn't holding a miniature milk can like the woman at the bookshop. "Go ahead." She hoped Marta would snap out of her drug stupor and answer the woman's question lucidly.

Bouffant stared down at Marta. "Tell us why we should keep buying yere books after ye murdered the Buttermilk Guild. I have to tell ye, it feels like an affront to Scotland!"

Jacques moved forward, as if to tackle the woman. Diana popped up and blocked him. She noticed Cheryl's cheeks were flushed, but apparently Cheryl wanted Marta to answer Bouffant's question, too, as she made no move to control one of her members.

Diana wished Cheryl would've done a better job of vetting the crowd. Or *non-crowd* as it were. *Except no one would've come.*

Marta's head tilted to the side as her hand shot in the air. "Free books for everyone!" Her words were slurred.

Diana took over, stepping in front of the signing table and putting her arms out, in case anything came flying in Marta's direction. "Yes, everyone will get a free copy of Marta's next book. I'll collect your addresses and make sure it happens."

They all crossed their arms as if they wanted no more books from the Buttermilk Guild killer. These quilters needed a diversion, anything to bring down the hostility.

Diana summoned her perkiest voice. "I see some of you brought quilts to have signed. How about you bring them up to Marta now?"

At that moment, there was a noise at the back of the room—the metal door leading from outside chafed the concrete floor. Everyone turned in their seat to see a man enter. And because Rory was right there and on guard, Diana put her attention back on the group.

"One at a time, bring your quilts up." *It won't take long.* "I have a fabric pen here for Marta to use."

Bouffant stood and slammed her hands on her hips. "I want to know how she—" Bouffant jabbed a finger at Marta "—has the nerve to come to Scotland after what she's done."

The new visitor rushed toward the circle of quilters. "Leave her alone!"

Diana didn't freak out. Rory kept pace with him, scanning him as if looking for a weapon. The Detective Chief Inspector had an air about him that said he was ready to take the intruder down, if the need arose. But mostly, Rory seemed interested in what the man was saying.

Marta looked up, coming to life. "Leo?"

This is Leo? At the office, people talked disparagingly about him. Diana was shocked to see he was very handsome. Tall, a head of blond hair, anchorman good looks.

Marta didn't get up, but cocked her head to the side. "What are you doing here? You're supposed to be at Malibu Hills Rehab, I mean, Resort...*resting.*"

Leo stopped and gazed at Marta with complete earnestness. "I got your message, sweetheart." He acted as if Bouffant and the rest of them had disappeared, and now he had Marta all to himself.

"What are you talking about?" Marta whined with confusion. "What message?"

"On the phone. Halloween night. I could tell you were missing me. I sensed you were ready to be rid of that hot-aired loser, Rance. You know I couldn't stand him. He wasn't right for you, punkin."

Marta emitted a choking sound. "Didn't you hear? Rance is dead."

"I know," Leo said. "I mean, I heard."

Marta rubbed her forehead, gazing at Leo.

He gave her a sad smile as if to tuck away the past. "I came to be with you. And I want you to know that I forgive you."

Marta seemed completely befuddled. Diana wasn't sure if it was the Valium or Leo's attempt at absolving her.

Bouffant stiffened at the words. "Well, we don't forgive her!"

Leo turned on Bouffant. "You better sit down and leave my woman alone."

His words riled the quilters, as they all came to their feet, speaking at once. "Ye have no right to be here!" "If ye know what's good for ye..." "Ye better leave!"

Rory interceded then, by taking Leo's arm. "I'll walk ye out."

But Leo wasn't done and broke away, rushing toward Marta. Jacques gently moved Diana aside and took up his post in front of his charge.

As Rory grabbed Leo's collar and brought him to a firm stop, Leo wailed to Marta, "Now that Rance is dead, we can be together, right?"

At Marta's look of shock, Diana wondered if she was thinking what Diana was thinking: *Did Leo kill Rance?*

There was some real merit to this theory. Leo had to know the particulars of Marta's books. And he had motive.

Diana watched as Rory dragged Leo away, wishing she

could go along with him to grill Leo with her questions. Rory had his ear to his phone before he even got him through the door.

She brought her attention back to the quilters, because apparently, Marta was too spaced out or too wigged out to get the meeting going again. "How about we get back to signing some quilts now?" she said brightly.

Only two of the seven people brought their quilts forward for a signature. And not one copy of the new book sold, only two earlier books. On the bright side, there wasn't a dead body outside as the evening concluded, and Diana was relieved.

Rory appeared again in the open room and came toward her.

"Where's Leo?" she asked.

"An officer came and took him to the police station for questioning."

"Here," Parker said. "Let me help you with the Rook quilt."

Diana wanted to know more about Leo, but held on to her questions for now.

With the Rook quilt off the stand, they took the corners and folded it. "I won't be going with you to the hotel."

"What's going on?" Diana asked.

"I'm going with Cheryl to the home of one of the members who couldn't come tonight, to photograph her collection of the Quilt to Death quilts. They're supposed to be works of art. Cheryl said she'll drop me off at the hotel afterward."

"Let me know when you've made it back safely, will you?" Diana said. Even though there wasn't a murder at the meeting tonight, it didn't mean they were in the clear just yet.

"Sure," Parker agreed.

The four of them—Parker, Cheryl, Diana, and Rory—hefted their boxes and headed for the door. Cheryl locked up the community center, said goodbye, and she and Parker walked off down the dark sidewalk.

Diana was alone with Rory and suddenly she was aware of her body. And his. She felt like she'd forgotten how to walk and how to talk. She forced herself to say something.

"I'm glad you came tonight." It felt stupid while she was saying it. But she was glad he'd come. Glad for the help to get things to her car, glad for the company, and especially glad he'd been there to circumvent Leo's intentions, whatever they were. "I'm grateful I don't have to do this alone. Spooky." And she felt stupider.

He glanced over at her, his gaze lingering for a moment, before he said, "Happy to do it."

They walked in silence to her car, the air thick with something. *Sexual tension?* Or probably more accurately, her imagination that there was something going on between them!

Diana unlocked the car. She wished he'd say something, anything, as they stowed each item.

Rory placed the last box in the back seat. "Is that everything?"

Her heart skipped a little. Was he *stalling* in order to spend more time with her? He had to know there were no more boxes to stow and the building was locked.

But he opened the driver's side door and waited for her to slide in.

"Thanks." Diana hesitated, not wanting him to go. She wished she had the nerve to take his hand or to make the first move, whatever that might be.

"Good night, Diana." He shut the door and shoved his hands into his jeans pockets. It all felt so final.

She held her hand up in a silent wave, knowing the truth. It wasn't just good night. It was goodbye.

She drove away feeling as if she'd missed out on something good.

At the hotel, she had to walk alone from the parking lot to the lobby. At her room, she had no manly Scot to search her place for anyone who might be lurking, waiting to kill her.

She locked the door, turned on every light, and made sure the window was latched. To calm the apprehension that had a stranglehold on her, she ran a bath. She needed a good soak to unravel her pent-up nerves. Of course, she was being ridiculous. Rance's murder was a fluke, and Rory—along with the rest of the police in Scotland—would soon find his killer.

She grabbed her phone and took it to the bathroom with her. Rory had told her to dial 999 in case of emergency and she meant to keep her phone close. She dipped her foot in the tub and then sank down in the warm water. Immediately, she relaxed. She laid her head back on the tile and closed her eyes, thinking of a certain police officer.

Her phone rang, and she jumped, nearly knocking her cell into the water as she scrambled for a washcloth to dry her hands.

"Hello," she said.

"Are ye okay?" Rory asked. "Ye sound out of breath."

"Your call startled me." She wasn't going to tell him she was in the tub, naked. She stood to grab a towel. Certainly, a couple yards of terrycloth would help calm her rampant heart.

"Is that water I'm hearing?"

She didn't answer him. "Give me a second." *To dry off!* She laid the phone on the counter to wrap-and-tuck the towel around her, before picking up the phone again. "What's going on?"

"I'm calling with bad news," he said.

Her heart went on a sprint. "Is Marta okay? Tilly? Parker?"

"The Ms. Dixons are fine. Marta wasn't picking up, so I called Jacques. They are safe at Marta's flat. Don't worry about Parker. She's fine. She's here with me."

"What?" Were they out together, having a drink? Diana had always liked Parker, but she certainly didn't harbor any warm feelings for her now. "Why are you calling then?"

"The Buttermilk Guild struck again."

Diana's lungs constricted. "What?" she barely squeaked out.

"Cheryl, the guild president, and Parker went to check on Judy Keith tonight after the event. You know, the woman whose quilt was used in the first murder? Apparently, Judy had told everyone she was coming to the meeting tonight and planned to bring the rest of her quilts to have Marta sign them."

"And?"

"Judy's dead."

Diana clutched her phone and used her other hand to steady herself against the wall. "Dead? It can't be."

"With a quilt wrapped around her shoulders, just like last night's victim," Rory said. "Cheryl confirmed it was the Buttermilk Guild's Sampler quilt with the same note attached as the first victim."

"Then it is a serial killer," Diana whispered, feeling more afraid than before. "Was Leo involved?" She felt a little dizzy. "But why would anyone go after Judy Keith? She was such a *nice* lady." Diana shouldn't have said that. She didn't mean to imply Rance got what he deserved because he wasn't nice.

"We don't know why Judy Keith was targeted. So far, the only theory we've come up with is the killer thought Judy saw him last night at the bookshop, when he took her quilt. Maybe he was afraid Ms. Keith could identify him to us."

That seemed logical. But awful. "Can you tell me how she died?" It was morbid, but Diana had to know. She figured it was because she was the daughter of a police officer.

"Strangled." He paused for a moment, as if he was struggling with whether to tell her more. "With a measuring tape."

"Like the second book!" Diana exclaimed.

"That's what Cheryl said, too, when I asked her if there was a correlation."

"Was Judy hit over the head like in the book?" Diana asked.

"Aye. A cast iron frying pan was lying beside her. Is your door locked?" The question seemed like a non sequitur.

"Yes." But just to be doubly sure, Diana padded to the door to click the lock again.

"I'm going to send someone over to the hotel to check on you anyway. I'll see if I can't get an officer to stay overnight, posted outside your door."

"That's not necessary."

But Rory had hung up.

She quickly dressed in a T-shirt and sweatpants, not knowing how much time she had before the officer arrived. Hopefully, after he or she checked on her, she'd be able to get into her pajamas. Though, after hearing about Judy Keith, and knowing Leo was nearby, Diana wasn't certain she'd be able to sleep.

Her first inclination was to go to Marta's apartment and see for herself that she was okay. She did the second-best thing. Diana retrieved her phone and called her.

Diana tried not to panic when there was no answer, telling herself Rory hadn't been able to reach Marta either.

Next, Diana tried Tilly, who picked up immediately.

"Hey, Tilly," Diana said. "I just wanted to make sure both of you are okay. Marta didn't answer her phone. Is she all right?"

"She's asleep."

"How did she take the news about Judy Keith?"

"Who?"

"The quilter, *um*, who was murdered. Detective Chief Inspector Crannach called, didn't he?"

"Oh, yes. *Her*."

"Did Marta freak out when she heard the news?"

"I haven't told her yet."

"Why?"

"She went straight to bed after the guild meeting." Tilly paused. "It might be best for *you* to tell her. Not now, of course. But tomorrow, when she's awake."

No! But Diana knew Tilly was right. She had a feeling Marta might otherwise take the bad news out on Tilly for being the messenger and all. "Sure, I'll do it." Diana paused, remembering there was something else. "Oh, yeah, tomorrow, we're heading out of Glasgow, first thing in the morning. I'll email you with the details." She walked over to her laptop and flipped open the lid. *Plan B will be starting tomorrow.* She'd meant to tell Tilly and Marta earlier, before the guild meeting, but Marta was so out of it that Diana forgot.

"I thought Marta had two more events in Glasgow," Tilly said.

"We've had a lot of cancellations," Diana said.

"Then where are we going?"

"Gandiegow," Diana answered. "The retreat has been moved up a week and a half. I understand that you and Marta have been there before?"

"Yes. At Gandiegow's first retreat. I really enjoyed the village."

"We need to leave by nine. It's quite a trek to get there." Diana found the info and sent it on to Tilly. "The email is sent."

"Thank you. Got it."

"Hey, I'm just wondering about Leo. Is he there with you and Marta?"

Tilly grunted. "Yes. In the bedroom with her. I told him she was out, but he insisted on sleeping next to her."

"I was just wondering." The police must've finished questioning him. "Thanks." Diana said goodbye and hung up. Had

Leo killed Judy Keith before he'd come to the quilt guild meeting tonight? She'd have to ask Rory about the time of death.

With so much on her mind, her head was spinning—*Marta, the new book, and murder.*

To counteract how helpless she was feeling, Diana sat down in front of her computer again and skimmed over the new itinerary. She opened her notebook and drew squiggles while she read, making notes also. The original plan was to spend the next week in Glasgow and Edinburgh, doing book signings and interviews. But plan B had them getting out of the city and filming interviews in charming—friendlier—settings which would give Marta a chance to explain why she had ended the series. The interviews would be conducted by Cait Buchanan, a reporter who was now married to the famous actor Graham Buchanan. After those three interviews were posted and hopefully going viral, Marta would lead a group of quilters at the Kilts & Quilts retreat in Gandiegow.

Cait had confirmed everything with Diana earlier in the day. Just reading over the plan helped Diana to feel calmer.

But then a knock sounded at Diana's door.

Yes, she was relieved the officer was finally here. But as she walked over to answer the door, she wished Rory hadn't hung up so quickly. They probably should've decided on a *code word* or phrase. It wouldn't do her any good to open her hotel room door and let a serial killer come waltzing in.

When she peered through the peephole, she relaxed.

Rory stood on the other side.

ℰꙨℭ℞

Rory ran a hand through his hair and hoped Diana checked first to make sure it was him.

It *shouldn't* be him, of course! He should've sent a junior officer to make sure she was all right. But he couldn't help himself.

She opened the door. "Hi." She tugged at her medium-length brown hair. The tips were wet, confirming what he'd thought earlier. She'd been in the bath when he called.

Man! She looked good in her white T-shirt and blue track-ies—wholesome, fresh, the girl-next-door. Quite the contrast from the purple number she'd had on last night, and the high heels, which were sexy as hell. But somehow, both looks fit her.

"May I come in and look around?" he asked before he checked with his brain...and his good sense.

She chewed her lip, then stepped back, opening the door wide.

But he didn't move, as he was mesmerized by her mouth.

"What about Parker? Where is she?" Diana asked.

He snapped out of it and walked over the threshold. "I gave her a ride here and checked her room as well. Naturally, she's shaken up, but she'll be okay." Perhaps he did have a valid excuse to be at the hotel. With both of the Americans lodged within rooms of each other, it made perfect sense. He sailed over to Diana's window and jiggled the latch.

"Am I in danger?" she asked.

He turned back and saw her worried face. "Honestly, I don't know." He went to check the bathroom, but the only thing he found was the tub still filled with water.

She skirted past him. "Nothing to see in there." She pulled the drain. "Anything else?"

"Are ye in a hurry to be rid of me?" He hoped not. He was drawn to her and he didn't know why. He'd like to stick around and see if he could figure it out.

"No, I'm not in a hurry for you to leave," she said quickly. Her answer seemed genuine.

He went to the small desk and stood by it like a guard. "It

would be best if ye returned to the United States." Best for her, for her safety. But he also knew it was to protect *himself*, too. He knew she could easily become a distraction for him. And he didn't have time for a distraction. He was all about the job. But apparently, not tonight.

Diana's eyebrows crashed together and he didn't like that he'd caused her pain.

He backpedaled a little. "I mean, it would be safer for all of you if ye went home."

She put her hands on her hips. "We can't go home. We're off to Gandiegow tomorrow."

"Gandiegow? Why would you want to go there?" He knew a little about Gandiegow. He pulled out his notebook and wrote it down. He'd have to get someone there to secure the place. "It's a fishing village the size of a midge."

She shrugged. "The reason we're going is kind of a secret."

He frowned at her. "What kind of secret? The kind that could get all of ye killed?" He planted himself in the chair in the corner, as if he was settling in for the night.

She watched him and then she carefully perched on the edge of the bed. "When the first Quilt to Death book came out, all the fans wrote in and wanted to know if the setting was real and where it was. Marta never told. Only a handful knew the real location. I only recently found out myself."

"I see." He'd heard that Gandiegow had set up some retreat center or something, having to do with quilting.

"I think now is the perfect time to reveal the inspiration behind the Buttermilk Guild."

"So, Ms. Dixon stole the idea from Gandiegow's quilt group."

"No, no. Gandiegow's Kilts & Quilts Retreat is the inspiration for her books' setting, but not the stories themselves. Now is the time to reveal it to the world, to steer them away from what Marta has done to the Buttermilk Guild."

"By the rising body count, it seems to me the Buttermilk Guild is fighting back," he said.

She cringed, but pressed on like a good soldier. "We're going to create some videos, podcasts, and do daily giveaways online. Hopefully, this will shut down the negativity and create some positive buzz for Marta's book and the series that's coming next. Surely, the bad press will die down soon."

He held out his hand for her notebook. "Show me what you have planned for Gandiegow."

Instead of handing it over, she clutched the notebook to her chest. "Why?"

"Because I need to know. And Jacques does, too. He'll need an hour by hour so he can devise a strategy to keep you safe, *I mean, Marta safe.*" Then as an afterthought, "And Tilly and Parker safe, too. It'll be my arse if another foreigner is murdered on Scottish soil."

"I'll email you my plan." She looked rather proud of herself for thinking up that one. Which only begged the question, *what was in her notebook she didn't want me to see?*

Just to test his theory, he held out his hand again. "Here. I'll write my email address down for you." Of course, she had his address already, since he'd given her his card.

Diana scooted away, pulling the pen from the top of the notebook, where it was clipped. "I'll write it down." Apparently, she'd forgotten about his card, which made this cat and mouse game more interesting. She opened to the back page, pen poised. "Go ahead."

He stood and moved closer to her, holding out his hand. "Forget the email. I'm in charge of this investigation. If ye insist on staying in Scotland, then yere plans have officially become my business. Hand the notebook over. Now."

"No," she said indignantly. "I have rights. I'm an American

citizen."

He lifted an eyebrow to let her know what he thought about her rights. "What's in there ye don't want me to see?"

"Nothing," she said too quickly, as she wildly looked around. Surely, she wasn't going to hide it from him! She shrugged. "It's personal. Okay?" She blew out a defeated breath. "Yes, I have our itinerary sketched out, but I also have other things in here, too. Just let me email you our plans, okay? "

Aye, something is in there. But he didn't want to scare her away so he let her off the hook, telling her his email address without pushing her further.

His own notepad was still in his hand. "While I'm here, do you know the particulars surrounding each of the Quilt to Death books? Where the murders occur, how they occur, what quilt, anything that might give us a heads up, if this really is a serial killer?"

"I made a list." She scooted back a little on the bed and cracked opened her notebook, but just barely.

He was going to be nice to her this time. "If you can't take a picture and text it to me, can you tell me what they are now?"

She read off the list, starting with book three.

Afterward she closed her notebook, pulled her legs up on the bed, and crossed them. "Do you want to watch some television with me?"

Surely she didn't mean to look seductive, but to his rattled brain that's what he saw. He could imagine climbing onto the bed and getting comfortable beside her, watching the telly holding hands, kissing. . .

But he wasn't on a date! He was supposed to be here to protect her. But who was going to protect her from him?

Suddenly, the room was too small for him. *Too cozy.* And dammit, he knew better than to mess around with someone involved in an investigation. He jumped to his feet. "Well, I better go." *Fast.*

"Oh?" Her inviting lips pouted and she looked disappointed.

Before he could do something stupid—even stupider *than coming here in the first place*—he headed for the door. "I have things to do. I'll check in with ye in the morning."

He practically sprinted for the door. But once outside her room, he felt a little lost. An idea came to him. He'd head downstairs to speak with the night manager. Surely, the hotel wouldn't mind finding a chair for a DCI so he could camp outside the American lass's door tonight.

5

DIANA STARED AT the door as it latched. "Wow. That was strange. One minute he takes a seat, as if to stay, and in the next minute, he's hightailing it for the door!" *Didn't he like what he saw?*

There was a knock and she froze.

"Deadbolt it," came Rory's muffled voice. "Now."

She hopped off the bed and rushed to the door, wondering if she should open it and give him some of her New York attitude. *No.* She really wasn't mad at him, just befuddled.

He knocked again.

She grabbed the handle and yanked the door open. "Hold your horses."

Mr. Rugged and Serious sighed. "Just do as I ask." He sounded like a man dealing with a petulant child. "I can't leave unless I know ye're safe."

"Okay." She stepped backwards. "Goodnight." She shut the door and secured both locks.

"Thank you, lass," came from the other side.

She looked through the peep hole and saw him running his hand through his hair, as he did frequently. Finally, he walked away, and so did she.

She climbed back on the bed and opened her notebook to the page where she'd been writing notes about Gandiegow. But that wasn't the only thing on the page. In the margin, she'd scribbled Rory's name about twenty times--with a few hearts thrown in for good measure.

She slammed her notebook shut. This wasn't her. She didn't daydream about men!

But wasn't it nice to be called lass?

Before she forgot, she went to her laptop and crafted an email for Rory of their itinerary for the rest of their stay in Scotland. She struggled with the closing: Hope to see you soon. She deleted that. For fun, she typed out: Love, Diana. But deleted that, too. In the end, she just signed her name.

At that point, she should've gone to sleep, but she was too wound up. She packed her bag and made more notes, but only ended up thinking about Rory. . ..

She woke with her alarm blaring and her notebook plastered to her face, feeling completely disoriented. She should've gone to bed like a sensible person. She stumbled into the bathroom to get ready, hoping today was better than the previous two.

But in the shower, Diana remembered she had to break the news to Marta about the second murder and wished she could take a day off—a *vacay* from the job she normally loved. Hurrying, she dried her hair, dressed in a black cami, a long ruffle-back blazer, and skinny black pants, before rolling her suitcase to Parker's room.

When Parker eased the door open, she appeared as ragged as Diana felt.

Diana gave her a quick hug. "Tell me how you're doing." She couldn't imagine seeing a second dead body. One had been enough.

Parker shook her head and blew out a breath as if the air in her lungs carried the weight of the world. "I'll be all right. I don't want to talk about it just yet, if that's okay?"

"Sure." They went down together to meet the shuttle. Once they were settled in the vehicle's third row, Diana texted Tilly. WE'RE ON OUR WAY. MEET US OUTSIDE.

In Diana's mind, she kept practicing different ways to tell Marta about Judith Keith's murder. Should she come right out with it or lay some groundwork first? In the short time Diana had known Marta, Marta always spoke directly, never filtering her words...unless she was in front of her fans. Should Diana tell her straight out about the murder, no hemming or hawing?

Too soon, the shuttle pulled up in front of Marta's flat. Diana called Tilly. "We're here."

"We're going to be a few minutes," Tilly whispered into the phone. "Marta isn't ready yet."

They waited twenty minutes, until Tilly appeared, wheeling three suitcases.

"Where's your sister?" Diana asked. The way the shuttle driver was grumbling, she was sure he wasn't happy about the delay. Neither was she.

"I'll go up and get the rest of her things," Tilly said. "We should be right down." But she didn't look certain.

Marta has more suitcases? But Diana shouldn't judge. Marta was *the talent* and she had a keen sense of how to play the part. Her taste was impeccable, even if her off-stage behavior could be downright diva-esque. Besides, Diana had overpacked for Scotland, too, expecting to dress up for every new event. All those nice outfits seemed a waste now.

"I'll be right back." Diana hopped out and followed Tilly upstairs to the apartment. Jacques stood at the door with his arms crossed over his chest.

Last night, she'd recognized he was imposing. But now she noticed he didn't have the serious all-work-and-no-play demeanor that Rory wore like his black leather jacket. However, Diana had a feeling Jacques could be more than a little dangerous, if provoked.

"I'm glad you'll be coming along with us to Gandiegow. I assume Marta is inside?"

Jacques nodded. Diana stepped around him and entered the apartment.

Leo met her at the door, dressed in a white suit; he was either auditioning for Miami Vice or he wanted to be Marta's twin. A man-purse hung from his shoulder.

Diana got the awful feeling that her day was about to get worse. "Are you going to Gandiegow with us?"

With his eyes, Leo shot poisoned arrows at Jacques's muscled back. "Someone has to keep an eye on Marta."

Oh, brother! Was Marta flirting with Jacques? In front of Leo? Marta had a reputation of going from one guy to another. But Rance had just died!

"Where's your luggage?" Diana asked.

"Tilly is getting it now. I've got a bad back, you know?"

Leo stood there impatiently as Tilly dragged two more suitcases from the bedroom.

Diana was *underwhelmed* with Leo so far. She ran over to relieve Tilly of her load. "Where's Marta?"

"She's just finishing up in the restroom," Tilly answered.

As if Marta was just waiting for someone to announce her entrance, the door was flung open and out she stepped in another one of her signature white designer suits. She wore a deep purple scarf that might have been chosen to downplay

63

her half-red face.

"We better get going." Diana ushered Marta out the door.

All the way down in the elevator, Diana looked for the right time and the right words to tell Marta what had happened to Judy Keith. But Leo wouldn't shut up, keeping a steady monologue running about absolutely nothing. He was probably trying to dominate Marta's attention to keep her from eyeing the overly muscled and manly Jacques.

Once out on the street, Diana and the shuttle driver loaded the extra suitcases, and then she positioned herself once more in the back with Parker. They didn't get to remain there comfortably for long, though.

"Leo, get in the back with Diana." Marta's voice held some irritation. "You know I need *my space* on long car rides."

Diana scooted over and made room for him and his overpowering cologne.

Marta took her place beside Tilly, but reached up and touched Jacques shoulder. "As I told you earlier, I really am glad you're here to protect me."

Leo scowled, and Diana felt a little sorry for him. But then she remembered that Leo could be the murderer. And here she was sitting right next to him!

"Punkin," Leo said sweetly, "if you need anything, I'm right here. I'm just going to close my eyes for a minute."

Marta only nodded.

"Love you," he said.

Marta didn't say it back.

Leo smiled as if she had. People in love could be selectively deaf and hear only what they wanted to hear. He leaned his head against the window and before they were even out of the city, he was snoring above the noise of the shuttle's engine.

What if Marta decided to take a nap, too? Diana leaned forward to tap Marta on the shoulder. "I have some bad news, and there's really no good time to do this." Diana saw Tilly grab her knitting bag and quickly pull out yarn and needles, as if she was too busy to get involved in this conversation.

"What is it?" Marta asked.

"Did you meet Judy Keith at the bookshop?" Diana knew she was hedging, but she wasn't sure how Marta was going to take the news.

Marta gave an irritated sigh. "I don't know. Why?"

"Judy came to your event so you could sign the first Quilt to Death quilt for her."

"So? A lot of them had quilts."

This wasn't going to be easy, and Tilly, with her head down and concentrating hard on *knit-one, purl-two*, was absolutely no help.

Diana shook her head and then blurted it out. "It was her quilt that was wrapped around Rance's body. Now she's been murdered as well."

Marta sucked in a scared breath and turned around, her eyes wide. "What?"

"I'm sorry to have been so blunt." Diana really was sorry, because Marta's eyes teared up and she grabbed her sister's arm.

"Tilly, there's been another murder." Marta sounded like a small, frightened child and Tilly finally looked her sister's way. "Fix it, Tilly?"

Tilly automatically put her knitting away and wrapped an arm around Marta. Marta laid her head on her sister's comforting shoulder, as if they'd been doing this all of their lives.

"There, there," Tilly soothed. "Your sister's here."

Diana knew she was witnessing an intimate moment, but she couldn't look away.

Tilly stroked Marta's hair. "Who took care of you after Mommy and Daddy died in the car accident?"

"You did," Marta whispered.

"Who made sure you were dressed and ready for school. Who packed your lunch?"

"You did," Marta said.

Some sort of weird power shift had occurred, with Tilly in charge now and Marta reduced to two-word whispers. It was easy to imagine the two sisters as little girls, clinging to each other after a tragedy had changed everything.

Tilly kissed the top of Marta's head. "I've always been there for you and I always will be. Now, close your eyes. When you wake up, everything will be better."

Marta nodded and relaxed against her sister.

Tilly began singing softly, a hypnotic lullaby which seemed to calm Marta more.

Diana did look away then and tried to focus on the scenery. Tilly and Marta's relationship might be a little odd, but Diana shouldn't judge. She and her own sister were living separate lives now, though once they'd been inseparable.

After Dad died, Mom was a mess and she and Liz had clung to one another. They'd had to. No one else was going to take care of them while their mother lay in bed, alternating between sleeping and sobbing.

Diana glanced at Tilly and Marta and couldn't help but draw parallels between the McKellan sisters and the Dixon sisters in front of her now. The difference was Marta and Tilly's lives were nearly conjoined, because Tilly was Marta's assistant.

Diana, though, couldn't remember the last time she'd seen Liz. Perhaps at Christmas? Or was it at the christening of Liz's youngest?

They'd never had a falling-out; it's just she and Liz seemed to have nothing in common anymore, except their mom. Liz lived in upstate New York, a busy mother of three, her life revolving around making dinner or taxiing her children to soccer and ballet. Diana couldn't imagine not having freedom to do as she pleased. But Liz had seemed happy at Christmas with her family around her. Diana could admit she'd been a bit jealous of her little sister then. But Diana had a full life, helping authors to make sure that their books thrived. Her job was important, and she loved it.

But sometimes...she wondered if there wasn't something more.

Diana looked at the two sisters in front of her and made up her mind to stop ignoring the nagging feeling that she was a bad sister.

As soon as she was settled in at Gandiegow, she was going to call Liz...and at least try again to have some semblance of family in her life, and to be a *good sister* to her sister again.

℘)(℃

Three hours later, the shuttle hit a pothole and Diana woke with a start. The last thing she remembered was Tilly's lullaby.

Jacques was quietly conversing with the driver. Marta was awake, the red half of her face visible to Diana while she spoke with her sister in hushed whispers. Leo was still snoring, and Parker had joined him, though not so robustly.

Diana gazed at the beautiful landscape of the Highlands stretched out before them. She'd always wanted to come to Scotland and she was kicking herself for sleeping through part of it. She blamed the murders for keeping her up last night, but it was really the Detective Chief Inspector's fault. *For being handsome, interesting, and confusing*, which did nothing to induce productive shuteye.

Finally, she glanced down at the pages spread across her lap—the latest threats to Marta—and began counting the less-than-friendly emails. Instead of waning, the death threats were growing. Diana made a mental note to email Rory the latest batch, something else to do when she arrived in Gandiegow.

Marta's low tones grew in volume, becoming angry and sarcastic sounding. What had happened to the sweet moment between them earlier?

Tilly straightened, looking indignant. "So, what *do* you propose I do, now that the Buttermilk Guild is gone?"

. "It's your life. Do whatever you want."

"Whatever I want? I want to keep writing the Quilt to Death series!"

What? Diana's attention was fully invested in their conversation now.

"Sorry, Tilly." Marta didn't sound sorry. "Writing more of that damn series is not an option. You're not supposed to be talking about it either."

Tilly looked down, defeated. "But all I have is the Quilt to Death series."

Marta glared. "Write something else."

"But--."

Diana tapped Marta on the shoulder. "Did I hear you correctly? Are you saying Tilly wrote the series and not you?"

The two sisters shared a look, but then Tilly squared her shoulders. "Yes. I wrote the Quilt to Death series."

Marta stared down her sister. "But I'm the reason the series has been successful. Tilly never could've done the public appearances."

Maybe Diana was having a bad dream. She just couldn't believe it. "So your name is on the covers but Tilly wrote *all* the books?"

Marta guffawed. "Not the last one. She's too much of a goody-goody to kill off the Buttermilk Guild. I had to put them out of their misery."

Diana's brain was spinning out of control. "Is this legal?" Of course, *ghostwriting* was legal—as long as you weren't lying to your publisher about it! "I mean, who knew about this?" Diana hadn't heard one word about it at the office.

From over her shoulder, Marta shot Diana the same annoyed look she'd been giving Tilly. "Relax. Once Rance became my editor, he fixed it with the lawyers at Three Seals."

But Rance had only edited the last few books. What about the rest? Dear lord, had she stumbled into the middle of a fraud?

Marta chuckled. "Stop looking so worried, Diana. The Quilt to Death series is a huge success."

Not is! WAS! Was a success. But not anymore.

"Weren't you worried the truth would get out?" Just another disaster waiting to haunt this book launch! And to haunt Diana. A skewed version of Milli Vanilli came to mind.

Tilly rubbed her forehead. "I signed away my rights."

"You signed a confidentiality agreement, too," Marta reminded her. "*Ironclad.* You can't tell a soul that you're my ghostwriter. Besides, big names use ghostwriters all the time to do the grunt work."

"Like writing?" Diana said sarcastically.

"Exactly." Marta dug around in her bag. "You're making too big a deal out of this." She pulled out an eye mask. "I'm going to shut my eyes for a while. I believe Tilly gave me way too much Valium last night." She slipped on the mask and leaned her head back on the rest.

Diana frowned at the back of Marta's head. Working with her was turning into a hell of a headache and there weren't enough aspirin in all of Scotland to make it go away. By the time this was over, Diana was certain she would be stripped of her *Fixer* title.

"How much longer until we get there?" Diana asked the

shuttle driver.

"Thirty minutes or so," he answered.

Diana steeled herself for the next obstacle. Gandiegow wasn't going to be the Scottish vacation she'd always dreamed of or a respite from her troubles. Before Diana left New York, all the arrangements for the upcoming retreat had been made through Cait Buchanan, owner of the Kilts & Quilts Retreat. But when Diana had switched to plan B, she'd gotten an earful from Deydie McCracken, Cait's cranky grandmother. Seems she didn't want Marta to step foot in Gandiegow, no matter the previous arrangements, because *she murdered my quilters!*

Minutes later, Cait called back and apologized, assuring Diana that Deydie wouldn't be a problem and that the Dixon sisters would be welcome in Gandiegow.

Still...

The only thing Diana was looking forward to, once they reached Gandiegow, was the possibility of running into Graham Buchanan, Cait's hottie movie star husband. Diana sighed. She and every woman in the world had a crush on the man.

Another manly Scot popped into Diana's head, but she banished Rory immediately. She didn't believe she would be seeing him again even if she wanted to.

Diana looked out the window. They were in the middle of nowhere—only sheep, a cottage here and there, and the occasional castle ruin could be seen. She decided to zone out and enjoy the scenery for the rest of the trip.

Thirty-one minutes later, the driver called out to them, "We're here."

But they weren't exactly. He turned onto an unmarked road and descended a very steep incline. The water was on their right as they made their way to the parking lot at the bottom, which butted up to the oceanfront. The village was exposed to the sea, sitting along a stone walkway that would provide no protection from a raging storm. Diana was grateful for calm waters today, though it was gray, misty, and cold.

She pulled out her phone. Cait had said to text her when they arrived in town. A moment later, she received a text back:

I'M SENDING RACHEL TO MEET YOU. SHE'LL GET YOU SETTLED IN.

By the time the shuttle driver had the van unloaded and Diana had paid him, they were approached by a cute woman and three gorgeous men—undeniably fishermen, judging by their raincoats and Wellies. Besides, she'd researched Gandiegow before coming to Scotland and knew this wasn't just a quilting destination, but a fishing village, too.

The men could've starred in a Ralph Lauren ad or on the cover of Scottish Hunks, a magazine Diana would certainly buy if it existed. She walked forward to meet them and stuck out her hand. "I'm Diana McKellen."

The woman shook it and answered in an American accent, "Rachel Wallace." She pointed to the men beside her. "This is my husband, Brodie, and these two are the Duffy brothers. I brought along a lot of muscle to carry your things. Gandiegow, you see, is a walking village. No cars beyond the parking lot." She beamed up at her husband as if he had invented this delightful system.

Diana introduced the rest of the group as the shuttle driver drove away. Brodie, the Duffys, and Jacques all grabbed bags and boxes and started toward the interior of the village.

Brodie spoke to Diana as he passed. "Leave the rest. We'll come back and get it."

"Thank you," Diana said.

"This way." Rachel took off toward the back of the cottages. "I've made up rooms for the Ms. Dixons and their bodyguard at Partridge House." She gave a worried glance in Leo's direction. "I hope you don't mind, Mr. Shamley, but you'll have to take the room over the pub. I just rented out the last two rooms of my B and B."

Leo grunted.

Diana should've thought to text Cait before they left Glasgow to warn her about Leo joining them unexpectedly.

Rachel pointed to a building. "Diana, you and your friend Parker will be staying at one of the quilting dorms—Duncan's Den. You don't mind sharing with the retreat goers when they arrive, do you?"

"Not at all." Actually, it would be perfect. Being at the quilting dorm would give Diana distance from Marta. It would also give her a chance to take the temperature of the retreat goers; if they had any animosity toward Marta, Diana should be able to defuse the situation before things got ugly and out of hand.

Marta could've made everyone's life easier if she hadn't killed off the Buttermilk Guild.

A crazy but possibly brilliant idea came to Diana, which was shocking because her brain had been *all-Rory-all-the-time* ever since she'd met him. As soon as she could, Diana needed to speak with Tilly alone.

A young woman dressed in a plaid jacket and a knit hat came towards them from between two cottages. "Hey, everyone," she called.

"This is Sinnie," said Rachel. "I'll give you and Parker a quick tour of Partridge House," she said. "Then Sinnie can take you to Duncan's Den."

Marta glanced around with disdain. "Why does Gandiegow have to be so gray and gloomy?"

Diana wondered if Tilly had more Valium tucked away to slip to Marta.

"The weather is verra *dreich* today," Sinnie said cheerily.

"I'm guessing that means dull, dreary, and depressing,"

Marta responded caustically.

Sinnie laughed. "Aye. Something like that."

"Maybe the sun will shine later," Rachel said, as if she was defending her home.

But the possibility of sunshine didn't help Marta's mood as they walked up to Partridge House's welcoming front door.

"We opened to the public two months ago," Rachel said. "I've been in the hotel business my whole life, but I've never worked anywhere that I've loved more." The new structure had been designed to fit in with the rest of the village, with stone walls and shuttered windows. "Wait until you see the inside. We used reclaimed wood from a sheep farm ten miles up the road."

"It's rather small for a B and B, isn't it?" Marta complained.

Rachel looked as if she'd dealt with difficult customers before and put a pleasant smile on her face as she pushed open the front door. "We have seven bedrooms. You and your sister each have a single occupancy room, as requested."

Diana and Parker left their backpacks at the entrance and followed Rachel as she gave them a tour. The woodwork was dark, as typical for Scotland, while the quilts hanging in the entryway made the area bright and cheery. Diana followed Rachel up the staircase, where the floral wallpaper countered the dark wood by whispering femininity. Diana found all of it cozy and inviting.

Rachel indicated the first bedroom at the top of the steps. "Each bedroom is named after a quilt block." On the door hung a rustic painted sign which read FLYING GEESE above a quilt block made of triangles. "You'll see the same design in the quilt on the wall." She pushed the door wide and pointed out the quilt on the far wall. The rest of the room was decorated in dark greens, browns, and blues. "Jacques, you'll have the Flying Geese Room."

Next, Rachel took Tilly and Marta to their bedrooms: the Dresden Plates and Kansas City Star rooms. Marta seemed anxious to shut her door and be alone.

Rachel pointed to the steps leading up. "Upstairs are our personal quarters."

Diana figured the tour was over, but Rachel surprised her.

She had a gleam in her eye. "I just have to show you something. Do you mind another flight of stairs?"

"Not at all," both Diana and Parker said together.

They followed Rachel, who spoke over her shoulder.

"My daughter, Hannah, has the cutest quilt which Deydie just made for her." When Rachel reached the top, she opened the door to a little girl's dream bedroom, complete with canopy. "See on the bed? Deydie calls the new quilt Let's Get Sheepy." The quilt consisted of wide vertical strips of sheep fabric of various colors alternating with white.

"That's delightful," Diana said.

"Hannah is very much into fishing, like my husband, but Deydie thought she needed to expand her repertoire." Rachel laughed. "Hannah acts like she just tolerates sheep, but I know she loves her new quilt."

They closed the door and headed downstairs to see the large living room and kitchen. When they were done, Rachel held the front door open for them. "I'll turn you over to Sinnie now and let you get settled in at Duncan's Den."

Diana picked up her backpack. "Thanks."

Once outside again, Sinnie guided them two doors down to Duncan's Den. The quilting dorm, it turned out, was simply a large cottage with extra beds set up in each bedroom. But it was cozy and would be a great place to hang out with the quilters when they arrived. Diana and Parker chose the bedroom at the end of the hall on the first floor.

Diana quickly set her things in their room, knowing they

needed to hurry to Quilting Central. Deydie McCracken had made herself clear on the phone, and Diana needed to head her off at the pass, in case she had thoughts of scalping Marta for killing off the colorful characters of the Buttermilk Guild.

It was only a few minutes' walk to Quilting Central through one of the byways between the cottages called *wynds.*

When Diana stepped from Thistles Wynd onto the walkway that faced the North Sea, the view took her breath away. She felt as if she were standing on the edge of the world. Such joy and peace filled her. But then she remembered the phone conversation with the cranky, old head quilter and her moment of peace evaporated.

Sinnie opened the door to Quilting Central and let them pass through the entrance. "That's Deydie over there," she whispered.

Deydie was a short stout woman, seemingly almost as wide as she was tall. She had a white bun wound at the back of her neck, a black skirt that hung nearly to the floor, and a pair of scuffed black Army boots. The soft expression on her face, as she held a baby against her shoulder, made Diana think she'd pegged the woman all wrong. Deydie was nothing but a softie! She was swaying and singing to the baby with such gentleness that the scene made Diana smile.

"Come," Sinnie said. "I'll introduce ye."

But as they made their way over, a woman about Diana's age leaned over and said something to Deydie. The old woman spun around quickly, stared at Diana as if she'd cut holes in her favorite quilt, then handed the baby to the woman who'd spoken to her.

Deydie's demeanor changed from loving granny to pissed-off wolf, as she barreled toward Diana. The change was so abrupt that Diana took a step back, wishing she was armed with more than her quick wits.

"Where is she?" Deydie demanded. "Where is that she-devil?"

Sinnie laid a hand on Diana's arm. "I think she means Marta Dixon."

Diana squared her shoulders and donned a modicum of false confidence, as if slipping into a business suit. "Marta is at Partridge House, settling in."

The woman shifted the baby and rushed to the door. "Hello, Diana, I'm Cait Buchanan. This is my gran, Deydie."

Cait seemed nice enough, but Deydie was looking for a fight.

Diana didn't take the bait. "Cait, it's nice to meet you. Deydie, it's nice to meet you, too. I appreciate you both letting us come early and extend our visit. And thanks, Cait, for agreeing to conduct Marta's interviews."

Deydie glowered at her. "Ye have quite the nerve to bring Marta Dixon here. Especially after what she's done."

Diana pulled out her logical argument, the one she'd been rehearsing for the village. "Marta coming here will be good for Gandiegow and the Kilts & Quilts Retreat. *Free publicity.* You have to be happy about that."

Deydie's glower intensified. "Happy about it? What would make me happy is if ye took the Buttermilk Guild killer to the end of the dock and dumped her in the sea! Get her out of Gandiegow now!"

Diana stood her ground. "I can't do that."

Deydie nodded, and for the slightest moment, Diana thought she'd won. But then Deydie went for the door.

Cait stepped into her path. "Gran, no. Ms. Dixon stays." Diana thought Cait was the bravest woman she'd ever seen. But maybe Cait knew Deydie wouldn't hurt her with the baby in her arms. "Besides, I told you Ms. Dixon's publishing company has sponsored this event. You don't want to give back all the money, do you?"

For a moment, Deydie's old face looked conflicted, but then she grabbed a broom by the door. "I'll let Marta Dixon decide whether she wants to stay or not—*after she meets the business-end of my broom!*" Deydie swung it as if batting a mangy dog out of her way. "Nay. She won't want to stay after I have a wee chat with her."

Cait stepped into Deydie's path again. "Ye can't do this. The retreat goers—who are expecting to meet Ms. Dixon—will be here in a week. We handpicked them."

"*Ye* handpicked them. I had nothing to do with this."

"Regardless, the retreat goers signed up for this special session and we have an obligation *to them* to provide the program that we said we would."

"Ye're all numpties," Deydie proclaimed. "And Caitie, ye should know better." Then the old woman blew through the door.

Diana followed and had to jog to keep up. Deydie might be ancient, but she was doing some serious power-walking.

"Wait," Diana said, but Deydie kept moving, ignoring her.

Diana caught up with Deydie and her broom as she slung open the door to Partridge House. "Marta Dixon! Get yere arse out here! Now!"

Jacques was the first to appear and blocked the old woman easily.

Deydie cranked her head this way and that, trying to see around him.

"Ms. Dixon is busy right now," he said, his French accent thicker than it was before.

"Do ye know who I am?" Deydie said, as if she owned the village. "I'll speak with Marta Dixon now."

"No. You won't." Jacques was as unmovable, and seemed as large, as the bluffs above the village.

Deydie tapped Jacques's chest with the handle of her broom. "Get out of my way. I didn't get a chance to speak with Marta Dixon at the bookshop in Glasgow. But I will now?"

"Wait a minute," Diana said. "You were at the bookshop? You drove all that way to see Marta?"

"No. I took the train. Sadie told me Marta was going to be there. Besides, I had been wanting to go to the wool shop in Glasgow for my winter knitting. Deydie gave a frightening grin. "I saw what happened ...that woman throwing blood all over *that murderer*." Her white bun flopped side to side as she shook her head. "Marta Dixon never should've killed my quilters that way!" She pointed a finger at Diana. "She got what she deserved at that bookshop! I only wish I'd thought of it first!"

"But were you there when the body was found?"

"What body?" Deydie asked impatiently.

"Marta's editor was murdered," Diana answered.

Deydie looked away, trying to peek around Jacques again. "I don't have time for yere jabberin'."

Diana was perplexed. "Where were you last night?"

"I was home," Deydie said irritably to Diana before turning back to Jacques. "Now out of my way, ye big French oaf. I'm going to find Marta Dixon." She tried to swat Jacques with her broom, but he blocked it with one beefy hand.

"Was anyone with you last night? Any witnesses?" Diana was sounding like the Detective Chief Inspector.

"I was alone, lassie. Me old bones were hurting and I went to bed early. I'm right as rain today, though." She glowered at Diana, as if she meant to wield her broom at her next, just for making her admit to a little arthritis. "Now, tell this bloke to move so I can take off Marta Dixon's head."

Diana touched the old woman's arm. "Deydie, there was a second murder last night."

"I know, there's murder in all the books. And murder is

what she did to the Buttermilk Guild!"

Diana wasn't sure how to get through to her. "No. There were two *real* murders. In Glasgow. Marta's editor," she repeated, "and a woman named Judy Keith. A quilter."

"A quilter?" Deydie slammed her hands on her hips. "What quilter? And why are ye talking about murder?"

"Because there is an honest-to-goodness murderer out there. And the two murders are somehow connected with the Quilt to Death series." Because her dad was a cop, Diana held back the bit about the quilts being the same as the quilts in books one and two. She finished with the bodyguard. "And this is Jacques. He's here to protect Marta." She nodded at the large man. "Give him a break. He's only doing his job."

Deydie stepped back and looked up at him, as if only now taking his measure. "Ye know I have to see her sometime."

"*Oui.* Sometime." Jacques was a man of few words.

The way Deydie was glaring at him, Diana was concerned Jacques might need to bring in reinforcements.

Diana motioned beyond the entryway but spoke to Jacques. "Can you let Marta and Tilly know that Parker and I will be ready to go in twenty minutes?"

"Where are ye heading?" Deydie said as if no one was going anywhere without her permission.

"We have an appointment at Spalding Farm to get some footage of Marta interacting with the animals."

"Aye. The beasties. They may be only farm animals, but I'm sure they'll want nothing to do with the she-devil. How are ye getting there anyway?"

"Cait said Sinnie offered to take us," Diana said.

"Oh, she did, did she?" Deydie took off, huffing and muttering, as she made her way back through the cottages for what looked like Quilting Central.

Poor Cait!

Jacques grinned at Deydie walking away, as if the old woman had been entertainment instead of a threat. "I'll let the Ms. Dixons know you're ready to leave soon." He went back inside and shut the door. Diana decided to forego witnessing the battle between Deydie and Cait. She'd text Cait and let her know that her grandmother was heading back to Quilting Central and Diana was at Duncan's Den. Diana's brain hurt, overloaded with what needed to be done and other worries. She still wanted to call her sister Liz. And she was wondering if she was going to see Rory again.

And there was more. *Much more.* Maybe at the farm, while Parker was filming Marta, Diana could pull Tilly aside and have that talk with her.

6

"**D**AMNED HAIRY COOS." Rory stepped on the gas as the last one meandered off the road. "Farmers really do need to check their fences," he said to his colleague in the passenger seat. "I wanted to get to Gandiegow before the Americans to make sure the village is secure." This wasn't the first time he'd said this today.

"We'll make a thorough sweep as soon as we get there." Reid McCartney was always looking on the bright side of things, which didn't seem to fit with the occupation of homicide detective.

Rory only grunted in response. Overnight, he'd gone through Parker's video of the book signing and found nothing of importance. He'd left his chair outside Diana's room early this morning, in plenty of time. But a flat tire on the way to McCartney's and then the hairy-coos road-barricade had frazzled Rory. Or maybe it was sleeping upright in a chair. Or maybe it was because he didn't sleep at all for thinking about the woman on the other side of the door.

McCartney, who hailed from this area of northeast Scotland, pointed. "Turn here. We'll be to Gandiegow in a couple of minutes."

They were in the middle of nowhere and there was no signpost at the turn. But then Rory saw the village down below. It was almost a drop-off.

"That's it," McCartney said. "Tucked right there between the ocean and the bluff. Make another right."

The road had a steep incline and Rory had to remember to ride the brakes to make it into the village safely. Though he was in a terrible hurry.

"Park here," McCartney said. "It's a walking village."

It felt like another delay to Rory. But the second he got out of the car, he saw Diana walking toward him with Parker at her side. His insides, which had been wound tight, relaxed and seemed to sigh. Which was ridiculous on so many counts. He'd only just met her.

Diana seemed to pause, too, and then resumed walking. He wondered if he'd surprised her like she had him.

Jacques, Marta, Tilly, and a young woman Rory didn't recognize were right behind Diana and Parker. Since they were all coming in his direction, Rory waited.

When Diana was close enough, he said, "Where are you going?" Now, why was he sounding so gruff?

She raised an eyebrow at him. "Colin Spalding's farm. Didn't you get the itinerary I sent you?"

"Yes." That had been another delay, when his printer at home had jammed. *But I'm here now and everyone is okay.*

"Hi," she said to McCartney. "Good to see you again."

Rory didn't like her cheery greeting to his inferior. But he decided it was harmless.

"Do you want to come along?" Diana asked.

Rory's brain froze, and McCartney cleared his throat and

took over.

"You go," McCartney said. "I'll stay and start surveying the village for problem areas." McCartney's eyes shifted to Diana and then back to him, as if looking for clues.

"Yes," Rory agreed. "I should go with Ms. Dixon."

Diana leaned toward Rory. "Just so you know, Leo came with us to Gandiegow. He's taking a nap in his room over the pub." Before he could respond she turned briskly to McCartney.

"You should check in with Quilting Central and tell them who you are. You'll want to speak with Deydie McCracken." She laughed wryly. "Good luck."

McCartney nodded, as if he was taking directives from Diana now.

"Call me if anything seems off," Rory said.

"Will do." McCartney said as he headed for the village.

"Ride with me," Rory said. "We'll follow the others."

The interior of the car buzzed with an energy that wasn't present when McCartney had been his passenger. Rory struggled to get the atmosphere more businesslike than personal. "So Leo?" he asked.

"I was certainly surprised when he was at Marta's this morning," Diana said. "So I guess he was questioned and released?"

"There was nothing to hold him on," Rory said. "How is Marta acting around him? Does she seem fearful?"

"No. Mostly indifferent, if I had to put a word to it. I think she's truly shocked by the two murders. We all are," Diana said, though she seemed calm.

"Anything else transpire that I need to know before we get to the farm and around the others?" he asked.

She shook her head. "Nothing murder-related, only publishing business."

"How did ye sleep last night?" he asked. As soon as the question came out, he realized he shouldn't have. It was too personal. He hadn't asked McCartney how he'd slept!

"Not very well," she admitted. "Too much on my mind. How about you?"

Too much on his mind, too. "I slept like a babe," he lied.

They glanced at each other at the same time, and Rory could have sworn there was an honest to goodness spark between them. He'd seen it. He'd even swear under oath that it had happened.

But when he looked away, there was another glint of light, and he realized that the *spark* had been nothing more than the sunlight bouncing off her chunky silver necklace!

He swore that when he got to the farm, he was going to stick his head in the nearest watering trough and wash away all the crazy thoughts that this American lass had put in his head. After that, he was going to do his damnedest to find the Quilt to Death murderer. Because if Diana didn't leave Scotland soon, he wasn't sure what he might see or say next. Or what he might do.

ଚ୨୦ଓ

"No!" Marta held her arms up, away from the offered rope. "Keep that nasty sheep away from me!"

It seemed as if the whole entourage rolled their eyes at once—Diana, Rory, Jacques, Tilly, and Parker.

Diana thought the sheep wasn't nasty at all. She looked over at Rory and they shared another moment—about fifty of them since they'd gotten to the farm. Diana put her thoughts back on the sheep. Miss Bo-Peep was the cleanest sheep she'd ever seen, though that wasn't saying much, as Diana had never before seen a sheep up-close and personal. Miss Bo-Peep, who belonged to Ewan McGillivray—the rope holder--was just a

84

visitor to Colin Spalding's farm, and was as adorable as the rest of her current surroundings. Five majestic Clydesdale horses were corralled within a wooden fence, whinnying for more of the fresh carrots and apples the human visitors had given them earlier. Fancy chickens with fluffy feathers atop their heads wandered around the yard along with white-as-snow ducks. And three large docile dogs stood guard beside their master, Colin Spalding, watching the strangers from America. Thank goodness, Parker looked to be getting it all on her video camera. Now, if only Marta would cooperate.

Ewan McGillivray, Laird and owner of Here Again Farms and Estates, dropped his sheep-rope-holding arm to his side and frowned. "Och, I gave Miss Bo-Peep her bath before we drove here." Right off, it was easy to read Ewan. He was good-natured, good-looking, nicely-dressed in a kilt and a polo with the Here Again logo over his heart. But he was no *Rory Crannach*. Perhaps Ewan's one flaw stuck out from under his golf cap—his large ears. But Diana liked him instantly.

Diana figured out immediately why Cait had volunteered Sinnie to drive them to Spalding Farm. It was clear she and Colin Spalding were an item.

Colin said, "Ewan came all this way. Can't ye do something to make Ms. Dixon get a picture with his prize sheep?"

Diana nodded, though she wasn't holding out hope. "I'll try." If Diana had any control at all—*and a time machine*—she'd force Marta to go back in time and undo the last book.

Marta had been a pill ever since they'd arrived in Gandiegow. She'd pitched a fit about coming to the farm this evening, saying she wanted to stay in and call a masseuse. As if she hadn't been to Gandiegow before and knew perfectly well there wasn't a spa within a hundred miles of the place.

"I'll do what I can with Marta," Diana added. "I thought coming to the farm was a brilliant idea. The tenth quilt is made of wool and flannel, so I figured readers would get a kick out of seeing the sheep who provided the wool for the fabric she used."

Sinnie gave Diana a pointed look. "Plus, ye hoped they'd forget all about what Marta did to the Buttermilk Guild."

"That, too," Diana confessed.

She smiled weakly at Colin. "Don't expect much. Marta doesn't understand that she has a serious image problem." Diana's own words gave her an idea. "I'll go talk to Marta now."

Colin grinned. "At least yere friend is enjoying the scenery."

True. Parker was falling all over herself flirting with Ewan McGillivray.

"Laird Ewan, how about I get a photo of you with the sheep?" Parker purred. "You can show Ms. Dixon how it's done."

Colin had introduced Ewan as Laird, explaining that he was the owner of a large estate that had been in his family for generations. Ewan had insisted they call him by his Christian name, but Parker was too besotted from the get-go for the words to sink in.

Ewan tipped his hat. "Certainly." *At least he has a full head of hair to go with those ears.*

As Parker snapped pictures, Diana made her way over to Marta, which meant she was also making her way over to Rory. Her insides did somersaults and back handsprings. *Calm yourself.* But Diana was pretty sure the pep talk wasn't going to work because her insides weren't listening.

She told herself to concentrate on Marta. There was only one way to motivate that massive ego.

Diana took the rope from Ewan and sidled up to Marta. "You're the consummate professional, Marta. Your image is everything. I know you can do this. You're the face of the Quilt to Death empire and this *one* picture will go miles to entice your readers to follow you to *your new series*." She held out the rope.

As expected, stroking Marta's ego worked. She took the rope and slapped on her game face. "Take the picture." She smiled brightly as Parker got the winning shot.

Diana glanced at her watch. "Let's wrap it up. We need to be back in Gandiegow for dinner, then you're going to have your interview with Cait Buchanan."

"Will Graham Buchanan be with her?" Marta asked.

I wish! But Diana said, "No. Cait said he can't make it."

Marta frowned and dropped the sheep's rope in the dirt. She walked away toward the edge of the barn, saying, "Get me a bucket of hand sanitizer."

Tilly ran after her sister, digging frantically in her bag.

Parker hurried over to Diana. "If it's okay with you, I'd like to hang around for a while. I want to get more shots of the farm."

And spend more time with Ewan! But Diana wouldn't waste her breath preaching to Parker. Diana was having her own troubles controlling herself with the Detective Chief Inspector around. Which was a problem she had to fix. She was the *Fixer* after all, and she had to fix her attraction to Rory. Stamp it out! She had to keep reminding herself that she didn't date cops under any circumstance, not even when they were as enticing as Rory. "Sure, Parker. You can stay. But I need you back within the next hour for the interview, remember?"

Ewan smiled brightly. "I'll give her a lift."

Diana gave Ewan points for knowing there was chemistry between him and Parker, and for taking the initiative.

Ewan kept his eyes on Parker, but seemed to be speaking to Diana. "I'm going to Gandiegow, too, as Deydie wants me to bring her three of my milking ewes. She said the milk would help some of the older women in the village with their osteoporosis."

Like Deydie wasn't one of the older women!

"I'll see you both there," Diana said.

Sinnie must've been listening in. "I can take you back now."

Colin pecked her on the cheek. "See you soon, luv."

Awww. Diana wished she had her own Scottish guy calling her *luv*. She couldn't help but glance over at Rory, who hadn't seen a thing, as he had his eyes on Marta. It was just as well.

Diana caught up with them. "Ready to go?"

"It's about time," Marta muttered.

Jacques ushered her toward the car.

Though Diana needed to figure out the carpool arrangements for the trip back, she ran after Tilly instead. "Can you hold up for a second?"

Tilly stopped and gave her a quizzical look.

"While we have a moment alone, I want to talk to you. From what I overheard, I gather you didn't know Marta was writing book ten?"

Tilly nodded cautiously.

"Does that mean you've been working on book ten as well?"

"Yes," Tilly said timidly, as if she might get in trouble for admitting the truth. "I'm nearly done."

"Can you do me a favor?" Diana asked. "Keep writing that book. I'm going to talk to Three Seals about how we might revive the Buttermilk Guild."

Tilly's face lit up. But a second later, her eyebrows crashed together, as if they'd been shot down with a single arrow. "Marta...Marta would never allow it."

"Don't worry about Marta." Diana could tell Tilly wasn't convinced. "Just keep writing the book." Surely Three Seals would want to continue the series, especially since Diana had come up with a possible way to get them out of the mess they were in. If she could get the publisher onboard soon, then maybe Marta's on-camera interviews could tease how the Buttermilk Guild might just be alive and kicking. But that begged the question, what would she do about Cait's interview with Marta this evening? *Maybe do the planned interview, but not post it until I can get an answer from Three Seals?*

Rory motioned to Diana. "Are ye riding back with me?"

Was it her imagination or did his voice sound hopeful?

She had to shut this down, for her own sake. "Tilly, can you ride with DCI Crannach?" Diana had heard him refer to himself that way earlier. "I need to go over the interview questions with Marta." Which wasn't exactly true.

Rory frowned, but quickly recovered as Tilly dutifully made her way to his vehicle.

As soon as Diana got in the car with Marta, she wished she'd gone with Rory. He was a much better conversationalist. He also didn't rail on Diana for not having the foresight to get Graham Buchanan in on the interviews with his wife.

Once back in Gandiegow, Diana watched as McCartney met Rory at the car. They left together down the walkway next to the ocean, both of them scanning the cottages and wynds. And leaving Diana, ridiculously, longing after Rory's presence.

Diana went with the others to Quilting Central, as directed by Deydie before they left for the farm. As soon as Diana got there, one of the elderly quilters pulled her aside.

"Me name is Bethia. It seems baby Hamish has a bit of a fever. Cait is at home with him now. She told me to give you her apologies."

"Not a problem," Diana replied. She breathed a sigh of relief. Not because the baby was sick, of course. But because pushing the interview off into the future would give her time to get ahold of Nicola Jacobson, the publisher of Three Seals, and pitch her idea of how to restore the successful Quilt to

Death series. "Thank you for letting me know."

Before she could tell Marta, Diana saw Rory out the large storefront window, by himself this time, carrying a duffel bag.

"Can you excuse me?" she said to Bethia.

Bethia smiled. "Go on."

Diana hustled outside and stopped Rory. "Where are you staying?" Duncan's Den she hoped.

"Partridge House," he said. "It was the only B and B I could find online." He studied her for a second and she wondered if he was trying to read her mind. "Where are ye staying?"

Before she opened her mouth, she made sure to sound upbeat. "I'm at Duncan's Den." Then, because she was foolish, she added, "It's two doors down from Partridge House."

"Good to know." His eyes skimmed the village. "I'm trying to get the lay of the land. Gandiegow is small so it won't be hard."

Which also meant she'd be running into him. "I better let you go unpack. See you around."

"Aye." He lingered for a moment, then took the wynd between the buildings to the back of the village, where Partridge House sat.

She watched him go and then turned to go back inside. Instead, she saw Parker and Ewan approaching with three sheep in tow.

"Making your sheep delivery?" she said with a grin.

"Aye," Ewan said. "I hope Deydie is at her cottage."

"She's inside," Diana said, and waved through the big window to get Deydie's attention. "Your sheep are here," she called.

Deydie emerged rubbing her hands together like a little kid. "Good. I think the women of Gandiegow are going to find the sheep's milk verra valuable to their fragile old bones."

"Parker," Diana said, "The interview is off for tonight. But I still need you to record. I want Marta to help the quilters of Gandiegow hang the Quilt to Death quilts on the wall." This was something Cait had suggested, since between them, the villagers had every Quilt to Death quilt.

"I'll only be a minute," Parker said.

Deydie took one of the ropes from Ewan and the three of them took off down the walkway to the other end of town.

Marta repeatedly complained about hanging the quilts, but when Parker came back, she turned on the charm for the camera, as Diana directed. Just as they were finishing up, Rory and McCartney came in and conferred with Jacques in the back corner of the room.

Deydie came over to Diana and said grouchily, "Dinner this evening is at Pastas & Pastries, Gandiegow's restaurant. How many of yere people will be coming?"

Diana glanced over at Marta and Tilly, who looked as if they were getting ready to leave. "I'll ask."

As she approached Marta, the men—Rory, McCartney, and Jacques—did, too.

"How about dinner at the restaurant tonight?" Diana asked casually, trying not to look at Rory. She didn't want to make it obvious that she wanted him to come along.

"I'm headed back to Partridge House," Marta said. "I'll just order in."

"We'll be going with Marta," Rory said on behalf of the men.

"Okay." Diana was disappointed but decided it was for the best. She was in Scotland to get a job done, not to have a cozy dinner with the Detective Chief Inspector.

All the quilters of Quilting Central joined them at the restaurant, and Diana enjoyed having dinner with them. What she didn't enjoy was going back to Duncan's Den alone. Parker, she decided, must've slipped out to be with Ewan.

Since she had Duncan's Den to herself, Diana settled herself on the sofa in front of the fireplace and pulled out her phone. Her first call would be to Nicola Jacobson, the publisher.

"Nicola Jacobson's office."

"Hi, it's Diana. I'm calling with an update."

"Oh yes, she wants to talk to you." Diana was surprised to get through immediately. And also a little disappointed the call hadn't gone to voicemail.

When Nicola picked up, Diana took a deep breath and explained her concept for publishing the book Tilly was working on.

"It would be a do-over and we can use Marta's upcoming interviews to promote the Buttermilk Guild's revival," Diana explained. "I know it will take some time for you to make a decision." But she hoped Nicola would hurry.

Nicola paused for a second. Diana could almost see her tapping her long, manicured fingernails on her mahogany desk. "I'll have to talk to Marketing and Sales and run some P&Ls to see if it's a viable solution." Nicola paused. "In the meantime, I want to see a heartfelt Marta Dixon splashed all over social media with that expensive quilt retreat you insisted upon. Right now, you have one job to do. I want you to fix Marta Dixon's image problem." Nicola didn't say *or else*, but it was implied. Her final words felt as sharp and clipped as Nicola's sleek New York haircut. She hung up.

Diana congratulated herself for not mentioning that it was Nicola who had signed off on killing the Buttermilk Guild in the first place. But Diana knew Nicola had tried to convince Marta otherwise. And no one could've anticipated the real murders that had happened since the book launch.

Diana took a deep breath. What if it took months for Nicola to make a decision? Publishing was known for being slower than a glacier, even when it was as time-sensitive as reviving the Buttermilk Guild before the whole fanbase revolted, dissolved, and couldn't be won back.

At least Diana had taken the first step. Next, she called her sister Liz and talked to her for almost an hour. It felt really good to catch up. When the call ended, she created a weekly reminder to check in with Liz. Diana was the older sister and it was her responsibility to keep in touch.

She put her phone away and got ready for bed. She lived alone in New York and never felt lonely. But here in Gandiegow, with Rory only two doors down, Diana felt isolated and unsettled, and wishing for his company.

There was nothing she could do about it. She left the hall light on for Parker and went to sleep.

The next morning when Diana woke, Parker was asleep in her bed. Diana hadn't heard her come in. She slipped out to make coffee. After she got it brewing, she looked in the refrigerator. Someone had stocked it with eggs, butter, juice and cream. On the counter sat a loaf of bread and a plate of scones. She wouldn't go hungry this morning.

When the coffee was ready, she slipped on her coat and sat on the back porch to drink it. The air was crisp and clean, and as the caffeine started to take effect, she felt like this new day was going to be great.

But an hour later, when she got to Quilting Central, Rory pulled her aside the second she walked in the door.

"I'm leaving," he said.

7

"WHY DO YOU HAVE to leave?" Diana asked, feeling irrational and letting her unfiltered words stand without backpedaling.

"McCartney and I have been called back. Jacques can handle things here." He didn't look happy about departing so soon. "Be safe, Diana."

"I will." She wanted to take his hand. She wanted to thank him for everything. There was no knowing if she would ever see him again.

"Goodbye," she said awkwardly. If only she was brave enough to kiss him, *even once,* it might help her let go of this overwhelming attraction she felt for him.

Or it might leave her desperate for more.

He walked away without touching her.

For a second, Diana considered running after him, but a young woman came over and introduced herself as Sadie. Diana was surprised that she, too, was an American.

"I run the library here at Quilting Central," Sadie said, giving her a welcoming smile. "Do you think Ms. Dixon would mind signing all the Quilt to Death books for us?" She gestured to the shelves.

Diana's first thought was maybe Tilly should sign the books. "I'll ask her." And then she amended her answer. "I'll ask her, when things calm down." Like when the taste of murder was out of their mouths and when Marta was in a better mood.

Sadie's nod said she understood, as everyone in Gandiegow must know about the two Quilt to Death murders. "Are you going to make the Rook quilt during the retreat?"

"I haven't sewn anything in years," Diana confessed. "And I've never pieced a quilt. The Rook quilt looks like it's for someone more advanced than me. I wouldn't know where to start." And she wouldn't know how to concentrate, either, with her thoughts swirling about Rory.

Sadie's smile was sympathetic, but then she looked as if she'd gotten an idea. "I have the perfect quilt for you to start with." She pulled out a sheet of paper from her clipboard and handed it over. "It's the Gandiegow Library quilt."

Sure enough, it depicted a bookcase filled with books, most shelved vertically, some stacked up, and a few tilted. Scattered about the shelves were other items—two potted thistles, a sheep figurine, and Wellies leaning against the shelf at the bottom. The rosette in the top left corner resembled the one Sadie wore pinned to her shoulder.

"This looks way too complicated for me," Diana said.

Sadie shook her head. "It isn't." She pointed to a row of books in the sketch. "Look, you could add all ten of the Quilt to Death novels right here."

"Thank you, but even back in the day I wasn't that good at sewing." Well, she *had* made some pretty cute outfits when she was in college.

"You'll be fine. I'll be with you every step of the way. Besides, you would be helping me out." She laughed, confirming she might have an ulterior motive. "You don't mind being my guinea pig, do you? Deydie wants me to teach a new quilt and this is what I came up with."

Diana studied the picture. "Do you really think I could make it?"

"Piece of cake."

ဆၣယ

If it wasn't for Sadie helping Diana with the Gandiegow Library quilt, the next seven days would've been agony. Diana missed Rory, and every day she thought about asking Jacques if he had talked to the Detective Chief Inspector. Of course, all Diana wanted to know was whether Rory had asked after *her*! But instead of making a fool of herself, she sewed.

The weather had been uncooperative and Parker struggled to get decent footage of Marta walking alongside the ocean with some of the quilters. They'd all been stuck inside Quilting Central, and Diana was grateful to have her sewing project. Parker had run out of things to record, which only played in Ewan's favor, as the two of them spent more and more time together.

Surprisingly—though Leo was annoying—Diana was grateful he was here. He worked hard to take care of Marta—making sure she had plenty to eat and drink, doing whatever he could to entertain her, and going to great lengths to make her smile. As the days went by, the wall Marta had erected between her and Leo began to crumble. There were whispers around Quilting Central that they might be getting back together.

The one thing Diana could've done without was Leo's complaining about Jacques. *He better keep his big mitts off of my lovebug!* It was ridiculous. Jacques didn't seem to have any interest in Marta at all, beyond keeping her safe.

Their first Sunday in the village had been another challenge that Diana could've done without. When Marta refused to go to church—or the *kirk* as the Gandiegowans called it—Deydie was so irate, Diana was worried she might drag Marta to church by her ear. In the end, Tilly stayed with Marta at Partridge House with Jacques watching them both, while Diana joined the rest of the quilters in their pew, singing hymns and enjoying the service.

Lastly, Diana was so tired of Marta arguing with her about every new idea to help her image. Cait had been busy with baby Hamish's ear infection so putting off the interviews wasn't a problem. Thank goodness the retreat was starting tonight, which would make for some great footage to post.

Diana looked out the window of Quilting Central, daydreaming. Possibly about Detective Chief Inspector Crannach, but she wasn't owning up to it. An hour ago, she'd finished her Gandiegow Library quilt top and Sadie had passed it off to Moira, another quilter. Moira put the quilt top on the longarm machine to quilt the top to the batting and the back. Being creative this last week had really helped Diana and she felt positive about the upcoming retreat. She pulled out her phone, deciding that clearing her email would be a more productive use of her time than thinking about Rory.

Her phone dinged with a text from Nicola at Three Seals.

SINCE YOU CAME UP WITH THIS CRAZY SCHEME, I WANT YOU TO PUT TOGETHER A COMPREHENSIVE PLAN FOR HOW TO PROMOTE THE CONTINUATION OF THE QUILT TO DEATH SERIES.

Diana wanted to jump for joy. But she held it together until she could pull Tilly to the kitchen area of Quilting Central, where they could be alone and no one could hear them.

"I just heard from Three Seals," Diana started.

"I get to publish the new book?" Tilly had never smiled this big.

"I don't know yet. But it's a great sign that they asked me to put together a promotional plan."

Tilly's face fell. "Oh." She glanced over at Marta, who was arguing with Deydie about something...again. "Even if they say *yes,* Marta will stand in my way."

"I told you not to worry about Marta." But Diana knew Tilly was right. There had to be some way to get Marta to see reason. "Anyway, we don't have to worry about that now. I'm going to get started on the plan right away. The quicker I get it done, the faster Three Seals will have an answer. Don't lose hope."

But Tilly's sullen expression said she already had. She wandered away, back to Marta's side, a sad loyal dog.

Just as Diana pulled out her notebook to start working on the promo plan, Deydie climbed up on the small stage.

Deydie clapped her hands. "All right, settle down now. The retreat goers will be here soon. Let's straighten things up for them."

Diana shut her notebook and helped the others.

An hour and a half later, Diana, Parker, some of the Gandiegow quilters and more than a few fishermen stood in the parking lot, as a small van pulled in.

"Everyone knows their jobs, right?" Deydie barked. "Dinner will be waiting for them at Quilting Central at half-past six."

"Yes, I'll take care of it," Rachel said patiently.

As the quilters climbed out of the van, Rachel and Deydie greeted them, and Diana gave them each a stack of fat quarter fabrics, the first of many goodies they'd been promised for participating in this retreat.

Diana tried to gauge the quilters' attitude toward Marta Dixon, but most of them seemed reserved, perhaps even wary.

She was going to have to do some quick damage control if she was going to get any video during the retreat that would soothe the angry fans.

As soon as Deydie and Rachel had led away the fishermen transporting the luggage, Diana addressed the quilters.

"Thank you all for coming to what I hope will be a wonderful and enlightening event. I'm *really* glad you could make it on such short notice."

"We weren't going to pass up a free retreat," one gray-haired lady said.

"Even though we aren't happy about what happened to the Buttermilk Guild, we're going to try and be nice to Marta Dixon, as Cait suggested on the phone. Marta, after all, is the reason we could come back here...*on her quid.*"

Well, it was really on Three Seals' dime, not Marta's.

"Thank you all in advance. Ms. Dixon is just devastated—" that was one way to put it "—at the idea that she has disappointed her readers. I would appreciate it if no one would question her about the Quilt to Death series. Just enjoy your retreat. We've brought along a lot of fun *quilty* prizes, so there's a lot to look forward to, starting with the lovely dinner tonight, which we're going to head to right now. Later, we'll have show-and-tell." The quilters perked up at the prospect of more free swag, and it was a much happier group walking to Quilting Central than they had been a few minutes earlier. Everyone carried a bag holding the quilt they planned to share at the show-and-tell, a traditional feature of many quilting retreats. When they arrived, Quilting Central had been transformed into *Dining Central*, with three long tables covered by autumn print quilts as tablecloths. On the back counter was an Italian buffet, compliments of *Pastas & Pastries*.

The quilters stowed their quilts in the library corner, which had been set up for the quilt stories and show-and-tell. They knew the drill and made their way to the counter, not hesitating to fill their plates. When everyone was seated, Diana texted Tilly:

TELL MARTA IT'S TIME FOR HER GRAND ENTRANCE.

Five minutes later, Tilly came in, holding the door for Marta.

"I'm here, everyone!" Marta announced gaily. It was fake cheer, but Diana was glad the sourpuss Marta-of-the-last-week hadn't come to Quilting Central tonight. Marta certainly knew how to get her audience worked up—in a good way, this time. "Are we going to have a great retreat or what?"

Diana saw Marta's eyes dart over to Parker and her camera, as if to make sure the red recording light was on.

"As you all know, Gandiegow is the hometown of Graham Buchanan. Who here would like to have *him* pop by Quilting Central?" Marta raised her hand and all the others' hands shot up, too. She turned and gave Diana a winning smile. "Let's see if we can make that happen."

Everyone applauded. Except Diana. Cait had made it clear the first time they'd spoken that she fiercely guarded Graham's time at home. He was going to be in Gandiegow for a few days during the retreat, which Diana hadn't shared with anyone. She didn't know what she was going to do now that Marta had strongly implied he'd come by to see them.

"Eat up now. We have a lot of fun events planned over the next several days," Marta said.

She then walked among the tables, and greeted each of the quilters like an old friend. She smiled, clasped hands, posed for an occasional selfie, and bantered with them all. Diana was awed at Marta's ability to act nice when she most definitely wasn't being sincere.

When she was done, she joined Diana and Parker, her back

to the group. "When's this going to be over?"

Diana kept herself from rolling her eyes. "I told you. Next we're going to do a quilt signing and giveaways." She didn't have to worry about Marta getting to eat. She'd insisted on having her dinner delivered earlier to Partridge House.

Five minutes later, the quilters started getting up from their tables and relaying their dishes to the kitchen.

"You're on." Diana handed Marta a pen and ignored her grumbles as the quilt fiction mogul sauntered over to the library area of Quilting Central.

"Okay, everyone," Marta sang out. "Let's all head over here." She motioned with her arms like she was guiding a plane of quilters into the gate.

"I understand that some of you have books with you for me to sign." She held up the pen. "I'm ready whenever you are," she said more to the camera than she did for the retreat goers.

The quilters took their seats, but no one offered her a book.

Marta easily pivoted. "But right now, how about we start the retreat off with soommee—" she held the word out to increase anticipation "—giveaways!"

Diana handed Tilly the box and Tilly hurried it over to Marta, as if they'd choreographed this moment.

"Kits for everyone!" Marta cheered. She really was charismatic.

The quilters clapped.

"The kit you're receiving is for the quilt from the new book. The Rook quilt." Marta pointed to the front wall. "Your bag has all the fabric you're going to need plus the quilt pattern. This is our project for the duration. What a treat!"

Marta passed around the kits—soaking up their *thanks* as if she'd been the one to cut out the wool and flannel pieces herself. Every quilter became absorbed in examining her kit, which would retail for almost 200 pounds in the quilt shops.

Jacques stood by the door, at the ready, watching the proceedings as if the quilters might attack Marta at any second. But free fabric would tame just about any group of quilters.

Deydie walked over to Diana. "Well, isn't *she* chipper? *Herself* acts as if she hasn't committed a crime." She glanced sideways at Diana. "Caitie tells me I have to stay away from Marta Dixon during the retreat. Normally, I do as I please, but *me* granddaughter has threatened to keep wee Hamish from me if I rip Marta apart. As I surely want to do! That banshee killed the Buttermilk Guild and acts as if she's done nothing wrong!" Deydie cleared her throat, perhaps giving herself a moment to pull herself together. "For now, I'll do as Caitie asks. But mark my words: I'll have a *nice* chat with Marta Dixon before she sees the last of me and Gandiegow."

Diana was determined to change the subject. "Are you going to eat?"

"Later," Deydie grumbled. "I need to prepare for the *stories*."

Diana wasn't quite sure what the *stories* were, though they'd been mentioned many times, and they were written into the itinerary. She hoped Deydie wasn't going to take the opportunity to roast Marta.

"Excuse me," Diana said to Deydie. "I need to check in with Parker."

Parker was following Marta around, catching her friendly exchanges with the quilters and filming their reactions to their kits.

Diana tapped her on the shoulder. "Parker, do you have a good place scoped out to tape show-and-tell?"

"Yes. I've chosen a few angles." Parker laughed as if she was musing over a private moment.

"What is it?" asked Diana.

"Ewan told me the funniest story, a joke actually. About a

sheep not knowing anything about cars. I can't remember all of it, but it was funny."

For the past week, Parker had talked nonstop about Ewan. During the day, that is; in the evenings, they went on dates. Diana didn't believe in love at first sight, but Parker insisted that's what had happened to her and Ewan. Which only sparked thoughts of Rory in Diana's mind...for about the thousandth time that day.

Parker grinned broadly. "Ewan is the sweetest, sexiest man I've ever met." She didn't give Diana a chance to respond. "He asked me to meet him at the pub when we're through here. Is that okay?"

Darn it! Diana had been planning for the two of them to work together to edit the footage immediately afterward. But who was she to stand in the way of *love*? "Sure. Just make certain to email me your video before you go off on your *date*. The sooner we get the positive buzz going, the better."

"Sure thing, boss."

"And Parker, I don't want to sound like your mother, but be careful with your heart. We're only in Scotland for a short while."

"A *short while* can be long enough." Parker smiled as if fairytales were true.

Tilly shuffled over, hunched down, and whispered to Diana, "Marta wants you to talk to Cait Buchanan about getting some pictures with her husband while we're here."

Diana sighed. "Tell her I'll check with Cait and get back to her." She really needed to ask Three Seals for a raise after this trip!

Deydie clapped her hands again, a technique she apparently used often. When she had everyone's attention, she spoke, "Okay, one by one, ye'll show the quilt ye've brought, and make sure to tell yere story about the quilt and not just hold the darn thing up. Every quilt has a story."

The retreat goers pulled their quilts from their bags. Most of them had brought a quilt featured in a Quilt to Death novel. She went to her own bag and pulled out a permanent fabric pen, slipping it to Tilly, who then handed it off to Marta for signing the quilts.

Diana stood up and said cheerily, "Marta will be happy to sign your quilts, if you'd like."

The retreat goers sat silently. Finally, one person sighed heavily—as if it was up to her to do the right thing. She dug around in her bag and produced a scrap of fabric. She rose and handed the scrap off to Marta.

"What's this?" Marta asked.

"For ye to sign," the woman said, as she glanced around to see if anyone was going to back her up.

Marta looked down her nose at the strip of fabric, as if she'd been offered a limp piece of cold bacon. After a moment's hesitation, she gingerly took the fabric between her thumb and forefinger, laid it on the table in front of her and scratched out her signature with the permanent ink marker, something she'd done a thousand times before. This time, though, it appeared she couldn't even muster up a fake smile, as her collagen-filled lips had been replaced by a severe red line. Deydie was standing with a gleam in her eyes, seeming to enjoy the sight of Marta getting put in her place. But Diana a felt a little sorry for Marta. She was accustomed to being presented stacks of beautiful quilts to autograph, instead of a scrap that might end up in the waste basket. *Oh, how the mighty have fallen.*

She gave Deydie a "what now?" look. Deydie pointed to a woman in the front row. "You, start us off. Stand up and tell us about yere quilt."

"My name is Lorna, and this is the Lover's Knot quilt from

book five in the Quilt to Death Series. I used fabric from my stash to make it."

Diana made her way to the back and listened as each person held up her quilt and told something personal about it—like the reason she'd made that particular quilt, who it was made for, or something special about the fabric. Diana was completely enthralled. She was beginning to understand why quilters were such a tight-knit group. They felt their emotions deeply and put those emotions into their beautiful creations.

When everyone had shared, Deydie hobbled to the front of the group. "Get to bed, lassies," she said good-naturedly. "For tomorrow, we go to Whussendale."

The quilters filed out happily and Diana felt relieved at how well things had gone. As she walked back to the quilting dorm, she actually felt hopeful that the bad luck surrounding the Quilt to Death series was behind them, and she couldn't wait to work on the promo plan before bed.

A noise came from the shadows between the houses on Thistles Wynd. Startled, she stopped to listen, but heard nothing but her pounding heart. Her mouth went dry. She'd felt safe in Gandiegow, but not now. She wished Rory were there to walk her the rest of the way. She figured she had two choices: spend precious time digging her phone out of her purse to use as a flashlight, or walk faster. Instead, she ran.

All the way to the lighted porch of Duncan's Den, she had the weird feeling she was being watched. She hurried inside, thankful she was bunking with the quilters and would have company for the rest of the night. She hoped Ewan would be a gentleman and walk Parker back to the quilting dorm, because Diana didn't want to go out again to get her. She sent a quick text to Parker to remind her to be careful.

Diana chatted with the two quilters who were in the kitchen, then excused herself to go work on Tilly's promo plan. She toiled over the strategy until she was nearly cross-eyed, then put the notebook on the nightstand and turned out the light.

She lay in the dark, thankful for the quilters snoring in the room next to hers. But she didn't have the feeling of safety that just a whiff of Rory would offer

The next morning, Diana woke to her alarm ringing. Groggily, she turned over to see that Parker's bed hadn't been slept in. A cold chill went down Diana's spine.

Parker hadn't come home to the quilting dorm last night.

8

WORRY HAD DIANA FULLY awake now. She snatched up her phone and called Parker.

On the fifth ring, she picked up. "Hello?" She sounded sleepy.

"Are you okay?"

"Sure. Why wouldn't I be?" Parker asked.

Diana heard someone in the background. A male someone.

"It's Diana," Parker said to him. "She's worried about me."

"Sorry," came Ewan's voice from a distance. Then louder, as if Parker had put the phone on speaker. "I kept her out all night. We stayed in the hunter's cottage by the loch, only a few miles from Gandiegow."

"Thank goodness you're okay." Diana wasn't sure when her racing heart was going to return to normal.

"I'll see you soon," Parker said and then she hung up.

Diana wanted to see Tilly first thing this morning and talk about the book signings and guild presentations that she would have to do to make her book ten a success. Maybe if Diana got over to Partridge House now, she'd catch Tilly before Marta rolled out of bed and monopolized her.

Diana slipped her feet to the floor, but instantly pulled them back, as the hardwood was cold. But she couldn't lie in bed all day. Finally, she stood and hurried to dress. As she threw on a pair of jeans, she became aware of the rain slashing her bedroom window. She peeked out and saw rivulets flowing down the pane and decided to dig out the dressy trench coat she'd picked up at Neiman Marcus. While her suitcase was open—and since she was freezing—she donned a white cowlneck sweater and her thickest socks—though she feared they'd be no match for the wilds of Scotland. After getting dressed, she rushed down the hall with her notebook. At the boot mat by the front door, she spied a pair of Wellies, kicked off her red flats, and commandeered the sturdy black boots before heading into the rain. At the door of Partridge House, she hesitated, but remembered Rachel's words: *Treat the B and B like a hotel, and come and go as you please.*

Quietly, she went in and took off her wet trench coat. She hung it on the hook and left her muddy boots on the boot mat. She listened for a moment, but no one seemed awake. Looking for signs of activity, she peeked into the living room, and spied Jacques lounging on the couch with his back to her. She assumed he was awake, because there was a mug sitting on the side table next to him. She wondered if Tilly was up, too.

Diana walked farther into the room and quietly said, "Morning."

Jacques must not have heard her.

She spoke a little louder. "Is Tilly up?"

But as she said the words, something felt off. The air was still. And Jacques was, too.

That's when her veins turned icy—not from Scotland's chilly weather, but from the quilt she noticed wrapped around his shoulders—the Bear Paw quilt from the eighth book in the Quilt to Death series!

Oh, no. "Jacques?" she said hoarsely. "Are you awake?" She felt sick. She didn't want to get any closer, as if death might be contagious.

She forced herself to the fireplace, where the fire had gone out. Finally, she turned around and faced him.

She'd expected blood or something gruesome, but his eyes were closed peacefully. The only thing amiss was that Jacques's face was a strange shade of gray.

"This can't be happening," she said aloud. *It has to be a bad dream.*

Tentatively, she inched forward and reached out a hand toward his shoulder, hoping he was only sleeping. She thought about grabbing the poker from the stand by the fireplace. But she'd look ridiculous if Jacques woke up and found her poking him with wrought iron. A note was pinned to the front of the quilt, but Diana ignored it. *This. Can. Not. Be. Happening.*

She finally touched him. "Jacques? Are you okay?"

He didn't move.

She didn't want to do it! She really, really didn't want to do it! But finally, she laid two fingers to his cold neck and checked for a pulse. . .

ജോൻ

Gravel skidded under Rory's tires as he came to a stop in Gandiegow's parking lot. He'd made record time, breaking more than a few traffic laws along the way, prepared to show his badge if he was pulled over.

To keep from thinking the unthinkable—Jacques—Rory concentrated on Diana, worried about her. She'd sounded calm on the phone to him, like one of the dispatchers at headquarters reporting a crime. He agonized over Diana, plain and simple. Which was strange. He wasn't the type to agonize over women. He may have let Jacques down, but he wouldn't let anything happen to Diana. Or to any of them. If his supervisor called him off this case again to attend mindless meetings, Rory would decline, no matter the consequences.

He turned off the car and pulled out his phone, texting Diana:

I'M HERE.

Rory got out and hurried toward Partridge House, which would only take a couple of minutes to reach. Diana could probably holler from the porch of the B and B and he'd be able to hear her above the crash of the waves.

A moment later, she stepped into the path in front of him. Without a second thought, he gathered her into his arms, glad he'd come alone.

She looked up at him. Rory had expected to find her red-eyed, if not hysterical, but she was as calm as she'd been on the phone, reporting the facts about Jacques. Rory decided she must be in shock. What else could explain why she wasn't distraught? She had the same cool head about her as she'd had around the American's body back in the alleyway of the bookshop.

"How are ye doing?" he asked.

Her face scrunched up in disbelief and she pulled away from him, her arms hanging at her sides. "I told you; Jacques is dead."

Okay, maybe she wasn't as calm as she seemed.

"The Dixon sisters? Did you get them out of the house okay?"

"Yes. The Gandiegowans are guarding them now. At Quilting Central." Diana started walking and he followed. "I had Rachel and Brodie take them. I stayed with Jacques."

He was amazed at how brave she was. Most people wouldn't

stand watch over a dead body.

"Marta is asking for another bodyguard. Two, if she can get them," she said as she walked briskly along. "Did you know Rachel, the owner of Partridge House, has a young daughter?" Diana shivered.

"Aye. I met her," Rory said.

"Thank goodness little Hannah had been spending the night at her great-grandfather's. I'm sure her parents are upset at the thought of their daughter being anywhere in the vicinity when *it* happened."

"My team will be here soon," Rory said soothingly. As though that explained how he was going to keep any of them safe.

When they reached Partridge House, Rory laid his hand on her arm. "Do you want to wait outside while I examine the crime scene?"

She hugged herself. "I'd rather stay with you."

He paused for a moment, then nodded. He didn't want to admit he wanted to keep her close, too.

Only to keep an eye on her. Nothing else.

Rory went into Partridge House and then slipped on a pair latex gloves and booties. "Where's the body?" It was best *not* to think of the victim as *Jacques.* A lesson he'd learned long ago. The only way to do this job, and to do it well, was to immediately disassociate himself from the victim...*even if they* had *been drinking buddies.*

She pointed. "In the living room."

He didn't expect two people to be waiting—Bethia and a tall man of thirtysomething. Rory felt nothing but relief at seeing them. Their presence meant Diana hadn't been babysitting Jacques's dead body alone.

Diana stepped forward and gestured to the pair. "You remember Bethia from Quilting Central. Doc, this is Detective

Chief Inspector Rory Crannach. Rory, Gabriel MacGregor is Gandiegow's doctor."

"Was the body covered like this when you found it?" Rory asked Diana.

Bethia answered. "Nay, I covered him with the sheet out of respect. I was careful not to touch anything."

Okay, he'd have to live with it. "Dr. MacGregor, help me remove the sheet. You get that end."

"Call me Gabe."

At opposite ends, the two of them carefully lifted the sheet and laid it on the desk by the hallway.

Rory didn't see any blood.

"No signs of blood," Gabe echoed his thoughts. "I wondered if he was poisoned."

Rory turned to Diana. "Is this quilt from one of the books?"

"Yes," she and Bethia said at the same time.

"It's the quilt from the eighth book," Bethia said.

"The victim was poisoned with foxglove," Diana added, as if she'd known what he was going to ask next.

"Possibly bradycardia or tachycardia, then," Gabe said. "Foxglove is essentially digitalis."

Rory noticed Diana staring at Jacques. "Are ye okay?" Maybe he should have Bethia take Diana to Quilting Central, away from the body. But she'd said she wanted to stay with him. And he wanted to keep her in his line of sight.

Instead of answering his question, she asked quietly, "Why would someone want to kill Jacques?"

"Maybe to get him out of the way." Rory didn't have to drive home the point that someone was killing people associated with the Quilt to Death series, even seemingly innocent bystanders like Judy Keith.

"Is there anything I can do?" Gabe asked.

"Stick around," Rory said.

Rory carefully examined the scene, knowing only a toxicology screen would confirm the foxglove theory. But he'd bet money on it.

"Any idea whose quilt this might be?" he asked.

"I have an idea." Bethia looked worried. "May I lift the corner there, where it's resting on his legs?"

"I'll do it." Rory pulled out the same pen he'd used when checking the crime scene at the bookshop. He carefully lifted the quilt and a tag appeared.

Bethia leaned over to look. "Oh, dear."

"What?" Rory asked. "Who does the quilt belong to? You?"

"Nay. It's Deydie MacCracken's."

9

DIANA BACKED AWAY and stood at Partridge House's fireplace. When she realized she was standing next to the wrought iron fireplace tools, she scooted away from them, too.

She couldn't stop thinking about the photos her dad would sometimes bring home and spread across the kitchen table as he worked. Those dead bodies hadn't fazed her. But those weren't of people she knew. Had spoken to. Had liked and known to be good people.

"Where's Deydie? Quilting Central?" Rory asked.

Diana's nerves were already a jumble, but now she was worried. Not for herself, but for the old quilter. *Deydie's no killer,* she thought. But maybe she should've told Rory earlier that Deydie was at the bookstore on Guy Fawkes Day. Or that Deydie had threatened Jacques the first night they were here. But that was ten days ago! Deydie hadn't had a run-in with Jacques since.

Bethia stepped in front of Rory. "Deydie couldn't hurt a fly."

She paused then, as if rethinking her position. "Aye, *a fly, maybe,* but she's my oldest and dearest friend."

Rory shot Diana a curious glance. Now, how the heck did he know she was feeling complicit? Guilty that she had information he didn't know yet—that the old woman had threatened Marta, Jacques, and everyone else who got in her way?

Rory opened his mouth, but his cellphone rang. He pulled it out and answered, never taking his eyes off her. "DCI Crannach." He nodded. "Partridge House. I'll send Doc MacGregor to show you the way." He hung up.

"You don't mind, do ye? MacTaggart, one of my team members, has arrived," Rory said to Gabe.

"Not at all," Gabe said.

"I'll go with him," Bethia offered. "I need to get to Quilting Central."

Probably to warn Deydie that she's a suspect.

"Ye'll stay here with us." Rory made sure his statement was a command. "Ye can take me to Quilting Central soon enough...to interview Deydie."

Doc left.

"Deydie wouldn't hurt a fly," Bethia repeated. "I've known her my whole life. She has a loving heart."

And a wicked broom, thought Diana.

Then she remembered how open Deydie was about being at the bookshop—she didn't try to cover it up. And when Diana had explained about the murders of Rance and Judy, Deydie had seemed genuinely surprised.

"Is Leo Shamley still here?" Rory asked.

Diana frowned. "Yes."

"Where is he now?"

"Quilting Central, with the others."

A few minutes later, Doc was back, and along with him were

Rory's team—Corey MacTaggart and Reid McCartney, carrying their equipment.

Rory walked to the entry to greet them. "Get some pictures. Bag and process the evidence. Did you call the Procurator Fiscal?"

"Aye. The coroner will be here soon to get the body," McCartney said.

"Where are ye going?" MacTaggart asked.

"To speak with the owner of the quilt that's wrapped around the body." Rory looked from Bethia to Diana. "Ladies, come along with me."

Once outside, Bethia stopped suddenly. "I need to go home. It's time for my morning remedy...for my arthritis."

"It'll have to wait," Rory said.

That's a little harsh, Diana thought, not letting the elderly Bethia have her medication, but she understood. Rory didn't want Bethia giving Deydie the heads up before he talked to her.

When they arrived at Quilting Central, Diana noticed right away how the eighth quilt was missing from its place on the wall. All the other quilts were still hanging in their spots.

And Quilting Central was packed. In addition to the quilters, seemingly all the men in the village were there. They must've felt like they needed to be there to protect the women. Though, from what Diana had seen of the women of Gandiegow, they could take care of themselves.

"Where do you think Deydie is?" Rory asked Bethia.

Bethia shoved her hands in her pockets and clamped her lips together tight.

Rory turned to Diana, but before he could speak, Deydie came out of the restroom with a baby on her shoulder. She handed him off to Cait Buchanan, who was sitting at a table.

Deydie walked to the stage. "Okay, now that Hamish's nappy is changed, let's get down to business."

"Thanks, Gran," Cait called, pushing her empty plate away.

Deydie nodded, then turned back to the group. "I've drawn up a schedule." She pulled a piece of paper from her skirt pocket and held it up. "I'll make copies and post it on the board by the front door here, and at the General Store."

There was a buzz around the room.

"Our strongest men will be guarding Quilting Central during the day," Deydie barked. "And no one goes out alone. Do ye hear?"

Rory stepped forward. "I agree. Everyone needs to pair up and use the buddy system when going out."

Deydie frowned at him. She clearly wasn't used to being interrupted.

"For those that haven't met me yet, I'm DCI Rory Crannach. I'm here to investigate the murder of Jacques Boucher. I'll be here for several days. I, or one of my associates, will speak with everyone in town." He stared down Deydie. "Starting with you, Ms. McCracken." The crowd looked at him as if he was crazy, or brave—*or both*—for speaking to Deydie this way. "Everyone else get comfortable. We're going to be here a while."

Deydie huffed. "Ye better hurry it up. Sunday service starts at 11:30."

Others nodded as Deydie lumbered off the stage toward Rory. She didn't wait until she was near to speak, but hollered at him from halfway across the room. "What's this all *aboot*? Why do ye want to speak with me first?"

"Is there somewhere we can talk?" he asked. "Someplace private?"

"I've nothing to hide." Deydie swept her old arms wide, as if encompassing the room, maybe the whole town. "And *nay*, there's no place private. Caitie wanted Quilting Central to be open-concept, whatever the hell that is. There is no separate room except the loo. But we can sit over on the sofa in the library area, if ye want."

As he made to follow her, he said to Diana, "The Ms. Dixons will have to find a place to stay other than Partridge House. It's a crime scene now. Will ye help with that?"

"But it's Rachel and Brodie's home," Deydie said indignantly.

"They, and anyone else residing there, will have to leave." He paused for a second. "Also, are there rooms in the village my associates and I can rent for the duration?"

Deydie put her hands on her hips. "No."

"Yes," Cait said coming toward them with baby Hamish asleep in a carrier strapped to her chest. "We have several options. Thistle Glen Lodge—the other quilting dorm—is available. Of course, we can always make a place for you and your colleagues at my house."

"Nay," Deydie protested, "not the Big House. Graham is coming in tonight."

Rory turned to Diana, his eyes dropping to her neck. Was he checking to see if her pulse raced at the sound of Graham's name?

"We'll get ye settled into Thistle Glen Lodge," Cait said, then turned to Rachel, her daughter, Hannah and her husband, Brodie. "I'll have Moira and Bethia help get you settled."

"What about Marta and Tilly's things?" Diana asked Rory. "Can we get them out of Partridge House now?"

He gave her a pointed look. "In a while."

Diana understood his meaning—*after the body is removed.*

Rory continued. "When it's time to fetch the Ms. Dixons' things, I'd like you to be with me."

Diana's stomach did a serious somersault. The Graham-

Buchanan flutterings from a moment ago had been less than a quiver in comparison.

But she stopped herself in mid-heartbeat. *Rory is a police officer! And I made my decision long ago about men like him.* When she was seventeen, to be exact.

Rory seemed to be waiting for Diana to respond, but for the life of her, she couldn't remember what she was supposed to be responding to.

"Ye'll go with me to Partridge House, when the Ms. Dixons go?"

"Oh. Yes. Sure." She stumbled over her words, as if she'd only learned to speak. "Yeah, of course."

He stared at her as if he was trying to solve a puzzle. And it all came back to her—everything she'd learned from her father about how cops could read people. And the notion scared the crap out of her.

Rory Crannach knew that she was thinking about him.

ℰ⌘ℛ

Rory motioned for Deydie to head to the couch. "Let's speak now, Ms. McCracken."

"I told you once before to call me Deydie."

He noticed Bethia was chewing the inside of her cheek. Apparently, Deydie's best friend had forgotten she was supposed to take her arthritis medicine.

Bethia put her arm around Diana. "There's something I mean to show ye, lass. Over there, by the library."

So that's what it is. Bethia was going to eavesdrop and make Diana an accomplice in her scheme.

Rory followed Deydie to the library area, which consisted of a sofa with shelves behind and perpendicular to the couch. As Rory took his place on the couch, near the perpendicular bookcase, Bethia and Diana tiptoed behind it. They weren't

119

fooling anyone; he could easily see them through the books. *Amateurs.*

He rolled his eyes at the whispered exchange going on behind the shelves. It sounded as if someone had stepped on the other one's foot.

Deydie settled on the couch next to him. "*Git* on with it."

He pulled out his notepad. "Where were you last night?"

"In *me* cottage," she said.

"Alone?"

"Of course, alone."

He pointed to the wall. "I see one of the quilts is missing."

"*Aye.* I don't know where my quilt has run off to," the old woman said. "When I find whoever took it without asking, I'll pin their ruddy arse up there next to it."

He made note of her quick temper and hoped his next question would render new information. "What can ye tell me about the quilt?"

Bethia and Diana were still making a small ruckus in their not so inconspicuous hiding place. He could hear every word Bethia said. "Yere detective is handsome, I'll grant ye that, but he's no match for Deydie. She's bound to turn him into mincemeat pie."

Diana gasped, and must've stumbled into the shelf, because a book launched into the air near his head and fell to the floor. He reached down to pick it up and caught a glimpse of her red cheeks between the tomes.

Deydie rubbed her chin and continued to frown at the wall where the other Quilt to Death quilts were displayed. "That quilt was here last night. I remember because I asked Ailsa and Aileen to straighten it a might before we left." She stopped and glared at him. "Why are ye asking about my quilt? Do ye know where it is?"

He sidestepped her question with one of his own. "Which

ones are Ailsa and Aileen?"

"There." She pointed to two middle-aged twins wearing matching plaid dresses, though one was a red tartan and the other one green.

"About the quilt," Rory started again. "Tell me about its design."

The old woman shrugged. "It's a bear paw quilt. The pattern comes from the eighth book in the Quilt to Death series."

"Do you know how the victim in the eighth book died?" Rory watched her wrinkled face closely, especially her rheumy eyes, for micro-emotions.

"What is this? Book club?" she spouted off.

"Just answer the question. How was the victim murdered in book eight?"

"*Poisoned.* Foxglove. In his herbal tea."

"Herbal tea?" Didn't Diana introduce Bethia on his first visit as the town's herbalist? He started to tell Bethia to come out from her hiding spot, but Deydie interrupted his thought.

"Aye, foxglove. From the fairy realm, ye know."

Good grief. Not the fairies! He couldn't believe how some of these remote villages still held strong to their superstitions of old. Not him, though. He believed in facts, not folklore. "What does foxglove have to do with the fairies?"

Deydie's face transformed into a glower. "In the book, the Buttermilk Guild is sure the fairies had played mischief by leaving the foxglove out on the counter for the killer to find."

"You seem to remember a lot of details from the books," Rory commented.

Deydie glared at him as if their eye contact was a game of chicken and she had no intention of flinching first. "Just because I remember the details, ye think I murdered that French giant?"

If she didn't avert her stare soon, she might burn holes

through Rory with her lethal gaze.

"Ye ninny! To prepare for the new novel coming out, I re-read all the Quilt to Death books, starting at the beginning. 'Tis fresh, ye see? I've got all the particulars right here." She tapped her wrinkled temple.

He hadn't encountered a geriatric serial killer before. And though his gut was telling him Deydie wasn't the *one*, he couldn't simply rule her out. "Let's start at the beginning. Where were you Guy Fawkes Night?"

"Oh, dear!" squeaked Bethia from behind the bookcase. There was some ruffling and she scooted around, rushing to sit beside Deydie on the sofa and putting her arm around her. "She was with me. At Quilting Central. We were working on a Row By Row."

Deydie brushed her words away. "Nay. I went to Glasgow to give Marta Dixon a piece of my mind." She laughed. "Someone beat me to it."

Rory was taken aback by her cavalier confession, but he had to hand it to her for being honest. "So, you were at the bookshop?"

Bethia was half-muttering to herself and half-groaning.

Deydie bobbed her white-haired head. "Aye. It was quite the sight to see."

"Did ye speak with any of the officers at the scene of the crime?"

"Nay. I never saw any officers." She glanced at Marta who was standing on the far side of the room and nodded with a smile. "I was only there long enough to see Marta Dixon get doused with blood and then I left. I had to catch the last train so I could start making my way back to Gandiegow."

He would check the security cameras. Maybe she spoke true. "Ye do know there was a murder that night at the bookshop?"

"I know *now*. What's that have to do with me?"

"Ye're a potential witness, are ye not? Did you see anyone suspicious among the crowd?"

"Nay."

"Did ye know Rance Bettus?"

"Who now?" Deydie said. "Speak up, lad."

"Rance Bettus," Rory repeated more slowly. He'd learned from an early age to respect his elders. His gran had boxed his ears enough times, until it had sunk in. "He is the one who was murdered outside the bookshop on Monday evening."

Deydie screwed up her face. "Ye're not making any sense. Why would I want to murder someone I don't know?"

"To exact revenge," Rory hypothesized. "Maybe ye thought since Marta Dixon killed off the Buttermilk Guild, someone close to Marta needed to die."

Deydie scratched her head and a few of her white tendrils escaped her bun. "That's a sound idea." She nodded her head toward the kitchen area. "But ye best be making yereself a cup of tea, if ye think I killed this Betty person. Yere head's all boggled up. Hopefully, a warm drink will help ye to clear it a bit."

Her response was exactly what his gran's would have been, if he'd been accusing her of murder. He pressed on. "Did ye get on all right with Jacques Boucher when he came to town?"

This time it was Diana who squeaked from behind the bookcase. He wished he could see the expression on her face to judge what she knew.

"Did ye have a run-in with Jacques?" He was only guessing, but apparently, he'd hit his mark, because Deydie nodded.

"Aye," she said. "The behemoth wouldn't let me in to speak with Marta Dixon...God rest his soul."

"Tell me what ye did the day after Guy Fawkes Night. Did you go anywhere? Did anyone go with ye?"

"Let me see." Deydie looked up at the ceiling.

Bethia cut into her silent recollection. "She was at Quilting Central for most of the day. Remember, Deydie?"

"Aye. Diana called about bringing her people here early, moving up the date of the retreat." She frowned. "It's not much of a retreat, though, is it?" She leaned over as if she was looking at Diana. "Stop hiding behind those shelves and come out where we can see ye."

Diana stepped out, looking more than a little sheepish.

"I say we're still holding the damned retreat, no matter who's dead. We're not gonna give back the money that yere publishing company gave us, either. Do ye hear?"

Diana nodded, but then she seemed to remember the retreat guests. "Don't you think you better ask the ladies what *they* want to do? They may not want to stay, now that there's been a murder."

"*Pish-posh.* They'll stay," Deydie said defiantly. "Scottish quilters aren't nearly the limp biscuits that American lassies seem to be."

"I think you should give them the choice, anyway," Diana responded, just as defiantly. Rory was impressed with her moxie.

But he needed to bring the women back to the matter at hand. "Ms. McCracken—"

"Deydie!" Deydie barked.

"Aye, Deydie. What time did ye speak with Diana, the day after Guy Fawkes Night?"

"I don't know. All's I know is that Diana gave me a headache with repeating all the talk about *vetting* the retreat goers. Caitie and I had to make sure these were the right ladies to have here for this retreat. Cooperative ones. Polite ones. Ones that wouldn't want to take off Marta Dixon's head, like I wanted to do." Deydie glared over at Marta. "*Still want* to do."

"Were ye in Glasgow, early in the morn on that Wednesday?" The coroner had calculated the time of death for Judy Keith to be around three or four in the morning.

"Nay. Why would I go back to Glasgow? I told ye, I was there at the bookshop until I had to catch the train."

He pressed further. "What about in the hours after midnight?"

"Ye're cracked if ye think I went gallivanting about Glasgow to the wee hours of the morn." She must've realized she should answer him more directly, because she added, "I came home and went to bed at 10:30."

"Is there anyone who can corroborate yere story?"

"I didn't see anyone when I made it back into Gandiegow, if that's what ye're asking." She glared at him. "And I sleep alone!"

No alibi, he noted. Deydie could've murdered both Rance and Judy Keith. Deydie could've also been the one to poison Jacques. But none of it seemed likely.

"Bethia, Diana said ye're the town's herbalist. Do you keep foxglove on hand?"

Bethia nodded. "It's tradition to put a few leaves in a newborn's cradle to protect the babe from being bewitched by the fairies."

"Isn't that dangerous?" he asked, incredulous.

Bethia nodded. "Aye, foxglove is nothing to play around with, but I know what I'm doing. I put only a few leaves in a plastic bag, seal it tight, then leave it in the bairn's cradle for just a moment."

He forged on. "Do ye keep yere herbs locked up? Especially the foxglove?"

"Aye," Bethia said. "Of course I do."

He went in for the big question. "If I go to your herbal stores, is there a chance I'll find Deydie's fingerprints on the container of foxglove?"

Deydie's face drained of color and she answered instead of Bethia. "Aye."

"Nay!" Bethia protested.

Deydie turned to her friend. "Remember? When wee Hamish was born? Ye stood right next to me while I took the bottle off the shelf. I'm the one who put the two leaves into the plastic bag, because wee Hamish is my great-grandson."

"Nay," Bethia said again. "Ye were only helping me because the arthritis in my hands was acting up."

Rory turned to Bethia. "I'll need that bottle. Stay here, and later, we'll walk together to your place to retrieve it."

"I haven't done anything wrong." Deydie wasn't pleading; her words were tough as nails and they sounded genuine.

He wanted to tell her that he believed her. She reminded him of his own prickly gran. But he couldn't say it.

Deydie glowered at him. "Are ye and I done here? I have things to do. We're set to take the retreat goers to Whussendale after Sunday Service to see a demonstration of their sheep-to-shawl program."

"Reschedule it for tomorrow," Rory said. "As I said earlier, no one is going anywhere. Today we will be interviewing everyone."

Deydie squished up her face and frowned, while Bethia patted her soothingly.

"Let's start the ladies on their quilts now, before we go to the kirk," said Bethia. "We'll do as the DCI says and go to Whussendale tomorrow. I'll call Sophie and let her know why we've been delayed."

"All right," Deydie acquiesced. She pushed herself off the couch and went to talk to the retreat goers gathered at one table.

"Sit," Rory commanded Diana. "I want to talk to ye now,

lass."

⋘⋙

Diana's heart skipped a beat. *No,* her heart did more than that. First it did a small victory dance, jogged a couple of laps, and then performed a backflip.

A little too late, she realized Rory was staring at her, his face stern. He oozed seriousness. *Yes,* of course, *murder is serious business.* But in her heart of hearts, she'd been longing to see him again.

He glanced across the room, as if to make sure Deydie and Bethia were out of earshot.

He stared at her for a long minute before turning a page in his notepad. "Tell me everything that has happened since you arrived in Gandiegow and while I've been gone. Don't leave anything out."

"More death threats have come in," she told him, then pointed to Leo and leaned in. "Leo has been complaining, wanting me to tell Jacques to keep his hands off Marta. It's been weird, but Marta and Leo seemed to be back together. I guess he was just making sure Jacques wasn't horning in on his territory."

"Was Jacques horning in?" Rory asked, but he looked like he already knew the answer.

"No! Of course not," Diana said. "He seemed too smart to want someone like her."

Rory frowned over at Leo. "I'll speak with Leo after I finish with ye."

Diana went back further and relayed the conversations in the shuttle between Marta and Tilly—both the intimate one and the one where Diana had found out Tilly had been the ghostwriter—*the true author*—on all the books. She even told him how Deydie tried to get past Jacques on the first night, but downplayed the interaction, making Deydie sound more like a folk hero than the tyrant she really was.

When Diana was done with her recitation of the facts, she delivered her opinion unasked. "I know it looks bad, but Deydie didn't do it. None of it. She's not capable." Though the old woman seemed more than capable of doing damage when she wielded her broom.

Rory had been writing everything down, but as Diana made her declaration, he glanced up. "It's not for ye to decide who did or didn't commit a crime. I have a duty to follow the evidence."

"She didn't do it," Diana said again, for good measure. She held his gaze. "I guess you should know that I believe someone was watching me last night from the shadows as I walked back to Duncan's Den."

Rory appeared infuriated. "Tell me that you had someone with you, preferably one of the big fishermen I'm seeing all over town."

She shook her head.

Deydie saved Diana from one of Rory's lectures by returning with the Duffy brothers. The old woman motioned for Rory to listen. "These two strapping lads, Hamilton and Gregor, have agreed to guard Marta Dixon. I figured with yere fellow, well, *gone*...someone needed to take his place. The Duffy boat is in for repairs the next couple of days and these lads ain't got nothing better to do."

The two men shared a look, as if they might have something better to do.

Rory gave the old quilter his full attention. "I appreciate it. I wasn't sure who I could get to watch Ms. Dixon, way up here in Gandiegow."

That was the wrong thing to say.

Deydie shot him a hard glare, conveying her displeasure at

the Detective Chief Inspector for blaspheming her village.

"I meant no offense," Rory said. "It's just Gandiegow is a long way from...*anywhere.*"

Deydie harrumphed and then went back to her previous topic. "The Duffys will not be the only ones. Once their boat is fixed, we'll have others helping to watch the *old Buttermilk Guild killer.*" Deydie sneered in Marta's direction. "But Hamilton and Gregor will be in charge of figuring out her—*what do ye call it?*"

"Detail," Rory answered. "Ms. Dixon's detail." He stood and spoke to the head quilter. "Thank you, Deydie. I really appreciate it." Then he focused on the Duffy brothers. "We'll get together later and talk about particulars."

Hamilton nodded. "We'll be around." He and Gregor walked over and took up their stations, where the women of Gandiegow and the retreat goers had surrounded Marta.

Deydie glared at Rory but pointed to Diana. "Are ye done with her? We could use her to get things rolling."

"Aye. I'm done," he said. "Lass, we'll speak more later." He walked over and called Leo out of the group, taking him to a table and sitting down.

Diana realized Deydie was halfway across the room before she followed the old woman to her desk, where Deydie picked up a basket.

"What's that?" Diana asked.

"I started book ten's quilt last night—the Rook quilt." Deydie pulled the pattern off the top and held it close as if to examine it. "I'm not fond of the rook. He's kind of sinister, don't ye think?" She glanced at Diana to make sure she agreed with her. "I don't mind the rest of the pattern, but I believe I'll switch out the rook for a puffin. Much friendlier bird in my eyes."

Deydie nodded toward the boxes Diana had brought with

her. "Might'n you have some extra bits of fabric in there, so I can change out the rook? I can give these already cut pieces of the Rook to one of the other retreat goers."

Diana smiled at her. "You bet. I brought plenty. I like your idea. Perhaps you'll allow Parker to take a video of you modifying the Rook quilt with your puffin?"

Deydie grinned at her. "Aye. I've always wanted to be on the telly."

Diana patted her shoulder. "Thank you." She hoped Marta would be as accommodating when it came time for her to teach the class on making the quilt. She'd know soon enough.

As they walked over to the Gandiegow quilters and out-of-town retreat goers, Diana pulled out her phone and texted Parker.

CAN YOU COME TO QUILTING CENTRAL NOW?

When she'd called Parker to tell her about Jacques, Ewan said he would bring her back to Duncan's Den and keep an eye on her, as she was upset.

Deydie was already speaking with the women. "Get to work and start cutting out the pattern until it's time to go to Sunday Service. I can attest to how easy it is. Ye'll make fast work of it." Deydie made a guttural noise, as if her next words might be caught in her throat. "At least Marta Dixon does a good job of writing a pattern."

Diana saw that the old quilter had things under control, so she went to Marta and Tilly. "We're going to start on the project today, instead of going on our field trip to Whussendale. Marta, are you up for being on camera?"

Marta glared at her. "You have to be kidding!" she snapped, and motioned to herself "I look hideous. That *Brodie* person rushed me out of Partridge House before I could get on a decent pair of slacks or make up my face."

Diana understood how important it was for Marta to keep

up appearances.

Marta put a fist on her hip. "Tilly and I will go back to Partridge House so I can shower and get ready. Come on, Tilly." She started to walk away.

But Diana rushed in front of her, raising a hand. "We can't go back until Rory says so."

Marta raised her eyebrows. "*Rory*, is it?"

"Detective Chief Inspector Crannach," Diana clarified. "He wants us to wait a while."

"Well, I'm not going to do any promotional work until I can take a shower and put on foundation and eye liner. I hope they catch whoever did this to me and throw the book at him." Marta was so worked up, she didn't even seem aware of the pun. She did look pretty awful. At least the dye on her face had faded, so it just looked like a sunburn on one side now. Make-up would tone it down.

She glanced over at her temporary bodyguards, Hamilton and Gregor. "It's bad enough that these two have to see me this way—not at my best." Judging by her *cougar ogle* the poor Duffy brothers might have to use their youth to fight off her advances.

Diana glanced around and found Rory. "Let me ask DCI Crannach when you can head back to Partridge House."

Rory was at the entrance, talking with MacTaggart and McCartney. He must've felt her coming, because his eyes shot in her direction as if she'd shouted to him.

"Deydie wants to get started," Diana said, "but Marta won't, until she can get changed. When can we get her stuff and get her moved to Thistle Glen Lodge, as Cait suggested?"

"Now," Rory said. "The body's been cleared from the premises. Just stay away from the crime scene." He gestured to his team. "MacTaggart and McCartney will take over here at Quilting Central until I can get back." He nodded toward the

Duffy brothers. "Have her new bodyguards come along."

"I'll see if Rachel wants to go with us now, too."

Diana found Rachel in the kitchen area. "We're headed back to Partridge House. Do you want to come?"

But it was Brodie who answered. "I'll go with ye to get our things."

Rachel nodded, looking more than a little shell-shocked. But she rallied. "I'll go along to make sure Thistle Glen Lodge is ready for our visitors." She squatted down to speak with her daughter. "Let's ask if you can stay here with Cait and help with baby Hamish while your dad and I see to getting things out of the house."

Hannah grabbed her Let's Get Sheepy quilt and ran to where Cait sat with the baby. Rachel didn't even have to go over as Cait waved back her consent.

Brodie caressed his wife's shoulder, his eyes darting to the two fishermen leaning against the far wall. "I'm going to see if either Ross or Ramsay can stay with you at Thistle Glen Lodge while I'm at the house. I don't want ye to be there alone."

"Okay," Rachel said. "Do we know how long before we'll be able to go home? Has anyone said?"

Brodie wrapped a protective arm around his wife. "I'll find out from the DCI." He had a determined look on his face, as if he wouldn't let a murder in his home ruin his perfect life. Brodie gave her shoulder a reassuring squeeze and then went to the fishermen by the wall.

Moments later, he came back with Ross. Diana headed to Deydie to break the news that the retreat would be delayed a bit longer.

Deydie listened, glowered, but then glanced over at Marta. "She looks like hell." She seemed to have a rare moment of compassion for the woman who'd killed off her favorite fictional quilters. "Who can blame her, though, after what she's been through in the last few days." Deydie gave Diana a dismissive wave. "Go on with ye. Bethia and I will stay with the retreat goers. Also, it'll give me a chance to show them the puffin I'm going to put in the center of my quilt. Just hurry back so Marta can get them going on the piecin' before the kirk bell rings."

Next Diana corralled Marta, Tilly, and the Duffy brothers and headed for the door. When they got outside, Tilly turned to her sister.

"Did you at least read through the Rook quilt directions?"

Marta rolled her eyes. "Don't act like I don't know what I'm doing, Tilly."

Diana got that sinking feeling again. "Marta, did you design the pattern for book ten?" *Or did Tilly?*

Marta turned around and gave Diana a look of disdain. "When would I have time to do that? I never design the quilts. I've been writing a book while running the Marta Dixon empire for Three Seals."

Tilly groaned a little, as if being crushed under the weight of Marta's ego...*while doing most of the heavy lifting for the Marta Dixon empire.*

"Well, this is a mess," Diana said aloud. This new revelation—that Tilly designed the quilts—wasn't the bombshell that Tilly writing the books was, but it was another secret that had been kept from the readers. Just another mess for Diana to fix.

Rory, who'd been leading the procession, held back until Diana caught up to him. He took her arm gently and stopped her, while giving her plenty of eye contact. *Serious eyes.* But something seemed to smolder in there, too, just below the surface. "Is there anything else I need to know?"

Diana sighed, feeling defeated. "I don't think it's going to impact your investigation. It's *me* who's been thrown an additional curveball." She exhaled another breath, glad she could vent a little. "Marta is going to be the death of me. We need to get footage of Marta leading a quilting lesson, but I don't even know if she can quilt. I just found out that Marta didn't design the Rook quilt, Tilly did." But an old memory popped into Diana's head. "Maybe everything's going to be okay. Last year, I saw a video of Marta teaching another of the Quilt to Death quilts and she did a really nice job of it." Diana breathed a little easier.

Rory went with Rachel up to the door of Thistle Glen Lodge first and he blanched when Rachel didn't produce a key but turned the doorknob and opened the door.

"It wasn't locked," Rory said flatly.

"No," Rachel said. "We normally leave the dorms open in case someone needs a place to stay in a pinch."

Ross added the next part. "Like if ye stay too late at the pub and yere wife won't let ye back into the cottage while ye're stinking drunk."

"I can't believe it," Rory said.

Rachel shrugged. "Most of the common buildings are unlocked here in Gandiegow. The General Store, the church, and of course, Quilting Central. We even leave Partridge House open in case a traveler comes into town late."

Rory shook his head, as if saltwater had lodged in his ears. He turned around on the porch and spoke to the whole group, making eye contact with each one of them. "Things are going to change. We're going to lock down the village tight until the killer is caught."

Everyone murmured their agreement.

Rory went inside by himself to make sure no one was lurking. He came out a few minutes later. "It's clear."

Brodie waved to his wife. "I'll only be a couple of minutes while I get you and Hannah a few items. Then I'll come to Thistle Glen Lodge to get you. Grandda will be happy to have us come stay."

Diana could tell Brodie hated leaving his wife for even a moment.

Brodie led them around to the back of Partridge House, through the kitchen, instead of entering through the front. Moments later, Diana figured out what a smart move it had been—as their procession passed through, they only got a glimpse of the living room. Diana saw Jacques's body was indeed gone, but it was definitely a crime scene. Yellow tape corded off the area with detectives and workers still milling about, gathering evidence and taking pictures.

Diana followed Brodie up the stairs so she could help Marta bring down her numerous suitcases. When Diana stepped into the room, Marta was telling the Duffy brothers, "Those are my bags there. After I get the last two suitcases packed, you can come back and get them, too."

Diana stepped forward. "Hamilton and Gregor, don't worry about coming back. I can bring the last two."

"Ham," the tall red-haired one said. "Everyone calls me Ham."

"And ye can call me Greg," the black-haired one said. "It's no trouble to come back and get the others."

Tilly came into the hallway from her bedroom, dragging an ancient wheel-less suitcase and started for the stairs.

"Here, Ms. Dixon," Ham said, giving her a smile as if she were his favorite aunt. "Let me get that for ye."

Tilly's utter surprise was nearly comical. "Thank you," she whispered shyly.

If Diana wasn't mistaken, Ham had just made a friend for life.

10

D IANA OPENED THE FRONT DOOR to Thistle Glen Lodge and stepped inside. As she explored the cottage, she found that this quilting dorm had a completely different feel to it than Duncan's Den.

A huge fireplace presided over the living room, big enough to roast a medium-sized pig. The downstairs bedrooms were nestled off the hallways on the other side of the living room, along with two restrooms. Diana headed upstairs to see two more modest bedrooms and another restroom. The upstairs view of the ocean was captivating and she stood there for some time, soaking in the peacefulness of the waves crashing against the walkway embankment. Duncan's Den had a comparable view, but with all its wood paneling it felt more like a hunter's cottage. She loved it— all warm plaids and coordinating tartan quilts. Something about it reminded her of her dad.

Ah, she remembered. Her father's recliner was dark blue and red plaid like the one at Duncan's Den. When Dad got off duty, he would come home and put his feet up with the TV remote in his hand. Mom would bring him a soft drink or a beer, and Diana and her sister would play at his feet until he was ready to have them crawl up on his recliner with him. Police officers needed a certain amount of downtime to adjust from work mode to family life.

Thinking about her father always made her feel sad...and empty. And angry. She trudged downstairs glumly, only to bump into Rory.

Rory stopped and stared at Diana. Possibly because she was staring at him and the backpack slung over his shoulder.

Her curiosity got the best of her. "Are you staying here?"

"Aye," he said in his deep burr. "To keep an eye on Marta."

"For how long?" She'd been brave for asking and possibly stupid, too.

"Depends." He didn't wait to see if she had more questions. Instead, he walked past her and disappeared up the stairs.

She didn't like how being around him made her jumpy, nervous, and—she hated to admit it—excited. All things she shouldn't feel around someone like him—*someone who carried a badge.*

A few minutes later, Ham appeared with Tilly and Marta, who was looking much better. "They're all moved in, Ms. McKellen. Where to next?"

"Back to Quilting Central." Diana checked her watch. "There's some time before church starts. Can you take them? I need to run over to Duncan's Den to get Parker."

"We'll walk ye there," Greg said, as he joined them in the living room.

"Aye," Rory said. He was midway down the stairs. "We'll all stay together."

But once outside, Tilly turned around. "I forgot my bag."

Tilly's bag was like Mary Poppins', stuffed with anything and everything Marta might need at a moment's notice.

"Ham, go with her," Rory said. "I meant it when I said no one is to be alone."

Ham did as he was told and the rest of them went on.

Next door at Duncan's Den, Rory went in with Diana. She noticed how he scanned the entry and the living room for danger. *Yes*, he made her feel safe. But it was the other emotions he elicited that were not so comfortable.

Diana walked back to her bedroom and knocked, not sure whether Ewan McGillivray would be in there or not. "Parker, it's me."

The door opened. Parker looked anxious. "I can't believe Jacques is dead."

"I know. It's awful," Diana said, looking past Parker's shoulder. "Where's Ewan? You shouldn't have been left here alone."

"Ewan went to the restaurant to pick us up something to eat. He's going to meet us at Quilting Central."

"Do you want to wait around a minute," Diana said. "I want to change into something dressier." Hoping it would raise her spirits, she pulled out her black mini skirt and some cute boots, quickly putting them on.

Outside, Parker gestured at the group. "I didn't expect a whole welcoming committee."

"Protection," Diana corrected her. "We aren't supposed to go out by ourselves. Make sure Ewan knows that."

Parker gave her a sad smile. "He's leaving in a little bit. He said he has to get back to Here Again Farm and Estates."

"Cheer up," Diana said. "We're headed to Whussendale tomorrow. You'll see him then."

"I know. It's just not the same." She lowered her voice. "We won't be *alone*."

This is moving too fast, Diana thought. Who gets lovesick over someone she just met? Unwittingly, Diana's gaze floated over to Rory. *No,* she wasn't lovesick like Parker. *Intrigued,* maybe. *A crush,* perhaps. But Diana wasn't going to get involved with *him* under any circumstances. She would never date a police officer. *Never.* And certainly not one from another country!

True to Deydie and Bethia's word, the quilters were nearly finished cutting out the pieces for their quilts.

The church bells rang.

"Okay, everyone, let's head over to the kirk." Deydie frowned at Marta, but this time didn't waste her breath telling her to come.

"We'll finish the interviews when you return," Rory said.

Tilly, Marta, and Rory stayed behind as the rest of the building cleared. Diana wished she could stay behind, too, but went to church instead, hoping the service would somehow straighten her out, especially concerning her attraction to a certain police officer.

∞∞

During the church service, the Episcopal priest did a good job of reminding them all that death wasn't the end, that they needed to celebrate Jacques's life in their hearts, though he hadn't been in Gandiegow long. Diana wished Rory had been there to hear the comforting words. She wished she was sitting beside him holding his hand, helping him through this difficult time.

After the service was over, Diana walked back to Quilting Central, feeling uplifted after the traumatic morning. The rest of the quilters seemed renewed, as well.

When Diana walked into Quilting Central, Rory nodded at her. It was a *polite* nod. Nothing untoward. But her insides did a delicious squeeze anyway. She decided it might take a lot of church services to straighten her out and get her back to how

139

things were before she'd met Rory.

Lunch had been laid out and the quilters got in line to make their plates. From the stage, Deydie pronounced, "As soon as yere done eating, and have washed yere hands, then ye need to get back to work. We have a lot of piecing to get through today.

Diana got in line behind Parker. "After lunch, will you be ready to start taping?"

"You bet, boss."

When everyone was done, Marta took over the class with confidence, showing off her knowledge and skill. Diana stood back watching, unable to help but ponder Marta. She was a mixed bag of good and. . . *not so good*. Which was kind of the human condition, if Diana was being honest.

"Tilly," she said, "Marta's really good at this!"

"I taught her how to sew when she was little." Tilly replied. "She took to quilting like she was born to do it."

"So why doesn't she make the quilts for the Quilt to Death series?" Diana asked. "Why have you been the one to do all the designing and sewing?" She knew Marta's take on it but wanted to hear Tilly's side, too.

"Marta says it's my job since I'm the one who comes up with the design while I'm writing the books. Besides, Marta only sews when inspiration strikes. She wouldn't do well with a deadline." But then Tilly's face screwed up. Was she remembering Marta *had* met a deadline, for the book that had killed off the Buttermilk Guild?

Diana put on a fake smile to push away the thought. "Well, I'm pleased we're getting some great footage. I'll have Three Seals send out an email blast with the video embedded. The team will also post it everywhere online. That should help."

But Tilly's expression said she didn't believe it would.

Maybe it wouldn't help, but Diana had to try. She leaned

over and whispered to Tilly. "I need to confirm some things for my promo plan for Three Seals. I need to know that you'll be able to do the front work—book signings, quilt guild visits, you know, all the public appearances?"

Tilly blanched. "I—I don't know. I'll think about it."

"Don't take too long." Diana hated to be pushy, but there was no reason to go to bat for the Buttermilk Guild if Tilly wouldn't be able to take over for Marta.

"I want to do it," Tilly whispered, her lips barely moving. "The Buttermilk Guild needs to carry on. But I just don't know if I can be in front of people like Marta."

They both directed their eyes to Marta, who was animatedly instructing the quilters from up on the stage.

Tilly looked conflicted. "She's going to be so mad," she murmured.

"I know," Diana said. She didn't have to ask what Tilly was referring to. Marta liked having Tilly in the background, and certainly didn't want to compete with her sister as an author. *Tilly will probably make me be the one to break it to Marta.* "Just keep writing."

"Diana!" Deydie hollered from her desk. "Isn't it time for another giveaway?"

"Yes." *Oh, crud!* She'd have to run to Thistle Glen Lodge to get it. Why hadn't she stopped Ham from taking that box upstairs and had him bring it to Quilting Central instead?

Probably because seeing Rory had distracted her from her job!

∞∞∞

With a notepad in front of him, Rory sat at one of the long tables at Quilting Central, working through the interviews with the quilters, fishermen, and retreat goers, one at a time. He'd hoped one of them had seen something unusual, *any-*

141

thing that might give him a lead into Jacques's death. Rory couldn't get out of his head what Diana had said about Leo resenting Jacques. Poisoning seemed like a weasel's way to commit murder, so that fit. Was Leo clearing people from Marta's life to make room for himself again?

All during the interviews, he kept an eye on Diana. She was busy flitting from this person to that—pouring tea, plating scones, retrieving sewing tools, and just generally making sure that everyone was comfortable. It was downright irritating! She hadn't asked him if *he* needed anything!

Now Diana was headed for the door. *Alone!*

"Thank you. We're done here," Rory said to the quilter he was interviewing. He stood and with a few long strides intercepted Diana. "Where do ye think ye're going?"

"You heard Deydie. I need to get the next giveaways. They're at Thistle Glen Lodge."

Rory crossed his arms. "I thought I made myself clear. Ye're not to go out alone. I'll go with ye." He wasn't sure why he'd offered. He could've gotten MacTaggart or McCartney to go. But the thought of one of them *buddying up* with Diana just didn't sit right with him.

"Don't be ridiculous," she argued. "You have an investigation to run. I'll get one of the Duffys to walk me." She looked over at the tall Gandiegowan brothers.

Rory had overheard the other women cooing over the Duffy brothers' good looks, describing Ham and Gregor as *studs*. Normally, Rory was as rational as they come, but he couldn't help imagining Diana as a butcher scanning the meat case, trying to select the best cut of beef as her escort.

"*Nay.* I'll go." Rory opened the door for her.

"You don't look happy about it, but suit yourself," she said flippantly, as she crossed the threshold.

Outside, a storm was brewing. The sea was whipping herself

into a lather. A cold breeze hit them and Diana shivered.

"Don't ye have something more appropriate to wear?" he asked.

"I didn't expect it to be so cold," she said defensively.

Well, her little trench coat wasn't doing her a bit of good against the lash of Scotland's north winds. Plus, he couldn't help but notice her black mini skirt wasn't covering much. But he certainly did enjoy the outline of her perfect bum. "Ye'll freeze to death if ye don't put on something warmer." He gazed at her long legs in her biker boots. *God, she was sexy.* She hadn't been able to keep his eyes off her whenever she'd bent over to speak with one of the quilters.

"Here." Rory slipped off his jacket and wrapped it around her shoulders. He was hot anyway.

She opened her mouth, but he shut her down. "No argument."

"Fine. I am a little chilly." She slipped her arms in the sleeves and zipped it up, swimming in his jacket. She looked both ridiculous and cute, and he couldn't have been more pleased with himself.

When they reached Thistle Glen Lodge, she opened the door.

"Wait a minute," he said, putting an arm out to stop her from going any farther. "Why isn't this locked?"

"I don't know," she said, looking at him nervously.

Damn but he had a clue. Tilly must've forgotten to lock it when she'd gone back to get her bag. He'd have a word with Ham, too, because he'd gone with her. It was infuriating that these villagers weren't heeding his instructions. Well, Rory knew who had the power in the village. He'd talk to Deydie about getting the dorms locked down tight and laying down the law about safety.

Cautiously, he opened the door and stepped inside. Diana

followed him.

There was a crash upstairs and Diana was instantly in Rory's arms, clutching him around the neck, her face only inches away from his. *Good lands*, her scent was intoxicating. But her eyes were big and her breath shallow. She was truly scared.

"What was that?" she whispered.

He was short of breath, too, but not from fright. The American lass must be taking up all the oxygen or his lungs had forgotten how to function.

Another crash came from upstairs and broke the spell.

"Stay here," he said. And though he knew he shouldn't, he brushed his lips against hers.

She breathed in and sighed, "Oh." An 'oh' that said she might want to do it again.

He gazed into her eyes for just a moment, then reluctantly unlatched himself before heading toward the noise.

But the lass didn't stay put as he'd urged. Gripping his bicep, she followed him down the hallway toward the stairs on the other side of the living room. She clung to him so closely, she could've been his body armor.

Whoever was upstairs didn't give a damn about making noise while they ransacked the place. But then it went quiet again. They crept the rest of the way up the steps and found that two of the three doors were closed. He assumed the criminal was behind one of the closed doors, but peeked through Marta's opened door first, just to be sure.

He took it in all at once. The room was a shambles. Clothes and towels were tossed everywhere, along with ripped magazines and an empty package of McVities Digestives. Sprinkled over the mess were cookie crumbs, feathers from a presumably shredded pillow, and pills of assorted colors. The strangest thing in the room, though, was lying in the center of the sunshine yellow quilt: a sleepy, or at least very relaxed, badger. He must've worn himself out from trashing the room. Or had swallowed one of the pills. The badger was still breathing, though, so he must be all right.

Diana poked Rory's shoulder and whispered, "What is it? Let me see."

Rory tried to back out slowly, but she wasn't having it. She dropped his arm and stepped around him.

"Uhhh," she uttered, no louder than a light breeze across his cheek.

He linked their hands and quietly pulled them into the hallway and closed the door.

"How do you suppose it got in there?" she asked quietly, as if to *let sleeping badgers lie.*

"I don't know."

"What are we going to do now?"

He pulled out his phone. "I'm going to call the SPCA. But first, please tell me yere box isn't in the room with that pest."

"No. Tilly would've had it stored in her room, not Marta's."

Rory made his call. The SPCA said it would be a couple of hours before they could get someone to Gandiegow. *Good,* Rory thought. It would give him time to conduct the rest of his interviews.

He opened Tilly's bedroom door and Diana went straight to the boxes stacked in the corner.

Once again, his mind wandered to a place it shouldn't. Three times he'd been in a bedroom with Diana. *Three times!* And not one thing had happened between them—except a chaste, harmless kiss. Which was ridiculous, since he wanted more from her than that. He'd liked her being in his arms, even if it was fear that had propelled her there. *Warm, soft, and smelling irresistible.* He'd ruined his opportunity to give her a proper kiss, to disarm her the way she was disarming

him with each and every glance in his direction. She was looking at him now, which made all his blood race southward like
a horny teenage lad. Rory decided he'd better focus on something else—*like the sleeping badger*—to keep from
embarrassing himself with Diana.

Seemingly oblivious to the heat he felt between them, she
went back to looking in the boxes. Suddenly, she pulled out a
feather boa, wrapped it around her neck, and turned to him
with the most compelling smile. He couldn't help but smile
back.

"This will keep me warmer, don't you think?" She picked up
a box and walked over to him.

He wanted to wrap himself around her like the boa. Instead, he straightened. He was on duty. And he was a
gentleman. He'd better start acting like it. But dammit, he was
also a red-blooded Scot, through and through. "Here. Let me
carry that box for ye."

She handed it off. "Thanks. I brought a few boas for fun, but
I also have fat quarters and book bling for everyone."

"Fat quarters? Book bling?" He lifted the box up and down
as if he was taking its weight.

"Just fun stuff for readers and quilters. I brought enough
for the ladies of Gandiegow, too. As a *thank you*."

He feigned weakness, like he could barely carry the box. "I
think ye've packed more than a few stones in here as well."

Her laughter filled the room. Then she did the damnedest
thing. She squeezed his bicep.

"You should work out more," she said, before sashaying
from the room.

They started their walk back to Quilting Central in comfortable silence. But all the while his brain was running wild,
imagining Diana in his arms again, and possibly horizontal
beneath him. He hadn't known many women like her. *Hell,*

none at all. So many birds tried to get their hooks into him right away, but not Diana. Though there was clearly an attraction between them, she knew how to keep her mind on business ...*bicep squeezing aside.* He smiled.

"What are you smiling about?" she asked.

"Just thinking." No way would he let her know how much he liked her *manhandling.* And how he wanted more of it.

"You have a nice smile," she commented matter-of-factly. She didn't seem to have any notion of how much her approval pleased him. "You smile like a leather-jacket type of guy, but you act more like a business suit."

"Are ye analyzing me, Ms. McKellan?"

The expression on her face said she was backpedaling. "Just an observation." She turned her face forward and didn't look at him again until they arrived at Quilting Central.

Adjusting the box, he reached for the doorknob just as she did, too. In the process, her left breast grazed his arm, making goosebumps break out on his triceps. Her hand landed over his and they stood frozen in time, gazing at each other, reading each other like a gripping novel they couldn't put down.

He wanted to confess that he'd never known a woman like her. That he knew she was something special. But being an investigator didn't allow for distractions. He looked away first, clearing his throat, as if that would help him reestablish a kind of distance from her.

She looked disappointed, then dipped her head, taking her blue eyes from him. Suddenly, he felt cold...which had nothing to do with the weather. They couldn't stand out here forever. He anchored his foot inside the door, so she could cross the threshold first.

Deydie waved a gnarled finger in Diana's direction and hollered, "Yere box will have to wait. We gave up on ye."

Diana looked around, as if to see who Deydie was yelling at.

The whole room was staring at them.

"What are ye wearing?" Deydie went on. "And what in damnation took ye so long?"

"A boa," Diana said, at the same time Rory said, "A badger."

Diana blushed and slipped off the purple boa and his jacket.

"There was a badger in Marta Dixon's room at Thistle Glen Lodge." Rory continued. "SPCA is on the way to humanely remove the animal."

"A badger?" Deydie snorted disbelievingly.

"A badger!" Marta roared dramatically. She turned to Tilly and began issuing orders.

Rory felt sorry for Tilly, who was clearly going to have to clean up after the badger. At the same time, he kind of enjoyed riling Deydie. "I wish I'd thought to take a picture of the badger for ye." *For both of them.* "Badgers aside, I need to speak with the rest of the quilters." He set the box on the nearest table.

"Nay," Deydie said. "We're on our way to Pastas & Pastries for afternoon tea. Dominic and Claire have put together something special for the retreat."

"I'm staying right here," Marta announced with a broad smile. "I'll be looking over my lesson plan so we can get right back to it. Enjoy your snack!"

McCartney approached Rory and solemnly handed him a report. "It's preliminary."

The coroner put Jacques's death somewhere around five this morning. Rory's blood ran cold. What if Diana had gone to Partridge House earlier? What if she'd encountered the killer? His eyes searched the room until he saw her. He relaxed, knowing she was safe.

"Would ye like to come with us, lad?" Bethia asked kindly. Her offer said a lot about her generous nature, since he hadn't made her *favorite* list when he didn't let her warn Deydie about being a murder suspect.

Food sounded good, but Rory couldn't. "Thank you, but no. However, it would be great, if you brought something—anything—back for me." He pulled out his wallet and handed her cash. "I'm going to stay here and work." To keep an eye on Marta.

Bethia took the twenty. "Very well."

As Deydie passed by, he said, "Can ye spare a minute, before ye head to the restaurant?" Now that he knew the time of death, he needed to speak with her.

Deydie frowned at him. "I haven't the time."

"Ye might as well get it over with," he said.

Bethia nodded to Deydie. "Sinnie, Sadie, and I can handle the quilters."

"I won't keep her long," Rory promised, before the women trailed out.

"Come sit at my desk." Deydie pointed to a rolltop covered with stacks of fabric. "I need to pull together the pieces for the next block." She gestured toward the front of the room, where a quilt block was stuck to the wall. "That's called a design wall, if ye were wondering."

"My gran would've loved this building. She was an avid quilter." It often helped to act chummy with a suspect, but Rory didn't normally speak about his family in interrogations! What was it about this old woman that brought out *the chat* in him?

Deydie turned her rheumy gaze on him, studying him as if her vision were as clear as if she were twenty again. "What about yere mum? Does she sew, too?"

"Gran raised us after our mum died—me and my brother, Kin." Rory's throat tightened. "Kin is a police officer, too."

Deydie gave a firm nod of approval. He got the feeling she could see right through him...that he hadn't had an easy time of it.

"Bethia said ye seem like a fine lad. Tell yere gran she's welcome here any time."

"I can't. Gran is gone, too." It still hurt to say the words. "She died a long time ago. . ." *on Guy Fawkes Night.*

"It's all right, lad." Deydie laid one of her arthritic hands on his shoulder and squeezed. She was surprisingly strong for one so old. "I, too, have had me share of losses. Now, I don't offer this to everyone, but since yere womenfolk are gone, whenever ye're in need of the company of old women, come see me and Bethia and the other quilters of Gandiegow. We'll share a tea biscuit and a cuppa with ye. *And* teach ye how to stitch, if ye like."

"Thank you," Rory said. He was shocked at how moved he felt. "I might just do that."

Deydie glanced at the man's watch pulled tight around her thick wrist. Then she picked up a stack of fabric from the desktop and held it to her chest, as if preparing to make a getaway. "Get on with yere questions now. I've a lot to do."

"Where were ye early this morning?" Rory expected Deydie to say she was in bed.

Deydie shook her head as if she was tired of his questions, but to his surprise she didn't argue with him. "I was up at the Big House by 4:30. Couldn't sleep, ye see."

"The Big House?"

"Where Caitie lives."

"Can anyone corroborate yere story?"

Deydie chuckled. "Oh, aye, Dingus can. I took him out for a shite by the cemetery." She gave Rory a toothy grin. "'Tis Graham's dog," she added unnecessarily.

Rory smiled back at her sauciness. On paper, she might look good for at least two of the three murders but his gut was certain she didn't do any of them.

Deydie stood. "Anything else ye want to know?"

"Not right now."

"Good. After I set these up, I'm going to get me my treat at the restaurant. Do ye want to come with me?" She gave him a stern look. "*A man has to eat.*"

"Another time."

"Suit yereself." Deydie waddled away to one of the front tables.

Rory scanned the room, cataloging those who'd stayed behind—Leo, Marta, Tilly, and Parker, all of whom he had already interviewed. Parker of course was alibied by Ewan. Leo claimed he'd been asleep in the room over the pub, but there was no way of verifying his story.

Diana was still there, too, working with Parker on the computer with the video camera between them. He was glad she hadn't left. He liked keeping an eye on her...keeping her close.

Marta marched up to the design wall and added a new quilt block beside the other one. "Stop hovering, Leo. I told you to go to the restaurant without me."

"What about you, darling? Aren't you hungry?" he asked.

"No," Marta said, "and anyway they have enough carbs sitting over there on the counter to put a horse into a sugar coma. I refuse to go to a restaurant to be force-fed more." She ran a hand down her thin hips. "That's the last thing I need."

Leo opened his mouth, but then seemed to think better of it. Rory wondered if Marta and Leo were having a tiff, even though Diana had said the two had been getting along.

Tilly handed another block to Marta, who positioned it by the other one.

"Tilly?" Leo cooed. "How would you like to go with me to the restaurant?"

If he was trying to make Marta jealous, it didn't seem to be working, as Marta was clearly ignoring him.

Tilly seemed genuinely surprised by Leo's offer, but then answered *no* with the shake of her head.

"Fine. I'll go alone." Leo stomped to the door, flung it open, and slammed it behind him.

"He's a temperamental mister," Deydie remarked to no one in particular.

Drama queen would describe Leo more accurately.

Rory liked Deydie. He really did. He flipped opened his notebook and jotted down a few more notes.

No sooner had Deydie gone—with McCartney as her protection—than the door opened again. It was Ewan, well bundled up except for his protruding ears.

"Parker? Are ye ready to go on our picnic?" Ewan said.

Rory thought it was crazy to picnic in this weather, but the bloke looked besotted and no doubt the two would find some way to keep warm.

Parker's smile was glowing. "I'll be right there."

Rory stepped over to Ewan. "Do ye have a moment?"

"Sure."

"Would you confirm where ye were last night?"

Those ears of his turned the color of beets. "Parker and I slept out by the loch. There's a small hunter's cottage about five miles away that I know about."

Which was basically what Parker had said.

Parker looked up and beamed at the man. But then her expression fell. "Ewan, I better stay here. I have to get these videos up on YouTube for Three Seals."

"Go on," Diana said. "I can finish it from here."

Parker looked hopeful. "Are you sure?"

"Oh yeah. They're almost ready to post anyway."

The two lovebirds turned to one another and practically cooed as they exited the building. For a moment, Rory was a bit envious of the two.

He walked over to Diana.

He knew she was busy, but he had to say something so she'd ask him to sit down beside her. "Not hungry then?"

She gave him a wary look, and he understood why. They'd had a connection—he'd kissed her, for heaven's sake—then he had cooled things down between them. He was regretting it now. He missed her smile.

He was such a confused idiot. He'd always been a man in control of his faculties, but apparently not around Diana McKellen. He wasn't sure of himself anymore. He knew she was a distraction that he couldn't afford to have and he wasn't certain what he might do next.

Like kiss her again.

11

THAT NIGHT, DIANA FILLED the electric kettle in the kitchen of Duncan's Den and flipped the switch to heat the water, while Parker stood by the back door, presumably texting Ewan. The chill from the evening had settled into Diana, or maybe it was the death of Jacques and then the long day that followed.

Back when she was watching Rory interview everyone at Quilting Central, Diana had expected the retreat guests to pack up and go home. Instead the quilters perked up when they settled themselves in front of their machines and began sewing. Maybe Bethia was right when she'd said, "Quilting helps ye forget yere troubles."

Diana's troubles, though, had increased exponentially since coming to Scotland. It was no easy task to restore Marta's scarred image, strategize a resurrection of the Buttermilk Guild, deal with the murders. . .and then there was the Rory problem. Though Diana tried, she couldn't help but be aware of his every movement. Fantasize about another kiss. Definitely longer than the one before.

The water boiled and the kettle shut off. Just a few more days, Diana told herself as she made instant cocoa for herself and Parker. The Rook quilts would be finished and she'd post the final few teasers about the big reveal, and then the real-life town that inspired the Quilt to Death series would be unveiled. After which Cait would have to be ready for the rush of quilters who would want to attend their Kilts & Quilts Retreats.

But right now, Diana needed to rest her mind and calm her nerves.

"Here." She handed a mug to Parker.

Diana pulled a quilt over her shoulders, grabbed her own mug, and followed Parker out to the back porch. They'd decided to give the retreat goers some time to themselves. After being on PR duty all day, it felt good for Diana to let her guard down. She was glad the wind was no longer blowing, but it was still cold outside.

Parker blew on her hot cocoa. "Ewan said he'll be in Whussendale tomorrow." She sounded relieved.

"I told you not to worry," Diana said.

A noise at Thistle Glen Lodge next door drew her attention, and she saw Rory stepping out onto his own back porch, holding a mug as well.

So much for letting my guard down.

Diana raised her mug to Rory as if in a toast. He nodded in return. *'Tis the season*, Diana thought, though Christmas wouldn't be for another five weeks. For a brief moment, she wondered what it would be like to celebrate Christmas in Scotland.

Cait knocked on the door frame and then walked out on the porch to join her and Parker. "Hey. I thought I'd stop by." She looked Diana over as she huddled under the quilt. "And maybe not a moment too soon. It's been brought to my attention that you're not dressing warm enough. By the way you're holding that quilt, I suspect *he's* right." She gave a cursory wave to Rory on the other porch. She held out a sack to Diana. "I think we're about the same size. Heavy shirts, insulated yoga pants, warm socks, gloves, and a hat."

"Thank you," Diana said. "The life of a popsicle is getting a little old. I've heard Scotland can even be cool in the summer, too."

Cait sighed. "Aye. But Gandiegow is beautiful in the summer. The gardens are lovely. The view from here and from Thistle Glen Lodge makes for some relaxing summer evenings."

Diana felt far from relaxed, which was all the fault of the handsome Detective Chief Inspector on the other porch, looking as calm as can be.

Diana snapped out of it and focused on Cait. "Would you like a cup of cocoa?"

"Thanks, but no. I have to get home to feed Hamish." She smiled at Diana and Parker. "Sleep well."

"Wait a second," Diana said. "You aren't out alone, are you?"

"Nay. Hamilton and Gregor walked me here. They're inside saying hello to the quilters. They'll get me home safely."

Diana stuck the hat on her head.

As soon as Cait disappeared back inside, Parker's phone rang.

Parker glanced at her screen. "It's Ewan. I'm going to take this in our room."

Suddenly Diana was alone. But she wasn't really. Rory was standing on the other porch, glancing at her every so often, as if keeping an eye out for impending danger.

Sure, she'd been around brooding, good-looking men before but this was different. It was probably just Rory's accent that exerted such a pull. Like right now. Even though he wasn't talking, just taking a drink from his cup.

Or maybe it was the magic of Scotland that made her attraction to him more powerful. After all, she could easily picture him in a kilt.

But whatever caused her to feel this way, she wanted it to stop.

At that thought, Diana should've gone inside to escape. From the cold. From the danger of wanting Rory to come over and put his arms around her...to keep her warm, of course, *and for no other reason.*

She waited too long to make a move, because Rory stepped off his porch and began walking toward her, maintaining eye contact, which seemed impossible in the moonlight, but he did.

The butterflies in Diana's stomach woke and fell over themselves, as if they wanted to get to Rory first. She desperately wished for someone to talk to about Rory. A sounding board. But her sounding board had died when she was seventeen. If her dad was alive now, he would give her sage advice, tell her how to handle the situation now, because she was way in over her head. Dad had been the one to listen to her from her first crush, to her first date, when Dad had told her not to listen to any of the bull that teenage boys tended to say. The night before Dad had died, they'd sat at the kitchen table and he'd given her advice about the football player who was flirting with her. *Dad, I wish I could call you now.* But Dad was gone and Rory had arrived.

"How are ye this evening?" Rory asked as he stepped up on the stone porch.

Diana looked Rory square in the eye. "Before today, had you ever lost someone you cared for?"

"Aye." He took a sip from his mug.

He paused so long, she wondered if that was all he was going to say.

"The first was my parents, and then my gran," he said.

"I'm sorry," Diana said sincerely. She knew how he felt.

"My gran is the reason I became a police officer."

"Oh?" Diana said, encouraging him to elaborate.

"Ye see, me and my brother, Kin, were hellions when we
were young, always up to trouble. But on Guy Fawkes Night,
when I was seventeen, my gran wanted me to walk her to the
market near our house in Glasgow. We didn't live in the best
of neighborhoods. I was to meet my friends and resented the
fact that I had to walk her to the store. I planned to leave off
once we were at the market, let her walk home alone. I was
such a fool. Before we even made it to the market, we were
mugged at knife point. The muggers walked away with her
benefit money. I received a couple of punches for trying to in-
tervene. Gran was very upset and collapsed in the street. Her
heart, it gave out. I decided then and there that my mischief-
making days were over. Kin joined the force as well. He works
out of Aberdeen." Rory seemed to get lost in thought then.

"What about Jacques?" she asked. "Were you two close?"

"Well, we met two years ago. He's done security for me a
number of times. A good man." They were both silent for a
moment, then he said, "And you? Why are ye so calm in the
face of death? Have you lost someone close to ye?"

She felt ambushed, like he could see right through her. But
she couldn't tell him about her father. It was something she
never spoke about. *Not to her sister. Not to her mother. No
one.* She was afraid if she spoke of him, she'd start crying and
never stop.

Rory came closer. "I didn't mean to upset ye."

She couldn't look at his face, as she felt a tear slide down
her cheek.

"Aww, lass." He pulled her into his arms and hugged her.

She shouldn't have let him. She should've pulled away. Instead, she soaked in his goodness, his warmth...just soaked in all of him. And imagined what it might be like if Prince Charming did exist. He'd probably look as gorgeous and feel as strong as this man that she was leaning into now.

Rory looked down and wiped away her tear. Then he leaned in and kissed her.

It wasn't the hurried kiss he'd given her earlier. It was a comforting kiss. She couldn't help herself, she held on to him tighter. Yes, he'd made her feel better, but also feel *more*. More than she'd ever felt before in a man's arms. He picked up the message as if she'd printed it out for him in bold type, because he held her tighter, too, and deepened the kiss.

She should've stopped. She meant to. But she couldn't, and the quilt slid from her shoulders.

He caught it in one smooth motion, never breaking the kiss, and wrapped it around both of them, cocooned.

Kissing Rory was heavenly. She could almost forget that police officers get shot in the line of duty.

Then it hit Diana. Was she turning into her mother? Falling for a man who would throw himself in front of bullets to save others?

Diana's inner thoughts battled her attraction to the man she was kissing. *I can't be falling for Rory. Not a police officer!* Diana had promised herself she'd never make that mistake. Falling for a cop only brought long nights of worry, days filled with anxiety, and then the possibility of crushing heartache. Mom had never smiled again the way she had when Dad was around.

Diana jerked away from Rory. The quilt fell to her feet.

Suddenly, she was cold.

೮つ◌ৎ

What the hell? Rory watched a battle play out on Diana's face as she moved away from him. "What's wrong?"

"Nothing's wrong." Not meeting his eyes, she knelt, grabbed the quilt, and then clutched it to her chest as if she was naked.

It was all going so well. "What happened? Tell me." Had he shared too much about himself? Had he come on too strong? He had no freaking idea what was up with her. Maybe he'd been wrong that she was a different kind of woman, one who didn't play mind games.

Yet...

"It's late," she said. But her explanation felt lame. "We have a big day planned for tomorrow." She headed for the door.

He held out his arm, blocking her way. "Ye can't go. Not until ye tell me what's going on." All she needed to do was to go underneath his arm. He wasn't touching her; he would never hold her against her will. He just wanted to know *why*. Why was she throwing up roadblocks?

He hadn't even told her of the other losses. How two years ago, he'd lost his partner in a grocery store robbery. And not a week later, a friend had died in a train bombing in France. So much loss that Rory hated to remember. For a second, while kissing this American lass, the pain had slid away, and he could breathe easier.

She hung her head and shook it. "I'm tired."

"Fine," he bit off. *Be that way.* He dropped his arm.

He didn't have time for female nonsense. He had a killer to catch. He should have no problem letting this bird go. No problem at all. *Except...*

He did.

Something was up with Diana. His gut knew she wasn't a flighty female. He was an investigator, wasn't he? He was going to get to the bottom of this and he knew just the person to ask, too.

Suddenly, the fire alarm next door rang out with an ear-piercing *meep, meep*. Two seconds later, the alarm went village-wide, sounding from the bullhorns atop the electrical poles.

He squeezed Diana's shoulders. "Stay here." He tore off for Thistle Glen Lodge to see what had happened.

୧୬

Hamilton Duffy smelled smoke. He rose from the kitchen table at Thistle Glen Lodge and sniffed again. Like all fishermen, he was acutely attuned to smoke; fire was one of the worst things that could happen on a boat.

The next second, the alarm went off, and Tilly jumped to her feet, too, both of them forgetting the late-night snack she'd fixed for them.

"What is it?" Tilly yelled above the blaring alarm. She looked frightened.

"I don't know," Ham said. "But I'm going to find out. You go outside!" He didn't wait to see if she did, but raced toward the living room. *Surely, the fireplace was the culprit.* But on the way, he saw smoke snaking down the stairs like an ominous cloud. He ran up two steps at a time.

What was upstairs that could cause a fire?

At the top, he saw tendrils of black smoke seeping from the crack under Marta's door. "Marta, are ye in there?" He grabbed the fire extinguisher from the wall and pulled the pin. He kept his ears sharp for her answer, but he heard nothing from the other side of the door. But who could tell with the alarm blaring?

He turned the doorknob, but the door was locked. "Stand back! I'm coming in." He rammed his shoulder into the hard-

161

wood and the door gave way, the trim shattering.

"Ham?" Rory called from the bottom of the stairs.

"Up here." Ham hurried into Marta's room, where the bed was on fire. Fortunately, Marta wasn't in it and he pulled the fire extinguisher's trigger; first on the flames that were licking the curtains, then on the counterpane lying over the bed. The acrid smoke stung the inside of his nose and burned his eyes.

Out of the corner of his eye, he saw Rory run into the room with a wet towel in his arms.

"Marta?" Rory called out.

"I'm here," she coughed. She was standing with her back plastered against the wall, looking too shocked to move.

"Here, lass." Rory pulled her toward him and wrapped the towel around her head and shoulders. "Let's get ye out of here."

The fire wasn't completely under control yet, so Ham continued to spray the bedside rug. Then Gregor burst into the room with a fire hose and doused everything...including Ham.

"Hey!" Ham yelled, but it only made him cough more.

"Sorry," Gregor said.

Ross and Ramsay were behind Ham, manning the back of the hose. Minutes later, the fire was drowned out.

The five of them were coughing now.

Ham set the extinguisher at his feet. "Are Marta and Tilly okay?"

Rory tilted his head toward the front of the house. "Tilly's fine. She's outside with the rest of the village. Doc MacGregor is with Marta. He says she's going to be okay." Rory scanned the room. "Now tell me. Was the fire in one location when you busted in?"

The door frame is a shambles, but the Dixons are okay. Thank the Almighty. "The bed," Ham said. "It was on fire when I came in."

Rory grabbed a sooty dress that was hanging on the closet door and used it as an oven mitt to pull the iron bed frame to the center of the room. Underneath was a melted pile of ash and plastic.

"What is it?" Ham asked.

The others moved closer to see what Ham saw.

Rory dropped Marta's dress, frowning. "I'm not a fire expert, but if I had to guess, I'd say that melted plastic was an incendiary device."

℘℘

Rory motioned to the door. All of them were wheezing and holding their shirts over their noses, using them as bandanas. "Let's get out of here." Hamilton, Gregor, Ross, and Ramsay headed out the door, and Rory followed them downstairs and outside.

The town descended upon them, inundating Rory with questions. "How did it start?" "Are ye okay?" "What are ye going to do about this?" But Rory had a few questions of his own. It would take time to get to the bottom of this latest crime.

He held up his hand to get the villagers' attention. "As soon as I know anything, I'll let ye know." But only if it was in the best interest of the investigation.

Doc seemed to be finishing up with Marta because he motioned Ross over with his stethoscope at the ready.

Rory pulled out his notepad and went to Marta. "Do you know how the fire started?"

Tilly joined them, standing protectively beside Marta.

"No. I don't have a clue," Marta said. "One minute I was drifting off to sleep, and the next minute, my room was filled with smoke."

"Was anyone with you?" Rory asked.

"No," Marta said.

Tilly cleared her throat. "Um, Leo was there a few minutes before. Remember, Mar-Mar?"

Marta frowned. "You don't think Leo started the fire, do you?"

"Where's Leo Shamley?" Rory asked the crowd.

"He was at Thistle Glen Lodge right before the fire started, just like Tilly said," Ham coughed out as he came forward. No one had seen him since.

"Okay," Rory said. "Have Doc MacGregor look at ye. Make sure yere lungs are all right."

Tilly had a hold of Marta's arm, supporting her while at the same time trying to brush ash from her ruined suit. The rest of the quilters swarmed Marta, encircling her as if to build a wall around her for protection. Which said a lot about the quilters. Rory knew for a fact they were less than thrilled with Marta for killing off their favorite characters, but apparently quilters took care of their own no matter what.

"What's going on here?" Leo said, running toward the group. "Marta? Are you all right, sweetie?"

Rory stalked toward him, but Diana stepped forward, looking as cool and calm as ever in a crisis. He'd seen her fielding questions from the quilters and villagers, plus making sure someone sorted a glass of water for Marta.

"Marta's fine," Diana said, blocking Leo from her.

Marta didn't look fine. Her face was a mess of soot and running mascara and her hair was flat and damp from the wet towel Rory had wrapped around her.

Rory roadblocked Leo with his hand, not letting him pass. "Not so fast. I have a few questions for you. Where were ye just now?"

"Out and about," Leo answered caustically, as if Rory had no right to know.

"Tell me where," Rory demanded.

"Exploring," Leo said, evasively.

But Rory had seen Leo emerge from the pathway that led up the bluff. Had Leo been hiding out to watch the fire from a distance?

Rory took Leo by the arm. "Ye're in a lot of trouble."

Leo jerked, trying to get away. "What for?"

"For being a cagey dobber after an arson's been committed."

"What?" He looked scared now.

"There was a fire at Thistle Glen Lodge. Didn't ye hear the alarm?"

"I didn't know what that sound meant," Leo whined.

"Tell me where ye were just now. *The truth.*"

Leo turned away, as if to give his answer some privacy. "I was up at Graham Buchanan's house."

"What were ye doing there? Casing the joint?"

"Good grief, no! I was just looking around," Leo said sheepishly, as if he was guilty as hell. Of what, Rory wasn't exactly sure.

"And?"

"I may have peeked in the windows," Leo went on. "I didn't do anything wrong."

Except skulking where ye shouldn't have been.

"What took ye so long to get here after the fire alarm went off?"

Leo exhaled, turned his head even more, and whispered out of the side of his mouth. "I didn't want anyone to know where I was. I had to find a different path back to the village. It's steep, you know. I had to take it slow."

"Let's go back," Rory said. "Were ye at Thistle Glen Lodge tonight?"

"Yes," Leo said. "I came to see Marta."

"Was she there?" Rory knew she was. He was right there

165

when Marta said she had a headache and needed to lie down. He was kicking himself for leaving Thistle Glen Lodge when he had. He never should've gone next door to Duncan's Den.

Leo looked down at his hands. "Marta was upstairs in her room."

"Did you speak with her?" Rory asked.

"Yes," Leo answered. "I offered to rub her back, hoping it would help with her headache."

"How long were ye in the room?"

"About five minutes," Leo said.

Just long enough to insert a time-delay incendiary device and get the hell out of there.

"Why didn't ye stay longer?" Rory asked.

"Marta insisted she wanted to be left alone. So I took a walk."

"Did ye speak with anyone beside Marta at Thistle Glen Lodge, before ye went for yere *walk*?"

"No. I saw Tilly and that Scottish guy in the kitchen, *Hamilton*—" Leo said it as if he didn't believe that was his name "— but I didn't speak to them." He looked around at the villagers. "I didn't speak with any of them either."

Rory was trying to put the pieces together. Leo was his number one suspect. Since he hadn't spoken with anyone on entering Thistle Glen Lodge, he could've snuck a small device under his coat and gotten it upstairs without it being seen.

"Ye're awfully lucky ye weren't with Marta when the fire started," Rory said, and then waited for some kind of reaction.

"Is she okay? Can I go to her now?" Leo pleaded.

"Nay. Ye're going to have to go to the police station in Inverness, to test yere person for chemicals, the kind which can ignite a fire."

"I'm innocent!" Leo's wail sounded strange coming from a tall, grown man. "I didn't do anything."

"Unfortunately for you," Rory said, "ye're the prime suspect for several crimes." He looked around for his team and found them. "MacTaggart, restrain Mr. Shamley and take him in."

"No!" Leo cried, trying to make a run for it again.

Rory reached out and pulled him to a stop. "Ye're only making this worse on yereself. MacTaggart, take him." Rory turned to the rest of the village. "Everyone to Quilting Central. We're going to start the interviews all over again."

The crimes were piling up. The complications. And he hadn't had a moment yet to figure out what had—or what hadn't—happened on the porch of Duncan's Den with Diana.

Everywhere he looked, things had turned to chaos.

He heaved a big breath and said, "I'll speak with ye first, Parker."

"Me?" Parker looked around as if another Parker had popped up in Gandiegow.

"Aye. Walk with me to Quilting Central."

Parker glanced around and he knew who she was looking for. Sure enough, her gaze landed on Diana. Then Parker gave Rory a pointed glare. "Are you trying to make Diana jealous? 'Cause if you are, stop it. She's my friend."

"I only need to ask you a few questions."

"About the fire?"

"No. About Diana."

Parker groaned. "You can ask, but I'm not sure I'll answer."

Now that he had an opening, he didn't know where to start. He couldn't tell her about kissing Diana and her pulling away when it got heated. But he could ask the other question that puzzled him the most. "How does Diana stay calm when everyone else is agitated and upset? Like when the body was found outside the bookshop?"

"I don't know," Parker said.

"Has she suffered some kind of trauma in her life, maybe?"

Rory asked.

Parker hesitated. "You'd have to ask her."

"Do ye think she'd tell me?"

"I don't know. Really. She hasn't talked to me, but I've heard things from other people at Three Seals."

"Like what?"

Parker shook her head. "It's not my place to say. I'm sure Diana has her reasons for whatever has caused you to ask these questions."

Rory saw Parker glance back at Diana again; she was following them, along with the rest of the villagers.

"Don't you want to ask me about the fire?" Parker said.

"Sure." *She was right.* He needed to think about the crime instead of Diana. "Were you asleep at Duncan's Den when the fire started?"

"I was on the phone with Ewan." Parker got a dreamy look in her eyes.

Rory made a note, but he knew Parker's interest didn't lie in making fires, unless it was with the Laird with the protruding ears.

"Okay. That's all for now." But Rory wasn't any closer to solving why Diana had acted the way she had on the back porch. He needed to know, so he could fix it. He liked having her in his arms. Liked it more than he should. And he wanted to kiss her again.

12

COMPLETELY MISERABLE, Diana sat at a table in Quilting Central, watching Rory pull on his jacket. He was leaving – she was devastated. She'd tried to keep from mooning over him, but nothing worked.

He'd finished interviewing all the villagers. Of course he didn't need to interview her, since *he* was her alibi--they had, after all, been in a lip-lock, or thereabouts, when the fire alarm went off--but Diana cringed, thinking about what Rory must've told his team.

And why couldn't he have come near enough for her to soak up a few more of his pheromones, enough to last her. . . how long? *Forever?* Oh, man, she was a train wreck.

At the door, Rory leaned over to speak with Deydie and Bethia, which made Diana's ears perk up. He said something about leaving for Inverness to interrogate Leo further and that he'd be back. But her mood—crushed from wanting Rory, but unable to have him—didn't budge from its place at the bottom of the pit. Diana knew enough about police procedure to know

Rory's next trip to Gandiegow would be a short one. He'd wrap things up in the fishing village and be off to the next case.

Her state of mind took a nosedive. Apparently, she'd only thought she was at rock bottom. She shouldn't have let him kiss her. She shouldn't have indulged herself and kissed him back.

She took a couple of deep breaths.

Enough already. She wasn't dating a police officer. It was an open-and-shut case.

Deydie and Bethia dropped down beside Diana, making her gasp with surprise.

"Ye need to quit making eyes at the DCI," Deydie commanded in her scratchy old voice.

"We've come to help." Bethia set a basket in front of Diana. "This is just the thing to occupy yere mind now that ye've finished piecing your Gandiegow Library quilt. Moira is nearly done quilting it on the longarm machine."

Deydie pulled pieces of fabric from the basket and positioned them on the flat surface. "'Tis the Kilts & Quilts Pillow Sham for ye to make. We've even cut the pieces for ye."

Bethia placed a graph paper drawing on the table and smoothed it out with her knotted, arthritic hands.

Deydie straightened her rounded shoulders. "I designed it just this morning," she said proudly.

Diana sighed heavily. Didn't these women understand she had too much to do already? She picked up Deydie's drawing to inspect it but ended up gaping at it instead. The design was stunning: a starry sky above three houses and three boats—mostly in plaids—with a ruffle around the edge. "I'm not an expert at piecing."

"'Tis not that difficult," Bethia said. "We'll help."

Deydie clapped Diana on the back several times. "An eighteen-inch sham is a grand way to pick up new skills."

Bethia nodded. "And a pillow sham is smaller than a quilt, ye see. Ye won't waste time or fabric, and ye won't get stuck if ye don't like doing a particular technique."

Diana stared at both women. "I suppose you won't let me get out of doing this, even if I tell you I'm too busy?"

"Damn straight we won't," Deydie said. "I've said it before, and I'll say it again: There's enough time, grace, and creativity to get done what needs to get done."

Diana hoped it was true. She also hoped their scheme would work—that the pillow sham would keep her from obsessing over Rory.

True to their word, the two women sat beside Diana and demonstrated, step by step, how to do foundation paper piecing and chain stitching. Meanwhile Marta and Tilly left, escorted by the Duffy brothers, to move into Duncan's Den. Marta didn't seem happy about doubling up with Tilly. Actually, she threw a fit about it.

As Diana was finishing up with the pillow sham top, Quilting Central began emptying for the night.

Deydie stood. "Ye've done good, Diana. I'll get this quilted and finished up for ye in the morn. 'Tis time to close up now."

"Aye," Bethia said, stretching while she rose from her chair. "I need to mix together some more herbs for Mrs. Bruce's migraines."

Diana switched off the machine and got to her feet as well. "Thank you both." She didn't have to say for what, because these two knew.

Deydie and Bethia walked Diana to Duncan's Den. McCartney was watching Marta, so Ham and Greg volunteered to escort the older women to their homes.

When they left, Diana put another log on the fire and wrapped herself in the quilt from the *back porch incident,*

171

when Rory had kissed her so thoroughly that she could still feel it. She was all alone—*everyone else must be in their rooms*—and her mind began to wander where it shouldn't. She plopped down on the couch, frowning.

She picked up a magazine but couldn't read.

She stared at the fire but couldn't relax.

She gazed at her phone but couldn't work.

She hated that she was waiting...for *him*.

She wasn't even sure if Rory was coming back to Duncan's Den tonight or not. McCartney was camping out upstairs outside of Marta and Tilly's bedroom. For a moment, really less than a second, Diana entertained the thought of embarrassing herself and asking, *Have you heard from the Detective Chief Inspector? When is he coming back?*

She made herself stay put and not seek out McCartney. She stretched her legs out in front of her and snuggled down into her quilt. Even though she was worried insomnia had settled in for the long haul, she laid her head back on the armrest. She listened for the door, but heard only the crackle of the fire. And the wind outside. And the earnest beating of her heart.

"Diana?"

She shot upright and cracked her head against his. She knew that voice, the voice she adored so much, which was now quietly swearing.

"Good grief, woman." Rory gripped her arms, as if to keep her from falling off the couch, or to keep her from whacking him again with her head. "Ye gave me a *bluidy* concussion."

"Sorry." But she was so glad to see him. "You startled me."

"Is yere head all right?" He let go of her and rubbed his forehead, but there was concern for her in his eyes.

"Don't worry. I have a hard head," she said.

He chuckled. "I came back to wrap things up. Not to knock heads with you." He looked so good to her. His five o'clock shadow had matured into a three a.m. beard, exuding masculinity and tempting her like crazy. Floundering for an excuse, she found one: *I'm dreaming.* And she gave herself permission to act out. She reached up and ran a hand over that manly stubble, sighing when it prickled her palm.

His gaze instantly turned hooded. She stayed right where she was, almost daring him. She didn't pull away when he leaned in to kiss her, wrapping her in his arms.

Yes, she'd started it. But in her defense, he'd caught her off guard by waking her with his sexy, gravelly voice. Besides, who could blame her for what she did at this hour, for surely her resolve must still be sleeping, too. Also, the glowing embers in the hearth blanketed the room in a magical cast of shadows and possibilities. For the life of her, she couldn't puzzle together why she'd ever objected to kissing a police officer.

When the kiss was over, he laid his forehead against hers. "Tell me why you pulled away from me earlier, when we were on the porch." He leaned down and brushed his lips against hers again, apparently considering them his best weapon to make her comply.

He might be right, because heck, she'd be willing to do *anything* for him right now.

He brushed her hair out of her face. "I asked Parker what your story was, but she said I would have to ask ye myself. The way she said it made me think ye do have a reason?"

Diana nodded silently.

Rory slipped his arms under her legs and lifted her up. For a second, she thought he might sweep her away, up the stairs like Rhett in *Gone with the Wind.* Instead, he sat on the couch, taking her with him, settling her head against his shoulder and her legs across his lap.

"Tell me," he said. "I want to know."

If it hadn't been the wee hours of the morning, or if she

hadn't been half-asleep, or if his arms cocooned around her hadn't felt better than any quilt she'd ever been snuggled into, maybe she would've been able to keep her father's story to herself.

"Ye're safe with me," he whispered. That was it. The words and his calming presence, which surrounded her like a fortress, convinced her to trust him.

But she needed a little distance to talk about her dad. She scooted back off Rory's lap and moved to the far end of the couch, her legs still outstretched. He set her right foot on his thigh and began massaging the sole.

She sighed, because it felt so good. Now, she really did owe him her story. "I started my last year in high school on top of the world. I was sure I had everything figured out. How my senior year would go. What university I was going to attend afterward. What I was going to do after that. Life at home was good. My parents were pretty cool, as parents went, though I thought my dad was overly protective."

"How so?"

She shrugged. "He'd seen a lot of bad things happen in New York." Now it was time for the big confession. "He was a police officer."

"Really?" Rory said thoughtfully. "That explains a lot."

"Like what?" she asked.

"From what I've seen, ye're good with cataloging details. Ye're extremely logical in yere thinking. Ye're able to compartmentalize--while others around ye are falling apart, you keep a cool head."

"Thanks." The way he was looking at her, Diana knew he meant it as a compliment.

"Is yere father still overly protective?"

She shook her head. "Dad died. That September."

"Was it 9/11?" Rory said gently, almost reverently, and she

appreciated the respect he was showing her dad.

"Not quite," she said, making sure her voice was steady. "He survived the collapse of the Twin Towers, though he was there. Many from his squad didn't make it out." There'd been tears of relief and gratitude in their home. But... "Dad was shot responding to an armed robbery on September 25th. Two weeks to the day after 9/11."

Rory's eyebrows crashed together. "Oh, lass, I'm so sorry. How did yere family cope?"

"My mother and my sister and I felt very alone," Diana said. "We were kind of lost in the shuffle. All of New York was grieving from 9/11. No one had any further bandwidth for our personal little tragedy."

"What a terrible feeling," Rory said somberly.

The memories flooded her—what it had been like the days following. Mom staying in bed, crying all day. Police officers stopping by briefly as they came off shift. They'd loved her dad, but they were exhausted from mourning dozens of friends. There'd been condolence letters that were heartfelt, she knew now, but they'd only felt hollow then. In one moment, Diana's life had gone from normal to disastrous. Nothing had ever felt *safe* again. "My mother was completely devastated and couldn't help Liz and me process what had happened, something I understand better now that I'm older. At the time, though, I was angry." Angry that her mother didn't have the strength to get out of bed. To comfort them. Worst of all, Diana hadn't been allowed to grieve. It had been up to her and Liz to get jobs, pay the bills, go shopping, get the laundry done, and deal with the creepy, *handsy* super of their building. Essentially, become adults overnight.

Rory leaned over, took her hand, and kissed it. "I'm truly sorry."

"My mom wasn't the same for a long time. Having grandchildren has helped bring joy back into her life."

Rory raised a questioning eyebrow.

"Not me. My sister Liz has three kids."

He nodded.

Diana paused, wondering if she should tell him the rest. But it felt right and easy with Rory gazing at her so compassionately. She went on. "Since I was little, I'd planned on following in my dad's footsteps. Even after the shooting." Maybe even more so then...to honor her father's memory. "But I couldn't do it to my mom, it would've crushed her." Back then, Diana would've done anything to make her mom bounce back, even give up her own dreams. "I figured I had to pick something safe, so I got a marketing degree."

"I'm sorry for all ye've been through." Rory sat back and took her other foot, rubbing it as if to erase her painful past. "I thank ye for trusting me enough to tell me." He gave her a look as if he was trying to see into her soul. "I see ye understand tragedy because ye've experienced it firsthand. Ye're calm in the face of a storm because you've survived the worst kind of storm." He frowned then. "What I don't understand is what's going through yere mind concerning *me*."

Diana couldn't answer. She felt like she'd been nicked by a razor. She turned her gaze away from him.

"Look at me, lass," Rory coaxed.

She did as he asked.

"Tell me why ye pulled away from me earlier on the porch...when we were only just getting to know each other."

≈≈≈

Rory was surprised when she jerked her feet from his lap and tucked them under her. She looked as if she didn't want to spell it out for him, but he was going to make her do it anyway. He wasn't trying to pile on to her hurt and pain, but he wanted to know if she was conscious of why she was doing what she was doing. He'd understood perfectly the moment she'd said her father was a cop.

Diana glared at him. "That's an interesting euphemism. What would you call it if things had gone farther?"

He scooted closer, making sure to maintain eye contact. "Ye're deflecting. Tell me why ye pulled away." He was a born interrogator. But this was no suspect. He'd have to tread lightly to make sure she was okay.

She crossed her arms and stared at him for a long stubborn moment, to the point where he thought she wouldn't answer him at all. But this lass had been forged from fire, and she was going to tell him how it was.

"It's nothing personal, Detective Chief Inspector. I don't date cops. Period."

He nodded, satisfied that at least she was aware of her motives. He liked women who knew their own mind. He liked *her*. But she'd thrown up a wall between them. Maybe he could coax her around with some teasing. "Okay, then. It's settled. We won't date. We'll just *get to know each other better*."

"You're impossible." She moved as if to get up and stomp away.

But she only made it halfway to her feet. He latched onto her hand and tugged, bringing her back down to his eye level, her face so close that he could've kissed her. For a moment, he stared into her steely eyes, but he wasn't deterred. His hands surrounded her waist and he planted her on his lap once again.

She squeaked, but she stayed where he put her. Gently, he cradled her in his arms, not forcing her to remain. With only his eyes, he willed her to stay.

She seemed as brittle as the stem of a wineglass. For a moment he faltered, not confident his brand of charm would work on a one-of-a-kind lass like her.

"What are your plans, Columbo? Or should I say Jimmy Perez, you know, from *Shetland*?" Her question threw him off, her voice harder than he expected, her tone a clear challenge.

His world twisted a little off kilter and he admitted the whole truth. "I do want to know ye better. I want to know everything about you. What makes ye tick. What makes ye laugh." What turned her on. Rory desperately wanted to find an empty room and make love to her. At the same time, he wondered if he shouldn't get the hell out of there.

The resolve in her eyes wavered. Maybe she was thinking about finding a bedroom, too. Or was that only wishful thinking on his part?

She tugged at her ear—buying time, perhaps—but she still didn't slip from his lap. "Where are you sleeping tonight? Duncan's Den is full." Her eyes scanned the room as if it was packed wall-to-wall people.

He chuckled. She was so damned cute in her uneasiness. "Aw, lass, ye've been waiting for me all evening, it seems, stretched out on *my bed*."

"I'll leave you to it." She tried to get up again, but he gently squeezed her, just enough to convey the request, *Please stay*.

Immediately she stilled. "Now what?"

"You're going to kiss me," he said boldly.

"I don't think so."

"Ye will." Slowly he ran his hands down her arms, and instantly goosebumps broke out under his caress. He examined the little bumps closely. "Are ye cold?" He didn't give her a chance to answer but took the opportunity to pull the quilt over the two of them.

Her eyes went wide.

"Relax, lass." He leaned his head back on the couch and closed his eyes. "Something about ye helps me to unwind," he admitted. "I'm grateful to ye."

She shifted and burrowed into him, too, as if she'd known he needed more.

His mind calmed. He could've let his hands explore her body, but they both needed sleep.

That's when she snaked her arms around his neck and pulled him down to kiss her.

In seconds, they were acting like a couple of teenagers, making out on the couch while the rest of the cottage was fast asleep in their beds. It was thrilling and passionate, and they were both still fully clothed!

When he was worried one or both of them might get carried away and take it farther, he pulled back. "We should sleep."

He meant for her to stay stretched out on him, but instead, she brushed her lips over his before rising. "I can't get caught out here."

"*Aye.*" He understood. She was here on business. He was, too. But understanding didn't fix how he'd gone instantly cold as she padded from the room. Or how all of the worries of the day flooded back in on him.

Then he was hit with a boulder of a thought. And, oh, God, he was in trouble. He'd crossed a line tonight. One moment he was perfectly content in his life. A life that had structure and purpose. A life he could control. But now he felt helpless with the realization his life could be so much more. *Richer. More fulfilling.* Challenging in ways he'd never dreamed of. ...if only Diana would agree to be part of it.

∞⃝

Sitting at her rolltop desk, Deydie chewed on her pencil, wrestling with how she should handle this new day. The retreat goers would be here any minute and Deydie wanted to do something special for them, besides the trip to Whussendale.

The poor lassies had been through a lot—*seen a lot*—since they'd come to this retreat. The Almighty knew the excitement had been hard on Deydie's old heart, too! At least it was all behind them now...with *that Leo Shamley* hauled off to prison.

The door blew open, carrying in a gust of wind, and with it, Diana and Parker. A blast of rain pellets showered Deydie, too.

"Shut the damn door," she complained. "Don't ye lassies understand how expensive bought heat is here in Gandiegow?"

"Sorry," Diana said as she pulled the door to, before shrugging out of her rain jacket.

Deydie frowned at the skinny American. "Lordy, aren't ye freezing in those scant threads ye're wearing? Ye're going to catch yere death."

"This is what I'd wear in New York." The Yank looked down at her black sheath dress, nude hosiery, and her pretty boots, which were good for nothing here in Scotland.

"Why aren't ye wearing a pair of jeans? I know ye have them. I saw them on ye the other day," Deydie said. "Och, ye young lassies need to care less about yere vanity and more about keeping warm."

"My jeans are fine, but I've worn all my tops," Diana explained. "Besides, I wanted to dress up for our trip to Whussendale."

"This is one problem I can fix." Deydie picked up her phone to ring up her granddaughter, while Diana gaped at her like a fish. "Caitie? Can ye bring a warm top down to Quilting Central for Diana? She's going to freeze if ye don't. I honestly don't think me heart can withstand another dead body this week. If this lass doesn't start wearing proper clothing, that's exactly what's going to happen. *Death by stupidity*."

Diana rolled her eyes. "Cait already brought me clothes."

Deydie ignored her and finished up with Caitie. "See ye soon."

After Deydie hung up, she nodded at Diana. "Git yere skinny arse back to Duncan's Den and get yere jeans on. Caitie will be by with a sweater for ye to wear. Ye're nearly the same size, though ye won't fill out her sweater as well as she does."

Diana looked down at her chest.

Deydie shook her head at her. "Stop wishing for teats ye don't have. Now tell me, do ye have any giveaways planned for today?" She didn't wait for her answer. "While ye're at Duncan's Den, gather up some goodies and bring them back with ye."

Diana held up her bag. "I brought them with me. We have charms for everyone. For your quilting ladies, too."

"Good...good," Deydie said. "Now off with ye."

But as Diana made her way to the door, all the quilters filed in with Marta in the lead. When the crowd flowed around her, Diana took a few steps before halting in her tracks: Rory had entered, shutting the door behind him.

Deydie observed the American lass' mooning and shook her head. She needed another good talking to, one more direct than the last time. "Diana, git over here."

The lass came out of her stupor and made her way over to the desk.

"I was leaving to put on jeans like you told me to," Diana complained.

Deydie whacked her desk with a pencil. "Snap out of it. The way ye act around the DCI, what's wrong with ye? It's as if ye've never seen a strapping Scotsman before. Are ye lovesick over the man?" Now that Deydie thought about it, they would look good standing up together.

"Nothing is wrong with me," Diana said, indignantly.

"Is that a bite mark I see on yere neck?"

Diana glared over at Rory first, then looked down—as if she was going to check her own neck. Her cheeks turned the color of red currants, nearly the same color as the border on Deydie's Puffin quilt.

Deydie stood and smacked her on the back, laughing. "Ye've no bite mark, ye ninny. Just testing ye. But ye proved there could've been one."

Diana glared at Deydie, but her gaze shifted to Rory again, as if she couldn't help herself.

"Pull yereself together, lassie, or I'll take my broom after ye, for yere own good." Deydie whacked her back again. "Now off with ye."

But as she started toward the exit, the door opened again. A rosy-cheeked and windblown Graham strolled in, causing the room to go silent.

"Hello, all," he said cheerily. "I thought I might stop by and have coffee with ye, before you head off to Whussendale."

The ladies were mesmerized, starstruck, right down to their warm stockings. Though Graham hailed from Gandiegow, he seldom visited Quilting Central during the Kilts & Quilts retreats. Deydie did everything within her power to make sure Graham wasn't bothered with people poking in his business when he was home. He was a son of Gandiegow and didn't have to worry about autographs here.

Caitie walked in behind him with wee Hamish strapped to her chest. Deydie's heart squeezed every time she saw the babe. And for Caitie to name Hamish after the grandda Caitie never met—Deydie's own dead husband—made Deydie love Caitie that much more, though she wouldn't have believed it was possible.

Graham gave the retreat goers one of his movie star smiles and chuckled. "Don't drink all the tea and eat all the pastries, ladies. Save some for me, as I have to help my wife with the bairn." He slipped the baby out of the carrier and bounced him a little as he made his way to the kitchen area. As if he was a trawl line and the retreat goers were a bunch of hooked haddock, they left their seats and were pulled in his direction.

Deydie hollered to Caitie. "Over here."

Cait smiled and joined her at the desk. "Hey, Diana—"

Deydie interrupted. "What a surprise! Graham coming to visit."

"Aye," Caitie said. "He's awfully generous to give them his time, as he needs to leave soon again. A trip to London. He said he wanted to say a quick hello to the quilters, as they've had a bad go of it since they arrived in Gandiegow."

"He's a good lad, Caitie. Ye couldn't have done better when ye picked him."

Caitie laughed. "*Aye.* We had a rough time of it, but it's all worked out well." She looked over at Graham and nodded. "He's making their day, ye know."

"I believe our troubles are behind us." Deydie glanced at Marta, who surprisingly stood back watching, letting Graham have the limelight for the moment. "Maybe I've been a wee bit wrong about Marta. Maybe everything going to hell isn't completely her fault. Maybe Marta isn't bad luck...*just a bad person.*"

Diana's eyebrows shot up as if she might say something, but then she clamped her lips shut.

Caitie held out a sack to Diana. "Let me know if you need anything else."

"Thanks," the American lass said.

Deydie glared at Diana. "Are ye still here? Git on with ye now and put on yere jeans. We're going to be leaving soon."

"Yes, ma'am." Diana gave her a mock salute.

Deydie scanned the room for her broom, but it was over by the door. "Don't be cheeky, missy."

Diana smiled and headed for the door, but her eyes were on Rory.

Caitie tapped Deydie's arm. "Do ye see what's going on there?"

"Aye," she said.

From across the room, Rory seemed to have been watching Diana's every move. As she opened the door, he strode toward her in a very determined fashion. Deydie opened her mouth to tell him to stay here; it wasn't proper for him to go, with Diana changing clothes and all. But Caitie slipped her arm through hers.

"Leave 'em alone, Gran. We both know how Gandiegow has a way of bringing hearts together." Caitie smiled blissfully at her own husband. "This village has magic."

Caitie and Graham's love was one for the books.

"All right," Deydie harrumphed. "Just this once, I'll let it go. But ye have to admit, we've had more than our fair share of lassies who have ended up with a bairn because of Gandiegow's so-called magic."

13

As Diana zipped up her raincoat, she spied Rory marching her way, definitely on a mission. He had on his rain jacket, but for some reason, he grabbed an umbrella from the milk can by the door.

"What are you doing?" she asked.

He reached out, turned the knob, and held the door wide for her. "Going with ye."

She started to argue, but the torrential rain was pouring into Quilting Central. Plus, everyone was gawking at them, as if they were watching a riveting reality TV show. Diana decided it was best to take their impending disagreement out into the storm.

When the door was shut behind them, she pulled him to a stop. "There's no need for you to escort me to Duncan's Den. Gandiegow is safe now, right?"

"Let's get out of this weather." He didn't answer her question.

"We'll talk now." Diana ignored how her legs were being

lashed with buckets of water from the sky and hosed down from below by the sea splashing and spraying under her dress.

"Fine," Rory said. "We're not 100% sure the village is safe yet. Ye shouldn't go out alone. That's why I'm with ye."

She wanted to know if there was another reason. Like, did he want to be with her? No way was she going to ask.

"You're not making sense," she finally said, diverting her crazy thoughts back to the case.

"Although the evidence points to Leo, it *doesnae* mean he did the crimes. Come, lass, let's keep walking." She started off. Not because she was inclined to do as he ordered, but seriously, she was going to either freeze to death from the cold or drown from the storm.

She let him hurry her along with his hand to her back. When Duncan's Den was in sight, she said, "I assumed, with Leo in jail, you'd be leaving. You even said so yourself—that you only came back to wrap things up." Which is why she'd let herself get caught up in him last night. The reason she'd let things go as far as they did. She figured she was telling Rory goodbye.

"Nay. Ye'll not be rid of me that easily." He opened the door to Duncan's Den and stood back, letting her go in first.

"And Whussendale? Are you going with us?" The thought of Rory hanging around had the strangest effect on her. Anticipation coated her insides like syrup over pancakes—sweet, delectable. But just like syrup and pancakes, especially in excess, Rory wasn't good for her.

"Aye. I'll be tagging along."

She slipped out of her jacket and kicked off her boots without looking him in the eye. She didn't want him to see her relief and excitement that he would be coming to Whussendale with them. "I need to change," she said, turning down the hall. "I'll be back in a moment."

She heard Rory's footsteps following close behind.

"I'm good with zippers," he said.

"I bet you are," she said under her breath.

"Let me know if ye need my help. *With anything.*" His deep baritone was so ridiculously sexy. She knew he was only teasing, but...

Don't tempt me, was on the tip of her tongue. Feeling suddenly brave, she turned, and like a linebacker, she threw up a hand to halt him. "You. Stay." *Don't come any farther, or I might not be able to resist.* Just thinking of how they'd made out on the couch last night had her warming up quickly.

Rory laughed, as if he could read every sensual thought racing through her mind. "I'll wait right here."

She slipped into her bedroom and closed the door, grateful for the barrier between them. She leaned back against the hardwood door.

Unfortunately, oak wasn't soundproof. "About last night..." Rory started.

There was a long pause. So long that Diana was beginning to wonder if he'd forgotten what he wanted to say. *Or* maybe he was trying to find the words to tell her that he regretted their *couch-capade* last night. Her heart sank. She searched for something to say so she wouldn't have to listen to the remorse in his voice. Maybe she could muster up: *Don't worry. Last night, when I kissed you, it didn't mean a thing.* But that wasn't true. So, she remained silent. Silence, she'd learned in the business world, forced the other person to speak. Especially since Rory had been the one to start the whole thing *about last night...*

He cleared his throat. It sounded like he was thumping the front of his boot against the door. "I'll wait to talk until you come out."

She pushed away from the door. "No. Go ahead. Say what

you were going to say." *Did she sound too eager?* Whatever he wanted to say, it would be better if she was behind the door and he couldn't see her face. "It will take me time to change."

As her luck would have it, her damned zipper got stuck halfway down. Really caught. Wouldn't budge a millimeter. She yanked and pulled, hoping she wouldn't have to take him up on his offer.

She heard him lay his hand against the door.

"Last night...was *nice*," he said.

They were both struggling—she, with her zipper, and he, with his words. Finally, *thank God*, the zipper gave way and she was able to slip out of the damp dress. She shivered, whether from the chilly room or his warming words, she couldn't say.

"Yes," she answered, though he hadn't actually asked a question. It had been nice. And exciting. And, and...beyond anything she'd ever known. She switched out of her wet bra into a dry one, still trying to process what he might have meant by *nice*. Had he measured the word, or had he been a typical man and said the first word that popped into his head? Had he actually tried and discarded numerous possibilities? God knew, he'd taken his time saying anything. She decided *that* nice was good. Was everything. Well, that's what she chose to believe. So as Diana pulled on Cait's stylish gray and black fringed sweater, she felt instantly better—warm and hugged by the soft wool. And warmed and hugged by his words.

There was a shuffle on the other side of the door. Had he just leaned against it?

"I thought, since last night went so well, maybe we should do it again." He paused. "Go on a proper date."

She sucked in a breath, not prepared for her heart to pound faster. Hurriedly, she slipped on her socks and black jeans, trying to piece together a response. But she was at war with herself.

She wanted him. But she couldn't have him!

Irritation gripped her. He shouldn't have asked for a date, proper or otherwise. Hadn't she been clear with him? She'd told him she could never date a cop.

She slung open the door, making him nearly tumble backward into the room. She reached out and steadied him, hating how she held him close for a moment too long before letting go.

"What's wrong with you?" she growled, feeling her don't-mess-with-a-New-Yorker attitude bubbling to the surface.

"What's the matter?" he said, straightening up. "I'm the one whose arse almost hit the floor."

"I'll tell you what's the matter." *Why was her voice so shrill?* She stopped to take a steadying breath, but it did no good, so she let him have it. "I *told* you. I. Don't. Date. Cops!"

He tilted his head at her and said calmly, "Aye. Ye did say that."

She opened her mouth, but he raised a hand, as if to halt her next tirade.

He gave her the most patient look. "But then ye kissed me, lass." His probing gaze was doing double duty. He was willing her to remember what they'd done last night, and it was clear that he was summoning an image of their make-out session, too. "The evidence suggests ye might've changed yere mind."

True. She looked away, clearly losing this game of chicken. A thrilling and dangerous game, which had turned her into a complete wreck. She took a moment to gather her wits. "Yes, I kissed you. But that was before I knew you weren't leaving Gandiegow."

He looked stumped. "Then ye were only kissing me because ye assumed I was on my way back to Glasgow and out of yere life for good?"

"Yes," she lied, staring down at her feet. Maybe she should've told him the truth. For when he'd woken her up on the couch, she hadn't cared about her long-standing convictions. Now, in this charged moment, a crazy idea whirled through her brain. *I bet I could keep him, if he'd be willing to change his line of work.* A safe job: Like an accountant. A dietician. Or perhaps a paperboy. She allowed herself to look at him then.

Any job would do, as long as it is one where bullets have no chance of hitting that gorgeous head of yours or piercing your strong chest.

But she knew he'd never give up being a cop.

Rory moved closer and brushed her hair from her face. "I don't believe ye, lass. I know when people are telling the truth and when they're not."

Apparently, he was still thinking about how good they'd been together, while she had been plunged into sadness. She leaned her head against his gentle hand, taking comfort, though he hadn't a clue as to what she was going through. "Rory, there's no way that you and I are going to happen. It would hurt too much." *To lose you.*

He pulled her in and held her close. "I do understand. Ye're thinking about yere da and the pain is as real as if someone has taken a dagger to yere heart."

She didn't want to feel this way. She just wanted to breathe with Rory—in and out, forever, quietly—and know peace.

He leaned his head against hers and spoke softly, as if telling her a secret no one had been privy to before. "Our parents died in a car accident, when we were wee lads. I told ye about my gran and what happened to her. I miss her every day. And then there's my partner on the force." He inhaled deeply, as if that would propel the rest of the words out. "Denny was killed in a grocery store robbery. There was nothing I could do about it, as I was running after one of the suspects." He kissed the top of Diana's head. "So ye see, I feel what you feel. But lass, ye can't stop living because of the terrible things that have happened. Ye have to have a little faith."

"Faith?" She pressed both hands against his chest. She wanted to tell him he had no idea...*but he did know.*

She pushed away from him as a frustrated sob escaped her. Something had broken loose. It was like Pandora's box had been opened, the lid yanked violently off. Frustration with him, the situation, even the past, escaped before she could rein in her emotions. "He was my dad! He was supposed to see me graduate college, to walk me down the aisle. He was supposed to bounce my own children on his knee, as he had done for me. He was supposed to *protect* me. When he died I lost my faith in God. And ever since I've felt alone and—and damaged."

The untamed words were running free, letting her true desires slip through the cracks of her stoicism. No one was supposed to see what she truly wanted. Not even her! She sucked in a breath and tried to step away from Rory, but he held on tight, as if the wind battering the windows had come inside, trying to carry her away. She knew, in her heart of hearts, that Rory would never let her get swept away, no matter what.

"It's okay, lass," he said, soothingly.

She felt exposed. He'd seen the real Diana, and she wished she could take it all back. She could think of only one way to erase the last few moments, but it was reckless. She did it anyway.

She wrapped her arms around him and kissed him. *Wildly. Frantically.* In the process, she bumped her nose against his, clanked their teeth together, all in an effort to make him forget. The kisses last night had been perfect. Her efforts now were pathetic.

He grabbed her arms. "Hold on there." He bent low to look her in the eyes. "*Now* isn't the time. Deydie and the others are expecting us back at Quilting Central, right?"

Ashamed, she nodded. She never should've allowed her grief out. Her grief was ugly and raging. Demanding and controlling. She liked her grief safely tucked away, where no one could see her anguish. But now Rory had exposed her: she wasn't the strong woman she pretended, the one who had her act together. Diana was a fraud. And no sweater in the world was heavy enough, impenetrable enough, to hide the dreadful truth.

As they walked back to Quilting Central, Diana had to accept how things would never be the same. Not just with Rory. But within herself. She was terrified by how her grief had suddenly changed her. How desperate it made her feel. When she was seventeen, there'd been no time for grief. There'd been school to finish and bills to pay. She'd been strong, a badass.

But now full-on grief had turned her into a limp noodle. Exhausted from keeping up the front for so long. Spent.

"Are ye okay?"

No! "Yes." She'd turned into quite the liar and was disgusted with herself. That emotion sparked a fresh batch of anger. It swelled up inside as if it was a wave picking up energy, ready to take out anything in its path.

Anger at the perp who'd shot her father *and gotten away.* Anger at her mother's inability to be strong for her children. And even anger at her sister, Liz, who'd successfully gotten on with her life—married to a dentist, living in the burbs with her three amazing children and doing good works on endless volunteer committees.

Diana had her job. Nothing else. No hope of a future filled

with children and volunteering. No hope of a happily-ever-after. Just a big fat void.

The injustice of it all was enough to make her sick. Truly sick of her life.

℘℃℃

Rory was worried about Diana as they walked back to Quilting Central. She had gone silent, like the wind had shifted suddenly and she'd crashed her ship against the rocky shore. He should've told her what grief had done to him. How, after his parents died, he and Kin were completely out of control. There weren't enough years left in his life to make up for the trouble he'd caused his grandmother, his teachers, and his neighborhood.

Rory and Kin had vandalized the school and the flower shop. They'd stolen bait from Dali's Fishery. They'd sprayed graffiti, shoplifted, cut classes, drank. And they'd mouthed off to Gran at every turn.

Gran would be proud of them now. Instead of ending up in jail—as she'd feared—the two of them had turned their lives around and ended up on the right side of the law. The irony didn't slip past Rory. Being a police officer helped atone for his sins, and at the same time, it was the one thing Diana couldn't accept about him. Life was screwed up that way.

Diana seemed to be in deep concentration as well. Or maybe the storm beating down on them kept her from talking. As she reached for the doorknob of Quilting Central, he stopped her.

"I didn't tell ye how nice ye looked when you came out of the bedroom," he said.

She gave him an expressionless nod. "The sweater is Cait's. She lent it to me." She turned the knob and walked in.

Bethia was speaking from the stage.

"Let's line up at the door. I just got a text from the coach driver. Yere bus is ready in the parking lot."

In the back of Rory's mind, he was trying to figure out a way he could sit with Diana on the bus, so they could continue their conversation. But the truth was he was on duty. His duty was to keep Marta safe and to gather more intel about the crime wave surrounding the author.

Deydie waddled hurriedly to the door, holding up her hand. "Be careful out there, lassies. The walkway is especially slippery during storms. We don't want any of *yees* to get washed away, now."

An ancient retreat goer tugged on Deydie's arm, her face lit with excitement. "Will Graham Buchanan be coming with us?" She acted as if she might call dibs to be his seatmate.

"Nay," Deydie said. "He's off to London."

The woman's face fell and with it, her wrinkles, making her look like a disappointed shar pei.

The plaid twins, Ailsa and Aileen, took up their post on either side of the woman and guided her out the door.

"Not to worry. There'll be a couple of nice-looking lads in Whussendale," Ailsa said.

"We promise," Aileen added.

Then Ailsa pointed to Rory. "And, of course, Deydie says DCI Crannach will be riding with us on the coach."

Rory wasn't sure how Deydie knew that. Had Deydie somehow been lurking in the shadows at Duncan's Den when he'd told Diana? But then he remembered the text he'd sent to McCartney about his plans.

Rory caught up to Marta. "Ye'll be sitting with me on the coach."

"Not that I don't want a handsome man for my seatmate, but I was going to stretch out and have some *me* time." Marta eyed him as if she was reconsidering her plans.

"Sit with me," Rory said. "I have yere witness statement for ye to go over and sign. It has to be done today."

"Very well."

"Take the back seat," Rory clarified. That way he could keep his eye on her *and* the rest of the quilters while they made their way to Whussendale.

"Sit in front of me in case I need something." Marta didn't even look at Tilly when she spoke, but Tilly nodded in response.

Marta climbed into the coach and took the rearmost window seat, with Rory in the aisle seat beside her. Surprisingly, Diana joined Tilly in the row in front of them.

Once everyone was on the bus, Bethia stood up, facing the group, and said, "We'll put on a wee bit of music for ye to listen to. How about some nice Scottish ballads?"

"Aye," the women on the coach chorused.

As the bus got underway Tilly and Diana put their heads together, and Rory wondered what they were talking about.

He pulled out the paperwork for Marta. "If ye can take a look at this and sign?"

She skimmed it, signed, and handed it back to him, then she stood, crouching because of the luggage compartment above her head. "Tilly, what are you typing?"

He heard Tilly close her laptop.

"Nothing," Tilly said.

"That didn't look like nothing," Marta said. "Diana, switch seats with me. Now."

Tilly looked up at Marta. "You should stay in your seat. The bus is moving."

"Do it," Marta commanded.

Diana sighed and vacated her seat. She waited in the aisle— not making eye contact with Rory—while Marta slid past and took the seat in front of him.

Now he stood up out of the way so Diana could climb into the window seat. He needed access to the aisle in case there was an emergency.

Suddenly Marta grabbed Tilly's laptop. Tilly lunged for it, but Marta held it out of reach and flipped open the lid. From where he stood, he could see it was a page of text. Marta scanned it quickly and then turned an angry red before spinning on Tilly.

"Why are you still working on the manuscript?" Marta's hissed words didn't sound like a question but an accusation. "It will never get published."

"Maybe it will," Tilly said bravely, as she snatched back the computer. "You never know."

"I do know," Marta said, her voice dropping to a whisper. She yanked Tilly's hair.

"Ouch!"

"That's what you get," Marta jeered. "You need to accept the truth, big sister. The Buttermilk Guild is over. Marta Dixon's books are all about True Crime now, not some namby-pamby quilters."

Rory sat down next to Diana and said quietly, "What's that about? Should I break it up before it turns ugly?"

Diana stared at the backs of the two sisters. "I think the row has calmed down. I'll tell you later what it's about."

True. Marta seemed to have won that round because Tilly's head was leaned against the window as she stared out at the rain.

Rory glanced over at Diana and instantly his insides turned into a blazing inferno. What was it about this lass that had him turned upside down? He'd always thought Gran was foolish for believing in fate, but since meeting Diana, he'd become a convert. He felt like the Almighty was giving him the thumbs up to pursue Diana, regardless of her refusal to ever date a cop.

Rory considered their circumstances and rationalized: *This isn't a date.* This was business. And because they were in the back seat, where nary a soul could see what he meant to do, he took Diana's hand and squeezed it. He looked at her with one eyebrow raised, daring her to complain. She frowned and stared back at him, her gaze full of steel. This was not a lass to back down, so he held on to her hand for dear life.

14

SINCE THE MOMENT MARTA had made Diana switch places with her, Diana had been a nervous wreck. Rory's handholding stunt certainly hadn't improved her composure. She was a hot mess. Literally--her face felt as if it'd been left too long on a panini press. She needed to fan herself or open a window. But since it was raining outside, the whole bus would crank their heads around to see who was letting in the cold, wet air. Then they'd see Rory, Diana's discomposure, and know. *Know everything!*

Maybe if she sucked in a couple of breaths she could get herself under control. But Rory took that moment to start making torturous circles into her palm. Could a person die from a heat stroke in winter? Of course, she could pull her hand away, but she didn't want to seem like a coward. He'd given her that challenging look—raised eyebrow and *daring her with his eyes*—and she wouldn't back down from him. Instead, she closed her eyes and pretended he was a boring accountant or a greeter at Walmart so she could ignore the sensation. However, the maelstrom he was causing inside her made her want to squirm in her seat.

Diana opened her eyes and focused on the Dixon sisters instead. They were still arguing quietly, but Marta was apparently bringing an end to the quarrel. She pulled out her compact and adjusted her lipstick, effectively blowing Tilly off. As she shifted the compact, Marta suddenly stopped.

Oh, no!

Marta spun around and peered between the seats.

"Awfully cozy back there, are we?" She laughed like Maleficent, which made Tilly turn, too. It took a second for her to see what Marta had seen.

Diana tried to pull her hand away, but the good detective held on tight.

"Eyes to the front, ladies," Rory said without a hint of embarrassment. Diana, though, wanted to crawl under the seat.

Tilly looked embarrassed enough for all of them and turned back around.

Marta nodded, giving Diana a congratulatory wink. "You're doing better than I did in that seat." She chuckled at her joke and then faced forward.

Rory leaned over and whispered in Diana's ear. "Relax."

Being able to relax was a distant memory, as his breath on her ear made her shiver.

"It's not like we're breaking the law," he said.

That had her slipping her hand from his. True, they weren't breaking any laws, but Diana was breaking her number one commandment: *Thou shalt not fall for a cop.* The words twisted around in her thoughts, almost laughing at her in a singsong fashion. *Too late, sugar plum. You already fell for this one.*

She kept her eyes on the scenery out the window, not letting herself glance over at Rory. She could feel the angry heat rolling off him at her rebuff. The man just didn't understand. It wasn't really a rebuff. Just self-preservation. For the rest of the trip, she and Rory sat in uncomfortable silence.

The landscape became thicker with trees and rolling hills, reminding Diana of the Midwest. Funny how things could be so similar to a place four-thousand miles away.

Not long afterward, they made a turn down a narrow road and stopped. Diana saw the sign for the wool mill and popped up. Without looking Rory in the eye, she squeezed past him by high-stepping over his knees. She rushed to the front of the bus to deliver instructions to the group. Never in her life had she been so grateful to be in charge.

"Pull your hoods up or put your rain caps on, while I head out to make sure Whussendale Woollens is ready for us."

Diana caught sight of a woman in the doorway of a stone building, giving the bus a wave.

"Come on," Deydie said. "Let's stop her from coming out in the storm."

Diana followed Bethia and Deydie from the bus.

Deydie hollered to the woman as soon as her feet hit the ground. "Stay there on the porch, Sophie. We'll come to ye."

In the pelting rain, the three of them ran to the awning in front of the building and the woman waiting there.

She stuck out her hand to Diana. "I'm Sophie McGillivray." She was young, probably in her twenties, and beneath her oil-skin duster she was wearing a tartan dress of red, green, and blue.

"The Laird's wife," Deydie interjected. "Laird Hugh McGillivray, that is."

Ewan had mentioned his cousin Hugh.

Diana took Sophie's hand and shook it. "Thank you for having our group and for being willing to change the date on such short notice."

Sophie smiled. "Let's get everyone off the bus and to the café. I'm sure the ladies will need a bathroom break and perhaps a cup of hot tea to warm themselves before we start our demonstration."

"Not just the ladies," Bethia interjected. "We have a man. DCI Crannach rode on the coach with us." A little smile sat at the edge of her mouth as she glanced in Diana's direction. Deydie's pointed stare was more obvious.

Diana wanted to run back to the bus to hide her face, but *he* was on the bus. Just hearing Rory's name made her breathing go a little shallow. She was a failure when it came to not thinking about him. But it was time to get back to business. "Which building is the wool mill?"

Sophie spread her arms wide. "All of them."

The wool mill consisted of a slew of buildings, some stone, some clapboard. It was raining too hard to make a complete examination, but Diana did see a little arching bridge over a rushing stream.

"I'll get the retreat-goers." Diana braved the storm and ran back to the bus. When the driver opened the door, she hustled up the steps. "Everyone ready?"

The quilters stood and made their way to the front. Diana refused to glance back to see if Rory was watching her.

As the women, *and one man,* filed off, Diana stood at the side of the bus, taking the hand of those who needed help stepping down onto the pavement. When she saw Rory's feet on the bus step, she looked down at her boots, pretending a stone was lodged in one of them. Rory walked right past her without saying a word. This was what she'd hoped for...and at the same time she was disappointed.

Sophie, Deydie, and Bethia led the way to a small green building with a café sign hanging above the door. Diana took up the caboose as the rest of the group piled inside, so many that Diana was worried the building couldn't hold all of them. When the last person went in, she poked her head in and scanned the room. Every seat was filled, making it standing room only for the stragglers. Rory stood across the room with an advantageous view of the door and of Marta. Diana couldn't help but see he had his eye on her as she squeezed in. She didn't want to block the doorway, so she sidled over next to two large, good-looking men who had clearly been in the café before the bus arrived.

Gorgeous One and Gorgeous Two eyed her and smiled. The one on the right offered his hand, though the space was cramped.

"Tavon MacLeish," he said, "and this is Declan Lyon. We work at the wool mill and will be helping out today."

She shook his hand. "Diana McKellen."

The two men looked at each other and grinned, but it was Declan who spoke. "American?"

"Yes," she said.

"A pleasure to know ye," Tavon replied.

They seemed like nice guys, but Diana *felt* the expression on Rory's face before she even saw it. The Detective Chief Inspector glared as if the two friendly hunks were really a pair of ex-cons trying to chat her up before abducting her.

"*Oi!*" Deydie pounded on the counter to get everyone's attention. "The restroom is through those doors. Mrs. McNabb has made tea and scones for each of ye. After ye have a few minutes to collect yereselves, we'll split into two groups—one to start the demonstration right away, while the other will follow in about fifteen minutes."

The sixty-ish woman standing next to Deydie, raised her hand. "*Me* name is Coira. I'll be escorting the first lot of ye to where we shear the sheep. We'll watch a film in the shearing shed, as there is no shearing in November, only *tupping*. Due to the rainy weather, I don't expect ye'll be seeing much of *that* going on out in the fields today either. Even if the randy rams were interested in the mating, I'm sure the ewes would have none of it." She laughed good-naturedly. "The tups and ewes won't be having their fun today."

A few *ayes* went up around the room, as if these ladies knew their way around sheep.

"Here, lass." Tavon passed Diana a mug of steaming tea. "Just the thing for a *dreich* day."

Even from across the room, Diana thought she heard a growl from Rory as he moved closer to them. Surely, she must've imagined it. Or maybe it was just wishful thinking. Immediately though, she felt ashamed; wanting Rory to be jealous was so shallow. She shook her head at the crazy, unrealistic fairytale playing out in her mind—Rory coming to defend her honor. Tavon and Declan had been gentlemen. Certainly, Rory could see that too.

Standing near the counter, Parker slipped off her coat and Diana caught her first glimpse of what she was wearing— Diana's own purple zip dress. Diana didn't care Parker had borrowed it; her sister had frequently raided her closet, and in college, she and her roommates had all shared clothes. It was just so out of character for Parker to wear anything other than blue jeans and her vast array of L.L. Bean activewear tops.

As if asking the question, Diana raised her eyebrows at Parker, and in reply, Parker shrugged apologetically.

Ten minutes later, Coira called for the first group and ushered them out. Marta was with them and Rory followed. Where Marta went, Diana and Parker went.

Parker grabbed her camera and put her coat back on while Diana caught up to her. Coira frowned at the two stragglers, but kept her thoughts to herself. Together, they ran across the compound to the shearing shed and stepped inside.

Parker pulled out her camera from under her raincoat's protection and examined her equipment.

"That's an awfully nice outfit you're wearing under your coat," Diana said. "I thought you liked to keep it casual, in case you have to climb on scaffolding to get a shot." This was something Parker had told her on their last photo shoot together. "I think it's the first time I've ever seen you in a dress."

Parker blushed. "I hope you don't mind. You had already gone to the bus when I decided to dress up a bit." She seemed giddy and nervous, which Diana chalked up to being in the presence of her Scottish beau.

Diana nodded toward Ewan, who stood with a border collie and two sheep. "Big date?" she said.

There was no doubt that Parker had it bad for Ewan; the evidence lay in how she smiled when she waved to him. "Excuse me. I want to say *hi* before he gets started."

Poor Ewan. His eyes nearly bugged out when he got a load of Parker in that dress.

Parker gave him a kiss on the cheek and then looked over at Diana as if to say, *See, I can show some restraint.* But she wasn't fooling anyone.

Ewan had it bad for Parker, too, but he pulled it together for the crowd. "Welcome. I'm Laird Ewan McGillivray, owner of Here Again Farm and Estates." He motioned to the animals next to him. "We—plus countless sheep and a large staff—provide the wool for Whussendale Woollens.

Parker ogled Ewan, making love to him with her eyes. He paused his spiel, as if he'd lost track of what he was about to say. Tavon and Declan cleared their throats until Ewan snapped out of it.

Ewan looked around the shed sheepishly before going on. "There are more sheep in Scotland than people. If this was

June, you'd be seeing a live demonstration of the sheep shearing. But since it's November, I have a wee film that starts out with us working the dogs in the field." He reached down and patted the border collie at his side. "The next bit will show a demonstration of shearing, the first part of our sheep-to-shawl experience, or—" he gestured to his attire "—*sheep-to-kilt*, if ye like." Using a remote, he hit the play button as the seventy-plus inch screen came to life. Diana thought the dogs were the stars of the film, but then the sheep shearers—both men and women—demonstrated how shearing was done in times past with scissors and how it was done now with electric clippers.

During the film, Ewan positioned himself next to Parker as she taped Marta watching the professional film of the sheep, farmhands, and the Laird of Here Again Farm and Estates.

When it was done, Ewan used the remote to click off the TV and then assumed his place at the front once again. "A point of interest, to add to the film...in recent years, there's been a shortage of shearers. Financial incentives are being offered to go through the training, and as a result, fifty percent of shearers are now women." There was a twinkle in his eye, and Diana caught a glimpse of what Parker saw in this interesting man. He held up a magazine with the title *Graze* on the front. "So if any of ye are interested, I can point ye in the right direction to get yere Blue Ribbon certification in Sheep Shearing." He laughed. "It's the best diet here in Scotland. Shearing can burn up to 5,000 calories a day!"

Though these women ranged from forty-five to eighty some *oohed* and *ahhed* at the prospect of switching careers for the weight-loss benefit alone.

Coira stepped forward with her phone in her hand. "Thank ye, Laird. We best move along. The next group is on its way."

Diana pulled up her hood against the rain and moved toward the exit. But Parker waved at her to wait.

Blushing, Parker held out her camera to Diana. "Do you mind taking video at the next stop? I'd like to stay here with Ewan, if that's okay. I'll catch up with you later. Promise."

Diana shook her head dramatically. "I can see my lectures have fallen on deaf ears. You're completely smitten, aren't you?"

"I am," Parker admitted. "I'm totally in love."

Diana couldn't help but glance back at Rory, feeling grateful she wasn't *lovesick* like her friend. Then why was she staring?

Disgusted with herself, she turned away. She had no willpower at all! She definitely should exchange the rose-colored glasses she was wearing for some *reality* ones. Falling for the Detective Chief Inspector would only cause heartache. There were other complications, too. Forget what her mother had gone through. Diana and Rory lived on two different continents!

She couldn't help but look at him again.

"Well?" Parker still held out the camera.

"Sure." Diana dragged her eyes away from Rory. "Stay. Have fun. I'll see you in a bit."

Parker hugged her really hard, which was uncharacteristic. But maybe what she was feeling for Ewan was overflowing onto others. "Thanks."

Diana followed Coira, Marta, and the quilters out, and did her best not to turn around to make sure Rory was following them across the compound. But she did turn. And he was looking at her, too. The rain, thank goodness, had tapered to a drizzle and Diana could only hope her rapid heartbeat would slow down, too.

Tavon and Declan would be leading the next leg of the tour. Before going into the building, they distributed pairs of disposable earplugs. Moments later, Diana understood why. The machines clacked and clanked loudly as the wool was carded and spun.

"First, a bit of business," Declan hollered above the noise. "All the machines in this building are very dangerous. We're a Victorian wool mill and enjoy preserving the old ways."

"Check the floor for the yellow lines, and *don't cross them.* If ye keep yere distance from the equipment, everyone will be fine," Tavon said.

With that they launched into an overview of the different machines in the building, Diana held up Parker's camera and recorded Marta pointing to various pieces of equipment wearing suitable expressions of awe. She also took a few still photos to add to an online slideshow for the readers following Marta's journey.

Diana thought about the video clip Nicola had sent her: Marta and the murders in Scotland had been the top story on the nightly news. Not the kind of press they needed.

Coira waved and shouted above the noise. "Let's move along."

Some people lagged behind to ask Tavon and Declan a few questions, but the majority of the group headed for the doorway.

Suddenly there was a strangled scream. Diana pushed her way forward and saw Tilly bent sideways, half-lying on a machine. Her dull gray scarf was caught in the cogs and wheels, choking her. With each turn, the noose tightened.

Tavon and Declan arrived at nearly the same time, with Rory close behind them. But it was Declan who hit the red emergency stop button. Instantly, the machine went dead, as if it hadn't been alive at all.

"What happened?" asked Rory, steadying Tilly. If she fell right now, her neck would probably break.

Still plastered against the machine, Tilly didn't answer but sobbed inconsolably as Tavon grabbed shears from the rack and began cutting her loose. Marta, watching from a few feet away, seemed gobsmacked, unable to move.

Diana wrapped an arm around Tilly, steadying her from the other side. With the last snip of the wool, Tilly was free and fell into Diana's arms.

Marta came alive then, stepping forward to take Tilly from Diana as the other quilters surrounded them, fussing over them both as if they were cherished members of their group.

Rory called for quiet. "Ms. Dixon, how did ye come to be caught in the carding machine?"

It was Deydie who spoke.

"It's just like in book six, don't ye see?" Deydie glanced around at them all. "Remember? The Buttermilk Guild had visited the wool mill and found the sheep farmer dead in the carding machine, wrapped in spun wool...suffocated. Of course, that devil got what he deserved. He'd doubled the price of wool to the Buttermilk Guild. But then all the lassies were suspects. *Poor things.*"

Aye, all the women agreed.

Rory frowned and asked once again for quiet. "Go on, Ms. Dixon. Tell us how this happened."

Tilly shook her head. "I--I think someone pushed me. One moment, I was gazing at the wool being carded and then I was hit from behind." She began to cry again.

Coira stepped forward and took Tilly's arm. "Now, now. I'm sure it was only an accident. We should've divided ye into three groups instead of two. Too many of ye jostling towards the door."

Tilly had a red ring around her neck from the strangling scarf, and Diana asked, "Coira, do you have any arnica to help with the bruising?"

"Aye," said Coira. "Tavon, get the first aid kit off the wall."

When he'd done as she bid, Bethia took the arnica and gently rubbed it onto Tilly's bruise.

"Oh, Tilly, I'll make sure you get a new scarf," Marta said. "I'm so sorry this happened." She seemed shaken up.

Coira clapped. "Let's head to the weaving building. After that, we'll watch our kiltmaker and his apprentice, Laird Hugh's wife, demonstrate how to make a kilt. Then I promise, we'll get ye lunch."

Feeling pretty shaky herself, Diana could have used some of Rory's reassuring warmth, but he rightly stayed close to Marta and Tilly all through the weaving mill and the kiltmaker's demonstration. After both groups were done, they piled back onto the bus and drove a winding mile to Kilheath Castle, where Laird Hugh and Sophie McGillivray lived.

They had a delightful lunch of fish and chips—fresh fish from the loch and hand-cut potatoes that had been fried to perfection by Mrs. McNabb. Diana had never tasted better. While they ate their dessert of cranachan—a wonderful combination of cream, raspberries, oats, and whisky—Hugh stood at the head of the table and entertained them with tales from the wool mill. Next, Coira told them stories about the quilt retreats they'd had since Kilts & Quilts had expanded into Whussendale. Diana recorded it all, looking up from the camera every so often to search for Parker, whose job she was doing.

"All right, ladies!" Coira got everyone's attention. "Let's make our way into the ballroom, where we'll be working on the medallion for the quilt—the rook himself."

Deydie held up a stack of papers, as she walked to the front of the room.

"I know some of ye have considered swapping out yere rook for a puffin," Deydie said. "I've made copies of the puffin template for those who are interested."

This would give Deydie her chance to be on the *telly* as she was promised.

"Ye don't mind, do ye?" Bethia asked Marta.

Diana thought Bethia was so sweet that no one could deny her anything. But then again, Rory had kept her from leaving Partridge House to warn Deydie that she'd need an alibi.

Thinking of alibis...Diana wondered where Deydie had been when Tilly was pushed into the machinery. She certainly had a motive to punish Marta for killing off the Buttermilk Guild. On the other hand, she'd been quick to jump in and point out the similarity to book six of the Quilt to Death series—would she do that if she was guilty?

"Where's yere sidekick?"

Rory's voice at Diana's shoulder almost made her drop the expensive camera. "You should wear a bell around your neck. You nearly gave me heart failure." How foolish was she? She'd been keeping tabs on Rory all day, and the one moment she let him out of her sight, there he was, sneaking up on her. "Where did you come from anyway?"

He pointed to the corner. "Over there."

"Do you think Tilly's accident was really an accident?" Diana asked.

"I do not."

"Did you see who pushed her?"

Rory shook his head. "I had my eye on Marta." He glanced around. "So where's Parker? I haven't seen her in a while."

A flare of jealousy went up in Diana. "She's crazy about Ewan, you know."

Rory gave a look like Diana's gun had misfired. "That doesn't exactly answer my question."

She felt stupid for being jealous. She didn't want Rory, right? So why should she care if he was interested in Parker? "She asked me to film for her while she stayed back with Ewan."

Rory frowned like he was trying to solve a puzzle. "I haven't seen Ewan lately either. Have ye?"

"No. Not since the shearing shed. I assumed he had to get back to his own estate."

"I better start asking around about him, too."

"Parker and Ewan just wanted some alone time," Diana said. "They probably found a secluded spot to slip off to." She pulled out her phone. "I'll text her and tell her to check in." She typed out a short note and hit Send. "You worry too much."

"It comes with the job."

How well Diana knew it. Her father's habits had worn off on her. But *surely Parker was fine, right?*

Rory was staring at her. "Are ye okay?"

She frowned at him, remembering how much she liked holding his hand. It wasn't just exciting and thrilling; it was calming and comforting, too. He was everything she'd ever wanted in a man. . .

"Diana?"

"Oh! Yes. Sure. Fine."

"We need to talk," he said, in no way seductively.

Even though he was using his *Do you have an alibi voice,* she knew he wanted to talk about *what-was-or-wasn't* going on between them.

"I'm working right now." She was glad she could use her job as a shield.

It did the trick. He stiffened. "Aye. Me, too." He walked away.

Immediately she wanted to call him back.

"Wait," she said. "Let me see if Parker has responded."

Rory sauntered back over, his professionalism surrounding him like a protective shell. They were so much alike!

He stopped inches away, so close she could soak up his

goodness. But then he lifted an eyebrow. "Well?"

"Oh." Diana pulled out her phone, pretty sure she hadn't gotten a message as her phone hadn't vibrated, but that didn't mean anything. Since she'd met the Detective Chief Inspector, she'd been distracted. Heck, a bull horn could sound right in her ear—and she wouldn't budge from gazing into his eyes.

She looked at her blank cell screen. "Nothing yet." Parker and Ewan were probably in the throes of passion. "Ewan probably took Parker to see his estate. I understand from Deydie that it butts up against this one."

"I'll go ask Deydie if she has Ewan's number."

Diana grabbed his arm to keep him from leaving. She'd caused the furrow between his brow and she wanted nothing more than to reach up and smooth it away.

He looked down at her hand. She did, too, not having any good reason to detain him longer.

"Tonight," she finally said.

"Tonight, what?" Rory asked.

"We can talk tonight. After we get back to Gandiegow. After everyone has gone to bed." But she shouldn't have used that word—bed. Rory might get the wrong idea once again. Even she might be getting the wrong idea. She scrambled for a location. "Let's meet at the pub." Anything would be better than the back porch, under *their* quilt.

He laid his hand over hers. "It's a date."

She started to say *I don't date cops!* But Rory had walked away. Diana was left with her mouth hanging open and her hand feeling warm and tingly where he'd touched her.

She looked at the phone in her other hand, wondering why it was out of her purse. *Oh, yeah, Parker. Why hadn't she texted back?* Worry crept over Diana. To keep it from taking her to a dark place, she had to act, to do something. Even though she'd already texted, she called Parker's cell phone.

She'll just have to forgive me for interrupting them. For surely, the two lovers had sequestered themselves someplace private.

The call went straight to voicemail. The rational side of Diana's brain said Parker had turned off her phone, or maybe she'd forgotten to charge it. But the other side—the side that knew evil did exist—had Diana chewing her lip. A chill passed through her.

15

R ORY MADE HIS WAY to the front of the ballroom where Deydie was holding court with Bethia. "Did Parker or Ewan say anything to either of you about leaving?"

The two older women looked around, as if the two missing people might be mingling with the quilters.

"Haven't seen them," Deydie said. "We've had our hands full with this lot."

Rory pulled out his phone. "Do ye have Ewan's mobile number?"

Deydie scoffed. "What do I look like? A telephone directory?"

Bethia touch Rory's arm. "Ask Sophie. She'll have it."

Rory smiled at Bethia, appreciating her kind nature. "Thanks." He walked back to the food table, where Sophie and the other women of Whussendale were laying out cookies and carafes of tea and coffee. When asked, she immediately gave Rory the number and then went back to work.

Rory dialed Ewan but didn't get him. He couldn't leave a

message, either, as Ewan's voicemailbox was full.

Using his browser, Rory searched for Here Again Farm and Estates. He spoke with the housekeeper first, then the estate manager. Neither knew where the young Laird was.

Rory glanced over at Diana, something he found himself doing a lot since meeting her. She was gazing at her phone apprehensively. He strode over to her. "Well? Has Parker gotten back to ye?"

Diana looked up at him with worry in her eyes, the opposite of what he'd seen earlier. "Nothing. When I called, it went directly to voicemail." Diana sagged a bit. "She's young and stupid in love. But I'm worried it's more than that."

"Why?" He was concerned, too, but he wanted to hear her theory.

She sighed. "It's about the fifth book in the Quilt to Death series, where several couples get murdered," she said.

"I know you sent me the list, but refresh my memory," he said.

"The first couple is lured to a cabin in the woods and murdered with a pitchfork."

Rory looked at her dubiously.

Diana bit her top lip. "They were caught unaware, because they were...you know. . ."

He helped her out. "Otherwise occupied?"

"Yes."

Rory looked worriedly out the window at the forest surrounding Kilheath Castle. "Tell me what else ye know about this book."

"A second couple is killed at the airport," she said.

"What quilt is featured in this book?" he asked.

"The Lover's Knot quilt." She looked embarrassed to say *lover*. Maybe because he'd kissed her, and she'd given him one *helluva* kiss back.

"I'm glad you made the list," he said.

"Amateur sleuth just trying to make sense of it all."

Like father, like daughter? But Rory didn't say it. He didn't want to do anything that would upset her further.

He nodded instead. "What does the Lover's Knot quilt look like?"

Diana pulled out her mobile, scrolled through her pictures, then handed her phone to him.

He examined the quilt, which was set on the diagonal. "Have ye seen anyone with this quilt? Any of the quilters here?"

Diana gestured to a woman standing over the table, examining her quilt blocks. "Lorna. Back in Gandiegow. She brought it for show-and-tell. The last I saw of the quilt, it was lying on her bed at Duncan's Den."

Rory eyed the woman with the long gray braid hanging down her back, dressed all in black with sturdy Wellies to match. She hadn't even been on his radar. Could Lorna have pushed Tilly into the carding machine? He sized her up; five-two, if that, he guessed, close to a foot shorter than Tilly. Lorna looked feeble but looks could be deceiving. His gran had been small in stature yet had no problem grabbing his ear and Kin's ear at the same time, and holding steady. Gran had the strength of a man twice her size. Scottish women were tough and scrappy that way.

He pulled out his phone and texted MacTaggart and McCartney. A search party would have to be organized.

"Stay here," he said to Diana. He would have a quick word with Lorna before he found the Laird, who would know which of his clan could help search the forest. It might be time wasted speaking with Lorna first, but he didn't want her to get away if she was involved.

As he walked toward Lorna, who was now placing quilt

blocks on the design wall, he saw out of the corner of his eye that Diana was following him. He wasn't surprised. She had a curiosity about her that would've made her an excellent detective. He shook his head in wonderment. Had she appointed herself his partner to help solve these murders? He hadn't had a partner on the police force since Denny died.

Rory walked to the design wall. "Lorna?"

The woman turned to face him, looking confused. "Aye."

"Do ye have a minute?" he asked. "I have a few questions."

"Sure?" She was definitely puzzled. She laid the rest of her quilt blocks on the table.

"I understand you brought a Lover's Knot quilt with ye to the retreat?" Rory said. "May I see it?"

She shook her head. "Nay. I left it back in Gandiegow. I carried it from home trying to decide whether I wanted to have Marta Dixon sign it or not." She shrugged. "I'm not sure even yet. We'll see what the verdict is by the time I go home. Marta *doesnae* seem sorry for killing off the Buttermilk Guild, now does she?"

He didn't have an answer. "Did ye happen to see how Tilly Dixon, Marta's sister, got caught in the carding machine?"

Lorna shook her head again. "Och, no."

"Where were ye when it happened?" Rory asked.

Her face turned red. "I was in the restroom. Probably too much tea this morn."

"Did anyone see ye in the restroom?"

Her embarrassment turned to anger. "Ye *cannae* think I would push that shy bird Tilly into the carding machine!" She glared at him as if *he* was nothing to be scared of. "Though I have to say that many of us quilters would like to have a go at Marta, the Buttermilk Guild killer!"

"Calm yereself. I'm just gathering information." Rory was realizing he needed to look into each retreat goer more thoroughly. "We'll talk later," he said to Lorna, and gave her a look to convey she better not go anywhere.

He left her standing with her mouth hanging open, and once more Diana followed him. "What are we going to do now?" she said. "Organize a search party?"

He rolled his eyes. "*We* aren't going to do anything. *I am.* I'll need someone to keep an eye on the quilters." *Especially Lorna.* He pulled out his phone.

"We can all help." Diana persisted. "We can look for them. Speed is important, am I right?"

He lifted his eyebrows at her, as if she should know better. "The quilters are all suspects, so the answer's no, I don't want them to help. Besides, what I need are locals. People who know the area. The woods."

"Let's talk to Sophie," Diana offered.

"I overheard it said that Sophie is a recent transplant. We'll talk to Hugh instead. The Laird will know where to look first." *But this particular criminal wouldn't necessarily know the forest, either.* Rory halted. "I need to sit down and draw up a timeline. Bring the quilters to me one at a time. We need to know which one of them saw Parker and Ewan last."

Hugh rushed into the room. "I just heard what happened."

That was quick. Was the ballroom bugged?

"Is Ms. Dixon all right? We'll gladly make it up to her by replacing her scarf. Or medical treatment. Anything she needs."

Oh, so Hugh was talking about the carding machine incident and not about the disappearance of Parker and Ewan.

Diana recovered first. "Tilly will be fine."

"We do need your help, Laird," Rory said. "We're looking for Ewan and Parker. Have ye seen them?"

"My cousin?" Hugh frowned, but pulled out his phone. "I'll ring him up."

"I already tried," Rory said. "His mailbox is full. Can you

call his estate to see if he and Parker have shown up since I called?"

"Certainly." Hugh hit a button and put the phone to his ear. "Aye. 'Tis Hugh. I'm looking for Ewan. Is he around?"

Rory could see the answer on Hugh's face.

"If he pops up, have him give me a ring," Hugh finished. He put his phone back in his pocket. "No one has seen or heard from him since he left this morn. I noticed his Here Again vehicle is still outside the shearing shed."

"Would he have borrowed someone else's auto?" Rory asked, hopeful.

"Nay. Not with his own vehicle here."

Rory had no choice but to ask the next question. He gestured toward the woods. "Do ye have any cabins on the estate?"

"Just the one. A small hunter's cottage." He gestured toward the large window. "There's a path leading into the woods through the trees."

"Can ye take me to it?" Rory said. If there was a crime scene, he wanted to be the one to find it.

"Aye," Hugh answered solemnly, not asking why.

"I need someone guarding Marta and the quilters while we're gone," Rory said.

Hugh was already tapping out something on his phone. "I'm on it."

"I'm coming, too," Diana piped in, her voice strong and steady.

"That's not a good idea. You should stay," Rory said.

She put her hands on her hips. "I'm going anyway."

He knew she would, no matter the rainy weather, no matter what they would find, and no matter if he forbade her to or not.

As Diana slipped her arms into her raincoat and zipped it

up, four men came into the room. They each nodded to Hugh, and then scattered to the four corners of the room. *Hugh's watchmen.*

Diana tapped Hugh on the arm. "Lead the way."

Rory followed the other two to the ballroom exit, praying they weren't about to find the Lover's Knot quilt with the dead bodies of Ewan and Parker wrapped inside.

Diana slipped away on a brief side-trip to Coira, probably to let her know she'd be gone for a while. In the kitchen, Hugh stopped at the door. "All the four-by-fours are in the shop for winter maintenance. We'll have to get there on foot."

Rory nodded. *Fine by me.* The adrenaline pulsing through his system needed a release anyway.

Out in the rain, side by side, they made their way across the pavement. Once they reached the forest path, they went single file—Hugh leading, Diana in the middle, and Rory bringing up the rear so he could keep Diana safe.

He had to hand it to her. For being a *girlie-girl*, she didn't mind traipsing through the mud and guck. But he wasn't all that surprised. From the start, he'd known she was made of sturdier stuff than what he imagined most Americans were. Diana was strong, impenetrable as steel—she either didn't have a squeamish side, or was choosing to ignore it.

There was one thing bugging Rory and he called to Hugh, "Who else knows about this cabin?"

Hugh glanced back. "Everyone, I expect. We have it listed on the website as a feature of the estate. We let it to tourists."

Well, crap.

They slogged through the woods for nearly fifteen minutes until they came into a clearing. In the middle was a large boulder, and on the other side was a rustic cottage. Diana took off running for the lodge. Hugh and Rory took off after her, but she'd gotten a head start and beat them to the door. They reached the porch just as she burst through the door.

There was no scream, but with Diana that didn't mean anything. Rory stepped around Hugh and peered inside.

The cottage was empty and looked as if no one had been there recently. Diana crossed the room to another door, which must lead to the bathroom. She pulled the door open and he could see there was no one inside there either.

She turned around. "What now?"

"We'll organize a search party," Rory answered. Diana looked visibly upset that they still had no answers, and he wanted to pull her into his arms to comfort her. If they'd been alone, he would have.

Hugh cleared his throat until Rory looked his way.

"I'll have Declan and Tavon head up the search," Hugh said. "They know Whussendale—the buildings and cottages—and will search every nook and cranny."

"And the castle?" Diana asked.

Hugh gave her an encouraging nod. "The castle, too."

Rory put his hand on Diana's back. "Let's get back." He wasn't so absorbed in his job that he was unaware of how he felt having Diana near. He liked it. He meant to tell her so, the first chance he got...when they were alone.

Back at the castle, the quilters were all abuzz. The news that they were looking for Ewan and Parker must have spread. It wouldn't be long until it was dark. While the locals were searching, Rory would repeat his interviews with the quilters, doublechecking their alibis. He drew a quick layout of the machines in the carding building, marked Tilly's position with a T and planned to pencil in the rest of the quilters as he took their statements.

An hour later, when MacTaggart and McCartney arrived, Rory filled them in about Tilly's accident and everything he knew about Parker and Ewan's disappearance. He had interviewed a handful of the quilters, but asked his team to go over their statements looking for inconsistencies.

From what he'd learned, he believed Deydie was the last to see Ewan and Parker before the two disappeared.

"I went back to the shearing shed to ask Ewan a few questions about my sheep." Deydie glowered, as if remembering the scene. "Those two lovebirds were so passionate that even his border collie looked embarrassed." She harrumphed. "I broke them apart and told them both to get back to work." She smoothed down her cotton dress. "That was the last I saw of them."

By the time Rory was done interviewing everyone, darkness had overtaken the sky, the rain had slowed to a mist, and the search party had returned from the forest because it was too dark to see their hand in front of their face. Still, there was no sign of Ewan and Parker. At first light tomorrow, they would begin again. *But will it be too late?* At times like these, Rory cursed the onset of winter that shortened the days.

Bethia and Deydie toddled over to him, followed by Sophie. There were only the three of them, but he felt descended upon just the same.

Bethia set a cup of tea in front of him.

Deydie sat down beside him. "We need to make some decisions about the quilters. Mrs. McNabb has dinner going, but we need to know what to do after that. Take the lassies back to Gandiegow or have them settle in here for the night?"

Sending the quilters back to Gandiegow could be a problem. Rory needed to keep an eye on them, but he needed to stay close by Whussendale, in case something turned up here.

"We have plenty of room, if they need to stay," Sophie put in.

Deydie grinned. "And with their sewing stations all set up in the ballroom, we could have a late-night stitch-in."

"A slumber party," Bethia said, digging up some enthusiasm.

"I could ask each of the Whussendale ladies for extra nighties for the retreat goers," Sophie suggested.

"This will be best for the DCI," Deydie affirmed.

Meanwhile Rory hadn't said a thing.

Deydie looked at Bethia and Sophie as if he wasn't even there. "Aye. The DCI will be able to keep the sheep all herded into one place."

"Then it's settled," Sophie said. "The retreat goers will stay. I better get to the kitchen to see if we have everything I need to make cocoa."

"I think ye should spike it with whisky. Something to take the edge off," Deydie suggested.

Sophie grinned. "Good idea. I'm sure I can scrounge up a bottle or two."

Dinner was a quiet affair, which wasn't surprising given the events of the day and his interrogation of the quilters.

But Rory was surprised when they didn't go back to the ballroom and sew after dinner, as Bethia and Deydie had planned. Instead, they'd all headed upstairs to their rooms, each one with some kind of bag of hand-stitching inside.

Rory checked to make sure Marta and Tilly were settled in for the night with McCartney posted outside their room, then wandered back downstairs. He found Diana in the parlor, sitting with a notebook in her lap in front of a low-burning fire.

"What are ye—"

Diana jumped before he could end his sentence.

"Doing?" he finished.

She didn't answer but asked her own question. "Any word on Parker and Ewan?"

"No. None. We'll pick back up in the morning." He hoped he didn't receive any bad news tonight. He wanted to hold out hope that Parker and Ewan had found a place for a tête-à-tête and were so wrapped up in each other that they'd forgotten to call. He changed the subject and pointed to her notebook. "Go on, then. Tell me what ye have there. Are ye trying to solve this case?"

She shrugged and blushed.

He wasn't stupid; he knew exactly what she was doing. "Don't ye realize, Miss Marple, that solving the case is my job, not yeres?"

She smiled at him and his pulse kicked up. "Everyone can use a little help now and then."

"Scoot over." He sat close to her. *To be near. To breathe her in.* He slipped the notebook from her lap. "Let me see what ye have here."

She'd constructed her own murder board, stretching across the two opened pages. Instead of pictures of the victims, she'd drawn boxes with their names inside. A quilt block was sketched next to each victim. Lines were drawn from each murdered person to potential suspects. On some of those lines, she'd scribbled in motives or rebuked some of their alibis as *bogus.*

"This is thorough," he commented.

"I like puzzles," she said. "I used to help my dad. He'd bring home cold cases and Liz and I would brainstorm with him at the kitchen table while we ate breakfast."

"He sounds like a great dad." Though Rory wasn't sure he knew what a great dad actually looked like. He could barely remember his own, the memories getting fuzzier and fewer as he got older. *Och,* but didn't he have a lot on his mind? He looked down at the notebook on his lap. Suddenly he wanted to make new memories, memories that didn't involve violence and death.

He shut the notebook and put his arm around Diana's

shoulder. "Enough for tonight."

"But—" she protested.

"Listen to me, lass. Through the years, I've learned ye have to let yere mind rest." Besides, he had more interesting things to think about besides murder. Like tasting Diana's soft lips again. He shifted his head and kissed her before she could argue with him further.

Her lips didn't debate his tender onslaught, but immediately complied, giving back as much as he gave her. She moved closer—which drove him crazy—and squeezed his biceps.

She pulled away, her breath coming out in rasps. "It's a little hot, don't you think?"

Was she speaking of the fire in the hearth, or the one blazing between them?

"We better head to bed," she said, as she scooted out of his embrace.

He could've reached out and told her to stop...that he wanted her to stay. He wanted to keep kissing her. But he accepted her *no* as graciously as he could, though the best he could do was to frown when she stood up.

She looked down at him with her own frown. It wasn't a look of disappointment like his. No, she seemed puzzled. "Aren't you coming with me?"

Had he heard her correctly?

She held out her hand, which made it clearer.

"Aye," he said quickly. He was afraid if he said more, his voice might crack as it had when he was a lad. He was bright enough to not make her ask him twice, and wasted no time getting to his feet.

Just to seal the deal, he pulled her in for a searing kiss.

16

D IANA SILENCED THE RATIONAL voice in her head, which insisted she scurry off to her bedroom alone. The same voice that told her to stop falling for the Detective Chief Inspector. The one that begged her to protect her heart. When he kissed her again, the only thing she heard was a resounding *yes* echo throughout her body.

Yes, to everything.

Inside her room, a nightlight illuminated their way to her bed. Though the light was dim, she could see his expressive eyes as he undressed her. His eyes told her so much, more than words ever could. In them she could see his desire, and his care. When she looked deeper, she saw his pain, his loss, his loneliness. His eyes revealed his vulnerability, but also how much he trusted and cherished her.

Their lovemaking was perfect—tender and passionate.

Although it seemed crazy, Rory made her feel loved—wholly and completely. Being with him felt like how love was depicted in the movies: warm, safe, magical, but also exciting and fun.

She was wrapped up in a fairy-tale she didn't want to end. She felt as if they could lie in each other's arms forever, so securely was she tucked under his chin. She listened to his heart pound, and reveled in the knowledge that she was the one who'd caused it to beat like a drum.

But then other thoughts intruded. She stopped caressing his arm and lifted her head.

"What's wrong, lass?" Rory asked.

Diana sat up. "I shouldn't be doing this. *Parker.* She's still missing." *And I'm lying in bed with you...without a care in the world!*

"I know, luv," he said soothingly. He gently pulled her back down and tucked her into his side, kissing her hair. "At first light, I'll be out looking for them. There's nothing we can do in the dead of night."

Did he have to say dead? "Parker could be calling out for help right this minute, while I'm here having the time of my life."

He shifted and was now gazing into her eyes. "HQ is sending people to help with the search. The best thing we can do right now is to get some rest. Tomorrow will be here shortly."

"I know you're right." But Diana didn't want to rest. Something primal welled up inside her and she kissed him wildly, as if this moment might be her last. No one had a guarantee on tomorrow. She could get hit by a car...or murdered by a serial killer.

Rory responded to her need and kissed her back, as if he could read her thoughts. When they made love again, Diana savored every single moment and sensation.

She thought she'd banished her fears. But before spooning her as she drifted off to sleep Rory had to kiss away her tears.

෪෬

Rory woke, nuzzling Diana. He wanted nothing more than to stay where he was and make love to her all day. Instead, he scooted as unobtrusively as he could from the bed and dressed quietly before leaving the room. He was deeply grateful to MacTaggart and McCartney for taking the nightshift with Marta and Tilly, but it was time to get back to work.

Maybe they would find Parker before Diana woke up, he thought hopefully as he descended the stairs.

What the devil? He'd wanted to get an early start, but the smell of coffee and the sound of conversation told him he was far from the first awake.

Mrs. McNabb was at the stove, worrying over a pan of Scotch eggs. The kitchen was filled with quilters dressed in warm clothes, and rows of Wellies were lined up by the door.

He looked at Deydie inquiringly—she always seemed to be in charge, after all—and she said, "After we have a quick bite to eat, we're heading out to find the Yank and Ewan McGillivray."

"Hugh will be down shortly," Sophie interjected, drawing Rory's scrutiny from Deydie.

Bethia walked over and touched his arm. "Ye can't expect us to stand by and do nothing."

"It's not necessary." Rory checked his watch. "Backup should be here any minute." But the women looked set on going and he wasn't certain he could change their minds. As he scanned the room, he realized something. "Where's Marta and Tilly?"

"Above stairs," Bethia said.

"Alone?" Rory asked.

"Yere man MacTaggart is watching them," Bethia answered. "We woke Marta and Tilly to see if they wanted to help." Bethia's face took on a stern look, the first Rory had seen from her. "Marta announced she was going back to bed and that Tilly had to stay with her."

At that moment, Rory's phone rang. "Crannach here."

It was Sergeant Grear from headquarters.

"I have two pieces of bad news," he said.

"Go ahead."

"Leo Shamley has been released on a technicality," the sergeant said roughly. "On our end, not yeres."

"When?" Rory asked.

"Yesterday afternoon," Grear said. "If I'd known about it sooner, I would've called."

Rory squelched the curse words that rose within him. Leo had known they were coming to the mill. He could've done something to Parker and Ewan and still have time to push Tilly into the carding machine. "What's the other news?"

"Two bodies were found in the baggage area at the Edinburgh Airport. A man and a woman in their thirties."

Oh, hell! The second couple murdered in book five! "Were they wrapped in a quilt?"

"I don't know. That's all the information I was given. We don't know if it's *your* missing couple."

A thousand questions crowded Rory's mind, from what had triggered Leo's release to the estimated time of death of the two victims. Could Leo have been so productive as to attack three people in Whussendale as well as the couple in Edinburgh? But Rory asked the most important question of all. "When will you have IDs on the victims?"

There was a sharp intake of air behind him. "What victims?"

He spun around to see Diana standing in the kitchen doorway with her hand covering her mouth.

"I have to go." Rory hung up and pocketed his phone. He hated that Diana was hurting. He wanted to pull her into his arms and kiss her worry away. His brain was such a jumble and nothing added up. Before meeting Diana, he'd had laser focus and nothing could distract him from his work.

He took a step forward, but Diana retreated backwards, her eyes as big as the saucers Mrs. McNabb had stacked on the table.

"What happened?" Diana whispered. "Is someone dead?"

Rory hated this part of his job. Finding a murderer was a puzzle; he was good at it. But explaining to family and friends that they'd lost a loved one was nearly unbearable. If only the victims would remain snapshots on his murder board. But when he spoke to families, empathy flooded him and he felt every ounce of their pain.

"We don't know anything yet," Rory said. "Keep that in mind, first and foremost."

"Tell me." Diana's voice was accusing, as if he was withholding vital information from her.

He closed the distance between them, not caring a whit that the room was watching him, as he gently placed his hands on her shoulders. She was trembling.

"Two bodies were found at the airport in Edinburgh."

"Were they Parker and Ewan?" she whispered.

"We only know it was a man and a woman." He wouldn't tell her that Leo had been released from jail.

He squeezed her shoulders. "Now, drink some coffee." He motioned to the room. "In a few minutes we're all going out to look for Ewan and Parker." Whether it was a futile endeavor or not. Everyone nodded or said *aye* in a show of support. Rory continued, "When our reinforcements arrive, we'll break into groups. I'll assign a Whussendalian and a police officer to each group." The reasons were obvious and these women were no dummies. "Every two hours, we'll meet back here at the kitchen."

Hugh came in carrying a rolled parchment and motioned to

Rory. "I have the map ye requested."

"The eggs are ready," said Mrs. McNabb, as if she'd taken her cue.

"Let's grid off the map," Rory said. He glanced at Diana, who seemed determined to follow him. Having something to do had transformed her from worried woman to woman on a mission. *Good.*

Diana sat with Rory and Hugh, as they worked on the map. McCartney strolled into the kitchen, looking as surprised as Rory felt when he'd seen the mob of quilters up so early.

"We have help this morning," Rory said. "Go relieve Mac-Taggart. Ye'll watch the Ms. Dixons while we go out and search."

Mrs. McNabb handed McCartney a mug and a plate overflowing with food.

A few minutes later, the additional team members arrived. The newcomers were plied with mugs of coffee and tea to counteract their long drive. Then the quilters rose as one and went for their coats and Wellies.

Rory handed out assignments and they were on their way. With Declan, Rory and Diana were tasked with searching the wool mill.

"It's going to take all day, especially if we're to return to the castle every few hours," Declan said. "There's a lot of buildings, lots of places to hide a body." He glanced in Diana's direction and must've seen her blanch, because he looked embarrassed to have chosen his words so carelessly.

Rory gave Diana a reassuring look, then addressed Declan's concern. "Returning every two hours isn't the most efficient way to go about this, but it's the safest." Rory didn't like it one bit that there was the possibility he was putting all the quilters in harm's way. "The mobile reception here isn't great. Also, it doesn't hurt to see each and every one of them every two hours...just to be sure."

Diana gave him a reassuring smile. "It's a good idea." Rory knew she felt responsible for the quilters as well.

Declan walked them to a Range Rover. "I usually walk to and from the castle, but this will give us more time to look."

Rory agreed. They piled into the vehicle and drove to the wool mill.

They started in the dye shack. It was small and didn't take long to search. Next they tackled the office building, finishing just in time to rush back to the castle for the first check-in.

No one had anything to report—good or bad.

As the day wore on, Rory became concerned. And Diana became frantic. After four hours,

Rory called Sergeant Grear, but the bodies hadn't been identified yet. When he requested photos, Grear told him it would do no good: dental records would be needed.

At lunchtime, they broke to have sandwiches and hot tattie soup.

"The quilters didn't sign up for this," Diana said. "They came to see Marta. I'm going to get her."

Fifteen minutes later, Diana appeared with her face set, towing Marta into the room by one arm.

Marta shook Diana off before plastering a smile on her face. She strolled forward as if she owned the joint instead of the Laird. "Afternoon, everyone."

The quilters remained impassive. They weren't going to let Marta off the hook so easily. Rory understood why the Scots were pissed. They couldn't comprehend why Marta hadn't gone out to help search. A part of him felt like he should come to her rescue and explain it was safer for her here. But he was curious to see how she would weasel her way out of this one and bring them back to her side. If she could...

"Hello, my darlings. I have a surprise for you." Marta dramatically flung her arms wide, as if a flock of turtle doves would spring from her embrace. "I know you have had a hard time on this multi-city retreat."

Multi-village is more like it, Rory corrected in his mind.

"I spoke with my publisher."

Rory could tell Marta was lying by the widening of Diana's eyes. He was certain Diana was the one who had talked with the publisher.

Marta continued on, unaware of how she was ticking off her publicist. "I am pleased to announce that we're about to have a *very* exciting prize drawing! There will be three lucky winners—one of the retreat goers, one of the Gandiegow ladies, and one of the Whussendale quilters, too."

The women looked at each other, their dismay changing into cautious excitement.

"What's the prize?" Deydie asked, pragmatically.

"A trip to the States for two. To the International Quilt Festival in Houston next fall."

Excited chatter broke out. Rory knew most of these women considered themselves lucky to take a trip into Edinburgh, let alone to another country.

"Diana, can you have everyone put their name on a piece of paper?"

Diana produced a small notepad and handed it to Deydie along with a pen. "Can you get this started while I find three bowls?" Mrs. McNabb passed her the bowls, one for each group of women, obviously. "You're included in the drawing, too," Diana said.

Mrs. McNabb beamed. "Thank ye."

Diana squeezed the old woman's hand. "We appreciate how well you've been taking care of us."

The women finished writing their names and dropped their slips of paper into the appropriate bowl. Marta held her arms out to Rory. "DCI Crannach, will you do us the honor of drawing one name from each bowl?"

Of course. It was like the doctor having the nurse give the shot instead of doing it himself. This way no one would blame Marta when they didn't win.

After an awkward embrace by Marta, he pulled out the three winning names: Lorna, Tally, Bethia.

The women smiled and looked delighted, but didn't squeal like contestants on the telly. He understood. They wouldn't want to rub their good fortune in everyone's face.

Finally, Deydie clapped her hands and stepped up beside Marta. "We've all had food and fun. Now, let's get back to the search."

Rory couldn't agree more. He caught up with Diana as she headed out the door. "Are ye all right?" he asked.

She shrugged. "It was weird having Marta do another giveaway while Parker is missing."

He leaned toward her. "Was it the only way you could get Marta to come downstairs?"

Diana nodded. "She wanted to play the hero. I had to call in all kinds of favors and..." she broke off.

"And what?"

"The PR department wanted to exploit Parker's disappearance, but. . ."

"But ye held yere ground," he finished for her.

"Yes. I guess you haven't heard anything about the victims at the airport?"

"No news." No news he would share with her.

Declan drove them back to the wool mill and they continued with the search.

For the remainder of daylight, they all did this dance, returning to the kitchen every two hours. When it got too dark to see, Rory called it for the night. The quilters drifted off to their rooms to rest before dinner. After Rory had a meeting with his expanded team and gave everyone their assignments, he headed to Diana's room and knocked.

When she opened the door, he saw she was more worried than she'd been before. He knew what she was feeling, because he was feeling it, too. The longer the disappearance, the less likely it would end well.

Rory pulled Diana into his arms and shut the door with his foot in one smooth motion. "Don't give up hope, lass."

"Where's Leo?" she asked, to his surprise. "Tell me he's still in jail."

Rory looked at her bed, scattered with papers. "Did ye turn yere bed into a murder board?"

"Answer the question, Inspector," she said.

He pulled her close again. "Leo was let go on a technicality."

"When?" she asked. "Before Parker and Ewan went missing?"

He nodded. "But I don't want ye to jump to any conclusions."

"I'm not jumping to conclusions. He seems the logical suspect."

"What would be his motive?"

"Hurt as many Three Seals employees as possible, I guess." She paused. "I don't know."

She looked so forlorn that he didn't know what to do. So he kissed her.

In response, she dragged him across the room to her bed and pulled him down as she swept the papers to the floor.

This wasn't the reason he'd come to her, but he wasn't going to put up a fight. Mrs. McNabb said dinner would be in thirty-five minutes, so he had time to help make his American lass forget her worries.

In half an hour, he reluctantly pulled away, giving Diana

one last kiss before he got out of bed. "I'll go downstairs first," he said as he dressed. "Give me about five minutes' head start."

In the hallway he pulled out his phone to check for messages. *None.*

He decided in this case *no news was good news.*

Rory wanted to linger on how Diana had lightened the pressure, the weight that had been pressing on his chest since Parker and Ewan had gone missing. Rory's step felt lighter, too, as he made his way down the stairs and walked into the kitchen.

His good feelings evaporated when he saw Leo standing by the large stone hearth, holding a mug of something hot, and having the brass to grin like the *effing* cat who'd eaten the canary.

"Hello, Detective Chief Inspector. I bet you didn't expect to see me here."

⁗)(⁗

Diana felt like she'd rather not get up at all, but after a few minutes, she dragged herself from bed and dressed.

She trotted downstairs and saw...*Leo?*

Before Diana could do or say anything, the phone in her pocket buzzed. She didn't take her eyes off Leo as she answered.

"This is Diana McKellen."

"Diana!" a voice squealed. "You'll never guess where I am!"

Diana's brain was trying to catch up to her shocked ears. "*Parker?*"

"Yes, it's me. You're not going to believe it--I just got married!"

17

"**H**OLD ON A SECOND," Diana said. As confused as she was, she wanted to let everyone know Parker was safe.

But Hugh burst into the kitchen and beat her to it. "Ewan and Parker are fine!" He held up his phone. "Ewan is on the line with me right now. They're in Las Vegas and they just got married!"

The whole room whooped and hollered, and then they all started talking at once. Rory turned to Diana, questioning her with his eyes. She couldn't answer him yet, as she already had the phone back to her ear. But she did reach out and grab his arm to let him know she'd speak to him in a minute...and to steady herself.

"You're in Las Vegas? How?"

"Ewan chartered a flight," Parker said.

"You just disappeared. Without a word." Diana couldn't help sounding accusatory, when she should just be happy her friend was alive.

"A shuttle picked us up at the wool mill." There were some

muffled words and then Parker said, "I have to run. We'll talk when I get home to Scotland." There was no goodbye, only dial tone.

Diana frowned at her phone, then looked up at Rory. "Well, she's okay. Alive. But I swear, I'm going to kill her for what she's put us through."

"It's okay now." Rory pulled Diana into his arms and hugged her. Immediately, he let go and looked around, as if the two of them had been caught in the act. But everyone was busy hugging everyone else.

Deydie clapped her hands, getting their attention. "Settle down, people. I know we've worked ourselves up worrying about them, but they're fine. And now, we have a lot of work to do."

Diana and Rory looked at each other and she knew he was having the same thought she was: *What kind of 'work'?*

Deydie answered their unspoken question. "If we all join together, we'll be able to get a wedding quilt done by the time the happy couple gets home. I have the perfect design. Everyone can help."

"How much time do we have?" asked Bethia.

Hugh laughed. "Twenty-four hours. They'll be here tomorrow evening around six. And," he added, "Sophie and I have decided to throw them a wedding reception when they arrive."

The room buzzed with chatter and excitement at the announcement.

"Laird," Lorna called out, "are ye going to bus in any men for us to dance with at this *céilidh*?"

Hugh laughed. "We have several bachelors on the estate and on Ewan's estate as well. Plenty of men to go around."

"I'll make sure a van full of men comes from Gandiegow as well!" Deydie hollered cheerfully.

"Now there's some good news!" Lorna plopped down and

everyone laughed.

"What's going on here?" Marta had just walked into the room with McCartney and MacTaggart.

Multiple voices responded about the elopement, the wedding quilt and the party, but Marta wasn't listening. She'd spotted Leo and looked dismayed, as if a lion had been let loose in the room.

A cowardly lion, Diana thought.

"Are you going to question him?" She whispered to Rory.

"Aye. In a minute. But first, I want to observe the happy reunion."

If by *happy* he meant awkward and unpleasant—then he'd nailed it.

"Come on, baby. I'm here to keep you safe," Leo said, pawing Marta. "My poor darling. I'm sorry I wasn't there to protect you from the fire. If I had known..."

Marta looked conflicted, as if she wanted to believe him, but didn't.

"Let's go up to your room to talk," Leo coaxed.

Rory stepped in then. "If Marta is willing, you can speak with her in the parlor. McCartney, you go with them."

"But—"

Rory cut Leo off. "Those are the conditions"

Leo put his hand on Marta's arm, but she pulled away and walked from the room under McCartney's watchful eyes.

"Those two are getting back together?" Diana asked.

"I don't see how, but maybe." Rory grimaced at the doorway, where they'd just left. "I'm going to have to check this out, too."

Sophie and several of the other quilters picked up trays loaded with food. "Everyone, come to the ballroom. We have a party to plan and a wedding quilt to piece."

Deydie hailed Diane as she entered the ballroom. "Lass, it's agreed. We're going to make a Gandiegow Rosette quilt for Parker and Ewan."

"This is so nice of all of you." Diana beamed at the happy bedlam. What a grand gesture—a wedding quilt! Even Marta was at the cutting mat with a rotary cutter and a stack of white fabric. Diana was still trying to wrap her head around the fact Parker had gotten married.

"I expect ye to participate, too." Deydie gave one of her Jedi stares designed to make her sit behind a machine. "'Tis yere friend, after all." She clamped a hand on Diana's arm. "Ye'll not argue. You can start by learning how to make a rosette, then ye can either hand-stitch it in place on the quilt or tack it down with the machine. I'll help ye." She guided Diana over to a sewing machine and sat right beside her, giving her instructions.

Diana had seen several women sporting a rosette on their sash and thought it would be complicated to make. Surprisingly, though, the rosette came together quickly, and Diana was proud of what she'd done. She hated to admit it; Deydie was a good teacher and only barked at her a couple of times.

Deydie dug in her bag and pulled out a quilt top. "It must've been fate that I put this in my bag before we left for Whussendale nearly-finished." She spread out the top made of stars around the edges and a panel of sheep in the center. She smoothed down the creases with her gnarled hands. "My new ewes inspired me. I looked through my stash and found this sheep fabric. I had just enough to make a small lap quilt. But I've decided to give it to yere friend and Laird Ewan. By the way those two look at each other, I'm sure Parker will be in the family way before the honeymoon is over." Deydie cackled then. "I'm going to call this quilt Feeling Sheepy. What do ye think?"

"I think it's wonderful!" Diana was so overcome by love for

this old woman that she couldn't help but hug her. "And I know the truth about you. You're an ol' softy." When Deydie tried to pull away, Diana whispered the rest. "I promise not to tell anyone."

Deydie hugged her back then. "Ye're not so bad for a Yank."

Sophie rushed over with a panicked look on her face. Not a *someone-died* look but a *help-me* look. "Deydie, Lorna wants to change up the Gandiegow Rosette quilt and add little rosettes for where your quilt calls for pinwheels."

Deydie forcefully scooted back her chair and stood. "Over my dead body, she will!" She hustled off with Sophie to fix the problem.

As Deydie left, Tilly grabbed her bag and headed in Diana's direction looking guiltily this way and that. *What is she up to?*

She sat beside Diana and set her bag at her feet.

"What's up?" Diana said.

"I have something for you." Tilly reached in, pulled out a drawstring bag, and held it out to Diana. "The first three chapters of the new Quilt to Death novel. I thought you might like to read it." She dropped her head and spoke to the parquet floor. "Since you're trying to save the Buttermilk Guild."

"I don't know what to say. Thank you, Tilly. I feel honored." Diana took the bundle and pulled at the drawstring, but Tilly stopped her by clutching her hand.

"No. Not here. Don't let Marta see."

"I won't," Diana said. "I'm still waiting on your answer about doing promotional appearances."

Tilly glanced over at Marta and then back at Diana. It looked as if she might cry. "I'll do it. But just don't expect me to be Marta."

Diana grasped her hand and gave her a fortifying smile. "I wouldn't dream of it."

Tilly got up and returned to her place at Marta's side, handing her pieces of fabric to cut.

Diana pulled up the promo document on her phone, reduced the number of appearances Tilly would be scheduled to make, and then emailed it to Nicola at Three Seals. When she was done, she was about to slip upstairs to read Tilly's pages when Deydie came roaring back.

"Have ye finished that second rosette yet?" the old woman hollered.

"Yes." Diana held it up for her to admire.

Deydie cocked her head to the side. "I guess that would do-- if seen from a galloping horse. Keep at it, lass."

Diana spent the rest of the evening with the relieved and happy quilters and didn't see Rory at all. *Which was good, right?* She needed distance. Perspective. Actually, she needed to get a grip. But she couldn't stop herself from wondering if he would sneak into her room again tonight.

When she opened her bedroom door, there he was, lying on her bed with his hands stacked behind his head.

She didn't hesitate but closed the door behind her and hurried into his arms. *I deserve this,* she thought. The past day and a half had been terrifying, and the Detective Chief Inspector had a way of making her forget her fears.

Diana just had to make sure she kept it light. There was no future for them. But they did have tonight.

༄༅

Last night, Rory had been studying the ceiling and asking himself why he'd come to Diana's room...and made himself at home in her bed. He just hadn't been able to stop his feet from bringing him there. It'd been wonderful having her in his arms again and holding her all night. But now that it was morning, he had work to do.

If he didn't get his head back in the game—get the job done

and catch the killer—he might as well give up being a detective altogether. For the life of him, he couldn't figure out why Diana distracted him so.

He had a job to do and, he needed to keep reminding himself, his job wasn't Diana.

ဆာ

When Diana woke in the morning, Rory was gone. The rest of the day was somewhat of a blur, as Deydie kept her busy sewing and prepping for the arrival of the newlyweds. Diana shouldn't have had any time to think about Rory. Or to look up to see if it was him every time someone came into the ballroom. Or when she was sent on an errand.

No time to think about him at all.

Except she did.

Diana escaped to the kitchen to pour a cup of tea. As she stirred in a teaspoon of sugar, she remembered last night and how she'd let her guard down. How another chink in her armor was exposed. Rory had touched more than her skin. He'd touched her heart and soul. So much for keeping it light.

She shook her head at the foolish thought and checked her watch before gazing out the window. Anyone watching would think she was waiting for Parker to arrive. But really, her eyes were searching for Rory. Not because she wanted to see him, per se, but because if she caught just a glimpse, she might be able to breathe again.

A vehicle pulled up outside. It wasn't Rory, it was Parker and Ewan!

Diana tore outside, forgetting all about putting on a coat. She ran to Parker and hugged her tightly, saying into her hair, "We were so worried about you! Why didn't you tell me you were running off to elope?" She pulled back to look at her.

Parker's nose crinkled and Diana knew she was chagrined.

"I'm sorry, I just couldn't. I knew you'd try to talk me out of it." Parker smiled. "I love him, Diana. When you know he's the right one, you just know."

"Well, then, I am very happy for you," Diana said sincerely. But already her mind had gone elsewhere. *When you know he's the right one, you just know.* That little voice inside—who'd been vying for Diana's attention since the start—was yelling at her now: *You know the truth. Rory is your one!*

Hugh came out to greet his cousin. "Ewan! Ye old married dog."

"Come on inside," Diana said. "It's cold out here."

Diana and Parker hurried into the warm kitchen, leaving Hugh in the driveway, pounding on Ewan's back and giving him his congratulations.

Parker chattered away excitedly about her whirlwind romance and wedding to Ewan.

"You do look happy," Diana observed.

"I am, *so* happy," Parker said. "But I feel terrible we made you and the others worry."

It was more than worry! There was a manhunt!

Parker continued without reading Diana's mind. "I knew you thought we were moving too fast but we knew it was right for us. We decided to slip away and come right back." She wrapped an arm around Diana. "Can you forgive me?"

"Of course I can." Diana felt guilty. If she hadn't repeatedly lectured Parker about taking things slow, maybe she would've let everyone know what they were up to. "I shouldn't have tried to tell you what to do. I hope you can forgive me, too."

They hugged some more, and the next hour passed quickly as Diana took Parker to the newly christened honeymoon suite and helped her get dressed for the *céilidh* in the flowy white dress they'd picked up in Las Vegas. Then, Diana hurried to her room to put on her purple dress—freshened in the dryer—

that Parker had returned. Diana's nerves had kicked into overdrive. Would Rory attend the dance?

At seven, Diana made her way downstairs and found Ewan and Parker at the doors to the ballroom, ready to make their entrance. Ewan, decked out in a kilt and suit jacket, stepped inside first, then offered his hand to Parker and presented her to the crowd with a little bow. Cheers and applause broke out. Diana, left standing alone, looked around the room at the smiling faces, but none of them were Rory.

When Bethia and Deydie made their way over to her, she slapped on a fake smile and gushed, "Everything looks wonderful."

"Aye," Deydie said. "Some of us are getting too old for these last-minute hijinks."

Bethia touched Diana's arm. "Are ye all right? Ye look a little sad."

"No! I'm happy Parker and Ewan are safe. I just haven't recovered yet. They gave me quite a scare."

Both Bethia and Deydie looked as if they knew Diana wasn't telling them the complete truth.

"Can I get you both something to drink?" Diana certainly needed a stiff one. But she was on the job and couldn't drink her worries away.

"Aye," Deydie said. "I'll take a dram of whisky."

"Me, too," Bethia said. "I feel a chill in the air."

Diana felt it as well. A chill that had started when Rory left her bed this morning.

Darn it, she was really starting to feel sorry for herself. At the bar in the corner, she ordered the old quilters' drinks and a water for herself.

"Ye're not celebrating with the rest?"

His voice made her jump, causing the drinks to slosh over the edges and drip onto her hands. Her insides felt raw and she had to wait a beat, so her voice wouldn't come out as shrill. She took a deep breath, trying to think of something benign to say. Something besides, *Where the hell have you been all day?*

"I need to get these to Deydie and Bethia. They're waiting on me." *Okay. That struck the right neutral tone.*

Before she could escape, though, the lights dimmed, and Hugh's voice came over the microphone. "Please join the bride and groom on the dance floor as they enjoy their first dance."

Diana gave an apologetic shrug and left Rory by the bar.

She was at war with herself. She wanted to run back to him and throw herself into his arms. But he'd left her alone all day to wonder what he was up to.

Diana got the drinks to Bethia and Deydie without further incident.

"Evening, ladies." *That voice* was behind her again. "Ye don't mind, do ye, if I borrow Ms. McKellen for a minute? *Police business.*"

"*Right,*" Deydie said sarcastically. She had his number, in other words. Rory's response was to give the two women his charming smile before ushering Diana away. She was too flustered to say anything and didn't protest as he opened the French doors and guided her out onto the balcony. She didn't even have to say she was cold, because he was already slipping off his jacket and wrapping it around her shoulders. The body heat it retained made her instantly cozy and warm. It was overwhelmingly intimate to have his heat wrapped around her like that.

"Did ye miss me today?" he said, smiling as if he already knew the answer.

She lifted a cocky eyebrow. "I was too busy to think of anything but Parker and Ewan's wedding reception." She wasn't going to tell him how she'd pined for him all day. She was going to be strong and ignore how much she wanted to be in his arms again...right now.

Rory must've seen the obstinacy in her eyes and accepted the challenge, because he reached for her. Fortunately, Diana would never know if she would've succumbed to his charms or not, because Bethia stuck her head outside. "Come in, Diana, come in. We're going to give Parker and Ewan their wedding quilt now."

"I'm coming."

Rory looked both frustrated and disappointed as Diana ducked under his arm and left him alone on the balcony.

⃝⃝

Rory watched Diana slip through his hands, wanting her to come back -- and glad she was gone. Really, he needed to break the spell that she'd put him under. He'd done well and managed to keep his distance all day. But seeing her across the ballroom, he'd felt compelled to get her alone. To kiss her. And more. There was so much he wanted to say to her.

Like, *When I see you, I lose all focus.*

Ah, hell. He had it bad for her, but a murderer was still on the loose. He should be happy Bethia had interrupted them.

Rory returned inside and watched as Ewan and Parker were called to the low-rise stage, where the band was located. Hugh and his wife, Sophie, stood behind a microphone.

"And now," Hugh said, "it's time to present yere wedding gift."

All the quilters came forward, Deydie and Bethia at the front, carrying a box with a large ribbon tied around it.

Parkers looked stunned, and Ewan simply beamed at his new bride, as if she was the greatest gift.

"Go on now," Deydie said. "Stop gawking and open it up."

Parker pulled the ribbon and the bow fell away. Ewan took

the top off the box and then Parker pulled back the tissue with a gasp.

"It's beautiful!"

Aye. The women had done a bang-up job, using Scottish rosettes of different tartans. Two more of the quilters took the corners and held it up for everyone to see. There were a lot of well-deserved *ooos* and *ahs*.

"Turn it around," Deydie said. "Show 'em the back."

The women turned in a big circle, exposing the back, which was made of stripes of white and tartan. Rory could see the quilters' signatures on each of the white strips. He wondered if Diana had signed her name as the others had. He saw her standing by the video camera, which was on a tripod, trained on the newlyweds. But she wasn't looking through the camera; she was looking at him.

Rory made his way over to her, not completely sure what he was going to do when he arrived. The lights dimmed again, and the band started up a slow tune. This felt like a sign. More like a hard nudge. He didn't give Diana a chance to turn him down, but pulled her into his arms and danced her out on the floor with the other couples who were swaying to the love ballad.

"Who's going to man the video camera?" Diana seemed proud of herself for coming up with the excuse.

"It'll be grand on its own." Rory wondered if the camera caught the spell Diana had put on him, for he was certainly feeling it now. He laid his cheek against her hair and breathed in, not caring one iota if the camera caught what he was doing or if anyone else saw that he was smitten.

He must've been doing something right because Diana relaxed in his arms, leaning into him.

"Better," he murmured into her ear. He felt a shiver go up her spine. In response, he nuzzled her neck. He tilted his head down, gazed into Diana's eyes for a moment, then kissed her.

The moment was full of promise and magic. *The music. The swaying.* It all spoke of things to come.

Diana didn't seem to mind they were kissing in front of everyone, because she kissed him back, long and sweet.

Then a scream pierced the room and Rory jerked away, his senses on full alert now.

"What is it?" Diana asked

"I'm going to find out," he said at once, and left her on the dance floor.

MacTaggart and McCartney caught up with him at the door but Rory instructed his team, "Watch Miss Dixon."

"Help!"

Rory ran toward the cry, which was coming from the kitchen. When he got there, he saw the upper half of Mrs. McNabb in an opening in the floor. She was clearly on the steps down to what had to be a cellar.

"He's in the root cellar," she wailed. "He's dead."

Rory didn't ask who, but instead rushed to Mrs. McNabb and helped her up and out of his way. Sophie and Hugh had followed him, and he asked them to take her from the kitchen.

Rory peered down the dark steps. A single bulb swung ominously back and forth, but he didn't see a body. He slipped on a pair of latex gloves before pulling a torch from his back pocket. He pointed the light at each dark corner as he descended the stairs, in case the killer was still down there with the body.

Before he reached the bottom, he saw what Mrs. McNabb had seen—Leo Shamley sprawled against a 100-pound sack of potatoes with a butcher knife stuck in his chest. Thrown across his legs was a quilt—the Lover's Knot quilt, the same quilt design that Diana had shown him earlier on her phone.

Leo's eyes were open, and his outstretched arm was cold.

"What is it?" Diana hollered down to him.

"Stay up there," Rory commanded.

It didn't surprise him when he heard Diana coming down the steps.

"I mean it, Diana. I need ye to stay put this time," he said. This was too grisly for her. "Please. Do as I ask."

"Okay," she answered. "I'll wait for you up here. Can you tell me what's going on?" she asked quietly.

"It's Leo," he said.

She was silent for a long minute. "But why him?"

"I suppose to hurt Marta?"

There was another noise at the top of the stairs. "It's Hugh. Can I come down?"

"Nay," Rory said, carefully checking the back of the quilt for a tag. He found none. "I'm coming up. No one is allowed down here." *The fewer people to disturb the crime scene, the better.*

When he got to the top, it was Diana who gave him a brave smile. "You okay?"

Rory nodded.

Hugh looked unsettled, not nearly as composed as Diana was. "Sophie's with Mrs. McNabb in the parlor. She told us what she saw."

Rory nodded. "Mrs. McNabb is to stay in the parlor. You and Sophie are to tell no one what she says. Got it?"

"Aye."

"The kitchen is now off limits, too," Rory said. "And Hugh, do me a favor?"

"Anything," Hugh said.

"Get Declan and Tavon to guard the entrances to the ballroom to keep everyone inside. I need to call Major Crimes to get a full team here."

"Aye." Hugh hurried from the kitchen.

Rory looked at Diana and saw lines of concentration etching

her face. "Are ye all right?"

She nodded. "I have a lot of questions, though, like how was he killed?"

"Not yet." He could trust Diana, but he wanted to keep the details to himself for as long as possible. "I need to speak with Deydie before I interview Mrs. McNabb." He had to determine the location of Lorna's Lover's Knot quilt before moving forward.

As Rory and Diana walked to the ballroom together, their intimate moment on the dance floor felt like a lifetime ago. Murder had a way of skewing the passage of time like that. He'd have a long night ahead of him with no more dances tonight.

He stopped just outside the ballroom. "Go on in, Diana. I need to call HQ."

Diana gave him an understanding smile and slipped past Declan and Tavon. Rory pulled out his phone and broke the news to headquarters that another American was dead.

When Rory entered the ballroom, he found the chandeliers had been switched from mood lighting to noonday bright. The band was silent, but the room buzzed with speculation. Rory was glad Mrs. McNabb had been sequestered in the parlor. There would be no containing the details, otherwise. He texted Hugh, reminding him again not to divulge any information that Mrs. McNabb might be sharing with them.

Rory found Deydie with her entourage. "May I speak with ye a moment in private? I need a favor."

She nodded and followed him. "What is it?"

"I need to know which Quilt to Death quilts are left in Gandiegow."

"By the retreat goers? Or by the Gandiegowans?" she asked.

"Both. I need a list of who has what quilt, and which quilts, if any, are missing," Rory said. "Ma'am, I'm counting on yere discretion... ye mustn't tell anyone what I'm asking for."

She nodded solemnly and pulled her mobile from her dress pocket. "I'll ask Moira to check the quilting dorms and then speak with the rest of the quilters in town, but I won't tell her why. This may take some time." She frowned, as if remembering that one of her beloved quilts was already evidence in a murder.

He appreciated Deydie for not asking him why he needed this information.

Rory eavesdropped as she gave instructions to Moira and watched her closely for signs that Deydie was guilty of Leo's murder, but he saw no trace. He'd taken a chance by asking this favor of her, but he had a feeling this loveable old bat was a safe bet.

Deydie finished and pocketed her phone. "Moira will get back to me straightaway. I told her not to tell anyone what she's doing. She's a good lass."

"Thank you."

Rory hurried to the parlor to speak to Mrs. McNabb, who was sandwiched between Hugh and Sophie on the settee. Mrs. McNabb had seen nothing suspicious. She was in the kitchen almost the entire day, but had just returned from having a half hour nap. When she needed some potatoes from the root cellar, she found Leo instead. Rory left Sophie and Hugh to console Mrs. McNabb and, with MacTaggart and McCartney, began the tedious task of interviewing everyone in the castle. He talked to Marta first, who claimed to be on the balcony having a cigarette while, waiting for Leo to come to the dance. As he interviewed each person, he heard the same answer over and over. No one had seen anything. But then again, everyone said they were focused on the evening's festivities, believing unwisely that the bad luck of the quilt retreat was behind them.

Deydie waddled over to him and held out a steaming mug. "Moira went through Duncan's Den with a fine-tooth comb and found one Quilt to Death Sampler and one Quilt to Death Bear Paw quilt. She's going from cottage to cottage now to make the rest of the list."

Lorna's Lover's Knot quilt had not been found.

Deydie looked at him shrewdly. "I know ye have murder on yere mind, but I have to tell ye that we saw ye kissing the American lass on the dance floor. Why don't ye pick some nice Scottish lass and not a foreigner? We've plenty of homegrown lassies right here in this room."

Whose average age was over sixty. But Rory kept his thoughts to himself and steered Deydie back to the investigation. "When do you think Moira will get back to ye about the rest?"

"She'll get back to me when she can. Gandiegow's a big place," Deydie said.

No, it isn't. "Can ye give me an estimate then?" he asked.

"It'll happen in due time." Deydie sized him up. "We need to talk about the American lass. What are ye doing with her?"

"There's nothing going on between myself and Diana." Nothing he wanted to discuss with Deydie, anyway.

"Just having a bit of fun then?" Deydie said disapprovingly. "Ye better break it off. I like Diana. We all do. Have yere fun with someone else. Besides, she'll be gone soon."

"Quite right." Deydie had hit the nail on the head. Diana was leaving soon. He looked down at his notepad, which reminded him of the duty he'd been half-assing because of his infatuation.

Deydie glared at him. "Then ye'll do as I bid and tell her it's over?"

"I told ye, there's nothing going on between Diana and myself." But as soon as the words left his mouth, he wanted to take them back. It felt all wrong. He wanted to tell the world the truth. There was a lot going on between him and Diana. The Almighty knew there was so much Rory still needed to learn about her. More about her family, her past. There was so much more he wanted to share with her. Like a hike up Ben Lomond. Or to take the ferry to Isle of May on Open Doors Day. He'd like to introduce her to Kin. He started to call Deydie back, but she was gone. And he didn't have time to go after her, because he suddenly knew he had to find Diana and tell her how he was feeling.

He twisted around, planning to scan the room to find her. He needed to speak with her in private. But right behind him, there she stood...glaring.

Oh, crap! He could tell she'd heard him say there was nothing going on between them.

He took a step toward her. "Diana—"

She put her hand out. "Don't!" She glared at him a millisecond longer, then spun around and fled.

18

DIANA RAN TO THE EXIT, wiping stupid tears from her cheeks. She'd always assumed if she'd dated a cop, it would end by him being shot and killed in the line of duty. It never occurred to her that the end would come by him dumping her...and at the urging of an octogenarian, no less!

Actually, it was worse. From his own mouth, he'd said there was nothing going on between them!

Declan stopped her at the door. "Ye can't leave, Ms. McKellen. Orders from the DCI."

She turned back to look at Rory—a reflex, as if the doctor at her annual physical had taken that little hammer to her. She hated herself for looking, because he was looking straight back at her with. . . pity in his eyes? *Pity!*

What she did next didn't make a whole lot of sense. She threw herself at Declan. Not to bust through the door, but to kiss him. She'd taken the poor guy by surprise, and he didn't respond to her kiss at first.

But then Declan kissed her back. It was nice. She tried to

enjoy it, but...

She couldn't. Because no one kissed like Rory.

And she didn't want to kiss anyone...but Rory.

A hand gripped her arm. It couldn't be Declan's hand, because his arms were wrapped around her. He was really *embracing* the idea of kissing her now.

Diana was pulled away from the kiss.

And the *pull-er* was growling. "Leave off, Declan."

Declan laughed. "Sorry. What can I say? The lass was willing."

"Nay." Rory's voice was laced with warning. "She was mistaken, 'tis all."

Diana was stunned, and okay, a little thrilled that Rory had come after her.

"Don't do it again," Rory said.

"Why not?" she snapped. "There's nothing going on between us."

He glared at her and for the first time, she saw he could be dangerous.

"Outside. Now! On the balcony." He didn't lay a hand on her, but his words felt like a shove.

She gave him a superior glare. "I'll go, but only because it's stuffy in here." And because she was curious as to what he wanted to say.

As she marched toward the balcony, she noticed many eyes on them. Her superior attitude faded, as she started to realize what a spectacle she'd made of herself, Declan, and Rory. She stopped and faced him.

"I'm sorry," she said to Rory.

Lorna and two of her fellow retreat goers leaned closer, as if not to miss a word of their conversation.

Diana moved nearer to him so others couldn't hear. "You have a case to solve." *And I'm acting like a lovesick idiot with a crush.* "Go do your job." She had a job to do as well. "We can talk later."

"Are ye sure?" He glanced skeptically at Declan, as if he couldn't trust him.

"I'm sure. I have calls to make." *And my crush on you...to crush! To obliterate!*

Rory walked back to the table where he'd been interviewing people. He didn't get to sit down, though. The forensics team arrived and he led them from the ballroom.

Diana pulled out her phone and texted Nicola at Three Seals to let her know about Leo. Next, she took her notebook to a small table in the far corner.

It was time for her to get serious.

Time to figure out who was committing all these murders...*and why.*

Time to solve the case, so she could fly home.

More importantly, it was time for her to finally be honest about what was going on. Because being in Scotland around the man she could never have was just too much for her heart to handle.

ৎ১৫৫

MacTaggart hurried over to Rory.

"What is it?" Rory asked.

"The newlyweds, Ewan and Parker, want to leave for their honeymoon. Are ye clearing them to go?" MacTaggart asked.

"Aye. Tell them to keep their phones on, in case we need to get a hold of them."

Rory saw MacTaggart deliver the news and then watched as Diana hugged Parker goodbye. Rory didn't wait around to see if she noticed him. There was a killer loose and he got the awful feeling the murderer was closing in for the finale. Where was Marta now?

With a quick scan, he searched the room and found Marta in the corner of the ballroom, dabbing her eyes, with McCartney standing guard.

Rory made his way to her, and caught the tail end of the conversation with her sister.

Tilly handed Marta another tissue. "I just don't understand why you're so upset. You said you were done with Leo."

"I don't know. I just am," Marta blubbered.

"You told him repeatedly to leave you alone," Tilly sounded genuinely puzzled.

"He's dead, Tilly," Marta wailed. "We had a history together, me and him."

This brought an empathetic look to Tilly's face. Rory could see she loved her overbearing sister very much. Tilly pulled out three tissues this time and handed them to Marta before wrapping an arm around her shoulder. "It's going to be okay, *Mar-Mar*. I'm here to take care of you." Tilly looked up at Rory. "Can I take her to our room now? She needs to lie down."

"Sure," Rory said. "McCartney, go with them. I'll send MacTaggart up to relieve you later."

Rory could feel Diana's eyes upon him as he left the room, but he wasn't going to give into temptation and look back. It occurred to him, then, that the sooner he caught the murderer, the sooner he could focus on Diana and see what was really going on between them.

One by one, he released people to go to their room or back home. When he was finished, he didn't have one clear suspect or one strong lead. Then a horrifying thought hit him.

What if the killer went after Diana next?

The killer seemed to be systematically getting closer to Marta by murdering those nearest to her.

"MacTaggart," Rory barked. *Why hadn't he considered this*

sooner? Because, since meeting Diana, his renowned rational thinking had been on hiatus.

"What is it?" MacTaggart asked.

"Someone needs to be posted outside Diana's door at all times," Rory said.

"Should I ask Declan and Tavon to help with the detail?" MacTaggart asked. "We could use the extra eyes."

Eyes aren't the problem. Lips are.

"No." It was a split-second decision, which he had no intention of explaining. "Ye're in charge of Diana. Ask one of the duty officers to take shifts with ye." *And make sure he isn't going to be someone Diana would find attractive!* "Text me with updates. I don't want her wandering around the castle alone."

One of MacTaggart's bushy eyebrows lifted slightly, and Rory realized he'd been too transparent.

"That goes for everyone. We're locked down tight," Rory said with authority. "The problem is, I don't know who we have locked down with us." A murderer, or just a bunch of quilters having the worst retreat in history.

"Understood." MacTaggart turned and left.

For the rest of the night, Rory worked with the forensic team to clear the crime scene. Now, he could only hope the killer would slip up and give himself away before another crime was committed.

Finally, just before dawn, Rory headed off to bed, hoping to get some sleep before they headed back to Gandiegow. Barely an hour later, there was a knock at his door.

"What?" he croaked, trying to clear the fog from his head. "What is it?"

"It's McCartney. Ye said to wake ye when the quilters were up."

"What's the time?"

"Seven,"

"Fine."

"Deydie says they're leaving for Gandiegow within the hour," McCartney added.

"Crud." Rory's exclamation wasn't completely under his breath. "I'll be down in a few." He wanted to get a look at the quilters to see if any of them had had a restless night's sleep from stabbing Leo and pushing him down the steps of the root cellar.

Rory took a quick shower and headed downstairs. Sewing machines were being carried out the massive double oak doors by Declan, Tavon, and the other men of Whussendale, whom Rory suspected were off to work at the wool mill after completing this chore. He found the quilters in the dining room, bellied up to the buffet. He tried not to look in Diana's direction as he loaded Scotch eggs and a couple of broiled tomato wedges on his plate, before sitting next to Bethia. He barred Diana from his mind, which wasn't easy; she was three chairs down, sitting across from Lorna. He scanned the table for guilty faces, and found none. Marta was the only one who was out of sorts with her red puffy eyes. There was real grief there and Rory couldn't help but feel sorry for her.

Deydie stood up at her place at the head of the table. "On behalf of Kilts & Quilts, we'd like to offer each of you a free two-day workshop, including tuition, room and board." She threw a disapproving look in Rory's direction, as though it was his fault and added, "Since this retreat has turned out to be more *eventful* than expected."

Approving murmurs filled the room.

Deydie glanced at the paper in her hands. "I'll send ye an email with the details, but I can tell ye that during yere mini retreat, the Love Coach will be stopping in to join ye."

Bethia jumped in. "Tell them what the Love Coach is."

Deydie leaned on the table, as if readying everyone to hear

the best gossip in the world. "Aye. The Love Coach is the invention of Gandiegow's own matchmaker, Kit Woodhouse-Armstrong, for mature singles."

The room, which was filled with mature singles, came to attention, their ears perked.

Deydie continued. "The coach will be carrying both golfers and quilters. All clients of Kit. Knowing her, they'll be a bunch of Americans among them. While the men are off golfing during the day, the coach will take the women to various *quilty* stops, like Gandiegow. Then, every evening, the lads and lassies will come back together for dinner and entertainment." Deydie motioned to somewhere out the window. "Declan, the lad who's been watching over Marta Dixon, is going to be the tour guide on the coach. He recently finished his Blue Badge Guide training."

At the mention of Declan, Rory's blood boiled. He couldn't help looking at Diana to see if she was remembering and reliving how she'd pawed and kissed Declan last night. *Gads!*

"Can we sign up for this Love Coach, too?" Lorna asked. "I could go for an American lad."

Rory thought her choice of words—*lad,* for instance—was ridiculous, as Lorna had to be sixty if she was a day.

All the women were buzzing now, and Deydie flapped her hands. "Settle down now. I don't know if the coach is full or not. But I'll find out and get ye the information when we get back to Gandiegow. Hurry and finish. I think we're all nearly ready to go."

Rory devoured the food on his plate and made a to-go cup of coffee to take with him, while McCartney escorted Marta from the room. Deydie stopped Rory as he was leaving Kilheath Castle.

"I've heard from Moira." Deydie handed Rory the list.

He scanned it quickly.

"All my quilters' Quilt to Death quilts are accounted for."

"Thanks for letting me know." Most likely, then, the quilt laid over Leo's body had been Lorna's.

He and Deydie walked out together and he helped her to board first. When Rory climbed into the coach, he didn't sit in the back, where he had sat with Diana on the trip here...and where she sat now. Instead, he took a seat in the middle of the bus—right behind Lorna and diagonal to Marta and Tilly. The decision was strategic, but it didn't feel good or right. Only once did he let himself glance back to see Diana's face. She didn't seem happy about where he was sitting, any more than he was. And somehow, seeing her disappointed, made him feel better.

Maybe she felt the same way for him as he did for her.

ഇൻൽ

The coach doors closed and they set off to Gandiegow. Diana pulled her gaze from the back of Rory's head and uncovered the first page of Tilly's manuscript, book ten in the Quilt to Death series. Before she could read the first sentence, Deydie stood up in the front of the bus.

"Bethia just had a suggestion," Deydie said. "She thought we could sing as we travel back to Gandiegow."

"Sing what?" Lorna asked, as she'd made herself the unofficial spokesperson of the quilters.

"I know it's early for Christmas caroling, but we could sing a few holiday songs to pass the time."

Bethia stood, too. "Let's begin with Jingle Bells." She started singing and most of the bus sang with her.

But Diana didn't hear a deep baritone voice joining in. In fact, Mr. Serious was glancing down at something. Oh, how she wished she was sitting with him so she could help him with this case.

Just like I used to help my dad. That thought sobered Diana and had her looking away from Rory. She stared down at the pages in her lap. With a lot of effort, she tuned out the singing and began reading. The pages were good, really good. Here and there, she made notes of things to ask Tilly, but overall Diana loved it, just like the other books in the Quilt to Death series.

Before she knew it, the bus was making the slow descent down the massive hill into Gandiegow. Deydie took that moment to start up her version of *Ninety-nine Bottles of Whisky on the Wall* and the quilters, laughingly, joined in.

When the bus came to a stop, Diana was surprised that a crew of Gandiegow men and women weren't waiting to take the sewing machines back to Quilting Central. "Why are the sewing machines remaining on the bus?" Diana asked Bethia.

"The quilters will be taking this coach back to Edinburgh in a few hours. They will pack the rest of their things, have a bite of lunch, and then be on their way."

Diana watched as the quilters walked toward the quilting dorms. They'd gotten more than they'd bargained for when they'd agreed to be the PR guinea pigs for Marta Dixon's blunder-of-a-book promo.

Rory hung back, too, and watched as things were unloaded.

Diana glanced over at him, trying to act like his pal instead a woman who was falling for him...*hard.* "I didn't hear you sing on the bus and I noticed you had your head bent." Okay, she'd said too much, like she'd been watching him like a hawk. She had to let him know otherwise. "Were you resting?" Still, she'd said too much. He'd probably deduce she was worried about him, being up all night, gathering evidence. "I, ah, assume you didn't get much sleep." Her ill-advised words were laced with *I certainly missed you in my bed.*

"Not much," he said, watching her closely.

Diana wanted to hide her face. At the same time, she wanted to gaze into his eyes, while running a hand over his beard stubble. It wasn't just his sex appeal she was drawn to; she loved his companionship, too. But a shredded heart—which would certainly happen if she let herself fall in love with the Detective Chief Inspector—was not worth the price of a few stolen moments.

"What did you do on the trip?" he asked. "Sing along with the crowd?"

If you'd turned around at least once, you would've seen that I wasn't.

But she kept her pout to herself. "I'll fill you in later. Too many ears. So...did you enjoy your nap?"

He held up his notebook. "I was going over evidence. I do have a couple of questions for you, though."

"Sure. Anything." Once again, she sounded too eager.

He hesitated for a second, waiting until the last person grabbed a suitcase and they were alone. "Let's walk."

They headed toward the village. The sea was feisty today, waves splashing over the walkway. Rory steered her toward the bluff to where the quilting dorms and Partridge House sat. For a moment, Diana wondered if he wanted her to take a siesta with him. Her foolish stomach warmed with anticipation.

"What I'm about to tell you can't be shared with anyone," he said in his serious detective voice.

Her stomach plummeted. *No fun-time siesta for me.*

"Sure. I'll tell no one," she agreed quickly, making sure her voice covered her disappointment.

"It's about the murder last night. I need details from you about the quilting series."

"Was there a quilt involved?"

"Aye. It's the one you showed me earlier—the Lover's Knot. But the one involved in the murder didn't look the same as the one you showed me on yere phone."

"Did it have a different colorway? Was it more blue than yellow?" Diana asked.

"Aye." Rory pulled out his phone. "I tried to take a picture of just the quilt." *Without showing Leo's body.* "Is this Lorna's?"

Diana looked at the picture. "It certainly looks like hers. But that doesn't mean that someone else hasn't made the same colorway."

Rory returned his phone to his pocket and put a hand to Diana's back. "Let's keep walking."

As she turned the corner, and the quilting dorms came into sight, she saw that while they'd been in Whussendale, work had begun on Thistle Glen Lodge to clean up after the fire. A pile of charred wood scraps and burnt rugs were piled outside the quilting dorm. The sound of hammering rang from the interior.

"I hope they can make the cottage good as new." She looked over at Duncan's Den, their destination. The quilters were rolling their suitcases out, heading for Quilting Central and their final hour in Gandiegow. Diana waved to them as they passed by, as she had more she wanted to say to Rory in private...about the murder, and nothing else.

"About Leo and the Lover's Knot quilt...was there a tag on the back?"

"Nay."

"Well, maybe it's not Lorna's. Not all quilts have tags," Diana commented. "Maybe Lorna's quilt is still at Duncan's Den."

"It isn't. Deydie had Moira check."

"Oh," Diana said.

"I should've asked someone in Gandiegow to check for the quilt, when we first thought Parker and Ewan were missing."

He looked irritated with himself.

Diana touched his arm. "Don't beat yourself up. You couldn't have stopped Leo's murder even if you'd known Lorna's quilt was missing." Diana was angry, too, but for a totally different reason. "If only Parker and Ewan would've let us know they were eloping."

"Aye," Rory said. "Wasted time and worry."

He completely understood her. The thought warmed her, though it shouldn't.

He pushed on. "What I need to know now is how the murders were committed in the fifth book."

"I told you. One couple was killed in a secluded cabin. The other was killed in baggage claim."

"Were there any other murders?"

"No. Though the killer definitely had plans to. You see, DI Abercrombie, a character in the story, and his love interest, Heather, acted as decoys and caught the killer red-handed."

"What are the details of the last one—the attempted murder?" Rory asked, as if not wanting to give her any information first.

"All the murders, it turns out, were connected through a website, which set up romantic getaways for couples in Scotland. Each of the female victims had ties to the Buttermilk Guild. The third murder setup was for a romantic dinner at a haunted castle. The killer came at the detective with a knife, but earlier, the Buttermilk Guild had set up trip wires to *trip* up the killer. Apparently, the killer was going to make it look like a murder-suicide—a stabbing and a hanging. He'd already positioned a noose over an exposed beam." She paused, watching Rory's face to see if any of this matched up with Leo's murder. "Well, does any of this sound like the crime scene?"

"Only the castle and the knife. But no rope," Rory confided.

"Either the murderer didn't have a chance to get the noose placed in time, or perhaps Leo's murder was a crime of passion."

"A crime of passion?" Diana asked. "The only person I can think who might want Leo dead is Marta. He might be the one who set fire to her bed. Where was she when it happened?"

"She said she was on the balcony having a cigarette."

"Do McCartney and MacTaggart corroborate her story?"

"My team admits they lost track of her for a moment. They reported she had gone to the restroom. Instead, she gave them the slip."

"Sounds suspicious," Diana said.

"I don't know," Rory replied. "When I was interviewing her, Marta said she needed space, that she was getting a headache from the music and the noise from the *céilidh*. She complained that McCartney and MacTaggart were hovering. Then she demanded to have Declan and Tavon added onto her detail." Rory rolled his eyes. "Declan and Tavon are too polite to tell her to shove off and keep her advances to herself."

Rory gave Diana a look, as if he was reliving how she'd put the moves on Declan.

Diana knew she'd acted stupidly and impulsively, but she wasn't going to apologize again. She gave Rory a hard stare to convey her sentiment. She wouldn't tell him that, even though Declan was certainly good-looking, it was DCI Crannach who did *it* for her.

Rory looked away, as if his murder board was off in the distance. "Perhaps I've been going at this all wrong. Maybe Marta's been committing these murders to give her new book and the series some major exposure."

"But why kill off her boyfriend—both current and ex?" she said.

"Publicity? Sympathy from the public? I don't know," Rory

said.

"That sounds like her," Diana said. "Marta has been brilliant in guiding the marketing team on how to showcase her, which has increased sales." But killing off the Buttermilk Guild for no good reason that Diana could see seemed like an epic fail. "Or maybe Marta needed a clean slate to make room for someone new. Perhaps there's a man waiting in the wings and she didn't want Rance or Leo interfering."

"Well," Rory said, "I'm putting Marta on the suspect list. She could have pushed Tilly into the carding machine. We've seen how she treats her."

"If Marta is behind all the murders, she'd have to be a criminal mastermind," Diana said.

"I agree." He pulled his notebook from his pocket. "I'm going to go through all her statements again and look for inconsistencies." He didn't open the notebook, though. "I'll need to be fresh to do it. I'm completely wiped out from nearly no sleep last night."

She could read his mind. Last night wasn't the only night in which he'd lost sleep. The two previous nights, they'd stayed up way past their bedtimes.

Diana touched his arm. "Do you want me to get McCartney or MacTaggart for you? So you can tell them what you're thinking about Marta?"

He laid a hand over hers and squeezed. "Nay. I'll go with ye to Quilting Central. I need to speak with Lorna, and I want to be there when the quilters leave. It shouldn't be too much longer. I'll talk to my team then."

"Okay. I'll see you there." She started toward the walkway leading to Duncan's Den.

Rory pulled her to a stop. "For a smart lass, ye're not very cautious. Remember the buddy system? I don't want ye to go anywhere alone."

"P_t." Didn't he know it was his fault she was a little ad-"
"being near him frazzled her brain."

d_y held on to her hand the rest of the way to Duncan's and opened the door.

I'll only be a minute to put my things away."

Rory went with her to the bedroom. She thought he might stay at the door and stand guard. Instead, he came in and shut the door. Her heart went giddy with anticipation.

He chuckled. "I see that look in yere eyes, lass. We haven't the time and I haven't the energy. Ye've worn me out."

"Then why close the door?" she asked, feeling let down and a bit rejected.

He crossed the room in three steps and pulled her into his arms. "For this." He bent his head down and kissed her. It was a crazy hot kiss, saying a lot more than his words had. When he was done, he pulled back a little. It wasn't just his lips that had some meaning to get across, his eyes were doing double duty, too, searching hers. "Ye needed a reminder of how a *real man* kisses. Especially after last night's debacle with Declan." Rory had tacked the last on the end, as if this one-sided conversation would put the matter to rest forever.

"Yeah," she breathed out. She agreed. Rory knew his way around her lips. "Right."

Laughing and looking satisfied with his powers of persuasion, he placed his hands on her shoulders and spun her back to the overnight bag she'd brought with her. "Put yere things away. I'll be waiting in the living room. Then we can get to Quilting Central."

It only took a moment before she was meeting up with him. When she walked into the living room, he was standing by the mantel, looking as if he was deep in thought. The man took her breath away! The fog from his kiss was only just beginning to clear and a thought was emerging.

"Are we alone?" she asked.

He looked up. "No one here but us."

"I was thinking more about your theory—that Marta m_ be behind the murders. Certainly she's cunning enough and, . I might add, malicious enough, at times. But if she did commit the murders, she is one hell of an actress. She seems truly upset over Leo's murder."

Rory shrugged. "I've seen plenty of criminals lie, put on a believable show, and still be as guilty as sin." He followed her out the door.

"You're right. I don't have firsthand knowledge of criminals." Though her dad certainly had. "I won't tell anyone of your suspicions. Or anything that we've discussed."

"I know you won't," Rory said.

Though the temperature outside was dropping, his trust in her was warming.

Diana's phone dinged. A text from Nicola at Three Seals.

CALL ME. WE NEED TO TALK.

There was no indication whether Nicola had good news or bad. Which was bad news for Diana, as she wished she had some assurances to offer Tilly.

"Is everything okay?" Rory asked.

"I need to call the office."

"Come." He put a hand to her back. "Let's get ye out of the cold first." He looked down at her short skirt. "Ye're going to have to dress warmer if ye plan to stay in Scotland."

She wheeled around to see if he was saying what she thought he was saying. Did he want her in Scotland for longer than just this job?

He only smiled, which cleared nothing up.

"Yes, well," she stammered, trying to pull herself together. "I'm a New York *lass* and I'm perfectly warm." Though the cold was starting to get to her. Or maybe it was her nerves. She turned back around and rushed to Quilting Central.

Once inside, she found the quilters putting on their coats.

"We're off to lunch," Deydie announced. "Hurry now. Dominic has the pasta almost ready and fresh bread is hot from the oven, too."

Rory stared at Diana apologetically. She understood he had to go to the restaurant to keep an eye on his new suspect.

"I'll be okay," she said. "I'm going to stay here and make that call."

Rory turned to MacTaggart. "Ye'll stay with her."

His words said he wanted her safe.

The tone behind them said he cared.

And the part of her that knew best didn't want him to feel something for her. They were just having a little Scottish fling, right? She also didn't want to care about him either. But she did. It was an impossible situation on so many levels. But mostly, she was in way over her head...in the deep end of the pool without a life jacket and no idea how to paddle to safe water.

MacTaggart wandered over to the coffee maker, while she settled herself on the sofa in the library area and waited for the call to connect.

"Nicola Jacobson here."

"Hi, it's Diana. What's the news? Did you read over the promo plan I sent you?"

"Yes. Marketing is taking a look at it now. They want more detail on how you plan to position the sister—since she would be coming out as the author now."

Diana thought that was encouraging. "I'll get right on it."

"*Dream sequence*," Nicola scoffed, which dashed Diana's rising hope that the Buttermilk Guild would ride again.

"Anything else?" Diana said, wanting to get off the phone so she could start on the new request.

"Yes," Nicola said. "Where's the footage you promised of Cait Buchanan interviewing Marta? And I hope you had the good sense to have Graham Buchanan sitting next to his wife."

Diana pointed out the obvious. "We've had a lot going on here with the murders. But we're back in Gandiegow now and we'll start the interviews today."

"You'll get them to me by 8 am tomorrow, New York time," Nicola said before she hung up.

Diana stared at the phone.

"All done?" asked MacTaggart, who sipped his coffee as he walked to the library area.

"Yeah." Diana was probably going to be fired over how this launch had gone. "I'm ready to go to the restaurant." Though she didn't think she could eat.

"I'm ready, too. I need something more substantial."

MacTaggart didn't realize it, but he'd hit the nail on the head. Diana needed something more substantial, too. *Not food*. But in life.

She'd always loved her job, but it wasn't fulfilling her like it used to.

She was in a semi-quasi relationship that wasn't going anywhere. Maybe once or twice, she'd fantasized about taking her fling with Rory to the next level, but the truth was there wasn't a next level. An ocean lay between them. And even more of an impediment...Diana didn't want to end up alone like her mother, when Rory ended up like her father...dead. As would surely happen. It was best to end things now with Rory and quit waffling back and forth.

She picked up her bag and headed out. She understood now, if she was going to have a relationship, she wanted someone like Rory. The world was full of people. Surely there was someone out there who would fit her requirements. *Rory-like*, but not as gallant. Someone who shied away from harm's way. Someone who wouldn't stand in front of another to take a bullet.

Suddenly, as if a spotlight had been illuminated on the truth, Diana realized that Rory was her soulmate. *But that doesn't change a thing.* She couldn't be with him. Soulmate or not, she couldn't end up with a cop. For the rest of her life, she'd cling to the memories of this time in Scotland, of being with him; these memories would keep her company in the days and years ahead. She just couldn't fool herself any longer. She couldn't both have him and preserve who she was.

Melancholy covered her, as if it was a second skin. She had to walk away from Rory. Starting now.

With purpose, she trudged to Pastas & Pastries and was proud of herself for not glancing in Rory's direction when she got there. She pulled out Parker's camera and recorded Marta chatting with the quilters, showing off how much Marta liked the everyday woman and how much they liked her.

Tilly sidled up beside her, checking for eavesdroppers as if they were plotting to overthrow the country.

"Have you heard back from Three Seals about you-know-what?"

Diana nodded solemnly.

"What did they say?" Tilly said eagerly.

"Marketing is looking at it." Remembering Nicola's tone on the phone, Diana put the camera on the table and gave Tilly her full attention. "You have to understand, there is no precedent for what we're suggesting. Publishers tend to play it safe. Even though Nicola asked for a promo plan, I'm not sure she's completely onboard with continuing the Quilt to Death series and calling the current book just a 'bad dream.' We should remain cautiously optimistic, and no more. Three Seals has made no promises."

Tilly's face fell, going from happy and expectant to utter

disappointment. She said nothing, just walked away.

Diana felt awful and started to go after her. But reassuring her that all would be well would only be self-serving, even cruel, if their plan to continue the Quilt to Death series didn't pan out. Diana's heart hurt for Tilly as the older woman's shoulders resumed their usual slump.

19

RORY COULDN'T HELP wondering what Tilly and Diana were talking about. After Tilly slunk away, he walked over to Diana and said the first thing that came to mind, forgetting he should've installed a filter first. "Do ye want to join me for my lie down?" At least no one was close by to hear his proposition.

Several emotions played out on her face. She seemed to be a lass at war with herself. "Sorry," she finally said. "Can't. I need to take video of Marta."

"Ye can video Marta later."

"No time. Later I have to tape Cait's interview with Marta in which she reveals Gandiegow as the inspiration for the series. We're leaving Gandiegow tomorrow."

"What?" *No!* There was still so much more he wanted to investigate about his relationship with Diana. Like...why he felt a little dizzy when she was around. And why his chest was tight, whenever he thought of her.

"After the quilters leave, I'll try to talk Marta into going up the bluff to get some scenic shots, too, before the interviews."

Rory knew the cemetery was up there and a cold chill passed through him.

"I don't want ye alone with her. Do ye hear?"

"And that should wrap things up here in Scotland." Diana went right on, like she was reciting lines in a play. "We'll be out of your hair in no time at all."

But I want you to stay!

"I'm sorry for the trouble we've brought to Scotland."

"Don't go!" he blurted. Emotion ripped through him, making him feel weak, powerless. He had to convince her. "Ye could hang around a bit longer, couldn't ye?" He felt like an idiot. "I could use you to bounce ideas off of--."

She flinched when he said *use*.

But he plowed on. "To talk about the case." He felt desperate.

She'd recovered, her mask firmly in place, covering the hurt he'd caused her. "You don't need me. You have everything under control."

I have nothing under control! He placed his fists on his hips. "I'm worried about your safety." He should've said he cared about her instead of acting like a police officer. But he couldn't help himself. "Who's going to watch out for you once you leave?"

"I'll be fine." Her worried expression made a brief appearance before going undercover once again. "I'm a New Yorker. Caution is second nature to me."

"I wonder if Bettus or Shamley might've said the same thing," Rory retorted. Anything to make her see the error in her logic.

She clutched the video camera. "I need to get back to work. Have a nice nap."

How could he? She wasn't going to be in his arms. Protected. Out of harm's way. For the first time, the job didn't feel like it was enough. He wanted more. But Diana had walked away.

She'd been clear. *I don't date cops. Period.* But couldn't she make an exception just this once?

He wouldn't ask her. One of the things he loved about her was her steeliness.

"Love?" He actually said it out loud. Was that what this was? "Well, hell." He didn't need to investigate his feelings to figure out what had him twisted into knots. Love had whacked him in the gut. "So, this is what it feels like."

Awful.

And wonderful.

He just had to convince her to stay in Scotland with him. For him.

He took one more look at her before heading back to Duncan's Den to sleep for a few hours. But no longer than that. Sleep was not going to help him face this challenge. But sleep would help him to say and do the right thing. For he had to say it right, do it right. He had to make Diana fall in love with him, too.

⳩

Diana walked around the café with the camera, feeling lost and not sure what to shoot. When she did raise the camera and point it in Marta's direction her hands were shaking too much to actually record anything. Why did she let Rory unsettle her so?

Over in the corner she saw Tilly looking as white as a ghost and as shaken up as Diana felt.

I should've really watched my words with her.

Tilly reached in her pocket but came up empty. Diana raised the camera and focused on Tilly's face, confirming the tears in her eyes. Tilly dug around in her bag before finally producing a packet of tissues. In the process, other items had tumbled out—one of Marta's bright scarves, a hand-stitching project, a notebook, and a small case with TOURNIQUET stamped on it in large capital letters. Diana zoomed in as Tilly scrambled for the tourniquet case, shoving it back into the bag first while allowing Marta's silk scarf to hit the floor.

Why did Tilly have a tourniquet? Did Marta have some kind of medical condition?

Diana focused on Tilly's face and was surprised and shocked to see Tilly glaring back at her.

She'd been around the Dixon sisters nearly around the clock and had thought Tilly was cut from a different cloth than Marta. But not now. Tilly didn't look as meek as Diana thought she was. In this moment, she looked like Marta and capable of the same emotional outbursts. Diana lowered the camera to her side, thinking about how she could smooth things over with Tilly. Diana started toward her, but Marta intervened by saying, "Tilly, get me an aspirin." Marta looked awful today. The trip to the wilds of Scotland appeared to have taken its toll on her. She seemed like a woman at her wit's end, her expression sour and her white suit looking like crumpled paper from the bus ride.

Maybe Marta looked like death-warmed-over because she'd killed off the series that was beloved by so many. Or maybe her guilt was about the murders, as Rory now suspected.

Diana pulled out her murder board notebook and wrote this down so she'd remember to run it past Rory later. And just because she had her notebook out, she added Tilly's tourniquet to the list of things Diana wanted to discuss with him.

"Aren't ye going to eat?"

Diana jumped at Deydie's words. "Not hungry. Especially after the scare you've just given me!"

Deydie harrumphed. "Ye need to keep up yere strength. A lass has to eat in this weather. I can feel in me old bones that snow is coming."

Diana glanced out the window but saw nothing. "This evening, I'd like to get some video of you making the Puffin quilt. Does that work for you?"

Deydie grinned. "Aye. I'm ready for me close-up."

Diana laughed. "What do you think? Is it time now to hand out the final giveaways?"

Deydie's grin was gone and her businesslike demeanor was back. "That's correct, lassie. The women will be leaving shortly."

Diana—still on a mission to apologize to Tilly—had to go to Marta instead.

"Are you ready to do the final giveaway? The parting gifts are set out over there." Diana motioned to the table by the front door.

Marta rose. "If I must."

Deydie joined Marta and hollered to get everyone's attention. "The citizens of Gandiegow have a few surprises for you before you go."

Marta looked confused. Diana felt a bit confused, too.

"Moira, tell Dominic and Claire that it's time," Deydie said.

Moira pushed back the swinging door to the restaurant's kitchen. "Deydie said she's ready."

Dominic and Claire each came out of the kitchen carrying a tray stacked with boxes.

"We're sending ye home with some delicious treats," Deydie said. "Compliments of Pastas & Pastries and the quilters of Gandiegow."

The retreat goers clapped as Dominic and Claire passed out the boxes.

"Pipe down," Deydie said. "We've another prize for ye. Each

one of you is getting a ticket to Gandiegow's first murder mystery dinner. We'll have a silent auction first to raise money for our new lifeboat, and then a murder to solve while we eat."

Diana thought this struck a little too close to home, but it *was* for charity.

"We're going to call it, *Kilt at Christmas*." Deydie said--smiling rather ghoulishly, Diana thought. "I named it meself."

Bethia and Moira walked among the tables handing out the tickets while Rachel stood and added, "Please let me know if you'd like to stay the night after the murder mystery dinner. Partridge House and the quilting dorms will fill up quickly for the event. Sooner is better than later."

"Thanks," Deydie said. "Well, ladies, I'll turn things over now to Marta Dixon."

Marta straightened her scarf, then lifted one of the bags with both hands like she was Mufasa in *The Lion King*. "I've put together a little something for you to take home." Her smile was full of fake benevolence.

The quilters beamed and several of them shouted, "Thanks, Marta." Diana was sure these ladies didn't give a whit about Marta's sincerity as long as there was free fabric beneath the perfectly arranged tissue paper sticking up out of the bags.

She put her hand up to get their attention. "I hope all of you will send me pictures of your completed quilts. My card is in each of your goody bags."

"Come on, ladies," Deydie said. "Time to get off yere arses. Yere coach is waiting to take ye home."

The women rose and headed for the coatrack and then the exit. Marta handed each a sack and thanked them as they departed.

Relieved that the quilters were finishing the retreat unharmed, Diana followed the group out to the parking lot, and wished each one well as they stepped up onto the bus.

When the bus left, Diana turned around to find that Rory had joined them. He looked good, all sexy in his stubble, but his serious face was back. Understandably, as he still had a series of murders to solve. And Diana was going home tomorrow. Suddenly, she didn't feel as relieved as she'd felt moments ago. She felt lonely and wanted nothing more than to reach out and touch him. But she couldn't.

She could, however, get him alone to discuss the case. At least in this one thing, they could connect -- and without her heart in danger of breaking.

"Everyone back to Quilting Central." Deydie glanced over at Diana. "Unless ye have more important things to do."

Since Deydie gave her permission, Diana turned to Rory. "Do you have a couple of minutes to discuss the case?" She made sure to speak at a normal volume to let those around her know that things were on the up-and-up.

Rory raised an eyebrow. "Is that code?" Apparently, he didn't care about the curious glances the Gandiegow quilters were giving them.

Diana rolled her eyes. "I really have some things to talk to you about." She gave him a hard look, hoping he would understand her seriousness.

"Sure." He pointed toward the back of the village. "Let's speak at Duncan's Den."

The two of them walked away from the others and started making their way to the quilting dorm.

While they walked, he glanced over at Diana. "Ye look worried. Is everything okay?"

"Fine."

"Tell me what's going on."

"It's this sense that we're missing something," Diana said, as they hurried along the cobblestones. "I can't quite put my finger on it."

He looked over at her with his eyes squinted, as if he was trying to read her mind. "What happened while I was away?"

"Marta might have some kind of medical condition," she said.

When they arrived at Duncan's Den, he stepped up on the porch, but turned to face her so his back was to the door. "What makes ye say that?"

"Tilly is carrying a tourniquet around in her bag," Diana said. "She acted weird about it when *she saw* that *I saw*."

Rory's eyebrows went up.

"Can you think of a condition that Marta might have that would need a tourniquet?"

But Rory wasn't listening. He was looking over her shoulder, in the direction of the ocean. "You?"

"What?" Diana said.

"No!" Rory lunged, pushing Diana to the side, essentially tackling her at the same moment a shot rang out.

With the wind knocked out of her, Diana tried to move, but Rory was dead weight. "Get up!"

But he didn't budge. From where she lay, she saw blood on the corner of the porch. "Rory! No!" Her lungs were constricting from panic. "Help! Someone help me!" Blood was oozing from the side of his head.

Sobbing, she tried to slide out from underneath him. "Rory, wake up! Wake up!"

"Hold on, lass!" someone yelled in the distance. It sounded like Hamilton. She heard his footfalls coming nearer. "I'm right here."

He shifted Rory off her. "Are you all right? I heard a shot-gun."

"I'm fine, it's Rory!" she cried. "Is he okay?" She was looking at his bloody head, but then noticed his shoulder was bleeding, too. "Get the doctor!" Her voice was a near screech as she laid Rory's head in her lap.

Ham pulled out his phone and dialed. "Come to Duncan's Den. Now. The DCI has been shot. I'm calling 9-9-9 for an ambulance." He listened for a second, then looked over at Rory. "He's bleeding from his head and his left shoulder." He listened again. "Right. Got it." He hung up and rushed to Rory, squatting down and applying pressure to Rory's shoulder. He handed the phone to Diana.

"You call 9-9-9. Doc will be right here."

With shaking hands, she dialed the number.

"Put it on speaker," Ham said.

When the dispatcher answered, Ham explained what had happened and where the ambulance needed to go.

By now, Diana had the vague sense that others had arrived. Someone laid a quilt over Rory. *For shock,* she thought foggily.

But another thought was clear. So very clear. Rory was going to die. Shot to death. *Just like my father.*

ဆာ

Deydie heard the gun go off. They all had, all the quilters of Gandiegow. They all jolted to their feet.

"Did you hear that?" "What was it?" "Someone was probably shooting some pesky animal."

But dread came over Deydie. When she'd gone home earlier to get her good pair of scissors, she'd noticed her shotgun wasn't standing in the corner, where she kept it handy for deterring varmints who raided her garden. But there was no garden in November. She meant to say something to Rory, when she saw him, but she'd forgotten.

She headed toward the door, but halted when Ramsay burst through first. His face was all contorted.

"It's DCI Crannach. He's been shot," Ramsay said.

"Is he going to be all right?"

Deydie was glad Bethia asked because she was afraid if she tried to speak now, nothing would come out.

"I don't know. Doc is with him now, outside Duncan's Den."

Deydie pushed past him as other questions were shouted and raced for Duncan's Den, her old heart pounding. She liked Rory. He was a good lad. She would hate it if it was her gun that shot him. But deep down, she knew the truth. The gun was hers.

When she rushed down the wynd between cottages, the scene at a distance looked dire. Doc was crouched over Rory, and Diana was standing over them, crying. Deydie pushed herself harder to get there faster.

She went straight to Diana, who couldn't wipe the tears from her cheeks as quickly as they were falling.

When Diana saw Deydie, she ran to her and Deydie wrapped her in her arms. "There, there."

"He's been shot," Diana wailed. "And then he hit his head when he went down. It's all my fault!"

Deydie patted her back. "How can it be yere fault?"

"He hit his head because he jumped in front of the bullet, protecting me."

Deydie tsk'ed. "It's his job. His training. I suspect he would've done it for anyone in the village."

"But he's going to die!" Diana cried.

Deydie didn't like it that Doc didn't contradict her, only kept working on Rory's wounds. She made a split-second decision. "Diana, I'm taking ye to the bosom of Quilting Central." She couldn't have the lass going to the hospital with Doc; it looked like bad news for the lad. Besides, it was safer for Diana to stay in Gandiegow; safety in numbers. "We'll keep an eye on ye until this nightmare is over.

"I have to stay with Rory," Diana sobbed.

"No," Doc said. Apparently, he'd found his voice. "Go with Deydie. I'll text with updates."

For a second, Diana dug in her heels, but Rachel arrived, and together, they got Diana to Quilting Central. The whole way there, Deydie felt the need to confess that her rifle had gone missing. But unfortunately, the one person she wanted to tell was the police officer who was unconscious. *If I can't speak with Rory, then I'll tell his men, MacTaggart and McCartney.*

But that wasn't enough. Her sin in keeping silent couldn't be washed away with speaking with mortal men. She needed an intercessory to the Almighty. Episcopalians didn't practice *confession* as part of the faith. But Deydie's old soul needed absolution anyway.

She glanced over at her quilters, who surrounded Diana. She was safe and sound. Deydie grabbed her peacoat and buttoned it to her chin as she headed back outside. She needed to see Father Andrew and tell him how she'd been a stupid old fool.

20

WITH CELLPHONE IN HAND, Diana sat in a stupor on the loveseat at Quilting Central. Deydie and Bethia flanked her, and Cait, Rachel, and Sadie buzzed around her, asking if there was anything they could do. Marta and Tilly sat across the room with MacTaggart, who was keeping guard. Marta looked upset, while Tilly stared vacantly at the floor.

Diana glanced down at the phone she was gripping so tightly it hurt. She willed it to ring with good news. If only she could talk to him, one more time before he died. And though it was futile, for Rory surely wasn't going to make it, she opened TEXT MESSAGES on her phone and began to type.

> I'M SORRY, RORY, FOR WASTING OUR TIME TOGETHER. INSTEAD OF SAVORING EVERY MOMENT, I SPENT EVERY SECOND PUSHING YOU AWAY. I RUINED EVERYTHING, BECAUSE I WAS SCARED THAT I WOULD LOSE YOU. I KNOW YOU'LL NEVER HAVE A CHANCE TO READ THESE WORDS, BUT I'M GOING TO TELL YOU ANYWAY. I LOVE YOU.

Tears dripped on her phone. She hit SEND. Then she looked around to see if anyone had seen how foolish she'd been.

She felt helpless, waiting to hear the inevitable, that Rory was dead. From off in the distance, she heard a siren. Something inside her stirred to life. She had to be with him, no matter what any of them said. Whether he was dead or alive, Diana had to be by his side.

With so many people watching her, there was no escape route, but she did see an excuse to leave her chaperones. She stood. "I have to use the restroom."

"I'll go with ye," Bethia offered.

"No. Please. I need privacy." Diana tried to look sincere. "I'll only be a minute," she lied.

Bethia and Deydie stared at her for a long moment.

"Go ahead," Deydie finally said, as if giving permission to a child. "Don't be long."

Bethia frowned at Deydie, as if she had an idea of what Diana might be up to.

Diana walked to the bathroom slowly, deliberately. Once the door was closed behind her, she rushed to the window and pushed up the sash. The window was small, but she felt certain she could get through. The siren had stopped, which meant she didn't have much time.

She stuck her head out the window and then had to maneuver the rest of her body through. She ignored the pinch of her belly and the tearing of her tights as she awkwardly crumpled to the ground on the other side, rolling in the dirt in the process. Finally, she made it to her feet, while dusting as much of the guck off as possible. When she glanced up, five of the Gandiegow quilters were waiting for her—Deydie, Bethia, Cait, Rachel, and Sadie.

Diana calculated whether she could push her way through them, but Deydie had her broom raised like she was ready to take a swing if Diana moved.

"What do ye think ye're doing?" Deydie asked.

"I—I—"

Bethia shook her head. "Ye have to stay here with us. There's nothing ye can do. Ye can't ride in the ambulance and no one is going to let ye drive in yere condition."

Cait and Sadie came forward together, slowly, as if afraid Diana might bolt. Which is exactly what she'd planned to do. The two reached out and latched on to her arms, both steadying her and making sure she stayed put.

"I have to see Rory!" Diana cried. "I have to go with him."

"I know you want to—" Cait started.

"Ye can't," Bethia reiterated. "Doc will call with news and will let us know when we should come to the hospital."

"I'm afraid I'm never going to see him again alive."

Deydie leaned her broom against the wall. "We'll all go together then." She led the way.

Cait and Sadie walked beside Diana with Bethia, Deydie, and Rachel bringing up the rear.

Unfortunately, when Duncan's Den came into view, Rory was gone. Doc, too. Only McCartney remained, taking pictures of a chalked outline.

Diana ran the rest of the way, shouting to McCartney, "How long have they been gone?"

McCartney pointed in the direction of the parking lot. "A few minutes."

Without looking back or asking permission, Diana took off. But halfway to the edge of town, the siren started up its wail again before slowly beginning to fade.

Diana wanted to wail, too. She kept running, even though she knew the ambulance had to be halfway up the bluff by now.

When she got to the parking lot, it was empty.

Her heart ached. She'd failed to see Rory. What if he'd come to and she'd missed her opportunity to tell him in person everything she felt in her heart? How her life was forever changed because of him. How he might be the most perfect man for her. And how she couldn't imagine going on without him.

She was breathing hard, and then hyperventilating.

The quilters arrived. Bethia laid a hand on her back and made Diana bend over.

"It's okay, Lass. It's going to be okay. Doc is with him."

But Diana understood how bullets ended lives. They'd ended her father's. In a way, her mother's too, as she'd never found love again.

Bethia pulled out her phone. "I'll text Doc right now and tell him to give us an update as soon as he can."

Deydie wrapped her arm around Diana's waist. "Let's get back to Quilting Central. Ye're going to freeze to death without yere coat." Deydie slipped out of hers and put it around Diana's shoulders. But it only brought back memories of wearing Rory's oversized coat.

Feeling defeated, Diana went along quietly with the quilters. The sea was calm, as if in deference to what had happened in Gandiegow today.

When they arrived at Quilting Central, Diana picked up her notebook and went to one of the tables to sit alone. Deydie and Bethia brought her a hot drink and a sandwich but she didn't touch them.

Diana twisted around to see who was left in Quilting Central and knocked her notebook to the floor. It fell open to her murder board. As she glanced at it and began scribbling, trying to draw parallels and get insight into who had shot Rory and was committing these murders.

A fire burned within. She would find the person who was avenging the Buttermilk Guild. She would put an end to this madness. If Deydie or anyone else tried to stop her, Diana would use Deydie's broom to ward them off.

Diana glanced over at Marta before compiling a list of questions for her. She wished she had access to Rory's notebook, the one he'd used during all the interviews he'd conducted.

A crazy idea came to her. Maybe his notepad had fallen out of his pocket during the shooting! She popped up and hurried for the door.

Deydie, apparently, had brought her broom inside, because she held it out now, blocking the doorway. "Ye're not going anywhere. We're to keep ye safe...here."

Ham walked through the door at that moment, stopping short at the sight of the broom.

"I'll take Ham with me for protection," Diana said impulsively. "I won't be gone long."

Deydie squinted at Diana, as if trying to read her mind. "Where do you mean to go?"

"Duncan's Den," Diana said honestly.

Hamilton nodded. "Aye. I can watch over her."

Deydie raised the broom like a drawbridge and let Diana pass through to the door.

Once outside, Ham gave her a sympathetic look. "Are ye all right?"

"I'm fine." Though Diana felt a sense of urgency.

"Ye've been through an ordeal--" he began.

"No." *Not me. Rory's the one who's been through an ordeal. And is fighting for his life.* "Let's hurry." Diana wanted to get this over with and then back to Quilting Central to see if there'd been any word from Doc MacGregor.

When they arrived at Duncan's Den, McCartney was standing outside, holding his phone to his ear. He said goodbye and hung up.

"Was that about Rory?" she asked.

He shook his head. "Forensics will be here in an hour. Unless there's cattle in the road like last time."

As inconspicuously as possible, Diana looked at the ground, her eyes darting here and there, hoping to see Rory's notebook lying in the bushes. *Why couldn't McCartney have been inside?* If she found the notebook, it might be considered evidence. At the very least, it was police property, and McCartney wouldn't let her have it.

"What are ye looking for, Ms. McKellan?" McCartney asked.

She cursed his keen observation.

She didn't see the notebook and decided it couldn't hurt to ask. "The Detective Chief Inspector's notebook. I was wondering if it fell out when he was...when he was..." She just couldn't bring herself to say *when he was shot.* She hated to think that Rory had taken a bullet for her, though she wasn't sure if she was the target or not. *Another item I'll have to add to my list.*

McCartney glanced around, too. "I haven't seen it. But it's an excellent question. When the hospital calls, I'll see if it's with the DCI's belongings." He eyed her closely. "Was there something else you needed?"

She shook her head, trying to cover her disappointment. "No. Just wondering if it had been found. Thanks for letting me know. If you hear anything about—" she'd almost said *Rory* "—the Detective Chief Inspector, will you let me know?"

"Aye. As soon as I know anything," McCartney promised.

"Thanks." She turned around and walked back to Quilting Central with Hamilton as her escort. She felt more determined than ever to find the killer on her own.

As she opened the door to Quilting Central, her eyes searched for Marta and found her sipping coffee with Cait. Diana went to her, grabbing the video camera from the table as she passed.

"Any word on Rory?" Cait asked. She didn't seem concerned about using his first name.

"Not yet," Diana said.

"It's too soon anyway," Cait said. "They probably haven't made it to the hospital yet."

That thought didn't ease Diana's fear.

"Here. Come sit," Cait said, looking concerned. She must've seen the blood drain from Diana's face.

Diana shook her head. "I can't. I'm on a mission. Marta? I need you." Diana held up the camera.

Reluctantly, Marta rose. "What do you want from me this time?"

"I want to take some footage of you working with the quilters." *And ask you a million questions.* Diana looked around the room. "Where's Tilly?"

"I'm not my sister's keeper." But then Marta frowned, as if giving in. "I don't know. She's probably in the restroom."

"Speaking of Tilly," Diana said nonchalantly. "Why does your sister carry a tourniquet with her?"

Marta rolled her eyes. "It's Tilly being Tilly."

"That's not much of an explanation."

"Tilly says it's part of her EDC."

"What's an EDC?" Diana asked.

Marta was clearly irritated, like she'd been asked to explain something to an idiot. "EDC means EVERY DAY CARRY. You see the bag she lugs around."

"I assumed it contained items for you," Diana said.

"Yes, some, but other things in there are for emergencies." Marta leaned closer to Diana. "Tilly's a little paranoid. She is constantly reading about crimes and murders and it's made her..." Marta's index finger circled near her temple, making the universal sign for crazy. "Wacky."

"So what's the tourniquet for?" Diana pushed. She remembered how angry Tilly had seemed when she saw Diana staring at it.

"I don't know," Marta said. "Tilly took a course in first aid, so she'd be prepared for anything."

Just then, Tilly emerged from the restroom with her large bag looped over her shoulder. She looked like a woman who had been beaten down by life. Maybe having her EDC helped her feel better, Diana surmised. As if she had some control over her life.

"Thanks, Marta," Diana said.

"For what?" Marta asked.

"Just because," Diana said. "Now, can you go stand by Deydie and Bethia? Pretend you're discussing how to make the Gandiegow Rosette quilt."

Marta did as she was asked, while Diana raised her camera and hit record. Just then, Bethia's phone rang. The elderly woman took it out of her pocket and answered.

Diana rushed over, forgetting all about the camera. "Is it about Rory?"

Bethia nodded, while listening intently. "Aye. Thanks for calling." She hung up.

"What is it?" Diana said, bracing herself for bad news.

"They've made it to the hospital," Bethia answered.

"And?" Diana wanted to shake the nice woman.

Bethia gave Diana a look of deep concern. "DCI Crannach is still unconscious. He's being examined now, and a surgery theatre is being prepared to remove the bullet fragments. There's really nothing else to report."

Diana was in a tug-of-war with herself, wanting to be by Rory's side, but also determined to solve this case.

Bethia rubbed her back. "As soon as Doc MacGregor lets us know that DCI Crannach is out of surgery, we'll go to the hospital."

"Does that mean Rory's going to be okay?"

Bethia gave her a sad kind of look. "We don't know yet, lass. To be honest Doc and the others are concerned that the lad hasn't woken up yet."

Diana went cold, as if the chill of death had passed through her. There was no denying the truth—Rory wasn't going to make it.

"Ye need to go lie down," Deydie commanded. "Ham will take ye. Bethia and Sadie will go with ye, too."

Tilly hurried over. "I'll go with ye." She looked over at Marta.

"Tilly, you don't have to come," Diana protested. "Stay here in case Marta needs you. Maybe you could take some video for me?" She held out the camera.

Tilly gently pushed the camera back to Diana. "I'd rather go. Marta says I'm hovering."

"Okay," Diana acquiesced, knowing Tilly needed a break from her sister, too.

Sadie grabbed her sewing basket. "I'll do some hand-stitching while ye rest."

But Diana wasn't planning on resting. She intended to work on her murder board, and dig into Marta's motives and opportunity for the murders.

Hamilton escorted them all to Duncan's Den and then left for the dock. Once inside, Bethia made a beeline for the kitchen, while Diana snuck off to her bedroom to be alone.

She laid the camera on the side table before pulling back her Gandiegow Library quilt and climbing underneath. She propped her head against the Kilts & Quilts sham that she'd made. At least she had these good things to remember Scotland by.

There was a knock at her door. Diana shoved her notebook under her quilt. "Come in."

Tilly entered with a tray and a mug of something steaming. "Bethia made you a cup of herbal tea to help you rest."

"Thanks." Diana didn't want to rest, but the liquid smelled

so inviting—lavender and chamomile—that she took a sip.

"Have a nice nap," Tilly said and quietly left the room.

Diana sipped and sipped at the delicious tea before downing the whole cup. As she went to set the mug on the side table, she had an interesting thought. *What if there's some hidden evidence on the video?*

She set the camera on her lap. But before she could start the playback, Diana felt overcome by sleepiness. She leaned her head back on the pillow.

But something was off. She felt foggy, too. Everything seemed to be going dark.

Off in a distant part of her mind, Diana wondered if Bethia or Tilly had drugged her. But before she could examine the thought any further, Diana slipped into blackness.

∽Ը∾

With night falling quickly, Ham pulled anchor on Brodie's boat and headed back to Gandiegow. He was glad he'd offered to do the evening haul for his friend. It was good Brodie and Rachel were getting out of the village for a date night, especially since their home had been the scene of a crime. Things in Gandiegow had been seriously screwed up since Marta Dixon and her entourage had arrived.

Gandiegow from the water was a sight to behold—idyllic, charming—and he was proud to be a life-long resident. As the darkness fell, streetlamps flickered on, glowing green at first, before turning to bright white. The cottages' windows lit up, too. From this distance, Ham could just make out the outline of his own boat that he shared with his brother. He was glad the boat was seaworthy again because no fisherman liked being anchored to the land for too long. But while he'd been on the water this evening, he couldn't help but worry about what had been happening back in the village. Although the view of

Gandiegow from the sea was beautiful, he was anxious to get to shore.

As he got closer, he saw a woman standing by the street-lamp, the one that sat closest to the harbor. The woman was smoking a cigarette and he could tell from her stance that it was Marta Dixon. She was looking toward the sea, with her back to the village.

What is she doing outside all alone? But it didn't exactly surprise Ham. Marta was always trying to slip away from him to have a private smoke. He guessed she'd given MacTaggart or McCartney the slip, too.

Ham steamed toward shore, ready to give Marta a piece of his mind. Hadn't the village seen enough calamity since she'd arrived? He certainly didn't want her to be the next victim.

As his boat chugged nearer, Ham saw a fisherman approaching Marta from behind, wearing Wellies and dressed in black raingear. *One of the locals was probably going to tell her to get her arse back to Quilting Central.* But as the fisherman got closer, he raised a long pole. *What the hell is he doing?*

Ham got the awful feeling that the fisherman wasn't there to protect Marta, but to waylay her.

Ham reached for the cord of the foghorn and gave it three short tugs. The low booming of the horn burst into the silent night and halted the fisherman, who turned to see what was making the noise. Ham tried to make out his face, but from this distance, he couldn't work out the features from under the fisherman's hood. The fisherman didn't wait around but ran off. Marta seemed annoyed at Ham's foghorn for wrecking her respite. As casual as can be, she dropped her cigarette on the concrete walkway, ground it out with the toe of her shoe, and then sauntered away. Without picking up the stub.

Ham pulled the boat into the harbor and tied off quickly.

He scrambled out, knowing he had to put the town on high alert. He made a split decision, running for Quilting Central, hoping Marta hadn't been accosted on her way there.

He yanked open the door, but didn't see Marta inside. Instead, he saw MacTaggart.

"Where's Marta?" Ham asked, out of breath.

"At Partridge House."

"Why is she at Partridge House? I thought she was to stay at Duncan's Den."

"She said she wanted more privacy. McCartney and I helped her and Tilly move their things over. Marta kicked us out so she could unpack *in peace*. McCartney is standing guard outside the B and B now."

"That was a mistake," Ham said urgently. "Ye need to go check to make sure Marta is all right."

"What's going on?" MacTaggart asked.

"As I was coming into the harbor, I saw a fisherman gettin' ready to attack Marta with some kind of weapon," Ham explained.

"Did ye get a good look at him?" MacTaggart asked. "What was he wearing?"

"Black raincoat. Black Wellies. He was tall. But I couldn't see his face, as the hood was up."

MacTaggart pulled out his notebook and jotted down his notes. "Tell me about the weapon."

"It looked like a pole," Ham said.

"Like a harpoon?" MacTaggart asked.

"No. He wasn't holding it like he was going to shoot Marta, but more like he was going to knock her over the head." Ham's eyes caught Deydie's broom leaning against the wall. "If I had to guess, I would say it was the size of a broom."

"A broom?" MacTaggart said.

"I know it sounds weird, but that's what it looked like from the deck of my boat," Ham replied, wishing he had more to report.

"Who in town wears black raingear?" MacTaggart asked.

Ham looked down at his own bright yellow gear. "Most of us wear yellow or orange. Only a few wear black." A sinking feeling came over him. He wished he'd taken a moment to gather his thoughts before reporting what he saw.

"What are their names?" MacTaggart asked.

It didn't feel right to rat out his fellow fishermen, but on the other hand Ham wanted the attacks on Gandiegow to stop. "Brodie Wallace, Ramsay Armstrong, and my brother, Gregor."

"Good. Do any of them resemble the man ye saw?"

"Well, all of them are tall." *Every blasted one of them, Gregor included.*

"Now, tell me where we can find these fishermen," MacTaggart said.

Why had Ham run in here, telling his tale, without thinking about the implications? He should've spoken to Gregor, Brodie, and Ramsay first. "I expect Gregor is at home. Ask Rachel—over there—where Brodie is. And Ramsay, well, he might be at home with his wife Kit, four cottages down."

MacTaggart wrote it in his notepad. "I'll check in with McCartney first to make sure Marta is okay. Then, I'll hunt down the owner of the black raingear. I'd like nothing more than to hand over the killer to Rory when he wakes up."

Ham had to say something. "I can vouch for all three men. Good blokes, all of them." Ham was worried the police might jump the gun and pin the crimes on them. He was sure the police were frustrated with the unsolved murders. "None of them could kill anyone. None of them have motive."

"We'll be the judge of that." MacTaggart slipped his notepad in his pocket and headed for the door.

Ham wished DCI Crannach was here! He seemed like a cautious man who didn't make snap judgements. What Gandiegow needed right now, more than anything, was a cool head overseeing the investigation.

Ham knew he shouldn't do it, but he called his brother.

He didn't give him a chance to say anything. "Is yere raingear hanging by the back door?"

"Why do ye want to know?"

"Just look and tell me." Ham felt a little crazed.

There was shuffling on the other end. Finally, Gregor spoke. "Nay. Did ye put it somewhere?"

"No. Listen, the police are on their way to question you about where ye've been."

"What? I've been in my easy chair, reading a book." Gregor paused. "Hold on. Both police officers are here."

"Be careful what ye say," Ham warned.

"Gotta go." Gregor hung up.

Ham thought about Diana, about how she seemed to be gathering evidence even before Rory was shot. He turned around and went out the door. He glanced in the direction of the boats, where he should secure everything for the night. But instead, he headed for Duncan's Den, where he'd left Diana. He wanted to tell her of this latest development. Maybe she could puzzle out why one of the fishermen was after Marta. With Rory gone, he figured she was the only objective one left in the village with a clue how to solve the mystery.

21

R ORY CAME AWAKE all at once. His eyes popped open; not at all like they showed on the telly, where the patient's eyes fluttered first. He turned his head and focused on the man in the room—Doc MacGregor, who was reading a chart.

Mother duck! Rory's head hurt. *The light. The movement.* His right arm hurt. But sheer terror had him sitting up. "Diana," he croaked. "Is she safe?"

"Aye. I just spoke with Bethia. Diana is lying down, resting. Perfectly fine." Doc set the chart back in the slot on the wall and pulled out his phone. "I'll call and tell them that ye're awake."

"No! Don't call. No one can know."

"What? Why wouldn't you want everyone to know ye're all right?" Doc sounded like he might reach for his mobile to call the psych ward.

Rory put his hand up to stop him. "I know it's not fair to those who might be worried." *Like Diana.* "But I have to put the case first. Even if others are worried about me."

"What's the plan then?" Doc asked.

"I need to sneak back into Gandiegow to find the bastard who tried to shoot Diana."

"Did ye see who it was?" Doc asked, hopefully.

"It's fuzzy. Except for the gun barrel. That I can picture perfectly." For a moment, Rory relived it—the fear of losing Diana. "But we must be getting close if the killer was stupid enough to fire a weapon in a small village. Not too many places to hide." Though, up till now, he *had* eluded Rory.

He swung his legs over the bed, stifling a groan of pain. "Where's my clothes?"

Doc dropped his phone on the bed and lunged to stop Rory from standing. "Whoa. Ye can't get up."

"The hell I can't." With his one good arm, Rory pushed him away and got to his feet like a newborn colt. He looked around the room. "Clothes. Now."

"Ye can't go," Doc said.

Rory leveled his gaze at Doc. "*Doesna* matter what ye say. I'm going anyway."

Doc sighed and went to the in-room closet, opening it. He pulled out a bag and laid it on the bed. "Here. Let me call a nurse to help ye dress."

"I don't need a damned nurse. I need out of here. Diana's in danger." Rory grabbed his pants and pulled them on, catching himself as he wobbled.

"Ye're in no condition to drive," Doc said. "You don't have a vehicle here, *ta boot*."

"Can I get a ride with ye to Gandiegow?" Rory asked.

Doc gave him a hard stare. "If I say no, will ye get back in bed to give yere body time to heal?"

Rory laughed, though it hurt to do so. "What do ye think?" He mentally scrolled through the officers he knew in Inverness. *Assuming that's where the ambulance had brought him!*

Doc held out Rory's shirt for him. "I'll take ye. Let me fill out the paperwork first."

"I'm indebted to ye." Rory picked up his mobile and shoved it in his pocket. He'd check it in the car. He prayed Doc would drive like a speed demon, once they were on the road.

ಬಂಗ

From a deep dark place, Diana stirred—only a very little—as something jostled her. Her brain felt rattled, as if filled with tumbling rocks.

"Wake up, ye ninny." Deydie gave her another shake. "We've something to tell ye. Hamilton is here to see ye, too."

"Give her a minute, dear heart." Bethia's voice was kind and sweet, where Deydie's wasn't.

"She needs to get up and hear what has happened," Deydie said loudly.

Diana's eyelids felt glued shut. She'd never been this groggy in her life. "I'm trying." Though she just wanted to sleep forever.

"Sit up. Now!" Deydie commanded. "Bethia has strong coffee for ye."

Diana finally cracked her eyes open. "What time is it?" There was darkness behind the windowpanes, but the room was blaring with light. She squeezed her eyes shut again. "What's going on?"

"It's seven o'clock," Bethia answered.

"Lass," Hamilton said, urgently. "I need to speak with ye. I fear my brother's in trouble."

Diana opened her eyes again. "Gregor? What's happened?" Things were coming back to her. *Awful things. A gunshot. Rory falling. Rory unconscious and taken to the hospital!* "How's Rory? Can I go see him now?"

"Drink this," Bethia said gently. "When I spoke with Doc a while ago, he said things were unchanged with the lad."

Diana's hopes plummeted. "I have to see him." She tried to move but she felt paralyzed. More thoughts broke through the fog. *Bethia making tea. Tilly carrying in the tray.* Diana looked up at Bethia accusingly. "Did you drug me?"

Bethia's hand shot to her chest. "Drugged? Lands, no! Herbal tea is all I made."

Diana believed her. "Well, someone did." And she'd have to find out why. But first, she'd have to literally gather her wits, because her brain felt scattered. She looked at the mug Bethia held out to her, hoping it wasn't drugged, too. Diana took it and sniffed the rich deep aroma.

"Drink the damned thing," Deydie said irritably.

"There's nothing in there except good-tasting Glen Lyon coffee," Bethia promised. "I brewed it meself."

Diana took a sip.

"Drink up now," Deydie urged, more kindly than before.

"Please hurry." Ham's words had Diana taking a long draw of the hot liquid.

Slowly, she swung her legs to the side of the bed, then gingerly used her toes to find the floor. "Okay." She looked up at Ham. "Tell me what's going on."

For the next few minutes Ham told her about what he saw, how Gregor's raingear was missing, and how MacTaggart was hellbent on solving the case for his injured boss.

At the mention of Rory, fear ripped through her, leaving jagged pain behind. *He's going to die.* She clutched the quilt, trying in vain to get herself under control before she spoke. "Give me a second to splash water on my face and then we'll head out to help Gregor."

Deydie and Bethia each took an arm as Diana wobbled to her feet. She felt like she was the old woman and not them.

Deydie shoved the coffee mug at her once more and she chugged the rest before tottering to the bathroom.

It only took a few minutes to get ready and leave with Ham. As they came outside, Diana glanced over at Partridge House, two doors over.

"Let me stop and make sure Marta is okay first." She had so many questions for that woman. Not to mention it would give Diana a chance to ask Tilly who had had access to her tea mug. "I'll only be a minute."

Hamilton looked torn, then he said, "Okay," and stopped at the end of the walkway to Partridge House. "You go inside and I'll wait for ye here."

"No," Diana insisted. "You go on. I'll be fine. I promise to text you for an escort when I'm done speaking with the Dixon sisters."

"I really do need to get to my brother," Ham said with a grateful but anxious smile on his face. He pointed to the back of a cottage. "We live just down the way. Not that far. Let me know when ye're ready." His look pleaded for her not to be long.

"I will."

Hamilton waited and watched as Diana made it safely to the porch. She waved to him before opening the door and going in.

The front entryway was surprisingly dark. Marta and Tilly must be upstairs, Diana thought, as she reached over for the switch.

When the room filled with light Diana found she wasn't alone, but she had a hard time processing the scene before her.

Marta was on the wooden bench by the door, where everyone sat to put on or take off their shoes. A pair of black Wellies sat on the mud mat beside her on the floor; they felt oddly significant to Diana. Next, she scanned Marta, trying to sort out and categorize what she saw. Marta's eyes were large and scared. She wore her dark gray puffy winter coat. Duct tape covered her mouth. Zip ties bound her hands in her lap.

Diana told herself to turn and make a run for it, but before she could move a muscle, the door shut behind her, and cold, hard steel poked her in the back.

Tilly's laugh was low and unnerving. "'Tis nice, isn't it? Having Marta gagged?"

Why is Tilly speaking with a Scottish accent? What in the world was going on?

Tilly nudged Diana toward Marta with what was inarguably the barrel of a gun. "I like *me* sister better this way...with her big trap shut, don't ye? And I'm glad you stopped by. It will be more fun with ye along."

As Diana took a step toward Marta, she looked behind her-- and was shocked at the change. There was a crazed look on Tilly's normally shy, awkward face, and her eyes were glazed. It was as if Tilly had transformed into a different person altogether. She was dressed in a black rain coat that hung loosely on her lean frame. To complete the bizarre scene, a shotgun was poking out of Tilly's sleeve.

That solves the mystery of who stole the black rain gear.

"Ye're in charge of me sister, do ye hear?" Tilly sounded as commanding as Deydie. "Make sure she keeps up." Tilly poked Diana again with the barrel. "Help her stand now. We have somewhere to be."

"Where are we going?" Diana asked, hoping to buy time. If she was gone long enough, surely Ham would come back to check on her.

But she also knew he might not. MacTaggart and McCartney were at the Duffy brothers' cottage now, interrogating Gregor. Ham would've forgotten all about Diana texting him, his hands full trying to convince the police officers that Gregor hadn't tried to kill Marta.

But it looks as if Tilly had.

"Stop shillyshallying," Tilly's Scottish burr was intensified, taking on more of Deydie's tone and mannerisms. "Ye'll know soon enough where we're goin', when we *git* there."

Diana prayed someone would see them. Gandiegowans looked out for one another. *Isn't that what Deydie had said?*

As Diana helped the frightened Marta to her feet, she kept one eye on Tilly, who was pulling her black hood over her head. Diana couldn't help but think Tilly looked like the grim reaper in a rain suit.

"Now out," *Tilly the Grim* growled.

Diana led Marta to the door and opened it. She glanced hopefully this way and that, but sadly, no one seemed to be outdoors. No one to shout to. No one to save them!

Diana heard her father's calm voice in her head.

Don't panic.

The ones who get out alive are the ones who keep their head.

Get Tilly talking and maybe she'll come back to being herself.

Tilly pointed with her gun arm to the silhouette cast by Partridge House. "Keep to the shadows. Or else." Her growl was feral and ominous.

Diana took a calming breath to counteract the apprehension trying to overtake her. She closed her eyes for a moment and imagined her father standing beside her with his loving hand resting on her shoulder, steadying her.

And just like that, Diana became composed, knowing exactly what she should do. "I read the pages you gave me for book ten. They're good. *Really good.*"

Tilly waved her off. "Ye're just saying that because I've got a gun."

"No, I'm not. I especially like how the Buttermilk Guild detained a suspect by pushing him into the carding machine."

Tilly nodded. "*Aye.* Just as Tilly was pushed into the carding machine at the wool mill."

Oh, no! Scottish-accented Tilly was talking as if *regular Tilly* was a separate person! She was off in her own little world, smiling. "One of my favorite things about writing mysteries is finding new and unusual ways for people to die."

The admission made a chill run down Diana's spine, but she tamped down her fear.

Tilly went on. "Ye never know when research might pay off: *Art imitating life.* It seemed such a happy accident when we were to go to the wool mill. I thought it was a good way to throw ye off Tilly's scent. 'Tis a shame Marta couldn't have been pushed into the machine, though. Carding machine accidents can be fatal, ye see." She sighed, as if disappointed. "But alas, *she* lives."

"It was a risky move, but ingenious," Diana said with phony admiration. "What else have you learned from your research? How to properly cut the brachial artery?"

"*Aye.*"

"Is that the reason you carry a tourniquet?"

"In case someone tries to cut *me* own brachial artery. I'd be equipped, ye see," Tilly said. "Of course, Rance wasn't...*prepared.*"

With the mystery of the tourniquet solved, Diana needed to know more. "Why did Rance have to...?" She was trying to pick her words carefully.

"To die?" Tilly offered.

"Yes," Diana said. "Why Rance?"

"For encouraging the end of the Quilt to Death series."

There were thousands of irate readers who might agree with

Tilly and not convict her for what she'd done.

Diana pressed on. "I thought it was clever to mirror what happened in the books. Vengeance for the Buttermilk Guild?"

"Aye," Tilly said proudly.

Diana would have to tread lightly as she stroked Tilly's ego. "But I am confused about a few things."

"Like what?"

"Judy Keith. Why did she have to go?" Diana was playing a dangerous game, but it served two purposes. One: To keep Tilly talking. Two: Diana had to know how and why everything happened the way it had.

"Judy Keith? Who is that?" Tilly said, clearly confused.

"Book two. The one killed with the tape measure. With the Buttermilk Guild's Sampler quilt wrapped around her?" Diana reminded her.

"Och, it couldn't be helped." Scottish Tilly seemed almost to regret this one. "I'm pretty sure she saw me as I was *aboot* to grab her quilt at the bookshop. I heard her explain to another woman that she'd be at the guild meeting the next night. I knew I couldn't let her see me again. I figured she'd put *two and two* together and know I was the one who'd taken her quilt."

"How did ye know where Judy lived?" Diana asked.

"I followed her home. She didn't live that far. I got back in plenty of time to get Marta to the flat. It was easy. I gave my sister a sleeping pill and then I slipped out to take care of the quilter."

"Yes, that makes sense," Diana said, though she was appalled at the nonchalance of Scottish Tilly's confession. The good news was that Tilly wasn't talking as if she were two separate people now. "And Jacques?"

"Ah, that one is yere fault."

"My fault?" Diana felt sick.

"Aye. It was ye who told me to keep writing the tenth Quilt to Death novel."

"I don't understand," Diana said honestly.

"Marta would never have allowed another *Quilt to Death* novel to be published. I decided Marta had to go if the Buttermilk Guild was to live."

"And Jacques?" Diana guessed at the answer, but she wanted to hear it from Tilly.

"He watched Marta like a hawk. There was no way I was getting to her with him around."

"Did you have foxglove with you all along?" Diana asked, trying to keep her guilt at bay so as to get to the truth.

"*Nay.* I gathered some while we were at Spalding Farm."

"But I didn't talk to you about continuing the Quilt to Death series until we were leaving Colin's farm."

"I know. What a happy accident that I was prepared."

Bile rose in Diana's throat. She was complicit in Jacques's death. If she hadn't told Tilly to keep working on book ten, he might still be alive. Standing beside her now, Marta made a gagged protest from under her taped mouth, presumably because Diana was the one who encouraged Tilly to continue writing the Quilt to Death series.

Diana tried not to vomit. "And Leo?" Though that one was easier. She'd seen the disdain on Tilly's face whenever Leo was around. "You framed him for the fire?"

"Actually, I'd hoped he would burn up with my sister, but the scoundrel slipped away unharmed."

"But you got him in the end."

"*Aye,*" Tilly bragged. "I got such delight in pushing him down the root cellar stairs and putting a knife through his *bluidy* heart." Tilly raised a hand, as if stopping Diana from asking the obvious question. "I know, I know. It was a deviation from the books, but at least he had the Lover's Knot quilt covering him." She chuckled again. "Lover's Knot is quite the pun, isn't it, dear sister?"

Marta looked as sickened as Diana felt.

Diana switched subjects. "So, I have to know. Are you the one who drugged my tea?"

"Of course," Scottish Tilly laughed. "'Twas so easy."

"But why?"

Tilly waved the gun, shrugging. "Ye were getting too close. Ye and the copper that ye fancy."

Diana could've corrected her, saying that she didn't *fancy* Rory. That she felt so much more.

Yes, she'd been happy as a single woman, perfectly fine with her life. But being with Rory made her life richer. She wished with all her heart that he would live. So that she could tell him how she really felt. She whispered a prayer to God, though she feared it was too late:

Please let him wake up and be okay. I've learned my lesson. I promise to cherish every moment I have with him. I will no longer live in fear. Moving forward, I'll embrace life, no matter that the world is a dangerous place for all of us.

If Rory lived, she would savor every moment with him. And if something happened—if he died in the line of duty—she would keep on living, because he'd want her to. Just like she was sure her father would've wanted her mother to keep living, too.

Diana's heart was so full of love for Rory. Oh, how she wanted to see his face, to see he was all right, to tell him everything she was feeling.

Diana's father came to her once more. *You have a rifle aimed at your chest and you have to deal with this problem first.*

"Stop it." Tilly leveled the gun at Diana. "Ye've been trying to stall me with all yere yammering. Now get moving. Go there between the buildings."

But Diana's job was to keep Tilly talking. "I've been nothing but nice to you. And supportive. Haven't I? I can't believe you would want to harm me."

"It's not personal. Self-preservation, ye see." Tilly acted as if she was commenting on the weather. Which in fact, wasn't looking all that great. Deydie had been right. The wind had lathered the ocean into quite a fury, making Diana hope they weren't headed toward the water. The choppy seas were sure to kill them if Tilly didn't.

Minutes felt like hours as they made their way toward the water. Diana's dad had said it was like that in the middle of an incident. "Please tell us where you're taking us. There's no harm in doing so now," Diana said, as if asking Tilly which restaurant they were heading to.

"To the harbor. To the Duffys' boat."

"Why the boat, Tilly?" Diana asked, remembering her father saying to use the perp's name over and over to remind them of their humanity. "There's no murder on a boat in any of the novels in the series."

"The Buttermilk Guild," Tilly said. "Remember? Marta had them die on a cruise ship."

Diana made a show of scanning the water. "I don't see a cruise ship anywhere in sight."

"There's no more time to waste. We'll have to use the Duffy brothers' boat."

"I don't understand, Tilly," Diana said, though she knew perfectly well what the deranged woman was up to.

"Bookending our story, don't you see?"

Diana shook her head.

"The Buttermilk Guild died at sea so Marta has to die at sea as well. There's poetic justice in it all." Tilly looked more than a little demented, as if she believed every word she said.

At Tilly's words, Marta began to struggle against Diana's grasp. Diana held on tight and tried to communicate with her eyes, *If you run away, Tilly will surely shoot us both.*

Which prompted Diana's next question. "I have to know, were you aiming at me or Detective Chief Inspector Crannach?"

"I was aiming in *yere* direction, but he jumped in the way." Tilly motioned with her gun arm as if she was wielding nothing more dangerous than a laser pointer during a PowerPoint presentation. "Shooting the DCI was a miscalculation. I should've waited until he wasn't around. I didn't think it through. Definitely a rookie mistake," she said, as if critiquing her own work. "I was only trying to scare ye."

Diana felt some satisfaction in that.

Tilly went on. "But when he got in the way, for a moment there, I thought I had killed two birds with one stone." She shook her head, smiling.

Tilly didn't deserve an ounce of Diana's sympathy, especially since Rory had taken the hit.

Off in the distance at the edge of town, Diana saw movement. Using only her peripheral vision, she took a second look. Hope grew. She definitely saw someone slipping stealthily from building to building. It wasn't just any someone. It was Rory in a sling, as if she'd conjured him up. Seeing him made her heart soar. Happy adrenaline rushed through her system and she had to stop herself from calling out to him, begging him to stay back, to stay safe...because she needed him. Oh, how she needed him!

She could almost hear her dad's patient, guiding voice. *You can get out of this unharmed. You know what you have to do. Just be careful while you're doing it.*

She took a calming breath. *Okay, Dad.* She willed herself to keep her emotions in check, to keep her expression as neutral as Switzerland. But it was easier said than done. With Rory in sight, she knew her life's path—*to love Rory forever*. But first she had to get past the next several moments. There was no skipping over them. Her job was to stop Tilly.

Diana could see her future, as crystal clear as if she could reach out and touch it. She had to get Tilly to surrender, or no one was going to get their happily ever after. It had to be fast, too. If Rory got too close, he'd put himself in danger again, and Diana couldn't let that happen.

Inspiration hit. Remind Tilly what she cared about most. And if Diana could keep Tilly's attention, she wouldn't see Rory approaching. "Tilly, if something happens to me, who's going to be your champion at Three Seals Publishing?"

Marta squirmed and groaned behind the gag, as if protesting the idea of Tilly having a champion of any sort.

Tilly glared at Marta, then Diana. "Three Seals isn't ever going to let me keep writing about the Buttermilk Guild. You said so yereself."

"That's not what I said. Because big publishing moves so slowly, I just didn't want you to think it was going to happen overnight. It's going to take time. I want you to keep writing the Quilt to Death series. When you finish book ten, I think you should jump right in and work on book eleven. So when Three Seals does get back to us, you'll have manuscripts ready to go right into the publishing schedule."

"But you said—"

Diana cut her off. "The first thing I was taught in PR was to *under-promise* so I could *over-deliver*. It makes the department look good. *It makes me look good, too.* I'm sorry if I gave you the wrong impression. Besides, Tilly, would I have gone to all the trouble of doing a second marketing plan for Three Seals if I didn't believe in you and the Buttermilk Guild?"

Tilly looked doubtful. "What are you talking about?" Her

brogue had disappeared, replaced with her soft, shy, awkward voice.

"It's on my phone. Nicola, the publisher, asked for more details on how to position you as the author. Here—" Diana reached in her pocket and Tilly flinched, raising the gun as if to fire.

Diana put her hands up. "Whoa! Nothing more dangerous here than my cellphone. No weapons. Promise, Tilly. Let me show you what I sent."

Tilly relaxed a little, the gun barrel lowering slightly.

Slowly, Diana pulled out her phone and tried not to watch as Rory crept closer. She opened her email and held out her phone. "Nicola says she received it and is looking it over now."

Tilly moved closer, took the phone, and studied it.

"See? All hope isn't lost," Diana said.

"But Marta would never let me continue writing the series." Tilly sounded small.

"She can't stop you, Tilly. You'll have your own deal with Three Seals." Diana wanted to tell her that she'd have her own life, too. But the truth was that the penal system would own her after what she'd done.

Diana tried a different tactic. "Also, Tilly," she said, "you care about the Buttermilk Guild. I promise, when you let us go, I'll make sure Three Seals continues on with the series. Just as you want."

"How can you guarantee that?"

"Because I'll quit if they don't. Three Seals values what I do for them. They won't want to lose their Fixer."

"Why do they call you the Fixer?" Tilly asked.

"Because I fix things that are messed up. Let me fix this with Three Seals. Together, the two of us can make sure the Buttermilk Guild lives."

Tilly seemed confused, completely back to her old self, the

crazy delusional Scottish persona gone.

Diana had another brainstorm. "Besides, you don't really want to drown Marta. You *love* your sister."

Tilly stopped and stared at Diana. "Drown?"

Diana continued. "I know you love Marta. I've seen it every day. I was there when you comforted Marta in the van. You're a wonderful sister to her." Diana nudged Marta, who took the hint, and nodded fervently.

The words must've seeped in because Tilly lowered the gun a little more.

Diana saw Rory was close. Too close! She had to wrap this up before he could pounce and get killed...like her dad.

Diana implored the real Tilly, "Yes, you love your sister! We all know it. It's the reason you were her ghostwriter for all those years. You wanted to make Marta happy." Diana recalled the words Tilly had said in the van and used them now. "You've always taken care of your little sister and you always will."

The gun drooped. Tilly looked over at Marta and it was obvious she was remembering Marta as a vulnerable child and not the demanding diva she'd become. "She was so helpless and so sweet." Tilly gazed at her sister. "She was my whole world when Mama and Papa died. She needed me and I needed her."

"She *still* needs you, Tilly." Diana felt a little nudge from her father. *Remember, Tilly will always take care of her sister.* Diana took the hint -- and tripped Marta.

Marta gave a muffled cry, her eyes widening as she started to fall. There was no way she could catch herself with her hands zip-tied. Tilly rushed to grab her. In the process, the gun fell from her sleeve and landed in a thorny bush. Diana dove for the rifle, though the thorns bit at her hands. Before she had a tight grip on the rifle, Rory rushed forward, grabbing Tilly, who was cradling Marta in her arms.

Tilly glanced over, her brow furrowing. "But you're in a coma."

"Sorry to disappoint ye," Rory said. "Ye're under arrest." He looked over at Diana. "Are ye okay?"

"I'm fine."

"Really?" He scanned her as if searching for bullet holes.

There was such concern in his voice, and across his face, that Diana wanted to run into his arms. But his arms were full of Tilly. "I'm okay. Really."

Rory yanked a set of steel cuffs from his belt and snapped them on Tilly. He then held out a knife to Diana. "Here. Cut Marta free."

Diana knelt down and sliced through the zip ties, then eased the tape from Marta's mouth.

The tape was barely off before Marta was scooting away and yelling. "Tilly, what the hell is wrong with you?"

Tilly hung her head. "You killed the Buttermilk Guild."

"And you were willing to kill me for revenge?"

Tilly looked confused by the question. "I'd never kill you, Mar-Mar. I just thought you should hurt a little."

But killing those who were in Tilly's way or that Marta cared about was okay?

Marta turned to Rory. "It really doesn't surprise me that my sister is the killer. She's always had a temper. Especially if she doesn't get her way."

A family trait.

Diana had so many questions for Tilly. She glanced over to see Deydie and Bethia hurrying toward them, huffing and puffing, their faces flushed with excitement and exertion.

"I told ye to stay inside," Rory said to them, looking mildly irritated, as he lifted Tilly to her feet.

Deydie was breathing hard, but her face was glowing with

animation. "We saw the DCI sneaking through town and knew something was up. We meant to come help ye, lass—"

"But Rory stopped us from leaving Quilting Central," Bethia finished.

At that moment, Diana could imagine them as young women, full of life and adventure. *Pretty much the way they are now.*

"I feel as if this is my fault." It seemed unusual for Deydie to take the blame. "I should've told ye my gun was missing."

He nodded to the gun in the bushes. "Is that yeres then?"

"Aye."

"We'll talk about it later," Rory said. "May I use Quilting Central to hold Tilly?"

"It'd be best, as I have questions for her, too," Deydie said resolutely.

Rory rolled his eyes at that, and said, "Diana, grab my phone and call MacTaggart or McCartney and tell them where we'll be."

Diana took the phone and texted them quickly as they all made their way to Quilting Central. When she was done, she once again leaned in, speaking quietly. "Why didn't you text them when you left the hospital?"

"I'd been shot," Rory said. "I fell asleep as soon as my arse hit the seat when I got into Doc's vehicle."

She didn't ask if he'd read her text. Instead, she continued, "But you should've called them when you got to town."

He stopped walking—pulling Tilly to a stop as well—and leveled a gaze at Diana. "I only had one thought in my head."

"And that was?" she said, holding her breath.

"To get to you." His eyes were full of emotion.

The rest of the questions in her head went silent as she savored those four little words. To Diana, it was as if he'd said much more.

Rory was grateful to see MacTaggart and McCartney running down the wynd toward him.

"Glad to see ye in one piece," MacTaggart said. "I heard back from headquarters. They have a man in custody for killing the couple at the airport. It had nothing to do with the books. What a lousy coincidence, eh?"

"Thanks for letting me know." Rory's head was killing him, but he knew he'd be all right once he got Diana in his arms and told her how he felt. "Take Tilly, will ye?"

"Where are you taking her?" Marta asked in a quavering voice. "I want to go with her!" The last was a plea.

Deydie put an arm around Marta. "There, there, lass." Rory had never seen the old woman be so kind, especially to Marta.

Bethia slipped her arm through Marta's. "Ye'll come to Deydie's cottage for a hot cuppa."

Deydie nodded solemnly.

But Marta was still looking at her sister fearfully. "What am I going to do without you, Tilly?"

"Bye, Mar-Mar," Tilly whispered. Her shoulders were slumped more than Rory had ever seen, and her head was bent so low, it looked like her neck might break.

Marta began to cry as MacTaggart and McCartney ushered Tilly away.

"Let's go now, lassie," Deydie said, as she took Marta's other arm, "and leave the DCI and Diana alone." Deydie grinned at them and said, "If ye'd like to get married here, me and my quilters will arrange one hell of a wedding for ye."

Rory smiled. "Thank you. Diana and I will discuss it."

"We will?" Diana couldn't conceal her surprise.

"Aye. We will." He pulled her into his arms, not caring if the old quilters were watching or not. "I love ye, lass. I feel like the moment I met you, I came alive. I don't want to think about my life without you."

"Me, either." Diana smiled, as mist came into her eyes. "I love you, too, Rory. I should've told you sooner. I should've listened to my heart and not been afraid I'd end up alone like my mom." She laughed. "I was so foolish. I've always been more like my dad."

"Strong?" Rory asked, but he knew she was.

"Yes." There was mischief in her eyes. "You get me."

"And ye have an exceptional mind, too," Rory said. "I think that's what I find most attractive about ye."

"But how are we going to do this?" she said.

"We'll work it out," Rory said confidently. "Whatever it takes." Even if he had to move to the States and clean toilets. "Whatever it takes," he repeated.

"I've been thinking about changing careers. I feel like I can finally follow in my dad's footsteps." She gave Rory a sheepish grin. "I saw online that Glasgow University has a degree in criminology."

A weight lifted from Rory's chest. "Aye, or we could live in Edinburgh. Or Stirling. Their universities have good programs, too. I can live anywhere ye want...but I can't live without ye."

She kissed him this time, and they lingered.

After a while, she pulled away. "In the meantime, I still want to work for Three Seals in a smaller capacity. Someone will need to promote the revival of the Buttermilk Guild. What do you think?"

"I think it's brilliant. I just want ye to be happy." He'd do whatever it took to make it so.

They weren't riding off into the sunset together, like in the movies. That was okay. They were real people, starting their life together right now, in this moment, here in Gandiegow.

What the future held, he didn't know. He didn't care. He had Diana, and that was all that mattered.

He gazed into her eyes. "Would ye like to have a Gandiegow wedding?"

"*Aye.*" She laughed and ran a hand across his cheek. "Kiss me."

Rory did, just as the snow began to fall.

COMING MARCH 2021

A NEW SERIES WITH PENGUIN RANDOM HOUSE, BERKLEY IMPRINT

HOME, SWEET HOME, ALASKA

Thirty-four-year-old Hope McKnight tried not to watch the clock, which hung on the dingy blue wall of her miniscule living room. But it was impossible to keep from glancing at it every other second. She turned and gazed out the frost-covered window into the pitch-black of night, and shivered, before peeking at the clock again.

Ten-thirty.

Ella should've been home an hour ago from the football game. Calling and texting Ella's cellphone hadn't eased Hope's worry, as her daughter hadn't responded.

Hope always agonized over Ella's safety when it snowed, even if it was only a dusting. Sweet Home, Alaska was remote, with winding roads leading in and out of the town, population 573— natives, transplants, and multigenerational Alaskans like herself. Hope knew better than anyone how treacherous the roads could be. And there was a deeper danger, hanging over their little house. For the past two Friday nights, her sixteen-year-old daughter had staggered in the front door, clearly drunk. Hope felt defeated…and guilty. Lecturing Ella from birth about the pitfalls of alcohol hadn't prevented her daughter from getting caught up in Alaska's number one pastime. Being the head volunteer of Mothers Against Drunk Driving in their borough hadn't solved anything either.

Is Ella doomed to repeat my mistakes?

She tried to shove the thought from her mind, but she couldn't stop from feeling—down to her bones—that Ella's drinking was inherently her fault.

Hope glanced at the car keys hanging on the hook by the front door. At least there was that; Ella wouldn't be driving. But that didn't mean she wasn't getting a ride home with another inebriated teen.

To stop fretting, Hope pushed herself off the couch and strode to the closet, pulling out a rucksack. "I'll start packing without her," she thought, more than a little annoyed. At least once a year they took a snow camping trip in the thick forests surrounding Sweet Home, where Hope could test Ella's survival skills.

Hope's gaze traveled to the clock once again. Yes, according to the experts, only five percent of what you worry about actually happens. But Hope knew that danger lurked around every corner, ready to ruin lives. She was living proof of how a good life could turn awful in an instant. And how, once things went bad, there was no way to turn back time and recapture the joy she once had. When her parents named her Hope, they'd made a grievous error...because she had none. Her job-one now? To prepare Ella for what lay ahead, good or bad.

Hope went to Ella's room and unearthed her daughter's backpack from a pile of clothes. As an exhausted and overworked single parent, she'd thrown in the towel about Ella keeping her room picked up. In the vast scheme of things, an untidy room wasn't important. Having skills to make it alone was. Knowing how to survive in the wild was key, too. Their camping trip would only be one night, but two days—Saturday and Sunday—the first two days Hope had off since September.

Before she could dig past the second layer of clothes on the floor to find Ella's wool socks, Hope's phone rang. She raced for the other room and caught it on the tail end of the second ring, knowing it had to be Ella.

"Where are you?"

But Hope was wrong; it was Piney Douglas, the closest thing she had to a mother now. Not that she didn't love Piney, but Hope's heart sank. *Where are you, Ella?*

"Where am I?" Piney chuckled. "I'm in my drafty apartment above the Hungry Bear," the grocery store/diner where Hope worked. "Where else would I be?"

"I thought you were Ella." Hope could've piped in that Piney could've been next door in the small wooden cabin with her boyfriend, Bill Morningstar, a sixtyish native, who was known throughout Sweet Home for making Alaskan quilts.

Piney clucked. "Ella is fine. I'd know if something was wrong."

Hope didn't believe in crystals, Tarot cards, tea leaf reading, and other psychic nonsense, like Piney did. Bill thought Piney's dealings with the other world was complete rubbish and didn't seem to think twice about voicing his opinion to Piney. Hope had to admit that at times Piney had the uncanny ability to know what was up with Ella, and thus decided that Piney was an intuitive. Piney maintained she was more in touch with the universe than regular folks because she was born on the Summer Solstice. She looked like Mother Earth— her gray hair curled at her shoulders, her Bohemian skirts flowing about her, and her wise smiling face, as if she was privy to the world's inner secrets. Piney had come to Alaska in 1970 at the age of twenty-two in search of the truth. A self-proclaimed hippie, she'd arrived in Sweet Home in her converted blue school bus, way ahead of the curve in the tiny home movement. Piney and her thirty-four-year-old daughter, Sparkle, had lived in that blue bus until just a few weeks ago, when two suits from Juneau had arrived, asking to purchase the bus for the state capitol as part of a pioneer sculpture. Piney took the money, telling everyone she'd outgrown the bus. But Hope knew money was tight since Sparkle's emergency appendectomy. It was perfect timing, too, as the apartment above the Hungry Bear had been vacated the week before.

"Keep your chin up, buttercup. Don't let your negative thinking carry you away. Besides, I'm calling to see if the rumor is true."

Once again, Hope glanced at the clock. Ten-forty. Maybe she should call the Alaska State Troopers to find Ella. "What rumor?"

"Mr. Brewster heard at the bank that Donovan Stone is coming home."

It felt like lightning struck. Hope couldn't breathe. Couldn't think either. "Donovan? Here?" *What am I going to do?* She hadn't seen him in seventeen years, not since his grandmother's funeral. Where he'd told Hope he never wanted to see her again. And he hadn't.

The front door creaked. For a second, Piney's call kept Hope from being able to move. But as Ella tripped on the threshold, Hope yelled into her phone, "Gotta go." She lunged for her daughter, breaking her fall and keeping Ella's head from hitting the corner of the side table.

Ella's response was to laugh as she went down. "You should see your face!"

Hope didn't think it was funny. "Where have you been?" She kicked the door shut with her foot. Winter was just getting started, and the baseboard heaters were expensive to run.

Ella stopped laughing. "Chill, Mom. I was just out with friends." Her words were slurred, and her breath smelled like cheap wine.

A smell that brought back awful memories.

"Who drove you home tonight?" Hope hadn't heard a vehicle. "Were they drinking, too?"

"I walked home from Lacey's."

"The trail through the forest?" Hope glanced up at the transom window to the black sky beyond. "Did you have your flashlight with you?"

"I was fine," Ella said. "I didn't need my flashlight. I know my way."

But Alaska was dangerous!

Sweet Home wasn't Anchorage, but someone could've kidnapped Ella and Hope would've never seen her again.

She got to her feet and helped Ella to her feet, too. "We're going to talk about this tomorrow. I know you're sad about Grandpa's passing—"

Ella swayed side to side. "Don't bring Grandpa into this. He has nothing to do with anything." She wobbled into her room.

Hope followed and caught the door before Ella slammed it shut. Hope's heart was heavy, so very heavy, as she watched her teenage daughter stagger across her room and fall into bed. Hope plodded over to Ella and pulled off her boots. "I think your drinking has everything to do with Grandpa's death."

Death was such a harsh word, but it had been harsh for Hope to see her dad lying in that casket, felled by a heart attack. There hadn't been time to fall apart, though. Hope had to keep it together for Ella. Remain strong. Even when she felt her life coming apart at the seams.

Ella stacked her hands behind her head. She glanced over at Hope before looking up at the ceiling. "Tell me a story. Tell me again about Aunt Izzie."

Had people been talking? Had Ella heard something, since the rumor was spreading about Donovan returning to town? "You haven't asked about her in a long time."

"I know. I just want to hear about her now." Ella reached over the side of the bed and pulled a ribbon from between the mattress and box spring. "I found this ribbon and want to tie it on the Memory Tree."

Hope reached out and ran her hand down the ribbon. "We can do that on our camping trip, okay?"

"Sure," Ella said.

Hope had started the Memory Tree after Izzie died. It was the same mountain hemlock where Donovan had carved Izzie's name— Isabella!—declaring the tree was now hers. At eight-years-old, Izzie had been thrilled. After Izzie's death, Hope had started visiting the tree, bringing treasures, things Izzie might like and decorated the tree. Over the years, Ella had enjoyed finding new treasures for Aunt Izzie and the two of them had continued the tradition.

"Go ahead. Talk about Aunt Izzie." Ella closed her eyes, as if she was six again, listening to a bedtime story.

Hope understood. There was only the two of them left. When Ella was little, Hope had started telling her stories about Izzie. It was one of the ways Hope kept her sister alive, and a way for Ella to know her namesake. Hope's mother had hated that she'd named her child after her dead sister, telling her it was cruel, making Mom despise Hope more.

Izzie was always a clear image in Hope's mind and Hope never tired of talking about her. "I loved Izzie. She was just a little thing with a big personality. Even though she was six years younger than me, she tried to act like we were the same age and wanted to do everything I did. Because your grandmother worked nights in the ER at Teklanika Regional Hospital, I babysat her a lot. It was fun. I taught her so much, from how to say her ABCs to how to tie her shoes. When we'd go with Mom to the Sisterhood of the Quilt stitch-ins, Izzie and I would set our sewing machines side-by-side and make all sorts of things from the fabric the Sisterhood would give us. Like matching pillowcases for the bedroom we shared, and blankets for Izzie's stuffed animals. We used to play Barbies together, bake cookies, and I didn't really mind if she tagged along with me and my friends." Most of the time, anyway. Donovan and his brother, Beau, were great about letting Izzie hang out with them, too.

"What happened to Aunt Izzie?" Ella said.

"I told you. She died," Hope said.

"You've never told me how," Ella said.

For the first time, it felt like the right moment, since Ella was clearly drunk. And sharing the story would be just one more way for Hope to atone for what she'd done to Izzie and their family. Tonight, especially tonight, Ella needed to hear the cautionary tale.

"Okay," Hope said. "I'll tell you now."

She started at the beginning of that awful night. "It was New Year's Eve, the day before I turned eighteen. I was at a party, celebrating with my friends."

Hope left out the part about Donovan, how they'd fought that night. How her friends had encouraged her to dull her anger and disappointment with alcohol after he'd dropped the bomb that he was going to stay in Alaska for college, not go to Boston like they'd planned. Maturity and years of adulting had Hope seeing things differently. She understood now why he couldn't turn down a full-ride, when every penny counted at his dad's house. Yes, Hope would leave out Donovan when telling Ella the story, but she wouldn't leave out the important part and shy away from her guilt in the tragedy. "I had a few sips of wine from one of those red Solo cups."

"So what? A few sips won't kill you, Mom," her inebriated daughter said. "I drank more than that tonight and I'm fine."

"Sure. You're fine. I should've videoed your swan-dive through the front door a few minutes ago. Even a few sips of alcohol can impair your reflexes." When you need them the most. It had been that way for Hope. She was lucky that when they tested her she was below the legal limit.

Hope crossed the room. "Scooch over so I can tell you the rest." She sat beside Ella on her twin bed. "While I was still at the party, Grandma Penny called from the hospital, telling me to pick up Izzie from a sleepover, because Izzie was complaining of a stomachache."

"I bet you didn't want to leave your friends," Ella said.

Guilt covered Hope, wrapped around her like a familiar, well-worn robe, the tie in the middle squeezing her stomach until it hurt.

It was true. Her senior year, she'd begun resenting how much of her time wasn't her own, how she had to drop everything to take care of Izzie. Izzie wanted her to play like they used to, but Hope only wanted to spend time alone with Donovan. After being best friends their whole lives, Donovan had finally stopped serial dating every girl in Sweet Home High and saw Hope as more than one of the guys. Hope, meanwhile, had loved him from the first day he'd moved in next door.

"Mom? Mom! You're doing it again," Ella said.

"What?"

"Zoning out. Get back to the story."

It wasn't just a story to Hope. She'd lived it. And she had to make her daughter understand how life could go wrong in an instant. She dropped into lecture mode. "From a young age, my mom told me to stay away from alcohol. Working the nightshift at the ER, she saw the disastrous outcomes of drinking and driving—mangled bodies, loss of life." It always hurt to say these words, but Hope was doing penance. "At the time, I didn't think it was a big deal to have a few sips. I didn't know I was going to be driving right away. But I was the one with the car keys and I shouldn't have drank at all." Also, Hope never understood those who couldn't have fun without knocking back a few. Donovan was one of them. She'd loved him, but she didn't like that he drank so much, and so often.

"So…you picked up Aunt Izzie…" Ella missing the point of what Hope had just said.

Hope sighed, feeling defeated, but plowed on anyway. "The point is, I should've listened to my mother and stayed away from alcohol."

Ella rolled her eyes. "Enough with the sermon, already. What happened next?"

"I yelled at Izzie for being a nuisance. For faking being sick." Hope had railed on her little sister, telling her that she'd ruined her night. Hope would never forget how Donovan had reached over and laid his hand on hers. *Don't take it out on Izzie. I know you're mad at me.*

"Then?"

This was always the hardest part, recalling those horrible details. "There was a snowplow in the other lane."

"Was it snowing bad out?" her daughter asked.

"Not when I'd left home, but by the time I left the party, visibility was bad, nearly a whiteout." Donovan had offered to drive, but Hope wouldn't let him. He'd had too much to drink. Sixteen-year-old Beau was three-sheets-to-the-wind, too. It was left to Hope to get them all home safely.

"But you've driven in snow your whole life. What's the big deal?" her daughter prompted.

"There was a moose. He charged into the road in front of the snowplow." Hope took a deep breath to get the next words out. "The snowplow hit the moose and sent it flying toward my side of the road. I hit it. The moose flipped backwards and crushed the back of my car." If only she'd had better reflexes to swerve and miss the bull. The biggest if only of her life.

She didn't remember too much after that, only what the snowplow driver had told her and the State Trooper at the hospital. She'd often wondered if she could've saved her sister if only she'd been prepared—stopped the bleeding, kept her from going into shock. It was one of the reasons Hope was adamant about teaching her daughter survival skills, beyond hunting and fishing, although those things were very important, too. Alaska was wild and anything could happen.

"I don't know why Donovan and I were brought to the hospital first."

"Donovan? Who's Donovan?" her daughter asked.

"Nobody," Hope said quickly. She'd never told her daughter that Donovan and Beau had been in the car that night, too. "I was dazed from the accident and only had a broken arm." Donovan just cuts and bruises. "Even though I confessed right away to my mom that I had drunk some wine, she didn't yell at me, but was only relieved I was okay." Beau arrived in the next ambulance and was pronounced dead on arrival. "When Izzie was wheeled in on the stretcher, she looked so small and broken. She only lived an hour before dying." Hope would never forget seeing her mother collapse with grief beside Izzie's hospital bed.

"And that's why I'm head of MADD in our area," Hope finished, though the story was far from complete. She left out the part where her mother never forgave her. How her parents split up over Izzie's death and her father moved to Fairbanks. How it was her mother who brought MADD to their borough, and then on her deathbed, insisted Hope take over.

"What happened to your mom? You and Grandpa never talked about her either."

Hope shrugged, not wanting to get into it. "She got sick— cancer—and died a few years later." Mom had been livid when Hope got up the courage two months after the accident to tell her that she was pregnant. *It's a slap in the face*, her mom had said, *Don't we have enough to worry about.* When baby Ella was born, Mom pretended her granddaughter didn't exist. After her death, Dad had moved back to Sweet Home to help, easing the load of raising a child alone. But now he was gone, too.

Ella looked stricken, then turned to face the wall. "Mom?"

"Yes?"

"What if you die, too?" Ella's voice was strained.

Hope understood. They didn't have anyone now, now that her dad was gone.

She wanted to tell her: There are worse things than death. Like being rejected at seventeen by your own mother, and being forced from the house, alone and pregnant. Whenever she thought about that dark time, Hope counted her blessings. She owed Piney so much: For giving her a job and letting her stay with them in the bus until after Mom died.

Hope wanted to reiterate how important it was to be ready for every contingency, how important it was that Ella be prepared...for accidents and to go it alone. If Hope had been prepared seventeen years ago, she might've handled her mother's rejection better, instead of letting grief and depression nearly consume her.

Maybe it was time to tell Ella more of the truth. How Donovan and Beau had been in the car that night. How her mother couldn't stand to look at Hope after she'd killed her sister. Maybe the truth would scare Ella straight.

But Ella had fallen asleep.

Hope brushed her daughter's light brown hair from her face. The same color hair as the father she'd never known. And Hope was sure she'd never tell Ella the truth about Donovan.

She turned off the light and left Ella's room, feeling drained. She'd spent the last seventeen years feeling tired. Exhausted to the bone.

Hope didn't have the energy to finish packing for their camping trip tonight or to worry about Donovan coming to town. She shuffled to her ten by ten-foot bedroom. She didn't turn on the lights but slipped off her slippers and jeans before climbing into bed with her turtleneck and sweater still on.

Before she fell asleep, Hope knew her eleven-year-old sister—*dead eleven-year-old sister*—would come to her in her dreams that night. Her sister Izzie had visited her on and off for the last seventeen years. But since Hope's daughter had started drinking, her sister Izzie had visited nearly every night. Her sister was always sparkling, almost glowing. Hope didn't shy away from her sister's pop-ins, as they comforted her in ways the town's platitudes never had. Her sister would be wearing the same red moose flannel pajamas she'd worn on the night Hope had picked her up from the sleepover. But instead of covered in blood, the pajamas would be clean and new. Hope never told anyone about the dreams that seemed so real.

For dreams they must be.

The first time her sister, Izzie, had visited Hope in a dream, was two days after she'd died. Her sister hadn't been chatty then, but sat cross-legged on the floor beside Hope's bed, something she'd done a million times in real life. But this time, she stared off into the distance, looking lost. When Hope called out to her, Izzie had shaken her head, as if she didn't want to talk. But these days, Hope couldn't get her to shut up. Eleven-year-old Izzie, still in her little girl body and her moose pajamas, spoke as a woman who'd lived a lifetime and had plenty of advice to give. Hope welcomed seeing her sister. It was hard to imagine that Izzie would've been twenty-eight a few months ago. If only Hope hadn't killed her.

Hope closed her eyes, and before she'd really drifted off to sleep, her sister Izzie appeared, sitting at the foot of Hope's bed.

"Piney certainly threw you for a loop." Izzie had a twinkle in her eye, as if she was having fun, stirring up trouble. "Didn't you ever suspect Donovan might come back after his grandfather died?"

"I suppose." Since Charles Stone had moved away seventeen years ago, the news of his death took nearly a month to reach Sweet Home.

Izzie reached out as if to pat the quilt covering Hope's legs, but she drew her hand back before touching it. "Do you think he's coming back to reopen the hardware store and the lodge?"

A Stone's Throw Hardware and Haberdashery had been everything to this town when Hope was growing up. And she loved going to Stone's Sweet Home Lodge with her mom and Izzie, when the Sisterhood of the Quilt gathered for their monthly get-togethers. But that was then.

Hope shook her head. "No. He wouldn't reopen his grandparents' businesses. He's probably just coming to Sweet Home to sign papers at the bank…if I had to guess."

Izzie slipped off the bed and put her hands on her hips. "Are you going to tell my namesake—my niece—that Donovan is her father?"

Hope shivered. She couldn't imagine telling anyone the truth. Though, she suspected all of Sweet Home had a clue.

"No. I'm not going to tell Ella about Donovan. I told you before. Ella thinks her father was an oil-worker who lived in the Yukon, that he died in a work-related accident when she was a baby."

"Are you at least going to tell Donovan that my niece belongs to him?"

"No!" Hope couldn't. Donovan had been crystal clear at his grandmother's funeral. *I never want to see you again.* There was such vehemence in his voice.

Her last act of love was to respect his wishes. Besides, she didn't want him to hate her more than he already did.

"Donovan might be coming to Sweet Home, but the fact is, my know-it-all-little-sister, I don't plan to see him at all."

If you enjoyed reading Kilt in Scotland, please *recommend* it to your friends or your book club. And please *write a review*. Readers love them and authors depend on them. If you write a review, please let me know. I would like to **thank you** personally.

Email: patience@patiencegriffin.com

For Signed copies, visit:

www.PatienceGriffin.com

JOIN Patience's Newsletter!
...to find out about events, contests, and more!

www.PatienceGriffin.com

The *Kilts and Quilts*™ Novels

BOOKS by
PATIENCE GRIFFIN

———— ෨෬ ————

KILTS AND QUILTS SERIES:
ROMANTIC WOMEN'S FICTION

#1   *TO SCOTLAND WITH LOVE*

#2   *MEET ME IN SCOTLAND*

#3   *SOME LIKE IT SCOTTISH*

#4   *THE ACCIDENTAL SCOT*

#5   *THE TROUBLE WITH SCOTLAND*

#6   *IT HAPPENED IN SCOTLAND*

#6.5 *THE LAIRD AND I*

#7   *BLAME IT ON SCOTLAND*

#8   *KILT IN SCOTLAND*

———— ෨෬ ————

To Scotland with Love
Book 1, Kilts and Quilts

Amazon #1 Best Seller
Publishers Weekly starred review*
New England Readers' Choice Best First Book
Golden Quill Best First Book

WELCOME TO THE CHARMING SCOTTISH seaside town of Gandiegow—where two people have returned home for different reasons, but to find the same thing....

Caitriona Macleod gave up her career as an investigative reporter for the role of perfect wife. But after her husband is found dead in his mistress's bed, a devastated Cait leaves Chicago for the birthplace she hasn't seen since she was a child. She's hoping to heal and to reconnect with her gran. The last thing she expects to find in Gandiegow is the Sexiest Man Alive! She just may have stumbled on the ticket to reigniting her career—if her heart doesn't get in the way.

Graham Buchanan is a movie star with many secrets. A Gandiegow native, he frequently hides out in his hometown between films. He also has a son he'll do anything to protect. But Cait Macleod is too damn appealing—even if she is a journalist.

Quilting with her gran and the other women of the village brings Cait a peace she hasn't known in years. But if she turns in the story about Graham, Gandiegow will never forgive her for betraying one of its own. Should she suffer the consequences to resurrect her career? Or listen to her battered and bruised heart and give love another chance?

"Griffin's lyrical and moving debut marks her as a most talented new-comer to the romance genre."
-Publishers Weekly starred review

Patience Griffin grew up in a small town along the Mississippi River. She has a master's degree in nuclear engineering but spends her days writing stories about hearth and home in the fictional small towns of Gandiegow and Whussendale, Scotland.

Connect online at www.PatienceGriffin.com

———————ဆၢ———————

All materials herewith are protected under U.S. copyright laws. Copyright © 2019 by Patience Griffi

Made in the USA
Middletown, DE
09 January 2021

31197086R00195